Marrying Up

A Right Royal
Romantic Comedy

wendy holden

sourcebooks
landmark

Sourcebooks and the colophon are registered trademarks of Sourcebooks, Inc.

Published by Sourcebooks Landmark, an imprint of Sourcebooks, Inc.
P.O. Box 4410, Naperville, Illinois 60567-4410
(630) 961-3900
Fax: (630) 961-2168
www.sourcebooks.com

Originally published in the UK in 2011 by Headline Review, an imprint of
Headline Publishing Group.

Library of Congress Cataloging-in-Publication Data

Holden, Wendy
  Marrying up : a right royal romantic comedy / by Wendy Holden.
     p. cm.
  (pbk. : alk. paper) 1. Single women—Fiction. 2. Aristocracy (Social class)—
England—Fiction. I. Title.
  PR6058.O436M37 2012
  823'.914—dc23
                        2012009863

Printed and bound in the United States of America.
VP 10 9 8 7 6 5 4 3 2 1

Also by Wendy Holden

Simply Divine
Bad Heir Day
Pastures Nouveaux
Farm Fatale
Azur Like It
The Wives of Bath
The School for Husbands
Filthy Rich
Beautiful People
Gallery Girl

To Noj, Andrew, and Isabella.

Chapter One

"Miss! Miss!" Squinting in the bright sunshine, the little boy with the trowel was waving at Polly. "I've found something, miss. It's Roman. *Definitely* Roman."

Polly grinned, got up from where she was crouched sieving soil, and went over.

"Let's have a look, Kyle."

The small, skinny boy with the buzz-cut hair proudly extended a filthy palm on which lay a small, dirty disk. He looked at her expectantly.

"It's a really interesting find, Kyle," Polly said. "But it's not a denarius—a Roman coin—not *exactly*. It's, um, actually a sixpenny piece dating from the nineteen fifties."

Far from being disappointed, Kyle looked thrilled. "Nineteen fifties!" he exclaimed excitedly. "That's *centuries* ago! That's, like, *ancient*, miss."

Polly giggled. She probably seemed ancient to eight-year-old Kyle, despite being only twenty-two. That time was relative was one thing you learned as an archaeologist.

"What's it worth, miss?" Kyle urged, his grubby face blazing with hope and bravado. "Millions?"

"Not *quite* millions," Polly explained tactfully. "But it's very pretty. And maybe it's a good thing that it's not Roman. Can anyone tell me why?"

The group of four children looked doubtful.

"Well, what is it we're digging up here?" Polly waved a hand around the wide, shallow trench whose reddish earth they had been exploring.

"Toilets!" they roared in unison, smiling broadly.

Polly nodded, tucking a stray dark brown curl behind her ear. "Exactly. This section"—she pointed at a low clump of narrow brown bricks—"used to be loos, and if it's a Roman coin, someone must have lost it in the loo. And remember what I told you about Roman loos?"

"Yes! Yes!" Four hands pumped into the air. Polly looked along the row of eager faces before picking Hannah, whose cloud of dark hair hid a lazy eye. Polly, who'd had a squint herself as a child, knew what it was to be less confident than the rest.

"They flushed," Hannah said shyly.

As everyone laughed derisively, Hannah went as red as her primary school sweatshirt. Polly leaped to her defense. "As a matter of fact, Hannah's quite right," she said. "And well done for remembering, Hannah, because I did mention very briefly that some Roman lavatories, in the forts on Hadrian's Wall for example, had a type of flushing system. But not this one here," she added. "So what else can you remember about Romans and toilets?"

The hands were pulsing in the air again. "Yes, Leo?" Polly invited a chubby boy whose face shone with exertion and excitement.

"You said"—Leo took his customary deep breath before beginning a long speech—"that they used to go to the loo all at once, and sit in long rows, and laugh and joke while they were...while they were..." He tailed off, embarrassed.

"Pooing!" shouted Kyle irrepressibly.

"Yuck!" said Poppy, a forthright child with bright green eyes and a pixie face. "Fancy pooing with other people."

"Better than what usually happened," Polly riposted, going on to explain that for most Romans, the communal loo was a large jar at the end of the street into which they tipped the contents of their chamber pots. As the children howled in disgusted disbelief, she thought, not for the first time, how the history of lavatories was the history of civilization. She had never intended to end up specializing in it, but her initial interest in tessellated flooring seemed to have drifted toward the privy and somehow never come back. There were good reasons for it to remain there too; Roman plumbing systems, being one of archaeology's less sexy areas, offered more opportunities for graduates.

How else, for example, would she have ended up here, in the gardens of the local stately home, after a pipe-laying project ended in historical discovery? Admittedly the dig had not unearthed the entire Roman palace foundations that Lord Shropshire, the landowner, had been hoping for. So far as he was concerned, a Roman villa, especially one this far north, would have been both a powerful tourist draw and a source of revenue, not to mention useful grants. Even a reality TV series had been mooted at one stage.

But once it became clear that nothing much beside the distinctly untelegenic lavatory foundations were to be found, interest, as it were, drained away. Even Polly herself, expert though she was, could not quite explain why the usually logical and practical Romans had apparently decided to build a loo block in the middle of nowhere, miles from the nearest road or settlement. But archaeology was full of mystery; you often unearthed more questions than answers.

She had been called in by the local council, who had been left with the necessity of recording the find and making sure there was nothing else of note on the site. The connection had come through a lecturer from her university who also happened to be the county archaeologist. Aware that Polly would be spending the summer at home, he had landed her the gig. The money—small though it was—was one benefit; another, more unexpected, was the pupils from the local primary school, which had taken an interest in the excavation.

Polly had never previously spent much time with children. She had been doubtful at first, imagining them rampaging on the ruins and throwing dirt at each other. In the end, it was themselves they had thrown—into the project with gusto—listening to Polly carefully and treating the excavations with respect. They had quickly mastered the various skills, such as making drawings of any finds and plotting their position carefully on a chart before removing them.

And while they were only allowed to poke and dig in a safe area removed from the Roman brickwork, their small, strong fingers had nonetheless managed to unearth all manner of treasures. Kyle had spent the best part of one afternoon painstakingly drawing his find of a broken Matchbox car, while Hannah had sieved up a contact lens.

"A bone, miss!" Leo called now. "I've found a yuman bone!"

He was waving something large and pale in the air. The other children were crowding around, shouting in excitement. Polly hurried over. A burial site? Unlikely, but you never knew.

"Miss? *Miss?*" Leo gasped, his dirt-smeared face red with agitation as he handed the object over to her.

"Maybe he got murdered in the loo," Kyle was theorizing.

"P'raps he'd been in too long," Poppy added. "People got fed up of waiting."

Polly looked up from the bone, hating to disappoint them. "It's a cow bone, I'm afraid. Probably from a beef joint. Not that old, either."

There was a howl of disappointment.

❖ ❖ ❖

A little later, Polly stood up and stretched in the hot afternoon sunshine. Archaeologist's back was a professional hazard, and as courses of physio were expensive, prevention was definitely better than cure. She was in no position to run up unnecessary bills at the moment.

A couple was passing, some of the many elderly shufflers who descended on the gardens in the afternoon. The old man stopped. "Digging for gold, are you?"

The old lady whooped with laughter and dug her husband in his pastel nylon V-necked ribs. "He's awful, he is. Always has to have his joke. Take no notice of him, love."

Polly smiled tolerantly, resisting the observation that this was not his joke, it was everyone's. At least ten people a day, all laboring under the delusion that it was wit of the highest order, asked if she was digging for gold. Others would inquire how long her university course was and then exclaim in rude amazement, "Four *years*? To learn to dig *holes*?"

"Found anything good yet?" was another sally.

"Yes," Polly would reply. "Everything we dig up is good. Bits of rock, shards of pottery, it's all good."

"Can I have a go?" some people asked, their joviality masking their obvious real hope. These were the ones Polly liked best. Her own passion for her subject had been sparked by seeing archaeologists uncovering a stretch of Roman road. It had been raining, and she had watched, fascinated, as mud-spattered people dressed like builders combed cheerfully through sludgy trenches. It had been love at first sight.

As it had been with Jake. But at that happy, head-spinning stage, she had not known that rats of the worst kind lurked in archaeologists' muddy pits. Love rats. She tightened her lips and rubbed her back harder.

As the old people moved off toward the garden café, she gazed across the lawns at the great pale stone mansion of Oakeshott House. The front unfolded in a succession of columns and windows, a carved baroque palace whose roofline bristled with muscular gods and horns of plenty. Beyond the house and gardens stretched the softly curving park, an enchanted valley whose grassy slopes rolled gently down to a broad silver river sliding slowly between banks of red earth topped with a rich fringe of green.

Perfectly positioned groups of mature trees stood about like guests at a garden party. Beneath them stood the deer: cinnamon, cream, and ginger in the sunlight. A magnificently macho stag was standing in the middle of his women and showing himself off, antlers branching proudly from his head like a crown. Now who, Polly thought sardonically, did *he* remind her of?

"Miss! Miss!" Poppy was jabbing her hand wildly in the air. "Piece of Roman glass!"

Polly examined it. Roman it wasn't; in fact, it was an early twentieth-century medicine bottle. She laid it beside her own growing pile of excavated alcohol bottles. That the Oakeshott gardeners of the Edwardian period were prone to heavy drinking on duty was the picture she was starting to build up. The Oakeshott of the past, it seemed, was not today's businesslike working estate cum tourist honeypot bristling with shops and cafés and run by its ducal owner with military zeal.

Polly had met the Duke of Shropshire for the first time yesterday; he had stopped by the dig and revealed nothing of his reported disappointment with the excavation. On the contrary, he had been charm itself. A tall, handsome man with gray hair and pronounced aquiline features, he had positively blazed with self-confidence yet treated the children with no hint of condescension. He had not missed a beat when Kyle had asked if he had a dungeon he tortured prisoners in. And when he had turned to Polly, His Grace had a definite twinkle in his eye.

"You're a very gorgeous archaeologist," he had said, rather

suggestively, which had made her blush and the children nudge each other.

Polly had returned determinedly to brushing soil off bricks with a toothbrush and ignoring the occasional giggles from the small helpers in the corner. She could not quite shake off the feeling that the Duke had been laughing at her. Glamorous? Her? The squint had been corrected now, but the feeling of having had it could never quite be removed, nor the memories of being teased at school entirely eradicated. Every time she looked in the mirror, whatever she was wearing, however elegant her hair, it was Boz eyes who looked back. And probably always would.

Archaeology was not glamorous either. It meant being out in all weathers, either broiled like a lobster in sunshine, as now, or fending off the lashing wind and rain in voluminous nylon coveralls, your hair flattened by a hard hat and your face as raw as an Arctic fisherman's. You got covered in mud, even in your ears and up your nose, your nails became split, and your hands became roughened, hard, and even bleeding. You ached constantly. Archaeology and drop-dead gorgeousness were, in Polly's experience, mutually exclusive. Apart from in Jake's case, of course...

"Have the children behaved?"

Polly was glad of the interruption. An assertive-looking woman in a red dress had materialized at the side of the pit. It was the primary school headmistress, Mrs. Butcher, come to reclaim her charges. Polly clambered to her feet, smiling. She liked Mrs. Butcher and her obvious ambition for her pupils. She alone among the heads of local schools had spotted the potential a real live Roman dig offered the children and had moved like the wind to secure permission to visit.

Mrs. Butcher's state primary was obviously very short of money; the small numbers who visited Polly were governed by how many could fit into the headmistress's car. Polly had once asked whether a school minibus would be a good idea, and Mrs. Butcher had given a short laugh and said it would indeed, as would the equally likely prospect of a school opera house.

"They've been great," Polly said, straightening up.

"We've been learning all about...*toilets*!" Kyle put in, to hysterical squeals from the others. He was silenced by one look from Mrs. Butcher.

"Sorry, Mrs. B," he muttered, reddening as he tried to dust the mud from his knees.

"Say thank you to Miss Stevenson," Mrs. Butcher instructed in her firm, friendly voice.

"Polly, please," Polly insisted. "They're a very bright bunch," she added.

"They are when you can engage them," the headmistress agreed. "When you can get them off the subject of their Xboxes and Nintendos." Her red breast heaved in a sigh.

Polly grinned. "The Romans can hold their own, though. Kyle couldn't believe it when I explained that they had an empire and a republic, not to mention a senate. He thought all that came from *Star Wars*."

Mrs. Butcher's warm brown eyes were rueful. "I wish we could do more about the Romans at school," she confessed. "But I have some very forceful governors—*very* forceful—and the curriculum committee insisted there was no point studying classical civilizations as they have no relevance to modern life."

"But," Polly began, as amazed as she was outraged, "they've *every* relevance. They're the foundation of *everything*. They're—"

Mrs. Butcher held up one small, capable hand. "I know! And I agree. But there's nothing much I can do—apart from bring the children here, of course. Even if it's only a few of them."

Polly's burning indignation switched to a burning generosity. "Well, I could always come to the school and give a talk or something," she offered. "Roman loos seem to go down well. As it were. Perhaps."

"That would be brilliant," Mrs. Butcher agreed enthusiastically. "You're a wonderful role model. It would be a real eye-opener for them to see someone young, fun, and attractive who's making a career out of an academic discipline. Most of the girls want to be Cheryl Cole."

"I'm not sure how much of a career it is," Polly said ruefully. "I've got to finish my degree, then somehow finance three more years of postgrad study with no definite job at the end of it. The only example I might be setting them is of a lifetime of debt and unemployment."

"No worse than they get at home, then," Mrs. Butcher said robustly. "Some of our kids come from families who think it's normal to be on benefits for your whole working life. I'll find you an assembly slot. I'd better go," she added, with a mock-exasperated glance at the children, now skidding up and down the graveled path bordering the lawn and sending arcs of tiny pebbles sailing through the sunny air. "Thank you again, Polly, if I may. I'm Aurelia, by the way."

Aurelia, Polly thought, as she watched the headmistress steer her charges decisively down the path. Latin for gold. She wouldn't have expected the forthright Mrs. B to have so elaborate a name. Another example of the surprises archaeology revealed.

It was quiet in the gardens, almost deafeningly so now the children had gone. Together with their forceful headmistress, they seemed to have taken the energy with them. Polly felt suddenly listless, and thinking of the long cycle ride home only made her feel worse. She had only herself to blame; Dad had offered to drop her off on his way to work and pick her up on his return. But she had insisted on making the daily journey to Oakeshott and back on Mrs. Pankhurst, her ancient, doughty university bike. Mrs. Pankhurst had no gears, weighed a ton, and bore the relationship to a normal bicycle that a medicine ball does to a football. She was, however, the best possible defense against Mum's irresistible syrup puddings.

Polly closed her eyes and breathed in the perfumed air from the flowers around her. Dozy bees, their back legs thick with pollen, buzzed in heavy, desultory fashion. Even now, at the end of the afternoon, the sun still blazed from a cloudless blue sky. It was hot. Too hot to be thinking of cycling off just yet.

Now the little ones were gone, she could remove the white shirt she wore over her tank top. As the cotton peeled away, she felt the warm air settle deliciously on her exposed skin.

Slowly she began to gather together the tools the children had used. Occasionally she glanced up. Afternoon was the most beautiful time of day at Oakeshott, and today was lovelier even than usual. On the lawns behind Polly, dazzling stripes of sunlight and the long shadows of trees stretched across shimmering grass. Before her, the afternoon sunshine blazed onto the front of the magnificent house, picking out the ripe fruit in the horns of plenty, the heaving breasts of the goddesses and the muscled thighs of the gods. From the center of the private knot garden to the side of the house rose a great fountain, its spume sparkling in the light.

What was that? A scrabbling noise. A panting. Something big. Something behind her.

Polly twisted around. To her horror, a large brown Labrador dog, apparently materializing from nowhere, had jumped down over the edge of the lawn into her pit and was frantically digging with big, swift paws right in the middle of her neat excavation. Soil flew over its heaving shoulders; the stakes and string, uprooted, lay tangled in the dirt.

"Stop it, you beast!" Polly stumbled toward the animal. "Stop it!"

She tugged with all her strength on the dog's collar, but he proved immovable as a block of stone. He was a big creature to start with; the muscles moved smoothly under his shiny chocolate coat, and to his size and weight was added the extra force of sheer determination. "Stop it, you *horrid* dog!" Polly yelled, further enraged by the sun in her eyes, feeling the sweat bead her brow as she continued yanking to no effect.

The strong light was suddenly blocked; Polly heard a thud and the crunch of heels on soil. Someone else was in the pit.

Looking up, she was fixed by a gaze from two deep-set dark eyes and felt a searing sensation through her lower insides like the passage of a bullet. She had a strange feeling of things slowing down. Realizing that her mouth was slightly open, she shut it. She felt winded somehow.

"Sorry about the dog," he said. He was, she estimated, a good foot and a half taller than her and about the same age. He wore an ancient check shirt and torn jeans, and his dark hair had a wild and undisciplined look, as if he often raked it deep in thought, or clutched it in despair or excitement. Polly was suddenly, hideously aware of her tiny tank top, exposing cleavage and midriff, and the fact that she wore no bra.

"Your dog has made a complete mess of this site," she snapped. In her agony of self-consciousness, attack was the only defense.

"I know. Sorry."

He had thick lashes, she noticed irrationally. His nose was long and straight and his mouth was wide and curved upward at the ends, as if it smiled a lot.

The dog had not stopped for a moment. His nose remained on the ground and his paws continued as a scrabbling blur. Polly glared at him, exasperated.

"He must have buried a bone there," the stranger suggested. His words sent a blinding flash of light through Polly. She dived for her rubbish bag and dragged out the bone, to which a banana skin from Poppy's lunch adhered.

"This one?" She chucked it at the dog, which fell on it with a growl of delight.

"Looks like it." The stranger was smiling. "Unless it's someone you dug up earlier?"

"It's a cow bone. The children found it." Polly seized her rake and scraped agitatedly at the ground. What was the matter with her? She frowned and stared at the earth, unable quite to pinpoint why, suddenly, she felt as churned up as it looked.

"Let me help tidy up," he was offering.

Polly shook her head. "I'm fine on my own."

"But…"

She looked him in the eye, finally. "Just take your dog away," she said in a low, steady voice. "*Please.*"

He shrugged shoulders that were wide but not bulky. His build was tall, rangy, slim-hipped. "OK. If that's what you want."

Was it what she wanted? She tore her glance away, feeling a churning in her breast. A warmth that had nothing to do with the sunshine burned in her cheeks. What she definitely didn't want, under any circumstances, was another good-looking, arrogant, brilliant, self-confident bastard like Jake.

Chapter Two

IT HAD BEEN A sunny summer morning by the river in Oxford; the trees were full of light and shimmered gently in the slight breeze. The dew made the grass dance with color, tiny glassy drops of pink, blue, and yellow, as if someone the night before had carelessly let fall a shower of diamonds.

"I'm going to miss you," Jake had said, looking down on her from his towering height and swinging her hand as they walked along.

"Sure you are." Polly had grinned. Jake, in the year above her and his course's star student, was going on a prestigious Roman dig in the South of France for the summer, unearthing the foundations of what promised to be a temple. What was probably unearthable, undiscoverable, Polly thought, was how Miranda had managed to land a place on it too. Miranda, in Jake's year, was celebrated less for her grasp of Roman worship sites than for turning up to digs in pink Hunter wellies and a leopard-skin bikini.

Jake had been outraged when, teasingly, tacitly, Polly had suggested that Miranda might try to seduce him. "I'm only warning you," she had protested. Beneath the tumble of golden hair, Jake's fine blond brows had drawn together in annoyance. Miranda, he explained, was a mere site bunny, the sort who infuriated the serious archaeologists by getting hand cream all over the digging tools. How could he ever be interested in someone like that?

Polly had been reassured. Until that evening, when she had gone around to Jake's college rooms unannounced and found an unscheduled piece of field work in full swing. Jake had been too occupied, groaning ecstatically as Miranda worked on an exposed site between his muscular legs, to notice Polly's white face as it stared, appalled, through the half-open bedroom door.

Too shocked to make a scene, she had reeled away down the narrow, twisting stairs. Next day, the university term over, she had gone home. After leaving messages—unanswered—on her mobile, Jake had called her at her parents', only to receive an indignant earful from Dad, who had gathered the gist, if not the details, of what had happened. After that, all communication had ceased. The relationship was buried forever. Archaeologist though she was, Polly had no intention of raking over this particular bit of the past. None of which, of course, meant that what had happened had not hurt.

And still did. The initial storm of misery had passed, but Jake had ebbed ever since at the edge of her consciousness, ready to break in at unguarded moments and twist her bruised heart anew. Now, however, as she heaved Mrs. Pankhurst along, Polly realized that for the first time in weeks, another man was filling her thoughts. The stranger with the dog, whom she had snapped at.

From the park at Oakeshott, the road home ascended through fields of hilly lime-green pasture scribbled with pale gray limestone walls. At the top were the moors, where a spectacular carpet of heather, purple as an emperor's robe, stretched away to the horizon. This was bordered by a gray stone wall supporting great javelins of willow herb, bright pink against the soft amethyst behind. A honeyish, herby scent was borne on the fitful breeze; Polly's ear caught the fizzing chatter of larks.

The stranger was still there in her mind's eye, dark eyes looking apologetically into hers. Polly felt a twist of guilt followed by a ripple of shame. Should she have been quite so cantankerous? The damage had been minimal after all; five minutes with a rake and the place looked as good as new, or rather, old.

She tried to push the uncomfortable thought away, but another, equally uncomfortable, immediately rushed in to replace it. This evening and what lay ahead.

It was all Mum's fault. "You'll never guess who I ran into today," she had said when Polly, exhausted, collapsed through the door the night before.

"Brad Pitt, Angelina, and the kids?"

"Janet Donald!"

Polly, puffed out, had slumped onto a kitchen chair. "Janet Donald?" The only Janet Donald Polly could think of was the mother of a girl she had known at school, a girl from the same village. But she had never been friends with Allison Donald, or even liked her very much.

"You'll never guess!" Mum had continued excitedly from the stove. "Allison's home from university as well! Isn't that a coincidence?"

Only in as far as all universities tended to break up for the summer, Polly had thought, moodily contemplating the salt and pepper shakers.

"We thought it would be lovely to get you two together," Mum had trilled as she tipped boiled potatoes into a drainer. "Do you good to catch up with an old friend."

Friend! Polly had frowned. Among those who had taunted her about her childhood squint, Allison Donald had been one of the ringleaders. She had straight black hair, a self-satisfied smile, and hooded eyes reminiscent of a snake's.

"You'll have a lovely time," Mum had said confidently, pounding away with the masher. "Allison's very keen to meet you again, Janet says."

"Really? Why?" Allison had never been keen before. But perhaps it was odd that she was even at home. Allison had always regarded the village as rather beneath her.

Mum, spreading the mash over the top of a shepherd's pie, had not seemed to hear the question. "We arranged that you should meet in the Shropshire Arms at eight o'clock tomorrow. They've done it up there—the duchess designed it all herself, apparently—and it's very nice, they say. Oh, and by the way"—she had looked up from making swirly patterns with her fork—"she's changed her name, apparently."

"The duchess?"

Mum had chuckled. "*Allison*. She calls herself Alexa."

"Why?"

"Janet's not sure," Mum had reported over her shoulder as she bore the finished shepherd's pie to the oven. "But you remember Allison. She always was—well—different. Between you and me, I think she thought she was a bit better than the rest of us."

Now Polly dragged Mrs. Pankhurst up the last few hundred yards to the top of the hill. Chest heaving with the effort, she slumped, clinging to her handlebars for support and trying to draw breath into her overstretched lungs. After a few moments admiring the view, she swung a leg over Mrs. Pankhurst's wide, cracked, yet supremely comfortable leather seat and pushed herself off.

After the agony of ascent, whizzing downhill was delightful. A breeze in every sense of the word.

Mrs. Pankhurst descended at first in dignified fashion between the dry-stone walls. With the slopes of twisting bracken stretching beyond on each side, it was like traveling down a gray parting in a great head of curly hair.

The road became steeper and the bracken gave way to slopes of brilliant sunlit green. Mrs. Pankhurst, whose great weight meant that downhill she was a force to be reckoned with, now dramatically picked up speed. The sunlight, dazzlingly bright, streamed through the branches of the overhead trees. Mrs. Pankhurst went faster and faster.

Polly tore around a bend and, unable to avoid a large, sharp stone in the middle of the road, went straight over it. Immediately the road beneath her felt hard and rattly through the wheel rims. A tire had gone. Mrs. Pankhurst had had a blowout.

Screeching to a halt, Polly pulled the heavy iron frame onto the grassy verge and stared in despair at the previously fat rear tire now hanging limply from the wheel. Damn. Damn. *Damn*. It would be a push of at least an hour from here.

Nor was that her only problem. She now felt a tiny shock on her hot forearm. Something had dropped on it: a bead of water. She had hardly noticed that the sun had suddenly gone; looking up, she saw that the hot blue sky was bunched with angry dark clouds. One of the storms summer was famous for was clearly about to do its worst.

Another tiny shock, and another. The beads of water became large spatters. Within seconds, it seemed, the landscape around became first blurry, then completely obliterated by a solid sheet of gray water. The black tarmac rippled with streaming wet, its edges a mass of muddy bubbles.

Polly huddled against the wall, taking what shelter she could from a somewhat sharp and inhospitable thorn bush. Salt water was running down her hair and dripping in her eyes. Her jeans clung wet and heavy to her thighs. Her shirt stuck to her breasts and back. It was like sitting under a power shower, only she was fully dressed and outside.

She waited, head bent, for the pounding of the rain on her skull to be over. She hooked dripping hanks of hair back over her ears with hands that were red and shiny with wet. Meanwhile, on the verge, Mrs. Pankhurst was slowly sinking into the softening mud.

She cocked an ear. Through the fizz of rain on the road and the drip of it in her ears, she could hear something. An engine, coming over the summit, grinding down the hill. It got closer, halted opposite her and she heard the yank of the handbrake.

"Are you all right?" someone shouted. Polly peeped through her streaming hair at an exceptionally dirty Land Rover, its tires thick and shiny with mud, spatters of the same decorating the doors. The windows were down, although she could not see the driver. It was difficult, through the rods of rain between her and the vehicle, to see at all, and anyway, a large dark-colored dog, turning around and around in the passenger seat, was blocking her view of anyone else.

"Fine," she shouted back. The storm would end as soon as it had begun; in any case, did she want to accept a lift from a stranger? The Land Rover did not drive off, however. She heard the driver's door bang and someone's feet on the wet road.

As a tall, dark shape approached through the rain, a thrill as unexpected as it was violent shot through Polly. It was him. The man with the dog from the dig.

"It's you," he said softly.

A powerful wave of self-consciousness had followed the thrill. She could feel her breasts sticking to her tank top. If she stood up, her nipples would protrude like coat pegs. And so she remained crouching despite the cramp in her calf.

"You're very wet," he remarked, a hint of a smile in his voice.

"So are you," she replied, although awkwardness gave it the quality of a retort.

"Yes," he agreed, laughing. The ferocious rain had turned his hair into a shining black slick. His checked shirt clung to his chest and shoulders. Polly felt suddenly breathless. She stared at the dripping grass.

He was examining Mrs. Pankhurst, sprawled in an undignified fashion across the verge. "This yours?"

"Yes."

"Wow. It's quite vintage."

"Yes."

"You've got a flat tire."

"Yes."

"Let me help you up," he said decisively. She tried to demur but his grip was strong. Pulled gently over the streaming ground, Polly struggled to maintain her bent posture.

"Have you hurt your back?" he asked her.

"Yes," Polly lied.

"Where do you live?" He sounded concerned. "I'll take you home."

He led her around to the passenger door. The dog, which evidently bore no ill will despite all the names she had called him, revolved excitedly on the passenger seat barking with delight. "In the back, you," his master commanded, hurriedly brushing the worst of the mud off the seat and gesturing to Polly to get in.

From the window, she watched him heave Mrs. Pankhurst out of the mud—a compliment the bicycle repaid by liberally smearing his clothes. Straining under the weight, he glanced up, saw her looking, and grinned.

He was being so cheerful, despite being soaked through and filthy on her account. She had, Polly realized as he finally swung himself into the driver's seat, caused him far more trouble than his dog had ever caused her.

"I'm sorry I was so rude to you earlier," she blurted at the exact moment the Land Rover engine started up. "I'M SORRY I WAS SO HORRID," she shouted, just as a gear change quieted the roar down. From the rear, the dog barked in alarm.

"Don't worry about it," he said lightly. His voice was level and warm. That he was well-spoken she had noticed before, although there was, she now detected, a hint of something else there too, a slight accent, possibly.

They drove the first few miles in silence. Polly could not think of anything to say and he, apparently perfectly relaxed, did not even seem to be trying. They rattled along, the tires hissing through the wetness of the road.

"I'm Max," he told her eventually.

"Polly."

"You like being an archaeologist?"

"I'm not one yet," Polly muttered. "Still studying." She realized she must sound as if she was contradicting him. Why was everything coming out so awkwardly?

The rain had slowed to a sprinkle; a strong sun was breaking through the clouds. His eyes, Polly saw, were not dark brown as she had thought but the rich dark blue of a warm night sky. Drops like diamonds were swelling on the ends of hair turned a glossy black by the rain.

"What do you do?" she asked bluntly.

"I'm a vet."

"Round here?" Polly was surprised. The local vet was a diminutive Scotsman whose manner was as short as his physique. It was hard to imagine this cheerful, solicitous creature working with him.

Max shook his damp, dark head. "No, still studying." He flashed her a smile. "Like you."

So he was home for the holidays too? "You live here?" And yet there was something about him that was ineffably un-local.

"No. Someone on the Oakeshott estate's a friend of"—he passed a hand through his hair and looked suddenly awkward—"my, um, family and so I jumped at the chance to work on the farm in the holidays. Tell me when to stop, by the way."

She had not noticed them driving into the village even. But now she saw they were passing the low stone wall that ran in front of her parents' cottage. "Here," she exclaimed, flustered.

Max slammed on the brakes hard and the vehicle stopped abruptly. "Sorry."

"It's OK," Polly muttered.

He leaned toward her, his eyes seeking hers. "Can I take you out for a drink?" The dark blue eyes crinkled. "To apologize?"

"Apologize?" Polly repeated cluelessly.

"About Napoleon and all that."

"Napoleon?" She was even more mystified. What had he had to do with it?

"The dog."

"Oh, him." It seemed so long ago. "That."

"Him and that, yes. Are you free tonight?"

Polly was about to nod, then she frowned, remembering Allison Donald. Her frown deepened as she weighed up the possibilities. Change Allison to another night? Blow her off altogether even—from what she remembered of Allison, she would not have hesitated in Polly's place.

"Just thought I'd ask," Max said easily, leaning over and shutting the door with a bang. As the vehicle roared away, she realized he had misinterpreted her frown. He thought she was turning him down.

The Land Rover was disappearing around the bend. Only now did Polly realize it had taken Mrs. Pankhurst with it.

Chapter Three

THE GLEAMING BRIDAL CARRIAGE with its plumes and ducal coat of arms drew up outside the Abbey's Great West Door. Alexa, helped out by liveried footmen, glided into the cool gloom of the ancient cathedral.

The Bach cantata corning from the great organ could barely be heard above the murmur of the crowd. The place was packed. Royalty was present, as well as nobles and notables from several counties around. Adding a particularly decorative touch were the friends of the bride and groom, the cream of the young London set of whom Alexa and her fiancé were the leaders. These occupied several pews in the middle of the nave, seats spilling over with long brown legs in short pale dresses and tumbling hair gleaming from the attentions of monogrammed silver hairbrushes and the best colorists in Chelsea.

Alexa wafted gracefully past in her long white satin dress. It was cut close to her slender figure and its neckline was demure, the better to show off the anything-but-demure gems above it. The diamond necklace had stones the size of apricots, and a pair of matching enormous pear-drops sparkled at her ears. Brought back by an ancestor who had been Viceroy of India, the celebrated parure contained some of the biggest gems outside the Crown Jewels. As Alexa passed beneath one of the medieval stained-glass windows, a rainbow shaft of light set the necklace and earrings ablaze with an almost painful brilliance.

Shutting her eyes against the dazzle, Alexa could see the facets imprinted on her retinas.

She glanced ahead, to the altar. There stood the man of her dreams, the man she had all her life longed to marry. He was no oil painting, but his family owned a lot of them. They had Holbeins, Rembrandts, and a Raphael, all of which he would one day inherit, along with an enormous and very ornate Victorian ancestral home bristling with towers, turrets, and heraldic beasts. The ancestral home, however, was only the beginning of it. He stood to inherit two additional piles, plus an estate in Scotland, a house on Mustique, and a villa on Cap Ferrat. And money. Vast and unbelievable amounts of it. Alexa had estimated that he would, even after death duties, be worth £80 million when he gained the dukedom. And that was in cash—quite separate from the property…

The boom from *Coronation Street* coming up through the purple shagpile jerked Alexa out of her favorite daydream. The copy of *Socialite* magazine she had been perusing slid off the bedspread and hit the floor.

Coronation Street—how ironic was that? Anything further from a genuine coronation was impossible to imagine. Alexa grabbed *Socialite* off the carpet and tried to lose herself in the social pages again.

> *The sleepy Scottish village of Stovie didn't know what had hit it when 400 close friends of Highland beauty Tara Gussett private-jetted in for her wedding to mobile-phone heir Orlando Smellie. The bride arrived at Boggie Cathedral wearing the Gussett family tiara, which had been brought by her mother the Duchess of Skegness by sleeper from Monte Carlo. Then it was back to Gussett Castle for dinner courtesy of party planners Orgasm and dancing by Lord Caractacus Smallpiece's Doo-Wop-A-Doggy-Doo-Doo Band.*

One of the bridesmaids, Alexa noticed, was a particularly beautiful, particularly lissom, particularly carefree-looking blond whose name, according to the caption, was Lady Florence Trevorigus-Whyske-Cleethorpe.

She turned to the next page of *Socialite*; photographs of a society party covered the whole of the subsequent spread. *Le tout jeune Belgravia turned out in force when titled twin Teutons Princesses Dodo and Fifi von Sauerkraut-Bogenfratzel held their joint twenty-first in the London Dungeon*...Alexa looked gloomily at the pairs of bronzed aristocratic legs in couture miniskirts cavorting among the racks and executioner's blocks. She noticed that the longest, bronzest, and most aristocratic of all belonged to a certain Lady Florence Trevorigus-Whyske-Cleethorpe. Her again.

Behind Lady Florence, evidently in hot pursuit, was a face Alexa recognized. It belonged to the son of a duke with whom she had been at university but upon whom she had singularly failed to make any impression. Lady Florence's face, however, betrayed no interest in who might be behind her; it was an absolute, beautiful blank. Alexa felt sick with envy.

In the small sitting room below—or the lounge, as they insisted on calling it—her parents sat transfixed by the latest events in working-class Manchester. There was the occasional boom of her father's laugh in response to some particularly salty televisual rejoinder. "You tell 'er, Ken!" chimed in her mother.

What was the point? Alexa stared miserably up at the paper ball shade that had been yellowish ten years ago and hadn't improved much with age. Far from it, it now looked more like a wasps' nest than ever. That shade had looked down on, had lit, so much of her youth.

Not just the dreaming she had done over magazines like *Socialite* and her subsequent ambition to have one of the glossy lives contained within them, but the very real work she had put in to make it happen.

As the best universities obviously attracted the best people, Alexa had slaved over her A levels. And while she had missed Oxbridge, she had managed St. Andrews, which had seemed more than fit for purpose. As a magnet for the upper classes, the place had form, and even if the biggest royal bag of all had been and gone, there were plenty of minor dukes and lords still littering the place.

Taking as her maxim that of the Boy Scouts—her interest in them otherwise being absolutely zero—Alexa went prepared. Money carefully hoarded from Christmas and birthday presents was equally carefully invested in elocution lessons. Answering an ad in a local newspaper entitled "Lose Your Ey Up Accent" proved the gateway to a paradise of long a's and the reassurance of knowing that never again could she be tripped up by hidden assassins such as "butcher" and "bush." While the lessons were kept a secret from her parents, the results could not be; her mother was mystified and her father openly annoyed. But it was not him, of course, that she was trying to impress.

As well as *Socialite*, her bible, Alexa devoured every etiquette manual she could lay her hands on for pointers about gracious living, absorbing like blotting paper the rules concerning not holding your knife like a pen, how to avoid taking someone else's bread roll by mistake, and the rights and wrongs of powdering one's nose at the table. The final piece of the jigsaw was clothes; there was no point speaking and acting the part if you didn't look it, too. As designer shops were, especially after the elocution lessons, out of the question, Alexa devoted her energies to scouring eBay and built up a respectable collection of secondhand designer wear.

"I hardly recognize you," Dad said disapprovingly, humping the luggage after her as she prepared to board the train to St. Andrew's.

And soon, she planned, he wouldn't recognize himself either; at university, when asked, Alexa would upgrade her father's job in a supermarket warehouse to "commodities dealer." Mum's part-time post in the pharmacist's shop, meanwhile, was repackaged as "consultant to a cosmetics house."

Things had gone well at first. As it was relatively straightforward during Freshers' Week to join the shooting, beagling, and hunting groups and the most right-wing political societies, Alexa was soon running after small yappy dogs through muddy woods and pondering the finer points of Conservative policy. She soon realized, however, that politics did not interest her and shooting was not only harder than it looked, but even less enjoyable.

Fortunately, this hardly mattered; Alexa had managed acceptance in a set who spent weekends in each other's country houses. Her calling card was her sexual availability; the warm and reliable welcome she gave to any titled corridor-creeper who happened to be passing her room, irrespective of whether he was attached or even married. As many of them were, however, the women affected took action and eventually even the thick-skinned Alexa realized that the nickname "Sit Up and Beg" stuck above her pigeonhole, posted on her Facebook page, and pinged through in anonymous text messages might refer to a reputation as the university bike.

But again, it didn't matter, as by then her efforts had paid off in the unprepossessing but nonetheless titled shape of a stammering Border baronet called Sir Lancelot Ffogge. His own prospects were unspectacular—he was the penniless heir to a ruin—but he had the connections Alexa needed. The somewhat ironically named Sir Lancelot, so physically unlike his dashing namesake, was her "starter" aristo; the boyfriend-cum-platform from which she would jump higher up the social tree.

"The *bugger*!" now boomed her father from downstairs, evidently in response to the TV again. In the room above, Alexa felt misery clench her concave stomach. Her mother had been concerned at her thinness on her return from university, but Alexa, used to picking at expensive morsels, was unable to eat the vast piles of mashed potatoes and sausages as thick as forearms, swimming in thick, viscous gravy, that were regularly plonked in front of her. "You need feeding up," her mother would chide in mid-chew from the other side of the sauce bottle.

It was a remark that filled Alexa with horror. There was nothing "up" about feeding. The grand were rarely fat; the women, never.

Alexa had stuck with Sir Lancelot for the first year, but the second had brought promotion to the etiolated and freakishly tall Lord Atticus Pump. From him, Alexa planned a raid on a duke's son—until fate unhelpfully intervened.

The relationship—and Pump's life—met a sudden end when, as high on crack as he was up the building, he fell out of a top-floor window at a party. Alexa's counter in the game of social snakes and ladders now slid down a python almost as long and thin as Lord Atticus himself.

This inconvenient setback had been reversed only when, out of sheer desperation, Alexa had at the start of the next term barged up to the richest freshman, a banking heir called Reinhardt Silverman, and introduced herself as his second-year mentor.

His actual mentor was a bombastic member of the female rowing team called Caroline Squareside, but by the time Reinhardt, who was not very bright, and the even-less-so Caroline found out, Alexa had been mentoring him for some time in her own very special way. Her hopes of an engagement were high. Then the shocking news broke that Reinhardt's father had absconded with the contents of his financial management portfolio and was wanted by Interpol.

As Reinhardt fled and markets plunged all about her, Alexa

was left only with her own wrecked dreams of riches. Worse still, as Reinhardt's conceit and appalling manners had alienated everyone whose acquaintance she had previously nurtured so carefully, she had become *persona non grata*. After three years of frantic social climbing, she was left right at the bottom with precisely nothing and no one.

Not even a degree, as studying had seemed irrelevant if she was going to marry Reinhardt, whose sexual demands had anyway precluded time in libraries, Alexa had failed her end-of-year exams. Back home she had come, her purse empty and her suitcase stuffed with tweed shooting suits and designer party outfits. She had had no money even for a cab home. Waiting at the railway station for her parents' battered Micra to come and collect her, she had restrained herself with difficulty from throwing herself under a passing express.

"Is anything wrong, Allison?" her mother kept turning to ask as they drove home. Alexa, in the dark safety of the back, shrank against the seat so the overhead streetlights could not illumine the expression of utter misery that for once even she could not disguise.

Once home, she was tortured by the possibility of redemption, of email invitations, of friendly messages on Facebook. The upper classes had short memories—most of those she had known had no idea what day it was; perhaps, in her absence, she had been forgiven. Rehabilitated. But as her parents had no computer, she had to walk miles to the local library, where invariably the computers were out of order. Or else monopolized by tramps or tense men in baseball caps jiggling their legs agitatedly as they pounded the keys. If she managed to log on, there would be only spam in her inbox, while on the Facebook pages of those few who hadn't yet managed to unfriend her, she saw her former acquaintances falling out of exclusive nightclubs, hanging with the band at hip music festivals, or playing drunken hide-and-seek at weekend house parties. None of which she was invited to, and obviously never would be again.

She would clench her fists with helpless envy at this glittering life she had once been so close to, but which now seemed further away than the moon.

Her social life these days consisted of sitting at the pine kitchen table opposite Dad with his mug of tea beside his brown-sauce-smeared plate as he made sausage sandwiches with Mother's Pride. But at least he rarely spoke, being more involved in squinting at the distant—and always on—television. Mum, on the other hand, liked to pore over the local freesheet, and in particular the large adverts for coach trips it contained. But at least if she was weighing up the opposing merits of "Lakeland Loveliness" and "Dutch Bulb Field Spectacular," she wasn't asking about Reinhardt, who Alexa had mentioned briefly in a rare unguarded moment and whose fate she could not bring herself to speak of, any more than she could bring herself to acquaint her parents with her failure in the exams.

Death seemed the only option; having briefly, histrionically, considered suicide, Alexa realized that a demise was in fact necessary. Allison Donald must be killed off. Only then would the social disaster of university be eradicated. She would change her name, regroup, rebrand. Allison Donald would die and Alexa *Mac*Donald rise from her ashes like a phoenix, smart-sounding in an untraceable, vague, castle-in-Scotland sort of way. She was pristine, full of potential, and had never been called Sit Up And Beg. She was the future.

But where, otherwise, was this future? Alexa had no idea. Certainly it was not at home. Home was so small! Horribly, *vilely* small. There was barely a stride between the entrance to her room and the side of her bed with its hideous frilly bedspread. Oh, the bedrooms she had stayed in at weekend country house parties! Bedrooms where you walked for minutes on end from the wide, high entrance before encountering any inanimate object, often human, male, and awaiting her services.

"You should get out," Mum had advised at tea earlier this week. "You should meet up with someone your own age," she had added, looking up from perusing the delights of "Torbay and the English Riviera." "An old friend from school, maybe. Do you good."

School! Alexa had been too shocked to speak. After life in the social fast lane, the thought of her late, despised schoolfellows made her almost want to retch.

"I saw Mary Stevenson today," Mum added. "She says Polly's home."

"Boz eyes, you mean," Alexa snarled, her lip remaining firmly curled.

Her mother's eyes widened behind her glasses. "I didn't realize *she'd* changed her name as well. It's quite the fashion, isn't it? But—Boz eyes…?" Mum looked puzzled.

"We used to call her that at school," Alexa snapped. "She squinted. Probably still does."

As Mum chuntered on, Alexa tuned out, then suddenly tuned back in again.

"What did you say?" she demanded.

"I was just saying that Polly's at Oxford," Mum repeated obligingly, frowning over "Cream, Crabs, and Coastline: A Cornish Cornucopia."

Alexa stared, her mind's eye filling with pictures of dreamy spires, of carefree, well-heeled young men in white tie drinking champagne. Oxford! Old Boz eyes had gone *there*? It was too bloody irritating to contemplate, except that, of course, it might be useful. A sly smile began to curve Alexa's thin lips.

Mum, most unexpectedly and possibly unprecedentedly, was right. It might be worth seeing Polly. One never knew who she knew.

Lots of people she had cultivated had relatives at Oxford; there could be a way back in.

Chapter Four

THE SHROPSHIRE ARMS HAD changed, Alexa thought, opening the door on what had been a room full of sticky carpets and fruit machines to find newly exposed flagstones and artfully mismatching wooden tables with vases of fresh flowers.

And Polly Stevenson had changed even more. That could not *possibly* be her. Panic and shock coursed through Alexa as the pretty, slender woman with shining brown hair waved from a corner table. Was it actually at her though? Alexa looked behind her to check, but there was nothing to see but the chic striped bucket chairs and exposed brickwork of the bijou new dining area.

Was this really Boz Eyes? But there was no sign of a squint; the eyes examining her as she approached were big, dark, thick-lashed, and absolutely regular. Cheekbones had come from somewhere. And had she had a lip job?

"Allison?"

"*Alexa*," Alexa corrected stiffly.

"Oh yes." Alexa noted, annoyed, that Polly seemed amused for some reason. "You've changed your name."

"As have you," Alexa shot back.

"How do you mean?" Polly's eyes widened in surprise.

"Well, whatever happened to Boz Eyes?" Alexa asked brightly, throwing her jacket on the back of the chair, pulling it out, and sitting down.

She saw Polly flinch. "The squint's gone. A while ago."

Still touchy about it, Alexa thought, half triumphant but half cautious too. She might need this woman. She had better be careful.

"You look the same, though," Polly added, to Alexa's silent fury. The remark was not, however, payback for the squint remark, or even intentionally provocative. The snapping snake eyes and black hair *were* the same, as were the thin lips and skinny frame. And even as a schoolgirl, she had given this same impression of both hiding something and knowing something the rest of the world didn't.

"I *can't* look the same," Alexa said indignantly.

Polly regarded her, head on one side again. Certainly, Alexa was more dressed up than before—the studded leather miniskirt and high-heeled sparkling sandals looked more nightclub than country pub, even if this one had been given an aristocratic makeover. She felt underdressed in comparison, in the same old white jeans that were her faithful standbys for any night out, teamed with the usual black top. There had been no time for makeup, not that she bothered with it much these days.

"Maybe your hair's a bit longer," she conceded. "Why *have* you changed your name by the way?"

Alexa smiled enigmatically and swung her hair about. The gesture concealed inner panic; Polly might know some useful people. The story must be got right. "It's not really changed," she said quickly. "Alexa was my middle name anyway. And my mother's maiden name was MacDonald."

Polly stared. "*Really?*"

"Mmm hmmm," Alexa confirmed smilingly. Now that danger was over, she could continue gathering clues from Polly's appearance. Thick hair, thin figure, she noted—the physical ideal of the upwardly mobile. And that white jeans/strappy black top look was totally Kate Middleton, absolute Liz Hurley. Especially with that long, shiny dark brown hair tumbling about those tanned shoulders.

That really was a serious yacht tan. A real villa bronzing. Who did she know? Alexa opened her mouth to ask.

"Can I get you a drink?" Polly asked suddenly. She felt rather unnerved by the other girl's stare.

"Oh...yeah...champagne, don't you think?" It seemed years since Alexa last tasted what she had previously enjoyed several times a day.

It was Polly's turn to stare; the Shropshire Arms had only ever served beer and lager before. But perhaps the duchess had made over the wine list too.

"Anything wrong?" said Polly, having arrived back at the table with a champagne flute and a glass of rosé for herself.

"I suppose I'm used to better vintages." Alexa put the flute down with a twist of her lips. She smiled patronizingly at Polly.

"I expect we both are."

"Not me." Polly shook her head. "After a long day's exploring ancient cultures, I usually relax with a beer." Or several, in the case of most of her colleagues. Archaeologists, on the whole, had less delicate tastes than champagne.

Alexa smiled. It was the Oxford point of entry she had been looking for. "I'm fascinated by ancient cultures, too," she drawled.

"*Are* you?" She wouldn't have guessed it by looking, Polly thought; although there was a definite touch of the site bunny about that miniskirt.

"Mmm, do you know Jamie Athelhampton? His family's the oldest in England."

"*Who?*"

"You *are* at Oxford, aren't you?" Alexa asked suspiciously. If Mum had got that wrong, this was an entire evening wasted.

As, to her relief, Polly nodded, she added, forcefully: "Then *surely* you know Piggy Athelhampton. Owns half of Dorset. Everyone knows Piggy."

"I don't know Piggy," Polly said. "Does he do archaeology?"

"*Archaeology?*" Alexa, taking a sip of champagne, almost choked in surprise. "Why would he do *that*? Why would *anybody*?"

"It's what I do," Polly said mildly, sipping her rosé.

Alexa's mouth dropped open. To go to Oxford and do *archaeology*? Was Polly mad? "But isn't archaeology all coveralls, huge boots, and hard hats?"

"To an extent."

"Wandering around in muddy holes with beardy men and snaggle-toothed women with glasses?" Alexa had once seen *Time Team*, but only by accident. She had assumed it to be a program about top-of-the-range watches.

It was an uncharitable way of describing some of her colleagues, Polly thought. But that there was a grain of truth could not be denied. She shrugged and took another sip.

Alexa was now frantically trying to connect the new idea of Polly being an archaeologist with the established one of her as a member of Oxford high society. "You specialize in castles?" she blurted desperately. "Stately homes?"

"Roman toilets, actually." Polly took another sip of wine.

Toilets? Alexa almost fell off the wooden cottage chair recently stripped and polished at the duchess's behest. Polly studied in a place where the streets were paved with peers. And had emerged with a passion for ancient privies.

"So what about you?" Polly asked calmly. "What are you studying?"

"I'm, um…" Alexa racked her brains. She had no intention of admitting to Polly Stevenson that she had failed her exams, was living with her parents, and had no prospects of any sort. "Actually, I'm taking a break from studying at the moment."

"Really?" Polly's archaeological instincts sensed something being concealed. "What are you doing with your break?"

Alexa's eyes dilated in panic. She had imagined herself doing this evening's cross-examining, not the other way around. Suddenly, out of the blue, *Socialite* magazine shot into her mind.

"I'm going to London," she said, in a rush. "I've got a job on… on…a glossy magazine."

"Which one?" Polly asked immediately.

"*Socialite*," Alexa shot back boldly.

Polly shook her head. "I don't know it," she said, finishing her wine with a smile.

Chapter Five

POLLY HAD FOUND IT oddly hard to explain what had happened to Mrs. Pankhurst. "You took a lift from a stranger?" Dad had deduced disapprovingly. "Then you forgot to take the bike out?" he had probed incredulously. "But where is it now? Where is he? Who was he?" Questions that were hard to avoid as she now depended on Dad to take her to Oakeshott every morning.

Mum, meanwhile, was teasing her about being distracted. She seemed convinced Polly had "met someone" the night of the glorious reunion with Allison Donald. "Do you good to have a boyfriend," she teased.

"So long as he's not like the last one," Dad had rejoined with feeling.

"Have you got a boyfriend, miss?"

Kyle's voice broke loudly into her thoughts. Polly looked up from where she was squatting in a corner of the trench, photographing the foundations from a previously uncaptured angle. "That's a rather impertinent question, Kyle," she said, trying to smile.

"Is it?" The boy looked genuinely surprised. "But Mrs. Butcher told us in assembly the other day that there was no such thing as impertinent questions, only impertinent answers. She said someone called Oscar Wilde had said that."

Polly raised her eyebrows. Mrs. Butcher's mission to raise her pupils' sights was as unceasing as it was impressive. "And anyway, miss," the irrepressible Kyle continued, "we were wondering. About your boyfriend. I said I thought you must have one, being so pretty and everything."

The other children, who were listening avidly, began to giggle.

Kyle pressed on. "Poppy thought you hadn't, didn't you, Poppy?" He looked accusingly at his schoolmate. "She said she thought you needed a nice man, didn't you, Pops?"

"I did *not*," riposted Poppy, obviously untruthfully. The class looked nervously at Polly.

"I'm grateful for your concern," she said good-humoredly. "Now just get back to work, the lot of you."

The site settled down, interrupted only by the occasional interested passerby. Polly had by now delegated the quips and question-fielding to Kyle, who reveled in the responsibility. "No, we're not digging for gold; we're digging for two-thousand-year-old toilets!" she heard him state now. "But if you want modern ones, there's some by the entrance."

When Polly, frowning into her viewfinder, heard a flutter of talk from the children, she assumed it was yet another ambling elderly couple and did not look up.

"She's over there, mate," she heard Kyle say.

Polly raised her head from her camera to find herself looking at a pair of legs in jeans, up, up, up and eventually meeting Max's dark blue eyes. Time stood still. The noise of the children faded far into the distance.

Napoleon, meanwhile, dived into the trench and began to lick her knuckles with a rough, warm tongue. Then he rolled over onto his back and lay, pleadingly waving his great paws.

The children roared. The Labrador wriggled in ecstasy, thumping his tail appreciatively on the ground.

"I think he wants to be forgiven," Max said gently, jolting Polly out of her trance. She blushed.

"Forgiven for what?" Kyle was demanding.

Napoleon gave Polly another grateful lick. She poked him. "You're forgiven, you old ham."

"Isn't he just." Max was shaking his head, smiling. "I've brought your bike back, by the way. The porter at the garden gate's got it. I didn't want to leave it in the bike racks in case someone stole it."

Polly glanced at him; was he teasing her? Who in their right mind, after all, would steal Mrs. Pankhurst? "Thank you," she muttered, as crowds of butterflies wheeled around her stomach.

"I mended the puncture," he said.

"Thank you."

"And I cleaned it."

"Thank you."

"So you have to come out for a drink with me now, don't you?"

Polly sensed the children listening. Self-consciousness rushed in on her like a tidal wave.

"You don't have to," she said, more grumpily than she'd intended.

"Oh, *miss!*" she heard Poppy say under her breath. Kyle, meanwhile, clutched his hands to his head as if his favorite team had missed a goal.

"I know," Max said easily, skating over her mood as if it was ice. "But I'd like to. I'll come and pick you up, shall I? I know where you live, as they say."

Alexa had spent the morning in her bedroom reading *Socialite* magazine. The idea of working there, which had suggested itself so unexpectedly in the pub, had gathered momentum overnight.

It had, Alexa was sure, come straight from the desperate depths of her unconscious. But as a solution to her problems, it could scarcely be bettered. An upmarket glossy magazine, the sort that covered the grandest weddings and parties and employed scions of the nobility in exchange for access to their address books was exactly where she needed to be in order to gatecrash her way back into society. Why had she not thought of it before?

And yet two considerable obstacles stood between Alexa and the realization of this ambition. Getting the job in the first place would be difficult. Positions on glossy magazines were highly sought after. Applying in the normal way would be pointless. She would be in competition with the best-connected people in the country.

The second problem was accommodations in London. Many of her university friends had homes in the capital. But thanks to the disaster that had been Reinhardt, Alexa was no longer in touch with any of them. She had burnt all her bridges, and with them all possibilities of free accommodations.

"Dinner!" yelled Mum from the bottom of the stairs. *Lunch*, Alexa corrected silently as she reluctantly sloped downstairs.

Dad, already tucking into pork pie and beans at the kitchen table, eyed her as she drifted through the door. No one at home ever waited for everyone to sit down, Alexa thought disdainfully. Still less stand behind their chairs until all diners were present.

"Got some news for you," Dad announced, tipping more ketchup on his pie. Alexa's stomach twisted in disgust. She *hated* ketchup.

"What news?" she asked haughtily, sitting down and deploring the absence of a napkin. Unless he was about to announce the acquisition of a penthouse in Mayfair or the takeover of the publishers that owned *Socialite*, nothing he could say could possibly interest her.

"Need a job, don't you?" Dad demanded. "Well, they've got vacancies at Tesco."

Alexa felt as if she had been shot. She doubted a more shocking thing had ever been said to her in the course of her entire life, Atticus's death and Reinhardt's father included. She choked, even though she had not eaten anything. "*Tesco!*" she managed after a glass of water.

"Yes," Dad said, fixing her with an oddly piercing stare. "Tesco. They treat their staff well. Perfectly good career."

It was crucial not to panic. Playing for time, Alexa slid her shaking knife into the enormous lump of greasy pork pie that lay on her plate. "I'm not sure Tesco's quite me," she said, dropping her voice to a frail whisper and looking appealingly at her mother.

"I'm university-educated," she added, choosing her words carefully.

Her father's face reddened. "That's not what I've heard," he said shortly, forking in another lump of pie and chewing violently.

"That university of yours rang us just now. Small matter of unsettled fees." His eyes glinted into hers from beneath his gathered brows.

Alexa quickly dropped her gaze.

"What *did* you spend your money on, eh?" Dad slammed the ketchup bottle down vehemently. "Not your course, by the sound of it. You haven't even passed, they said."

Alexa stared at the jelly—its clear amber color so ironically reminiscent of a yellow diamond—between the pork pie crust and the lumpy pink meat. Tired, frustrated, and, rarely for her, slightly frightened, she was tempted to throw herself on her parents' mercy. But was honesty really the best policy? Telling her father the truth—that the money had gone on cases of champagne for cocktail parties and bespoke tweed suits for shooting weekends—was unlikely to calm him down.

She therefore took the only other course open to her. Shoving aside the plate of pie, she buried her head in her arms and wept hysterically. After a few seconds, after which she calculated her eyes would be piteously red and bloodshot, she looked up and directed her anguished gaze at her mother. "I didn't want to tell you about the breakdown," she heaved between sobs.

Her mother responded magnificently. "Breakdown! Oh, *love*!" she said, reaching clumsily for her daughter's hand, her voice so warm with sympathy and concern that Alexa almost felt guilty.

"Breakdown?" Dad echoed suspiciously. Although the heat, Alexa noted with relief, seemed to have gone from his fury.

Alexa propped herself on her elbows, pushed back her hair dramatically, and placed her hands over her face. "I just couldn't cope," she sobbed into her palms. "I needed the money for the medicine. The therapy sessions. The, um, doctors."

Neither of her parents said anything, although their silence took different forms. Alexa, an expert in social temperature, felt the loving and concerned warmth from her mother's side of the table meeting, over the ketchup bottle, the chill blast of suspicion and disbelief from her father's. There was clearly more work to do.

She stood up, still sobbing, and threw Dad an impassioned and accusing glance. "It was hell!" she cried dramatically. "You've got no idea. You can't even begin to imagine what I've been through!"

As she fled through the sliding door of the kitchen, she reflected that her parting shot had the advantage of being true, at least. The rest, of course, could be disproved by one single phone call to her tutor.

In her bedroom, Alexa buried her ears in her nylon pillows, expecting a storm of fury to break downstairs. Yet the house remained calm. After some minutes had passed, there was a knock at the door and her mother came in.

"Hello, love," Mum said gently.

Alexa, edging away at this dangerous display of maternal closeness, winced inwardly at Mum's brown nylon trousers, lemon cotton blouse, and the worn gray toweling slippers that completed the outfit. How *could* this woman be her mother? It was many years since she had finally, regretfully, abandoned her childhood fantasies about being a princess who'd been swapped at birth. But occasions like this brought it all back.

Her mother, as usual, was clutching the local freesheet. Was it bloody welded to her or something? It was even open at one of the coach tour ads.

"What do you think of this, Allison, love?" Mum asked brightly, holding the page closer for Alexa to see.

Alexa, wincing at the use of her real name, stared at the newsprint a few inches from her face. What was she supposed to be looking at? Her eyes were running up and down the columns, but beside the half-page ad for Vernon's Bus Trips, she could see nothing but a report about the local Women's Institute enjoying a knitting demonstration.

Her mother angled the paper away, and her thick forefinger, a forefinger that for as long as Alexa could remember had been plunged in washing-up bowls, grappling with peelers, hanging out washing, or stirring mugs of instant coffee, now stabbed repeatedly at the bus tour ad. "You can go all sorts of places. Scotland, Wales, even Dutch bulb fields."

"Very nice," Alexa said acidly. Coach tours, how unbelievably dreary. How unbelievably cheap and miserable and provincial. The ad was inviting readers to book Christmas trips already, for something called a Turkey and Tinsel Tour. She felt almost physically nauseous.

"They're nice coaches these days," Mum was saying. "Got lovely toilets and everything."

Toilets! Alexa shuddered with horror. *No one* said toilet. Or lounge. Or pardon.

"Pardon?" Mum said, looking at her.

"I didn't say anything," Alexa muttered.

"No, but you made a funny noise. Anyway, love, come on. Which one do you fancy?" Her mother's face was bright beside the newspaper.

"*Fancy?*" Alexa's brain, normally so quick, was struggling to understand.

"I thought it'd be just the thing to cheer you up. You and me could go on one, I thought. There's a Lincolnshire Cheese Weekend…"

Her mother was suggesting she went on a *coach tour*?

"A Whiskey and Haggis Tour of Scotland…" Mum went on cheerfully.

The words fell on Alexa's amazed ears like cymbals on a stone floor. Lincolnshire *Cheese* Weekend? When she had stayed at Lincolnshire's finest stately homes? Whiskey and Haggis Tour of Scotland? When her previous experience of Caledonia was baronial piles with stalking, fishing, shooting, and maids who packed up your clothes in tissue paper?

There was a painful sensation in her heart; was it breaking, or was this organ failure?

"Or there's Choirs and Steam Trains—that's a three-day tour of Wales," Mum continued blithely.

Alexa was gasping for air. *Wales!* The only thing about Wales she cared about was the Prince of it.

"I can't," she managed in strangled tones. "I'm going to…to…to…*London*! Tomorrow!"

Mum looked amazed. "You what, love? *London*?"

She made it sound like Mars, Alexa thought contemptuously. "Yes. London. I've got a job interview there," she snapped, adding, in a wheedling voice, "although I'm going to need you to lend me the train fare."

Once Mum, stunned, had reeled back downstairs, Alexa snatched up the latest copy of *Socialite* from the top of the pile by her bed.

She had almost forgotten what optimism felt like. But now all her old determination came roaring back. Working at *Socialite*, she would meet more influential people in a week than she had managed in three years at university. Once she had installed herself, she could spin the web in which she intended to catch a very grand fly indeed.

She flicked to the magazine's party pages. She was not the only one catching a grand fly, by the looks of it. Leading London socialite Lady Florence Trevorigus-Whyske-Cleethorpe seemed to have been promoted.

> *Frotton Park's celebrated annual charity polo competition got off to a dramatic start when the Hon. Fizzy Slutt slid out of the saddle after scoring. Fortunately billionheir fiancé James Hugh-Fortune was on hand to mop Fizzy's fevered brow, as was best friend Lady Florrie Trevorigus-Whyske-Cleethorpe, who, as is increasingly the case these days, had HRH in tow.*

Had the ubiquitous, all-conquering Lady Florrie managed to attain official royal girlfriend status?

Chapter Six

THE FRONT DOOR OF the flat slammed shatteringly. Lady Beatrice Trevorigus-Whyske-Cleethorpe, deep in the pillows and even deeper in dreams, reared up from under the bedclothes in panic. For a disoriented moment of blind-dark terror, she felt certain that someone, somehow, had breached the cast-iron security of the Palace Gate flat and she was about to feel the chill edge of a murderer's ax in her skull. Then she realized what it really was. Her sister. Back from a night out.

"Florrie," she growled into the pillow. "Bloody Florrie."

Beatrice wondered angrily what time it was. She'd gone to bed at midnight herself, and hours must have passed since then.

She sat up, rolled over, and fumbled for where the alarm clock was buried Through bleary eyes, she saw that it was three a.m. Fury seized her. Three bloody a.m.! If her sister *had* to come back at this hour, then why in God's name couldn't she open the front door *quietly*? But never in her life had Florrie evinced the smallest degree of concern for others. Which was infuriating enough in itself; what was more infuriating still was that she had always got away with it.

Too angry now to go to sleep, Beatrice flung her legs out of bed, padded across her bedroom carpet, and opened the big white-paneled door of her room. Down the shadowy, picture-hung corridor, she could see the sitting room at the end—brilliantly lit; Florrie had turned all the lights on—and Florrie herself sprawled out with her shoes on over the pale yellow sofa.

"My head!" Beatrice could hear her moaning. "Beattie!" came the sudden sharp yell. "Omigod, I'm dying, I swear it. Get up and get me some Nurofen, would you, there's a darling."

Beatrice winced. She hated being called Beattie; her name was bad enough without being abbreviated to sound like a cockney char, even if that seemed roughly the relationship she enjoyed with respect to her sister. She marched down the passage to the sitting room in her pajamas and stood over her prone sibling, arms akimbo.

"It's three in the morning, for God's sake."

Yet despite occupying, as she almost always did, the moral high ground, there was, Beatrice sinkingly felt, something about Florrie that made this seem redundant.

It was that she was so lovely. The fact that normal rules simply didn't apply to people who looked like her was something Florrie, in her sister's view, took full advantage of. She was possessed of the kind of beauty that had people rushing up to give her flowers in the street, striking up conversations from the other side of the road, and exiting Tube carriages and re-entering them just to have the pleasure of looking at her again. It was the sort that prompted streams of men to follow her down the pavement, and for some of them even to propose marriage. Beatrice knew this because all these things had happened, some more than once, at times when she had been out with her sister.

Even now, despite the beginnings of what would doubtless be one of Florrie's famous hangovers, her sister still appeared far younger than her twenty years and as pure as if the mere thought of alcohol had never so much as crossed her alabaster brow.

One slender white arm was draped languidly over her lovely oval face with its perfect bow-shaped lips and flawless skin. Florrie's beauty had an old-fashioned quality; it was easy to imagine her floating about thirties salons in shimmery column dresses, laughing tinklingly into martinis.

It was so bloody unfair, Beatrice thought. By most people's standards, she herself was very attractive, being tall and slender as most of the family was. But next to Florrie, she was nothing.

She had her father's black hair and dark complexion, while Florrie had inherited the golden beauty of their mother. But it wasn't simply that she was dark and Florrie was fair. It was more subtle than that.

Florrie spoke in a lower, huskier voice that made all the difference. Her eyebrows were spread at a better angle. Beatrice had gazed often enough in the mirror to know that her nose, while similar to Florrie's, was longer, lacking absolutely her sister's delicious retroussé. Her mouth was also thinner and flatter than Florrie's pert, peachy pout. More elongated here, more squashed there, in some ways the same, but ultimately absolutely not. Her face was like Florrie's—but reflected in a hall of mirrors.

Florrie's great big eyes—violet-blue to her own dark brown—were closed. Her long pale blond hair was pulled back, revealing neat little ears adorned with, Beatrice noticed with a stab of fury, a pearl earring that looked suspiciously like one of her own. And which, more to the point, she had already refused to lend Florrie some days ago. Draped carelessly over the sofa, Florrie's long, slender body, with its elegant small breasts, looked longer, more slender, and paler than ever in a mini-dress of some thick, pale, pearly material. Beatrice recognized the Valentino that Igor, the oligarch's son, had recently presented Florrie with. There was a big orange stain on the front of it that looked like ketchup.

Pale high-heeled sandals, one of which had smeared mud on the cushions and one of which had its strap broken, hung off long, delicate white feet. The sandals were hers too, Beatrice saw, outraged. Her new ones. She hadn't even worn them yet.

Please God, Beatrice prayed, let her leave this flat soon. Please God let Ned propose so she, Beatrice, could become Marchioness Dymchurch, have her own estate and fortune, and get away from her bloody sister.

He had, she was sure, been within a hair's breadth of asking her to marry him tonight, but then the waiter had interrupted and asked whether he wanted gravy. The result was that Ned, incapable of holding two thoughts in his head at once, had never got back to the subject, for all her efforts to lead him there.

"The Nurofen, darling?" Florrie drawled.

"Get it yourself," Beatrice said unsympathetically. But it *was* three in the morning—probably quarter past by now—and Florrie had wrecked her new sandals and, by the look of it, lost one of her earrings.

Her sister opened the huge, dewy, violet-blue eyes that could look so bored and blank but which now expressed hurt, surprised innocence. "Darling!" she chided. "You might get it for me. You really might. I feel terrible." She rolled over and groaned, but she even did that beautifully, Beatrice noticed, the deep-cut back of the dress emphasizing her pale and delicate shoulder blades. "Perhaps I should lay off those Aladdin's Cave cocktails," Florrie muttered into the pale primrose sofa cushions.

"They're the ones that cost two hundred pounds each, aren't they?"

Florrie rolled back, her expression impish, and nodded her head enthusiastically before clutching a cushion to it and groaning. "They're yummy."

"How did you afford them?" Beatrice demanded, knowing that her sister had spent her way through her entire monthly allowance a fortnight ago.

"Oh darling," Florrie sighed. "Not all that Genghis Khan stuff again."

"Genghis Khan?"

"Oh, silly me, I mean Nelson Mandela."

"Nelson Mandela?"

"You know what I mean. Financial responsibility and all that." Florrie yawned.

Not for the first time, Beatrice reflected that the hundreds of thousands that had been poured into her sister's education might just as well have been poured into a black hole and to all intents and purposes had.

She and Florrie were two of ten children, although only they and their brother had that particular combination of mother and father. Lord Whyske and Lady Annabel had had six marriages between them, of which the union producing herself and Florrie was their second in both cases. She, Ed, and Florrie were, as Beatrice saw it, the center of the family Venn diagram, although it was painfully obvious that hardly ever were they the center of their parents' thoughts. Lady Annabel moved constantly between social events; Lord Whyske, meanwhile, seemed always to be in meetings with lawyers—about business or his latest divorce. And when he wasn't, he made a point of disagreeing with whatever Lady Annabel had said on any topic. There was no love lost between them; Beatrice had learned that the only constant of her parents' behavior was that they always took opposite viewpoints. Was it any wonder, she would muse, that of the three children her parents had had together, she herself was unnaturally controlling, Florrie was semi-feral, and of Ed the least said the better?

She emerged from these thoughts to find her sister looking at her pleadingly from behind her cushion.

"I really do need a Nurofen, darling. I had several Aladdin's Caves practically to myself. And then I danced for ages." She began to hum "Brown Sugar" and moved her arms languidly about. "Omigod, we had such fun. HRH and I were sticking our tongues out at each other. He was on great form."

Dread reared up in Beatrice like a terrified horse. Of course, it had always been a danger. Florrie had been a member of the young royals' set for some time, albeit a star in one of the more distant galaxies. But now the papers were beginning to pick up on it. There had been something in *Socialite* just the other day.

The idea of her sister being linked romantically to the ruling house was too ghastly for words. For one thing, it would completely overshadow her own wedding—always presuming it happened. For what was a mere marchioness compared with a princess, especially a princess who looked like Florrie?

"I thought you were out with Igor," she said accusingly.

"We're taking a break from each other," Florrie said vaguely.

This was not, so far as Beatrice was concerned, good news. Admittedly she had never liked Florrie's Russian lover and the way he sat about their flat demanding, in a rolling accent, the answers to questions like "Why have one London mansion when you can have two?" and "Why line up with the losers in first class when you can have a plane to yourself?" Igor's father owned, among other things, an airline business, and Igor had his own Learjet on permanent standby. "Igot" seemed a more suitable name, Beatrice thought, given how frequently his listeners were reminded of his possessions and his father's wealth. According to his son, Igor Senior earned ten thousand pounds an hour just in interest.

Ned had been disgusted the weekend Igor had crashed a shooting party at the Whyske family seat and blasted everything in sight with a Kalashnikov with "Rock and Roll" stamped on the side. When, apparently for fun, he shot the bowler off the head of the butler delivering the guns' lunch to the moor, Beatrice had found her calls to Ned unanswered for weeks.

But while Igor was a liability, he was less of a risk to her own happiness than a prince of the blood royal. Oligarchs' sons attracted little general attention; they were two a penny after all.

"Why the break with Igor?" Beatrice asked nervously.

Florrie stretched her arms in the air and gave a voluptuous sigh. "He's a bit demanding," she said with a smile.

She wasn't joking, Beatrice knew. Some of Igor's requirements were most unusual, even though Florrie had accepted them in her usual breezy way. Her sister was, Beatrice had discovered since they had started sharing the flat, quite startlingly open about sex, usually in the kitchen on Sunday mornings as Beatrice made tea and the Russian snored in Florrie's bedroom. Beatrice, narrowly avoiding slopping boiling water over her wrists, felt the insight into Igor's preferences didn't make liking him any easier.

"Oh, I'm going to make a cup of tea," Beatrice said jumpily, twisting so hard on her bare heel that her skin burnt against the carpet.

"Make me one, will you, darling?" Florrie called as Beatrice stomped in the direction of the flat's smart black and stainless-steel galley kitchen.

As she waited for the kettle to boil, Beatrice strove to calm herself down. Florrie had been out with the prince. But so what? The prince had taken lots of girls out. It was not a serious gesture, nor was Florrie, Beatrice was fairly sure, seriously interested in him, whether as a person or a prince. And particularly the latter. Social class was not a subject that interested Florrie. Duke, dustman, it was all the same. All that mattered was whether they amused her. Or whether she wanted to sleep with them.

Besides, making an effort, pursuing something, was not Florrie's style. She never made a play for anyone. Not even her worst enemy—which is what Beatrice frequently felt like—could accuse her of man-eating. The far more depressing truth was that

Florrie just attracted men like jam drew wasps, simply by virtue of existing. She never tried in the least, which of course made her all the more irresistible.

Beatrice poured the water into two mugs and carried one through to Florrie, who had now left the sitting room and was settled happily in Beatrice's bed. "Mine's all unmade." She smiled beseechingly.

"Your trouble is that you're lazy, Florrie," Beatrice grumbled as she passed the tea into her sister's frail hands. "You really must be the idlest girl in Britain."

"I know!" Florrie beamed, her smile lighting up her face and showing a row of small, even, pearly-white teeth. "Aren't I awful?"

Chapter Seven

IT WAS A FEW days afterward, and in the sitting room of the flat, the telephone was ringing. Beatrice dived between the antique furniture to answer it.

"Darling!" exploded the other end.

"Mummy!" Beatrice beamed, relieved that her mother had finally responded to her frantic texts and voice mails transmitting the triumphant news. Ned Dymchurch had proposed at last, which meant that Lady Annabel, whose organizational skills were as formidable as the rest of her, could finally sink her teeth into the wedding.

"It's fantastic, isn't it?" she burst out, unable to stop herself.

"Amazing!" cried Lady Annabel.

"I can't believe it!" Beatrice exclaimed. It had indeed been a close-run thing. The sommelier, tiptoeing purposefully toward their ice bucket, had almost done for it this time. Only Beatrice seizing the bottle herself and sloshing it violently into both their glasses had saved the moment.

"Me neither, darling. All my dreams have come true!" There was a little yelp of ecstasy at the end of Lady Annabel's sentence. "So, is our princess there?" she added.

"Princess?" Beatrice frowned. Her heart began to hammer. "Princess who?"

She realized in a flash that they were talking at cross-purposes. Of course they were, she chided herself bitterly. What had she been thinking of, to imagine her mother was remotely interested in her?

"Oh *really*. Princess who do you think?" Lady Annabel's tone was scornful. "Just a mo, I've got it here…yes…ahem…" Lady Annabel cleared her throat as if preparing to address the nation. "Lady Florrie Trevorigus-Whyske-Cleethorpe…seen dancing cheek to cheek with HRH—and we're not talking faces…"

"Oh God!" groaned Beatrice, clasping her forehead with an icy hand.

It was too cruel. After what seemed like years of working on him, Ned Dymchurch was finally going to take her up the aisle. But now Florrie looked set to steal her wedding thunder, as she had always stolen everything else. Shoes, earrings, attention most particularly.

"Awfully funny, don't you think?" Lady Annabel gurgled. "Cheek to cheek and we don't mean faces!"

"What else does the article say?" Beatrice asked miserably.

"Now where was I, oh yes…Lady Florrie, blah blah…deep in intense conversation…"

Beatrice relieved some of her feelings in a hot, savage snort. "Intense conversation! Florrie!"

"Don't underestimate her," Lady Annabel ordered. "Florrie is full of surprises."

Beatrice didn't disagree. The latest, provoked by the arrival of a clutch of bills, had been the discovery—unbelievable with anyone but her sister—that Florrie had no idea one paid for utilities and thought electricity came out free from the wall.

She took a deep breath and made a determined effort to return the subject to herself. "Er, Mummy, now the wedding's definitely on, we need to think about the venue."

"Yes! St. Paul's or Westminster Abbey?" Lady Annabel sighed

happily. "I prefer the Abbey myself, *so* romantic, although of course we need to remember it's a royal wedding and you can get more people in the Cathedral…"

Beatrice did not reply. Her smoldering sense of resentment had become an angry blaze. It was so unfair.

"And, of course, Florrie would look fabulous in a tiara," Lady Annabel wittered on. "But no doubt Her Majesty will want to lend a crown from her collection; she usually does on these occasions…"

She was, Beatrice realized, going to be entirely eclipsed. A sickening sense of hopelessness swept through her. Back rammed against the Chinese floral wallpaper, she sank slowly down to the thick-pile beige hall carpet.

"It will be so lovely to see the dear Prince of Wales again," Lady Annabel carried on. "Perhaps at Highgrove…"

One of the few addresses, Beatrice knew, that the socially rocket-fueled Lady Annabel had not wedged her foot in the door of over the years.

Her mother finally rang off, but immediately the telephone shrilled again. Beatrice hesitated before answering it. A journalist, wanting the inside track on her possibly soon-to-be-royal sister?

But no, it was her father. He had not yet spoken to her about her engagement. Beatrice's heart leaped with the hope that he, at least, was calling to congratulate her.

"Beatrice?" Lord Whyske barked in his testy baritone, as usual dispensing with time-wasting expressions of affection.

"Hello, Papa! You've heard about…?"

"Florrie, yes. Is she there?"

"No, Papa. Isn't it great news about Ned, though?"

He was speaking over her, however. "Busy being measured for her crown, eh?" Self-satisfaction softened the hard edges of Lord Whyske's voice.

"But you have heard?" Beatrice persisted. "About me getting married to Ned…"

"Must go. Spot of trouble on the Cornish estate to sort out."

The phone went abruptly dead at her father's end.

Beatrice stared miserably at the receiver. If Florrie became royal, what about the consequences for her? Had her parents even stopped to consider them?

The whole point of going up the aisle with Ned Dymchurch was to show the world—and especially her parents—that she, Beatrice Trevorigus-Whyske-Cleethorpe, was not as hopeless as everyone had always thought. She might have grown up in the shadow of her beautiful and beguiling sister, but she was the first to marry, and marry spectacularly well. Marry a mansion, an ancient title, and, most of all, money. But who was going to care now?

Nor was this all. Apart from the disaster it would be for her own nuptials, the idea that her sister could join the royal family was absurd. For all her gentle birth and patrician upbringing, anyone less suited than Florrie to the rule-bound rigor of court life was impossible to imagine. The royals had, after all, only just recovered from the last havoc-wreaking blond.

She needed a drink, Beatrice decided. She opened one of the many bottles of vodka that stood on the kitchen shelf, presents from the Pole who did the ironing. She reached into the freezer and flung some ice cubes into a tumbler. As an idea started to bloom in her mind, Beatrice stopped gulping the spirit and sipped thoughtfully.

Twenty minutes later, she lifted up the phone to call the diary page of a leading tabloid newspaper.

"Er, I'm calling with a story about Florrie—um, sorry, Lady Florence Trevorigus-Whyske-Cleethorpe. Yes. The one who was dancing cheek to cheek with HRH. Er, who am I? I'm an, er, friend. Yes, that's it. A close friend. And I just happened to hear her saying something rather amusing and terribly personal. It seems she's not quite so keen on him as everyone imagines…"

The journalist was fascinated, delighted, grateful, and awfully nice. After a few minutes, Beatrice put the phone down feeling a mixture of guilt and relief. But mostly, it had to be said, the latter.

Chapter Eight

"Is my darling Florrie there?" gasped a hysterical Lady Annabel over the telephone the following day.

"She's out," Beatrice said flatly. *Hello, Mother. Yes, I'm fine, thank you. Yes, I'm very excited about my wedding. I'm so glad you are too. Yes, absolutely we need to get together about the guest list. When are you free?*

"Out with…?" Her mother's voice was plangent with enormous hope. "With…the Prince?"

Beatrice bit her lip. Her mother's obvious anguish was unexpectedly affecting. "Well, sort of yes and no," she muttered.

"*Yes and no?*" shrieked Lady Annabel, as if someone had come up behind her and inserted a cattle prod in her rectum. "Yes *and* no?"

"I mean, she's having lunch with a prince. Only," Beatrice pressed on as her mother threatened excitably to interrupt, "not that one."

"Which one, then?" screamed their mother, who probably, Beatrice felt, didn't need a telephone to make herself heard at the moment.

"Erm, a German one she met in a nightclub. Prince Von Something Zu Something Else. Erm, Mummy," Beatrice added swiftly as Lady Annabel tried to butt in again, "you know, um, with the other prince… That's…actually…over. It was in the paper this morning," Beatrice added in a tone perfectly poised between innocence and surprise.

There was a silence, then the other end burst into cataclysmic, eardrum-busting grief. "Yes, I know! I've just read it!"

Beatrice hastily reminded herself that it was the best thing for everyone. She had to keep strong and concentrate on that. That and her mother's utter lack of interest in her own nuptials.

"How *could* she have said that?" heaved out Lady Annabel between racking sobs. "How could she have been so...*stupid*?"

"I've no idea, Mother," said Beatrice, as if nothing could be more astounding than Florrie's being stupid.

"And who is this...this *friend*...anyway?" spat the Belgrave Square end.

"Can't help you there, either." Beatrice crossed the fingers of her free hand and looked guiltily upward.

"I've a good mind to ring the editor," Lady Annabel thundered, her mood changing from abject to belligerent in an instant. "Challenge them to name this...*friend* or face legal action. Does the blasted newspaper realize what's at stake here? I've already ordered my hat! Lots of little crowns entwined with the Prince of Wales's feathers..."

"I wouldn't," Beatrice said quickly.

"Wouldn't what?" Lady Annabel demanded. "It's fabulous. Monarchist with a twist and very stylish..."

"I'm not talking about your hat. I mean, don't ring the paper. You'll only make things worse."

"I don't see how they *could* be worse." All the air had gone from Lady Annabel's voice. She sounded flat and crumpled, like a burst paper bag.

"It won't make any difference," Beatrice advised gently. "The Palace says the relationship's over. I'm afraid you'll just have to accept it, Mother."

Hysterical, heartbroken sobbing greeted this advice. "My poor princess! My poor princess!" lamented Lady Annabel, in the manner of a Greek tragedian.

"My life is over. Everything I worked for, everything I believed in, is *over*."

"There's always my wedding…" Beatrice began eagerly, but the line had gone dead.

Almost immediately, the door of the flat opened and the woman at the center of the drama appeared. Florrie looked absurdly young, fresh, and pretty in a white dress and black ballerina flats, which, Beatrice recognized crossly, were once again her own. Her bag's mine too, Beatrice thought indignantly, recognizing the seventies plum patchwork suede tote she had bought in a junk shop in a moment of madness. Florrie, somehow, made it look like new-season Bottega Veneta.

"I didn't expect you back so early," Beatrice said cautiously.

Florrie smiled, shook her blond hair, tossed the bag to the carpet, and sank down on the sofa. "I started to feel a bit rotten," she announced cheerfully.

"Was it the food?" Beatrice had no idea what one ate at lunches with party-going German princes. Perhaps piles of sauerkraut to keep the strength up.

"No, it was him," Florrie declared. "He said my legs were like a foal's and my eyes were pools and my hands were like a dancer's and my neck like the stem of a flower…" She yawned. "It was ghastly. I felt that he was trying to chop me up and bury all the pieces."

"Oh dear," said Beatrice, reflecting sardonically that it must be nice to be complimented so routinely that you literally got sick of it.

"Oh deer, you mean." Florrie giggled. "Because he compared me to a beautiful doe as well, starting shyly at the approach of the huntsman or some such crap. It makes me rather long for Igor. He never said *anything* nice to me, the poppet. I'm rather wondering if we should get back together." She pushed herself up off the sofa.

It was, Beatrice thought, difficult not to admire the way Florrie shrugged off trouble like a duck did water. To watch her tripping about the flat like Tinkerbell, one would never suspect that her fledgling romance with a prince of the blood had died a brutal and public death in the newspapers that very day. On the other hand, she reflected, it proved she had been right to assume that Florrie did not care two hoots about her royal relationship.

The telephone rang.

"Will you get it for me, darling?" Florrie sang. "It might be one of those horrid papers and I don't want to talk to them. I'll only say something silly and get myself into even worse trouble." She giggled, gathered up Beatrice's bag, and flounced out of the room.

As she passed, Beatrice's nostrils caught a delicious floral scent. This, too, had the ring of familiarity. The bottle of Joy Ned had given her for her last birthday, possibly?

Annoyed, Beatrice picked up the receiver.

"Florrie?" boomed the voice on the other end. "What the devil…?"

"It's Beatrice, Papa," Beatrice said hastily.

"*Give me Florrie!*" The lord roared painfully into the tender inside of her ear. He was as angry as she had ever heard him, and that was saying something. Beatrice had heard him angry a lot.

"Hang on, Papa. Florrie! *Flor-ree!*" Beatrice laid the receiver on the thick carpet and rushed down the corridor to her sister's room. "*Florrie!* Papa wants you."

"Tell him I'm out," Florrie pleaded, looking what was for her that most unusual of all things—scared. Of all the people in the world, their father held the distinction of having some small impact on his daughter, not least because he was the conduit through which her money flowed.

Beatrice returned reluctantly to the phone. "Sorry, Papa. Thought it was her, but it was Maria, the cleaner."

"Is it true?" Sir George demanded.

"About Maria?"

"Grrrr! Is it true what I read in the papers? Florrie's buggered it up with HRH?"

Beatrice confirmed that it was.

"It's a bloody disaster," Lord Whyske ranted.

Beatrice, for whom it was just the opposite, bit her lip.

"I've had enough!" His Lordship boomed. "It's time that girl was taught a lesson. I'm cutting off her allowance, tell her. She'll have to get a job."

Chapter Nine

MAX HAD ARRIVED TO pick her up in a Land Rover almost unrecognizable because it was so sparkling clean. Polly, watching for him out of the kitchen window, sprang up in excitement. Could he possibly have washed it just for her? She watched him jump out, his white shirt spotless and his jeans old-looking but clean. His dark hair shone in the sun and the sight of his brown forearms, finely muscled and corded, made her heart thump.

Until, that was, Dad, who had opened the door to Max, cast a suspicious look over him and expressed, in a voice heavy with warning, the hope that he wouldn't "mess her about like the last one had."

Polly wanted to sink through the floor. "*Oh, Dad!*" she hissed through gritted teeth, squeezing past him in the doorway.

They had driven to the pub in awkward silence, Polly racking her brains for something light and amusing to say, something to dissolve the tension.

"Where's Napoleon?" was all she managed in the end.

"He's not mine," Max said, frowning through the windshield. "He belongs to the people I'm staying with."

"Who are they again?" Polly asked; Max had never really explained. His hands tightened on the steering wheel and he did not explain now.

"Here we are," he said, drawing up in front of the pub. Like its sister pub the Shropshire, the Oakeshott Arms had recently received a makeover at the delicate hands of the duchess.

"They do champagne by the glass," he told her, waving the wine list.

"No thanks," Polly replied in alarm, remembering Alexa. She wanted this evening to be as different as possible.

But then she saw how surprised he looked and realized she had been too vehement. Possibly she had sounded ungrateful. Rude, even. A great start. Even greater than the one Dad had given the evening. Oh *why* had he said that? He was trying to protect her, Polly knew, but surely there were subtler ways? She had no idea what Max had made of it; he had said nothing. But it was unlikely he was impressed.

And so, while Max approached the bar, Polly hung her head and stared at the pub's rustic flagged stone floor. He returned, handed her a glass of rosé, and straightaway an embarrassed silence fell, made worse by the fact that the Oakeshott Arms, previously thumping with landlord-sponsored heavy metal, was now a Muzak-free zone.

"Shall we go outside?" Max suggested eventually.

"That would be lovely," Polly replied politely. Their exchanges, she felt gloomily, had every bit of the excitement of those between the vicar and local spinster in a bonnets-and-shawls BBC drama.

They took their drinks outside to where several wooden tables and benches nestled against the pub's rough, sun-warmed stone wall.

They smiled at each other self-consciously, then looked awkwardly away at the same moment. "It's very pretty here," Max said rather stiffly.

"Yes," Polly agreed, feeling more Cranford-like than ever. Judi Dench was going to walk past in a crinoline at any moment.

She would have fitted in; Oakeshott village was a Victorian ducal fantasy dating from the days when the owners of the big house determined the entire surrounding landscape. Every cottage bordering the green reflected a different architectural style. One was half-timbered Tudor, with red herringbone brickwork filling in the spaces between the black oak beams. A miniature Italian villa stood next door, and beyond that a tiny medieval castle and a Swiss chateau. The gardens were as picturesque as the houses, the hollyhocks mighty and magnificent, and with vegetable patches neater even than Mr. McGregor's in *Peter Rabbit*. The apple trees along the old brick back walls were bent double with the weight of the fruit. Around the cottage doors, roses foamed in pink profusion.

A more charming setting, particularly on a soft summer evening, full of scent, sunshine, the calls of sheep, and swooping birds, was difficult to imagine. And yet Polly was suppressing a rising sense of panic.

Self-doubt had set in. Polly was increasingly sure that Max was desperately regretting inviting her out and only asking questions to be polite. Nervously, in a monotone, her eyes not quite lifting to his, she answered his questions about the excavation.

Gradually, however, things warmed up. It was impossible for Polly to talk about her subject without enthusiasm, and even to her self-critical eye and ear, Max's interest began to seem less feigned. He seemed particularly intrigued by the children, snorting at some of Kyle's more choice remarks.

"He's completely fascinated with the fact that they're toilets." Polly chuckled. "None of the children can get over the idea that we're working on an ancient loo. But loos *are* fascinating."

"Why?" Max asked, his expression hovering somewhere between incredulous and amused.

"Because they show that people haven't changed over the centuries."

Max laughed. "I suppose so. There's not much variation in what happens after all."

"Quite," Polly said, about to expand on the point. Then, realizing it perhaps wasn't the ideal subject for a romantic first date, she blushed and twiddled with her glass stem.

His expression, as he looked at her, was serious. "What's the most amazing thing you've ever discovered?" he asked her.

The question pulled her up short; Polly could not think what to say. She fought the sudden, insane urge to shout, "You! *You* are!"

"I suppose," she said slowly, trying to gather her scattered wits, "it was something we found in a dig in Dorset. A skeleton that had been buried with a dog."

"Dog?" Max's eyes lit up.

"Yes, we thought it was a grave offering, or even a sacrifice. But then we found both of the skeleton's arms arranged so that they were cradling it."

"So it was a pet?" Max leaned forward, intent.

"Yes. It was moving, seeing the demonstration of a relationship like that." Polly smiled fondly at the memory. "The love a person had for their pet, thousands of years ago."

Neither of them said anything for a moment.

"Like you say," Max remarked, breaking the silence, "people aren't all that different. I'd probably want to be buried with my dog, frankly."

"What sort of dog is it?" A much-loved one, obviously; his eyes were shining with affection.

"He's a spaniel called Beano." Max's voice was soft. "Been my pet since I was a little boy. Only got one eye, though, poor old devil."

"One eye?" Polly was immediately interested.

"Blind in the other. Squints a bit too. He's always been funny-looking." Max flashed her a grin. "But I love his squint. He's more interesting because he's not perfect."

Polly stared at him. She felt a rush of something like adoration. She had suffered so much of her childhood because of her squint. And here was Max, who loved his dog all the more because of his.

"I'd love to meet Beano," Polly said sincerely. "He sounds like my kind of dog. You see," she added shyly, "I had a squint as a child. We'd have a lot in common."

Max looked at her eyes for a long time, perhaps longer than was strictly necessary. "A squint?" he said softly. "You can't tell at all now. Which eye was it in?"

Polly's face was warm with self-consciousness. "This one." She lowered her right eyelid in a wink. "They used to call me Boz eyes at school," she added, embarrassed.

He frowned. "Boz eyes?" he repeated in his slight accent. "What is that? It doesn't sound very polite."

"It's not." She smiled suddenly. "But who cares now? It was ages ago. Anyway, I'd love to meet Beano. Is he with you?"

Max shook his dark head. "No, at home."

She was about to ask where home was when she saw that something had distracted him. He was staring over her shoulder, toward the village green.

"Excuse me," he said softly, standing up.

Polly twisted around. There was a dog on the green, a Jack Russell. She had vaguely noticed it before; it had been galumphing about in the center, bolting backward and forward, crouching, then leaping, as dogs did at play. But now it had stopped, she saw, and was standing in the middle of the green, one paw raised in the air, whining sadly.

Max was already crossing the grass toward it. She got up and followed him. When she reached him, he had dropped to the ground and was examining the animal's hurt paw. The dog had sunk its head on its uninjured one and was emanating a sad keening noise like an alarm.

The paw Max held had a cut on it. Blood was smeared across the white fur.

"Poor thing!" winced Polly, who was helplessly squeamish and hated the sight of blood.

"It's not as bad as it looks. Broken glass, I suppose." Max's eyes narrowed as he looked around the green. "People just chuck things; they don't realize how dangerous it can be for animals. Here, just hold this, would you?"

While he rummaged in his pockets, Polly found the Jack Russell's bloody paw plonked matter-of-factly in her own. She held on to the twitching limb and realized to her surprise that her feelings of nausea had faded. Max clearly expected her to cope and be calm, so cope and be calm she would.

"Thanks, Nurse." He flashed her a grin. Taking back the paw, his hand accidentally touched hers, and she felt suddenly breathless.

Max, meanwhile, had calmly produced a small can of antiseptic spray from the pocket of his jeans. It was like the Tardis in there, Polly thought, as he dragged out some cotton wool balls and bandages. Talking softly to the dog all the time, he swiftly cleaned and dried its wound. His head was very close to Polly's; she could see faint threads of glittering brown in the glossy black.

He glanced at her and saw her looking; hurriedly, Polly transferred her attention to the dog. "His name's Archie," she observed, flipping up the disc on the dog's tartan collar. "There's a phone number. I'll ring it, shall I?"

Max, busy, grunted assent. She scrambled to her feet, rummaged in her bag for her phone, and paced around the green as she dialed. No one answered at Archie's home; Polly left a brief message on the voice mail.

She returned to find that Archie was calm now, and Max was wrapping his paw.

"You've done a great job," Polly said admiringly.

"Did you talk to his owners?" was all Max wanted to know.

"Voice mail."

He muttered something under his breath.

"Perhaps they're out looking for him," Polly suggested.

He looked up, his face lit with a soft smile. "You always think the best of people, don't you?"

She shrugged and dropped down to tickle the dog's rough fur. "He's sweet."

"Can I see you again?" Max asked her, so quietly that at first she thought he was addressing the dog. She nodded, her heart hammering so hard she felt she might be knocked off balance.

His fingers brushed hers; fire juddered up her arm. "I really like you, Polly," he said quietly. His dark head moved toward her; she gasped softly.

"*Archie!*"

They both looked up.

An enormous woman in muddy jodhpurs was striding over the green. Prominent blue eyes bulged from a wide, red, weather-beaten face framed by a short gray bob.

Archie struggled to his feet. He managed a weak bark of welcome.

The woman gave a fruity roar, "Archie!" She broke into a heavy run. "Archie! I've looked everywhere for you! I've been all over the village! Where did you go to, you silly, *silly* dog? And what have you *done* to yourself?"

"You were right," Max muttered to Polly. He leaped to his feet and passed Archie to his tearful owner, who hugged him to her great fawn bosom, exclaiming with love and relief and crooning into the top of his head. "Silly baby!" she was murmuring.

Polly looked at Max. They grinned at each other.

The woman looked up from fondling Archie's ears. Her veiny face was purple with emotion. "I can't thank you enough. I'm Lavinia Butts-Upward, by the way."

"It's just a cut, Mrs. Butts-Upward," Max told her politely. "It won't take long to heal. It was fairly clean."

After more thanks, Mrs. Butts-Upward hurried off with her prize. Left alone with Max, Polly braced herself. Would he remember what he had been about to say? Or had the moment passed?

It seemed as if it had. They walked back across the green. Their shadows slid ahead over the bright grass; his tall and broad-shouldered, striding confidently; hers smaller, more awkward, trailing slightly behind. Had she merely imagined he was about to kiss her?

She felt dreary with disappointment. If only Mrs. Butts-Upward hadn't barged in…but no. The poor woman had been ecstatic to be reunited with her dog.

Max, as he walked, seemed to be lost in thought and stared into the distance. She guessed he had forgotten all about her.

"Well," Polly said resignedly. "Thanks for the drink. I guess I'd better be going."

He was all attention in an instant. "No," he said. "Don't go." He stopped and turned to her. She had the head-spinning feeling that something was about to happen.

Silently, gently, he drew her into his arms. She looked up at him, wide-eyed; his mouth approached hers and grazed her lips lightly. Then it grazed them again, more firmly this time, and suddenly he was kissing her. She rose into him, kissing him back, ablaze with a sudden overwhelming want.

"This is ridiculous," she murmured, dizzy with desire. "We've only just met, after all."

"No we haven't." His eyes, deep midnight blue, were searching hers. She felt she was looking into infinity. "I feel I've always known you," he said softly. "Don't you feel that?"

"Yes," she said with a sigh. "Yes. I do."

Chapter Ten

THE CHATEAU OF SEDONA looked down to the blue Mediterranean from its position high in the hills. Originally a small defensive fort, it had been, over the centuries, enlarged and embellished by the de Sedonas, successive rulers of this tiny mountain kingdom that had broken away from its Italian city-state rulers in the fourteenth century. Fortunately it was so small and insignificant that no one seemed to notice, medieval Italian city-states being, in those days, far too busy fighting each other to worry about piffling little villages declaring UDI.

Yet Sedona's rulers had been successful over the centuries, and now the chateau spread over a wide area. Four great round towers with conical tops marked the outer limits of a romantic riot of turrets and castellations, mostly decorative and entirely delightful when, as now, each tower fluttered with a colorful flag. Were a child to draw its ideal palace, the ancient castle of the kings of Sedona was exactly what it would come up with.

The sunshine was pouring down cheerfully over Sedona this morning. The Old Town flowed out behind the palace, a rough cloak of red roofs over a picturesque knot of narrow medieval lanes whose shape and length had been dictated by the rise and fall of the rocky terrain. The lanes were ten feet across at the widest, and the walls were so close at their narrowest that you could shake hands over the street.

The walls of the lanes were painted in ice-cream colors: vanilla, lemon yellow, and apricot orange enlivened by the occasional pink. The lanes themselves were a mixture of houses, shops, and cafés, linked by shady passages and arcades that led to fountained courtyards and neat, tree-planted squares before well-kept official buildings over which fluttered the royal standard: three golden keys against an azure background.

The pumping, parping sound of a brass band came from the cobbled square in front of the chateau gates. Here, every morning when the King of Sedona was in residence—as almost invariably he was—the Royal Sedona Regimental Band went through its paces.

The sun caught the whirling white pompoms beating the big bass drum and the gold braid glittering on the front of the musicians' red coats. From nine a.m. until noon, the band bashed and blew, making up in spectacle and gusto what it lacked in musical finesse. Its repertoire harked back to the visit of Victoria, Queen of Great Britain and empress of India, in the 1880s. Sedona liked to remind itself of its most famous royal visitor, and so "Land of Hope and Glory," "Oh I Do Like to Be Beside the Seaside," "Cwm Rhonnda," "The Skye Boat Song," and other British favorites could be enjoyed daily by resident and visitor alike.

Behind the scrolled wrought-iron gates, before the sea-facing façade of the great building, a sequence of terraced gardens followed, like wide grassy steps, the contours of the hillside on which the chateau was built. While Sedona was generally a warm and sunny place, its high, exposed position and the occasional appearance of those dry Mediterranean winds, the dreaded mistral, meant that flowers could be difficult to grow.

Despite these limitations, the Queen of Sedona had managed, with her customary patience and diligence, to produce a surprising number of roses. Two varieties, which she had named after her sons Maxim and Giacomo, were even registered with Britain's Royal Horticultural

Society. These roses, along with others, now formed the colorful middles of borders placed symmetrically about the palace lawns.

At the other end of the town from the pinnacles and towers of the palace reared the answering spiry bulk of Sedona's twelfth-century cathedral, built at the very edge of the mountain plateau and commanding the principality's most magnificent view. Anyone standing atop the sweep of the cathedral steps enjoyed a stunning prospect as mountains and valleys tipped away to a distant sea where yachts sat about like tiny white toys on a giant blue silk rug. The views extended up and down the coast from Monte Carlo to the north and Bordighera in Italy to the south.

It was at the great Gothic cathedral, vaulting soaring within, gargoyles and statues bristling without, that all the main ceremonies of Sedona royal life were conducted. Every king since Engelbert the Fat had been baptized in the black marble font, while lined up like a spread deck of cards by the high altar were gold-lettered marble tombstones going back to Engelbert the Ugly. The impressive nave, meanwhile, had resounded to the footsteps of every marrying royal couple since the thirteenth century, the latest being those of current monarchs Engelbert XVIII and his consort Astrid.

The Old Town this morning was peaceful, the red herringbone brick-paved lanes still drying in the sun after the daily clean and cheerful with the sounds of people calling greetings or good-byes as they opened or shut the glass doors of the various bakeries and cafés. The air was filled with the scents of fresh coffee and freshly baked coeurs de Sedona: the small, icing-dusted, custard-filled pastries that were a specialty of the town.

The owners of the souvenir shops were opening up too, arranging their piles of glossy paperback guides and laying out pennants, pencils, flags, and key rings displaying the royal coat of arms. The same three golden keys against a blue background were available on sweatshirts, bags, T-shirts, and baseball caps; one particularly go-ahead retailer had recently introduced a screenprinted Warholesque version.

On the postcard stands, the Sedona royal family beamed out at passersby. Dark-haired Prince Maxim, eldest son of the King and Queen, had the serious expression appropriate for someone poised to inherit the responsibilities of a throne. The Crown Prince was currently at university in England.

His younger brother Prince Giacomo had not, to employ one of his mother's favorite euphemisms, gone down the university route. To his parents' dismay, he had gone down the hedonism and girls route. At only eighteen, the prince already enjoyed a fearsome reputation in what nightclubs Sedona possessed, and in most others up and down the coast.

Giacomo's expression on the postcard was something between a smolder and a smirk. His striking looks were of an entirely different variety to his brother's. Smirk aside, Giacomo was the image of his mother; Sedona's popular, gentle, and kind Queen Astrid, who was fair-skinned, blue-eyed, and blond.

The postcards of the monarch showed King Engelbert looking short, gray-haired, and stern. Both he and the Queen were magnificent in golden crowns and red velvet robes edged with ermine. These had the effect of making them look as if they ruled an entire empire, not a small and somewhat eccentric kingdom less than five miles across at its widest point and with fewer than five thousand subjects.

Most residents of Sedona were there by virtue of the favorable tax status the principality offered and maintained a luxurious lifestyle. Quietly so, however; Sedona had traditionally distinguished itself from its flashier neighbor Monaco by attracting people who, while possessed of equal wealth, were more discreet in displaying it. If Monaco shouted, Sedona whispered.

The problem was, fewer and fewer people were hearing it. And as a result, financial trouble loomed. Sedona's few indigenous industries were in the service sector and required tourism to give them life blood. Tourism drove hotels, restaurants, and retail. It drove, by association, the building trade. It had, for the last 150 years, been the principality's main source of income, but now it was dwindling.

The fact that, for the first time in its history, Sedona was about to slide into deficit had plunged King Engelbert into panic. Like all rulers of ancient fiefdoms, he prided himself on his ability to hand over a flourishing inheritance to the next generation.

How could Sedona get its visitor rates back up again? How could it promote a glittering and youthful image to compete with its glitzy neighbor? Monaco was seemingly invincible, its tourist-attracting advantages including a reputation as a celebrity playground, a Grand Prix, and a recent royal wedding. In comparison, Sedona's claim to have one doctor for every five head of population and the best wheelchair access on the Mediterranean lacked razzmatazz. There may well have been celebrities in Sedona, but no one alive could remember who they were.

To address the issue, Engelbert had just engaged at vast expense Sedona's first ever public relations consultant, a man in red spectacles who spoke about audience mapping, mood boards, message development sessions, and thought leadership platforms. Yet despite all this, and the time the King spent with him, the solution had yet to be arrived at.

The fact Sedona lacked the port and harbor that had enabled Monaco to develop so spectacularly was, the PR consultant had said, clicking his mouse and moving his arrows about, the main reason for its relative poverty. He had recommended that Sedona develop its own marina, down on the coast some ten miles from the mountain principality itself. The international luxury yachting scene, at its most international and luxurious in the immediate area of the

Mediterranean, could bring much-needed wealth to the kingdom through vast annual fees levied to berth boats. The marina could also be an events venue. The problem was, or at least so Astrid had gathered, that a building project of that scale needed investors, and in a time of international downturn, they were not forthcoming. Something needed to be dreamt up to bring them in.

Engelbert was in conference with his PR adviser this morning, dreaming of just that something. Astrid, who wriggled out of all such meetings if she could, was in her garden, among her roses. She snipped busily at her Rosa Mundi, noting with satisfaction how pronounced the deep pink stripes were this year.

There was no one else in the garden apart from Beano, the spaniel who had been her elder son's childhood pet. She was charged with looking after him while Max was away. Beano was old and had been blind in one eye since birth. He still had a squint in the other. This, however, did not stop him pacing suspiciously about the lawns as if on the lookout for intruders.

"Come on, Beano," the Queen coaxed, picking up a stick from the carpet of brown needles beneath the tree and throwing it for him. But instead of galloping off in an auburn blur as in his youth, Beano moved slowly across the grass, his lustrous white plume of tail—looking perhaps less lustrous now—waving less keenly than it had. "Come on, boy," urged Astrid, noting sadly the dog's arthritic legs. Beano was not as young as he had been, but then who was?

Beano didn't seem to know he was old, though. He ambled toward her with his spaniel's grin, the light of pride in his one working eye. She ruffled the top of his head; he dropped the stick and licked her hand. Astrid stooped and picked him up, not caring that his damp paws marked her dress. To bury her nose in Beano was the nearest she could now come to hugging her beloved elder son, without whom, it had to be said, Beano would very probably not exist.

He had been the runt of the litter, and the intention had originally been that the royal dog would be the pride of his species. But once Max had seen the tiny, half-blind puppy cowering at the back of the breeder's kennel, no other dog in the world would do. When, finally, he had left for England and the course he longed to take, his only regret, Astrid suspected, was leaving Beano. She had been required to make all manner of solemn promises to look after him, which she had fulfilled to the letter.

Beano looked into her eyes; a question was there, as always. "He'll come back soon," the Queen assured him. "There are holidays."

Astrid missed her son more than she had ever imagined or would admit, particularly to his father, who had been doubtful about the English veterinary course in the first place. But she was happy in the knowledge that Max was doing what he wanted. It was more than she had ever been allowed herself.

She closed her eyes and tried to ignore the distant sound of the brass band thumping away. Astrid was not a fan of brass. But over the years she had trained herself to accept it, as she had trained herself to accept everything else about Sedona.

At least so she had thought. Lately, however, she had been plagued by the same dream. It was twenty-five years ago and she was back in the palace of her parents, twenty-two and trembling as she was shown into the heavily furnished office of her redoubtable father the King. There came the doomy closing click of the double doors behind her. Her father looked up over a pile of state papers and regarded her sternly for a couple of seconds before brusquely gesturing that she should sit.

Astrid could feel again the scratchy red brocade material beneath her fingers as she sank down to be told that she had, for the sake of her family, to break with the handsome American scholarship student she had met when presenting prizes at a university degree ceremony. He was not noble, he was not rich, and so she had to marry Crown Prince Engelbert of Sedona, who was both. As well as being perfectly nice and eminently suitable, but not what she had wanted, not at all.

After this dream she would wake trembling and tearful, and Engelbert, concerned, would ask what the matter was. Astrid hated to lie, but telling her husband that it had been a nightmare about black spot on her roses seemed the lesser evil.

Now, hugging the dog, she admired the surrounding flora. Jasmine bushes clustered thickly on the decorative balustrades beside the short flights of steps dividing one descending terrace from another. Astrid closed her eyes and inhaled the heavenly scent.

At that precise moment, the band stopped. The Queen's ears rang with the welcome silence. Then:

"Astrid!"

The King, his square, tanned face perspiring in the sunshine, was hurrying across the lawn in his gray suit.

"Very useful meeting," Engelbert gasped, as he drew level. "We've had a marvelous idea."

"Good," Astrid said absently, her attention on her rose stems. Was that an aphid?

"Don't you want to know what it is?" the King demanded.

Astrid suppressed a sigh and forced a smile. "I'd love to."

"We're going to generate world headlines, boost the monarchy's popularity, attract massive numbers of visitors, and promote a positive new image of Sedona." He rubbed his hands with glee.

Astrid nodded. "Yes, I know. The marina."

"No, no, no." Engelbert was shaking his large head of thick, well-combed gray hair. "Not yet. Things must get moving financially first. And this will make them. At one stroke, Sedona will become the most glamorous place on earth. Visitors will pour in, the hotels will be full, the economy will take off like a rocket." He paused for breath. "It's such a simple idea. I can't imagine why I didn't think of it before."

"But what *is* it?" Astrid pressed.

Engelbert beamed. "We'll put on a royal wedding."

His wife stared. "*Wedding?* But whose wedding? No one in the royal family is getting married."

"On the contrary, my dear," the King said gleefully. "Max is."

Chapter Eleven

THE QUEEN WAS SO surprised, she dropped her secateurs. "What!" One hand flew to her mouth. "I knew nothing…he didn't tell me…" She felt confused, but more than this she felt wounded, sick even. Why had her beloved son, to whom she had always considered herself close, not confided in her?

Engelbert chorded. "Of course he didn't tell you! He doesn't know himself!"

"Doesn't *know*…?" None of this was making sense to Astrid. She glanced warily at her husband. Had worry about his country's future finally driven him out of his wits?

"He'll understand, once it's all explained to him," the King claimed bumptiously.

"Once what is explained?" queried the Queen.

"That it's his duty to get married. That a royal wedding is exactly what we need to bring glamour back to Sedona and give the economy a boost." Engelbert began talking about hotel revenues and modernizing the legal framework for business.

"Understand?" Astrid was aghast. "But Max is at university! He's not even halfway through his course. He…he…loves it," she added, her voice rising as she saw that none of this had any impact on the King. "He doesn't want to leave. He doesn't want to get married; I'm not even sure he has a girlfriend."

Engelbert snorted. "Well, we'll find one for him"

The Queen gasped. "Find one for him?"

"Absolutely." The King nodded vigorously. "There's bound to be some suitable gel knocking about spare in one or other of the royal houses. We just need to make some inquiries."

"Inquiries? Suitable gel?" Astrid shook her head disbelievingly. "Engelbert," she said, after taking a deep breath. "I don't know what to say. Except that you sound like a complete dinosaur."

The King looked unabashed. "Dinosaurs are big business, my dear. People can't get enough of them. The Natural History Museum in London being just one example."

There was silence for a few minutes.

"Of course he can't come back," Astrid said furiously, dead-heading rapidly to relieve her feelings.

The King squinted angrily at his wife in the sunshine. He really needed glasses, she knew. The perfect eyesight of his younger days had long since blurred at the edges. But as Sedona monarchs traditionally never wore spectacles—weak-sighted men being by definition poorly bred and thereby unfit to rule—Engelbert must stumble through the rest of his public life more or less unable to see. Monocles were acceptable, apparently, but to Astrid's secret relief, even Engelbert drew the line at those. In private, he wore bifocals, but whipped them off whenever a servant entered the room.

"Do you mind if we go back inside?" the King grumped. It was unforgivingly hot.

As the Queen did not reply, he drummed his fingers testily against the warm stone. His crested signet ring flashed agitatedly. "My dear, our son is going to be King of Sedona. Sooner or later, he needs a suitable queen. Preferably a rich one," he added, thinking of the marina project. While it would be funded mainly by the rejuvenated state, a private fortune would undoubtedly be useful.

Still the Queen said nothing. Engelbert looked at her crossly.

Astrid was wonderful in every possible way, from her even temper to her never-altering slender figure, clad today, as always, in one of her well-cut sleeveless dresses in flattering shades of pastel. But there was no doubt she could be difficult to get through to at times. He leaned against the lichened urn beside which his wife was working and tried to shade his glistening head behind a bulge of Floribunda.

"We should never have sent him to university in England," he complained. "That was your idea."

"He wanted to be a vet. It's a very good course," the Queen said shortly.

"Well, you should never have encouraged him. Vet! What business has a future King of Sedona got being a vet?"

"He's doing brilliantly well," Astrid reminded her husband tartly. "He gets top marks in every exam."

Her robust defense of her son masked a growing terror. Engelbert was obviously serious. And Max, she was certain, would refuse point blank to obey his father. Come back and marry a stranger when he was doing the course of his dreams in England? There was no possibility, no chance at all.

"He should have gone to university in Paris," the King was grumbling. "We wouldn't have had to look for anyone then. Paris is choked with eligible heiresses. Rich, beautiful girls from the very best families. You can hardly avoid them." There was a wistful note in his voice.

"Is that so?" The Queen's secateurs gleamed in the sunlight.

"Absolutely it is," her husband affirmed. "When I was at the Sorbonne, I was going out with a *duchesse*, a princess, and a *comtesse* all at the same time. At the same time…"

It was at this moment, meeting the uncharacteristically icy glare of his wife, that the King realized to whom he was speaking. "But of course," he added hurriedly, "none of them could hold a candle to you, my dear."

The Queen snipped viciously at her bushes. "Max will refuse, and there's an end to it," she said tightly.

"Well, he'd better not," Engelbert riposted.

"He will. It's out of the question. He's a good boy," the Queen said, "but he will not be forced. Please don't make him," she added, impassioned.

The King smacked his forehead. "Where," he groaned, "did I go wrong with Max?"

"When you put him in military uniform at the age of six?" the Queen suggested icily.

Her husband rounded on her furiously. "All crown princes of Sedona wear military uniform from the age of six. It's—"

"Traditional?" offered the Queen, meeting his gaze boldly.

The King stared irritably at the manicured lawns before him. "It's not a question of forcing."

"Isn't it?" Astrid fought not to sound shrill.

"No," Engelbert said decisively. "We need to *encourage* him. He'll be twenty-one soon, the age at which all the Sedona princes get married."

"Used to get married," Astrid corrected. "We've dropped that particular rule, remember?"

The King looked her boldly in the eye. "Well, the PR man thought it would be a good time to bring it back. Have a competition for his hand, almost. Like one of those TV talent shows."

"*Never!*" Astrid's hand, holding her rose clippers, was shaking. "*Never* that."

"All right, all right, perhaps that's not appropriate." Engelbert's plump hands were held aloft. "But we need a wedding," he said stubbornly. "That's the bottom line."

Astrid recognized one of the PR man's stock phrases. Out of sheer desperation, an idea now struck her. "If someone has to get married, why can't it be Giacomo?" she suggested.

"*Giacomo?*" The King seemed stunned. "My dear, where do I begin? Because he's not the Crown Prince? Because he needs to learn how to behave first? According to Hippolyte, Giacomo was just going to bed as he came into the office this morning."

Monsieur Hippolyte was the King's long-serving private secretary, now doubling as the palace press officer. The PR consultant had been unable to believe, on arrival, that the royal family had no media representative whatsoever.

Astrid suppressed a groan. Their younger son's all-night visits to the local nightclub, La Cage Aux Princes, seemed worryingly frequent. While the place was exclusive in the sense that only the richest were allowed in, this did not, she feared, make for the most morally elevated company. Still, as Engelbert would remind her, young men had to sow their wild oats, and at least Giacomo's club of choice wasn't Madame Whiplash, an establishment of even more doubtful morality than La Cage and whose existence in genteel Sedona the Queen did her best to ignore.

"He's not doing anything else," the Queen pointed out with persuasive speed. "Marriage would give him a role, do him some good."

But the King was shaking his head.

Astrid felt desperate. She had to save Max somehow. Having experienced it herself, she knew the full horror of the situation now threatening him: sudden marriage to an unknown someone for the sake of the future of the state. Yet the state in question was her state; she was queen of it.

What should she do?

At her coronation she had sworn under oath, before the Archbishop of Sedona, to put her country first in all things. Nursing her firstborn in the quiet of the palace nursery, she had put her lips to his downy head and sworn to protect him and love him for life. Whose side should she be on? Her country's good versus her son's happiness. Her duty as a mother versus her duty as monarch. To which of her responsibilities should she be loyal?

Her only hope, for the moment, was that Engelbert would not insist she became directly involved. If she were given time, she might think of a way around this appalling dilemma. A way out, even.

"Obviously. So if you could just ring Max," the King was saying, with a casual expectation that made her see red.

"Me! Why *me*?" Astrid flared. "It's *your* idea. Why don't you ring him?"

The King looked surprised. "Because you're the best at talking him round," he said. "Max will do anything for you."

His words twisted the knife so agonizingly that Astrid wanted to scream. *Because he loves me, and because he knows I love him and want the best for him. I don't want to "Talk him round," as you put it. I know what it feels like to be made to do what you don't want to.*

"I won't," she muttered stubbornly, slashing at the bushes with her blade.

Her husband watched her for a few minutes.

"You have no choice," the King said. His tone was light but matter of fact. "You're Queen of Sedona. Your duty is to your country. You should keep your personal feelings—which I don't pretend to understand, by the way—out of this. Max's marriage is a matter of state, and you must support it—and me. I'm your husband, remember."

Astrid looked up; Engelbert's eyes were flinty and his square, rather heavy face was set in a manner that brooked no argument. The royal mind was made up. Even so, Astrid thought hotly, she would resist it all the way.

"So you'll call Max?"

"I can't," she said stubbornly. "He's at Oakeshott House, at Stonker Shropshire's."

A mighty jolt of panic now shook Engelbert's composure. He swallowed, and his myopic eyes narrowed. Stonker Shropshire! That settled it. If Max was with Stonker Shropshire…

The handsome English duke, with his imposing height, silver hair, libidinous reputation, and the allegedly enormous manhood to which his nickname referred, was something of a lady-killer even in his mid-sixties. He and Astrid had been friends for many years. Had they ever been more? the King often wondered.

For all his bombast and bluster, Engelbert was deeply insecure. He was aware that in marrying Astrid, he had strayed significantly out of his league looks-wise. He adored his wife, but the fear that she had never really wanted to marry him lurked deep within, and sometimes, like now, it rose to the surface.

"What's he doing with Stonker?" the King growled.

"I did tell you about it," Astrid snapped back.

"When? *When?*" the King demanded. Had he really been informed? He cast Astrid a suspicious look.

"I've told you several times," the Queen snorted. "But the only person you seem able to listen to at the moment," she added, her voice rising sharply, "is that *ghastly* PR man."

"He's not ghastly," the King retorted. "He's saving Sedona. Look, just tell Max he has to come home and get married. He's the eldest. The Crown Prince, the heir. It's his duty to his king and his country. He has no choice."

Chapter Twelve

In a garden square just south of Oxford Street in central London, a dark-haired woman in a red coat and high black heels was sitting on a bench. She was keenly watching the entrance of an imposing thirties office block across the road. Above the revolving door were the words "Fashion House," although, strictly speaking, the building did not require this announcement that it was the home of *Fashion*, the hugely influential glossy magazine. The leggy, polished creatures who kept the door in a constant spin were proof enough.

Alexa had watched them arrive, one by one. In Porsches, Ferraris, and Aston Martins they had come, driven by glamorous men who kissed them lingeringly before roaring off around the square in a cloud of smoke and money. None of these sophisticated creatures seemed to walk from the Tube, as she had done.

She knew, however, that to feel bitter was an indulgence she could not afford. She had nowhere to stay that night, nor did she have a job. And if she didn't get both before the end of the day, she was lost. She could either sleep on the streets or return to Mum and Dad's; the former option seemed by far the most attractive.

She looked glumly across at Fashion House. *Fashion* magazine was not her quarry; a job on its sister publication, *Socialite*, was her aim. On the train, it had seemed a possibility; Alexa had pictured herself swanning in, passing security with a light sally, and ascending in the elevator to waylay the *Socialite* editor, impress her with her irresistible chutzpah, and talk her way into a job.

Now, she felt less certain. She had been close enough to the doors to see that security was hardly the sort one just flounced past; two mean-looking men in uniform sat behind the gold-sprayed front desk. Alexa's hastily concocted alternative plan had been to persuade an employee to accompany her in, but the idea of approaching any of them made even Alexa quail. There was something so disdainful about the privileged beauties who scampered through the door, tossing their hair and swinging their It bags. Seeing one look her over haughtily as she swept past in a cloud of delicious perfume, Alexa had retreated to the garden square to regroup. How was she ever—ever—going to penetrate this citadel of privilege and power?

She stared hard at the square metal-framed windows of Fashion House. Behind which of those anonymous apertures was the office of *Socialite*? That el Dorado whose desks were no doubt piled high with invitations to the parties she so longed to go to.

While the façade of Fashion House shone in the morning sun, the garden square remained plunged in shadow and was chilly, despite being the height of summer. On the bench opposite, a tramp was just waking up, rustling in his filthy sleeping bag among his plastic bags and paper carriers. Alexa shuddered. Was she looking at her own future?

Quickly, she pulled the much-thumbed copy of *Socialite* out of her bag. If this couldn't galvanize her, nothing could.

Not every parent would willingly throw open their Elizabethan mansion to 500 teenage ravers, but Lord and Lady Huddersfield were characteristically relaxed about holding their own music festival for People Like Them. Classtonbury, brainchild of their spirited daughters Ratty and Moley Huddersfield, saw every funky titled teenager in Britain cram into the stately pile. Lady Florrie Trevorigus-Whyske-Cleethorpe thrilled onlookers by tippexing a bikini on her otherwise naked form and bareback-riding a Belted Galloway after one too many cracktails...

Alexa mused over the accompanying illustration of Lady Florrie in action. Despite being covered in correction fluid, mounted on a cow, and obviously zonked on drugs, she somehow managed to look serene and beautiful. Of course, quite apart from her spectacular looks, she was the daughter of a rich and titled family. Oh, to have that sort of confidence, thought Alexa. To have that sort of anything. But she would, she would!

"All right, darlin'?"

Alexa jumped in shock as the ragged figure loomed; it was the tramp, arisen from his couch and now stumbling confusedly around the path to her side. The stubbly face with the rheumy eyes came near; the toothless lips made a smacking sound. "Gi's a kiss, darlin'!"

Alexa screamed, leaped to her feet, and beat him off with the copy of *Socialite*. Then, wobbling on her high heels, she hurried across the road to Fashion House. She needed to make progress. She was running out of time.

The morning was melting away; soon, all the Fashion House girls would have arrived at work. She had to find someone to admit her. But who?

Rather than stand looking hopeless outside the Fashion House revolving door, Alexa took the more dignified route of buying a cappuccino from the café next to the magazine offices. Fishing out three pound coins from her dwindling funds Alexa briefly assessed the likelihood of being discovered as a magazine genius while working as a full-time barista. It seemed, at the very best, to be a somewhat meandering route to her object.

She carried the coffee to one of the rickety aluminum tables outside and sipped meditatively. Her agitations were interrupted by a terrifying roar in the square and an enormous, shining black vehicle swung into view. It had tractor-sized wheels, a gleaming, tank-like body, and bristled with lamps, bull bars, and exhaust pipes. At first she wondered if the Third World War had broken out and she had been too busy reading *Socialite* to notice. Then she realized, as the terrifying machine screeched to a thunderous halt outside Fashion House, that yet another employee was being delivered.

There was a girl in the passenger seat, a very beautiful girl of about twenty, with long blond hair. She clutched a very short black mackintosh over long, slim, bare white legs. Was she wearing anything at all? Alexa wondered. She could see no trace of a neckline inside the flaps of the mackintosh collar. As the girl swung her legs fully out, Alexa saw that her feet were bare.

The girl seemed blissfully unconcerned by her undressed state, however. Having reached the level of the road, she then sprang back into the vehicle to bestow a protracted kiss on the driver, a stockily handsome man with fair hair and a wide face. Alexa could not see clearly, but he appeared to be dressed in a pinstriped suit over a string vest, with several gold chains around his neck. His wrists and fingers blazed with bracelets, rings, and watches.

As Alexa, too fascinated to look away, kept her gaze trained on the couple, they disappeared from sight below the steering wheel. She could hear gasps and shrieks. "Omigod! Not now, Igor!"

The girl, squealing with laughter, bobbed up again and scrambled out, her blond hair wheeling, her coat swinging open to reveal, as Alexa had expected, a body without a stitch on it. She wondered why the girl seemed so familiar, then realized. This was none other than Lady Florence Trevorigus-Whyske-Cleethorpe, seen naked, painted in Tippex, and mounted on a large bovine not ten minutes before.

Chapter Thirteen

ALEXA, SITTING STOCK STILL at the pavement cafe, felt tremendous excitement. Could this be what she had been waiting for?

"Come back!" Igor was urging in a thick, heavy accent.

"I've got to go to work!" Florrie laughed up at him from the pavement. Alexa recognized the green leopard skin bag she swung as one of this season's most lusted-after models.

"Work? Work he is for losers!" Igor's contemptuous laugh sounded like a hail of bullets. As he roared off, mowing down anything in his path, Lady Florrie sighed, pulled her short black coat about her, and stared around cluelessly.

Her large violet-blue eyes came to rest, rather helplessly, on Alexa. "Er, hi there. I'm looking for Fashion House. Have you seen it?"

It was, of course, straight in front of her and so clearly marked that only an idiot could have missed it. But Alexa was in no hurry to point this out. She had been given an introduction, a way in; she could make capital out of this, she could just *feel* it.

She jumped to her feet. "Florrie! I *thought* it was you!" As Florrie looked at her uncertainly, she added forcefully, "Alexa MacDonald. We met at Classtonbury! You *must* remember."

"Omigod, did we really?" Florrie gasped. "I can't remember a thing. I was stoned out of my mind all weekend."

This was exactly what Alexa had been banking on. "Well, we had a *great* time together," she insisted. "You and me and Igor—"

"Igor wasn't there, was he?," Florrie said vaguely. "No, he wasn't," she added more certainly. "He was busy murdering someone with his father, or whatever those Russian gangsters get up to. Omigod, can you believe I just said that?" She giggled and her long fingers flew to her lips.

"I was about to say," Alexa rejoined smoothly, "that it was almost as if Igor *was* there because you talked about him so much. You're obviously *very* much in love."

"No, we just fuck all the time." Florrie's angelic features were split by a grin of pure naughtiness. "So you know Ratty and Moley Huddersfield?"

"Absolutely…er, like a coffee?" Alexa was anxious to avoid potentially compromising detail.

Florrie's beam wavered. "Actually, that might be an idea. I've got the most awful headache."

She slumped back in the aluminum chair and flipped her magnificent hair back. Up close and in the flesh, Alexa saw, Lady Florence Trevorigus-Whyske-Cleethorpe was more beautiful even than her pictures. Perfect cheekbones, bow lips, and flawless skin. Her makeup was smudged and looked like it had been applied the night before, but this only added to her allure.

"Poor you," Alexa cooed sycophantically. "Drink a tiny bit too much last night?"

"Igor bought a methuselah." Florrie giggled. "It cost fifty K."

Alexa almost fell off her chair. Fifty K! On a bottle of champagne! "That must be thousands of pounds per glass," she couldn't help exclaiming.

"Really?" Florrie said vaguely. "Well, I spilled mine. The first two, actually." She gave a sudden, uproarious laugh, then winced and clutched her head. "Omigod, it was just so mad. After the champagne, we all went off back to his penthouse—it's the size of a football field. And he—omigod, this is so crazy—he got out his gun and—actually shot the television! Where's my coffee, by the way?"

Twisting around in her aluminum seat, Alexa waved wildly in the direction of the back of the café, hoping a waitress would see her and come out. There was no chance she was going in there; the bird might have flown on her return.

Florrie, meanwhile, had spotted Fashion House. "Omigod, look, there it is. Right in front of me all the time. Can you believe I didn't see it?"

Alexa smiled politely. "What are you going to do there?"

"I'm supposed to be starting work," Florrie groaned. "On *Socialist* magazine."

"You mean *Socialite?*"

"Yes, that's what I said, wasn't it?" Florrie blinked in surprise.

"No, you said *Socialist.*"

"Well, what's the difference?"

Alexa started to laugh, then realized Florrie wasn't joking.

"Anyway," Florrie said, "it's a mega-yawn, whatever it's called. Work's such a drag. I mean, why do people do it?" The waitress was finally approaching, and Florrie beamed dazzlingly at her. "Omigod, you wouldn't have any champagne, would you? I could really do with some hair of the dog."

"We only do champagne in bottles, madam," the waitress said in a flat eastern European accent.

"Great," Florrie said excitedly. "Bring a bottle."

Chapter Fourteen

WAS SHE MAKING PROGRESS, Alexa wondered, raising her glass to her lips. The upside was that she was sipping champagne with the celebrated socialite Lady Florence Trevorigus-Whyske-Cleethorpe. On the downside, she still lacked a job and somewhere to sleep tonight. There was no time to lose.

"You've done so well to have got a job at *Socialite*," she began sycophantically.

"Have I?" Florrie rolled her violet eyes. "Nothing to do with me. Daddy sorted it out. The managing director was at school with him."

Alexa could not afford to dwell on the unfairness of this. "Well," she said brightly, "I've got an appointment at *Socialite* this morning. Why don't I come in with you? You could sign me in."

Florrie was busy tapping the screen of her iPhone. Alexa was obliged to repeat herself and Florrie looked up. "Omigod, but you know, I can't."

"Can't?" Alexa swallowed.

"We're not supposed to sign people in. I actually got a letter about it. Apparently all sorts of sad sacks try and crash the security; they want to work on magazines for some reason. Can you imagine?" Florrie gave a disdainful giggle.

Alexa's insides felt as if they were in free fall. That was it, her last hope. The end of the road had been reached right outside *Socialite*'s door.

She almost couldn't help it. She burst into passionate tears.

Thanks to her absorption in her iPhone, Florrie did not immediately notice that Alexa was racked by agonizing sobs.

Alexa sobbed louder and eventually she looked up. "You're crying," Florrie remarked in the same tone she might have used to observe that it was raining.

Alexa waited for Florrie to inquire into the cause of her grief, but she just continued humming and fiddling with her screen.

Alexa racked her brains. The job was a non-starter, but was there hope with Florrie on the accommodations front? She was bound to have a large apartment. If there was even a spare closet she could sleep in, it would be something. Otherwise...

Her eye caught the tramp, shuffling out of the park across the road with his plastic bags. He was muttering to himself.

"I'm crying because I've been thrown out of my flat," Alexa said dramatically.

Florrie's eyes flicked up from her iPhone. "Omigod, that's, like, so *weird*. How can anyone throw you out of your own flat?"

"It's not my flat," Alexa explained.

This was amazing enough for Florrie to raise her entire head. "Not your flat?"

Alexa shook her head.

"But it must be," Florrie persisted. "Who else's can it be?"

"I rent it," Alexa lied.

"What's renting? I've never heard of it." Florrie took a slug of champagne.

Alexa, who had never imagined having to go into such details, was forced to invent wildly. "It, er, means it belongs to my landlord. He's come back unexpectedly and wants me out." Her eyes sought Florrie's pleadingly. "I need somewhere to stay. Just for a few days. Overnight, even."

Florrie picked up her glass of champagne again. "Oh," she said, smiling at something that seemed just to have appeared on the screen.

Alexa leaned forward over the aluminum table. "I'm homeless," she urged with unfeigned desperation. "I need a roof over my head; otherwise I'll be sleeping on the streets of London."

Florrie looked up excitedly. "But, you know, that's quite fashionable. Wills—Prince William—slept on them, I think."

Subtlety—in so far as this was subtle—was a waste of time, Alexa realized. "It would," she began, slowly and emphatically, "be just so wonderful if I knew someone who had a spare room in their flat."

Florrie, her attention back on her iPhone, did not seem to hear this.

"Or even a bit of floor space," Alexa continued to spell it out loudly. "A closet, anything. Even the bath. Just somewhere I could shelter for a few days until I found somewhere else."

"Mmm," Florrie said absorbedly.

"You don't know anyone who does, do you?" Alexa raised her voice.

"Does what?" This, vaguely.

"Has some spare room in their flat."

Florrie's beautiful brow creased with what was clearly the enormous effort of thinking. "No," she said eventually. "I live with my sister…"

Alexa's heart sank. She had officially hit rock bottom. Frozen with misery despite the warm sunshine, she heard Florrie complete the sentence.

"…except that she's moving out today—she's getting married."

Alexa, computing the possibilities at lightning speed, felt her heartbeat race with a new, almost painful excitement. Not only a flat with an empty room, but a looming society wedding and all its attendant opportunities to meet the eligible elite. None of this could be allowed to slip through her fingers. No! No! No!

She poured the rest of the champagne into Florrie's glass and spoke slowly and emphatically, as if to a child. "You Don't Have A Spare Room Coming Up In Your Flat, Do you?"

"Hey, girls, sorry to interrupt…"

Alexa, staring up at the long-haired young man in vast black sunglasses with a large boxy bag suspended from one shoulder, felt she had never wanted to kill anyone more in her life.

"…but I'm a photographer, and I was just wondering," his eyes were on Florrie, "whether you'd ever considered modeling."

Possibly as a result of reaching for the iPhone, Florrie's coat had slid down her arms and her pearly shoulders rose in perfect contrast to the black material; her hair, meanwhile, was streaming everywhere in a golden mass. She looked like the most glamorous magazine front cover in the world.

Florrie rolled her lovely eyes. "People are always, like, asking me, but I'm, you know, not sure I can really be bothered." She yawned.

There was no answer to this, and the photographer did not try to come up with one. He merely shrugged and sloped off.

"I'd better go," Florrie observed regretfully, draining the wine in her glass. "Anyway, great to see you again, er…" She looked at Alexa vaguely.

"Alexa," Alexa supplied rapidly. "We met at Classtonbury. I'm a friend of the Huddersfields. We were"—she hesitated only fractionally—"just talking about me crashing for a while in your flat."

"Were we?" As Florrie looked at her, puzzled, Alexa could almost hear the rusty cogs—or possibly cog—struggling to turn in her brain. The question was, were they turning the right way?

"Sure, why not. You can crash there for a bit if you like now Beattie's gone," Florrie said casually as she rummaged in her green leopard skin bag.

Alexa, deeply relieved, expected the keys to emerge, followed by the purse to pay for the drinks. But Florrie looked up, grinning. "Omigod, I've left my dosh at home. You OK to get the champagne?"

Chapter Fifteen

BACK IN SEDONA, QUEEN Astrid had endured yet another sleepless night. She walked, heavy-eyed, into the white and gold breakfast room.

The big French windows, as usual at this time of year, were open to the breathtaking panorama of mountains. Brightness and air poured in. But the Queen's mood remained sunken and glum. She had lain awake pondering the absolute impossibility of dragging her son away from the studies he loved, and was so good at, and of making him marry someone he didn't want to for the sake of king and country, as she had been forced to do herself.

Muttering a greeting, she joined her husband at the oval breakfast table. He looked up and rattled the newspaper at her. "The PR chap's done a poll," he announced. "Ninety-nine percent of the public, when asked, were in favor of the Crown Prince marrying."

"I see," Astrid said levelly, taking a tea cup with a shaking hand. She tried to focus on the court circular, where her day was set out for her. *At half past ten this morning, His Majesty King Engelbert of Sedona, accompanied by Her Majesty Queen Astrid of Sedona, will formally open the new kitchens of the Bougainvillea Rest Home, Sedona. They will then proceed to open the new sunroom at the Amaryllis Rest Home, Sedona.*

The queen was gloomily aware that, apart from anything else, today's poll would give people license to ask more personal questions than usual. Old people were particularly shameless on the prying front, taking advantage of the immunity of age. Knowing they had little time to live, and little to lose, they asked anything and everything. Astrid expected the worst. She wriggled with reluctance in her shift dress and dug the heels of her beige court shoes into the Savonnerie carpet.

"You've called Max, I take it," the King said casually. Only the fierce way his hands were gripping his newspaper betrayed the tension with which he awaited the answer.

"I couldn't get through," Astrid lied.

"What? Again?" The King slammed his cup down in his saucer so hard that the Queen winced. She took great pride in the palace china collection.

"You haven't been able to get through for days," Engelbert said suspiciously.

Astrid felt panicked. "Max," she explained, "is doing some hands-on experience at Stonker's."

"I bet he is," snarled the King.

"On the farm," Astrid hurriedly continued. "But it means he's outside a lot and out of range."

"Well, he goes inside sometimes, doesn't he?" Engelbert blustered, recognizing a feeble excuse when he heard one. "He's not a cow out at pasture."

The King took up his silver spoon and dug violently into his boiled egg. It was detectably three or four seconds over the four-minute limit he preferred. This did not improve his mood.

The breakfast room door opened and Prince Giacomo, yawning, his unbrushed golden hair cascading over his face, shuffled through in baggy jeans and unlaced white trainers.

"Good morning, Giacomo," said his father pointedly. "You're late. Again."

"Keep your hair on, Pops," replied the young prince blithely.

The King stared upward as if seeking divine guidance, or

perhaps a shaft of lightning to reduce his troublesome younger son to a smoking cinder.

Giacomo dragged out a delicate gold chair and plonked himself down on it. "So wossup, man?" He grabbed a slice of toast.

"If you mean what have we been talking about," his mother replied patiently, "the answer is that we've been talking about Max."

"Max?"

"Your brother, remember," Engelbert said ironically. "Maxim Albert William Carl Philip Emanuel Gothenburg de Sedona."

Giacomo blinked. "Wow. Does he really have so many names?"

"We need to find him a wife." Engelbert gestured at one of the white-gloved footmen to take his unsatisfactory egg away. "He's got to come home and get married. For the good of his country," the monarch added stirringly.

"Marry? *Max?*" Giacomo was so astounded that he dropped his toast onto the antique carpet. "Marry who? He's not even got a bird, not so far as I know."

"Quite," muttered the Queen.

"We're going to find him a bird, as you call it," the King said briskly, clattering his tea cup down in its saucer. "A bride will be chosen," he added pompously, "from among the leading families of Europe."

Giacomo looked puzzled. "I'm probably being a bit thick…" he began, frowning.

"Surely not," the King put in witheringly. The Queen shot him a look.

"…but," Giacomo continued slowly, "you're actually going to make the poor sod come back from sticking his arm up cow's arses or whatever it is he's doing and marry some old munter he's never seen before, just because it's his royal duty?"

Engelbert sighed so hard in exasperation that the linen napkin covering his suit front fluttered with the force of it. "Well, I wouldn't have put it quite that way, but in essence I suppose that sums it up reasonably accurately."

Giacomo was reaching for another piece of toast. "Bit heavy, Pops, don't you think?"

"I don't disagree," muttered Astrid.

The King, now feeling rather persecuted, was swift to counterattack. "Come on, Astrid," he snapped. "You're supposed to be supporting me. It's your royal duty, remember? It could be worse. Max isn't interested in anyone else, after all. We're not insisting he tears himself away from the love of his life or anything, are we?"

Astrid flinched. Was there something knowing, something barbed, in her husband's tone? She dared not raise her eyes and show him the pain in them, or see any unexpected insight in his. She remained staring at the table, hands out of sight, clenched agitatedly on her knees. "I'm not aware of him being in love with a *person*," she said in a monotone. "But he adores what he's doing and he won't want to leave it."

"He's going to be a king; kings can't be vets," Engelbert was ranting when, in the service kitchen outside the large gold and white door, there was a shattering crash as someone dropped a plate onto the stone-flagged floor. The entire family jumped in shock. Engelbert's angry gaze remained on his wife. "You have to call him," he said accusingly. "*Now.*"

Chapter Sixteen

MAX WAS ON HIS knees in a grubby cowshed when his mobile shrilled. Politely, he ignored it at first, being deep in conversation with one of the Duke of Shropshire's dairy girls about the mastitis from which one of the herd was suffering. Max was enjoying himself immensely; the comforting, earthy smell of the shed, the warmth of Daisy's flank, the certain knowledge that he could cure the animal, all conspired to give him a feeling of ineffable satisfaction.

"Shouldn't you get that?" Tamsin, the dairy girl, asked as Max's mobile rang insistently in the depths of the battered jacket he had thrown casually over the wall of Daisy's byre. "It might be something important." She shook her loose red hair over her shoulders, rather hopelessly by now, it had to be said. It had been obvious from the moment the handsome young vet had arrived that the only female in the shed he was interested in had four legs and a pair of horns.

It occurred to Max that it might be Polly. They had arranged to meet later for supper. He felt a thousand pinpricks of fear in his stomach; was she calling to cancel?

Tamsin watched as he hurriedly pulled the mobile out and turned his back. A girlfriend? There must be some reason why he had so utterly failed to respond to the considerable efforts the farmyard assistants had made to interest him. Even the guinea pig girls had turned out daily in full makeup.

"Oh, Mum, it's you," she heard him exclaim warmly. That he

had a good relationship with his mother somehow made him more attractive than ever. She sighed and patted Daisy, who was turning her large, square head and lowing inquiringly, evidently wondering where Max had gone.

"How's Beano?" Tamsin heard as Max walked into the cobbled yard. "Oh, good. Good boy. What? Yes, I can talk, but make it quick," he said happily, glancing back and giving Tamsin a smile that made her heart turn right over. "I've got an important lady awaiting my attentions."

"An important *lady*?" Astrid, at the other end, gasped. How important? Hope soared within her. Royal, rich, marriageable important? It might be all right after all…

"Yes, I'm just sorting out her teats." Max chuckled. He felt, as he increasingly did these days, in an uncharacteristically skittish mood. He was doing exactly what he wanted. And if he wasn't madly in love quite yet, he was, he knew, closer to it than he'd ever been.

"*Teats?*" Astrid had almost dropped the phone. Her hands were shaking.

"Just an old cow," Max explained, wondering why his mother sounded tense. She was usually the first to get a joke.

"*What?*" she squealed.

"A *real* old cow. C'mon, Mum. What's happened to your sense of humor?"

Exactly what's going to happen to yours in a minute, Astrid thought sadly. She clung to the final, few precious minutes in the knowledge that she was being loved and esteemed by her favorite son. After she had broken the news, things between them would be different forever.

"I just hoped you meant you'd met someone," she said wistfully.

"Oh, I have met someone," Max said happily.

"What did you just say?" she demanded, and Max repeated himself.

"*Someone?*" Astrid yelped. "You're not teasing me? Not the cow? A real person?"

He was laughing. "No, not the cow. Yes, a person. A girl." Astrid's hopes soared again. If this girl had a title of some sort, was someone with wealth and connections that Engelbert would consider worthy…Her fingers crossed around the receiver.

"She's an archaeologist," Max was saying.

Astrid's ears buzzed. The line from Sedona was a bit crackly, but had he really said *aristocrat*? "A what?" she croaked.

"Archaeologist," he repeated cheerfully.

An *archaeologist*? Astrid came to earth with a bump.

Archaeologist. There were some of those in the principality at the moment; she had passed them several times en route to official engagements. They spent their time up to their knees in dirt. Most of the men had beards, and the women were very plain, apart from one who hung around at the edge in a leopard-skin bikini and pink wellingtons. It seemed unlikely that an archaeologist would fit the crown princess template.

"Have you," she began cautiously, "have you, er, told this archaeologist who you *are*, darling?"

"That I'm a prince, you mean?" Max lowered his voice and glanced around. "Course not."

"Why of course not?" his mother pursued patiently.

"Well, no one here knows who I am," Max told her, making double sure Tamsin was out of earshot. "Apart from Stonker, that is." A slight impatience, Astrid noticed, had crept into his happy tone. "I don't want them to. I want people to behave normally around me. Because it's not as if I *am* anyone, in the sense that I'm more important or anything."

Astrid suppressed a sigh. Max's egalitarian streak was another reason why he had always been on a collision course with his father.

She tried to look on the bright side; if this girl was unaware, at least she could not be interested in Max for the wrong reasons.

"But you must have told her *something*," she pressed.

"I told her that Dad ran a family firm and worked in tourism," Max said shortly. He had been rather pleased with this neat précis. It wasn't a lie, and it didn't offend anyone. "Also that the rest of my family lived abroad."

"I see," was all Astrid could think of to say.

"Hey, Mum, you OK?"

"Yes, of course," the Queen said hurriedly.

"You sound a bit funny, that's all. Look, were you ringing for a reason? Was there something you wanted to tell me?"

"Oh…nothing, darling," Astrid said. "Nothing important."

Chapter Seventeen

FLORRIE'S WORLD WAS EVEN grander than Alexa had anticipated. The flat in Belgravia was huge: vast and luxurious, with oversized window whose thick lined curtains were big enough to fit a stage, it had lofty corniced ceilings, white fireplaces, and fat four-seater sofas upholstered in yellow chintz.

The other thing Alexa had underestimated was the epic scale of Florrie's laziness and fecklessness. But this, as it happened, was entirely to her advantage. The fact that Florrie took it for granted that the rest of the world was at her service meant that Alexa had not only prime accommodations, but a full-time job as well.

Florrie happily allowed her to wait on her hand and foot, serve at her dinner parties, collect her dry-cleaning, and even update her Facebook page. For Alexa, this was yet another opportunity; she could collect for her own page—now relaunched under her new name—the entire range of Florrie's contacts, who, discovering she lived with Florrie, were usually happy to befriend her.

Alexa's own Facebook page contained, besides wild fabrications about her background and schooling (she was careful not to be too specific, however), various images of her hunting, grouse-shooting, partying with royalty, and frolicking on the yachts of the rich and titled.

But were the images really her? As they were almost always from the back, and taken in bad light, these pictures of the woman with long dark hair passed the only test that mattered; the very brief scrutiny that the attention spans of her target audience would allot them.

After he told her he had completely forgotten how to log in, Alexa had offered to update Ed's page too. Ed was the most wonderful opportunity of all, the heaven-sent chance, the almost unbelievable bonus. He was Florrie's inebriated viscount brother, offspring of Lord Whyske's first marriage and, thanks to primogeniture, heir to three stately homes, walls full of old Master paintings, various glamorous properties abroad, and millions of pounds after death duties. And, more importantly still, he was single.

Desperate, therefore, to make herself useful, Alexa happily repositioned to their best advantage pictures of the viscount looking red-faced in a deerstalker or red-faced in white tie waving a jeroboam of champagne. His status had not been changed for several months. "Bloody freezing after shooting," it said, which sounded odd in midsummer. Alexa altered it to: "Looking forward to my sister's wedding bash; maybe I'm in the mood for love myself." It hadn't taken her long to work out that Ed was the kind of person who had to be told to feel things. And feel things for her, in particular.

How she wished to change his status permanently to "married." She had lost no time in laying plans to snare him. Being alone and intimate with him was the first step, and a simpler business than Alexa had expected, thanks to the poor communication between brother and sister. Whenever Ed rang up to make a date with Florrie, Alexa would invite him around at a time when she knew Florrie would be out and neglect to mention to her roommate that the arrangement had been made at all.

It worked beautifully; around Ed would trot and up in the elevator he would come. Waiting for him at the door would be a scantily clad Alexa; she would ask him in, sit him on the sofa, and practically push her breasts into his face. Despite all this, so far she had not managed to tempt him into bed; Ed, a keen field sportsman, had no interests whatsoever beyond hunting, shooting, and fishing.

Only once had Alexa's hopes risen: greeting him in an unfastened flimsy negligee, having ostensibly arisen from the bath, she had been thrilled by the viscount's gasp of pleasure.

"That's fantastic," Ed had panted. "I've been *desperate* to open my flies." It emerged, however, that his requirement was not sexual relief, but for Alexa to return to the bath, lie down, submerge her head, and pretend to be a salmon, so he could test his fishing lures.

Nor was this Alexa's only challenge.

Was Ed's—and Florrie's—mother suspicious of her? The terrifyingly well-groomed Lady Annabel had been chummy at first, vocally delighted that her daughter had a reliable companion staying with her, even applying to be Alexa's friend on Facebook. But of late she had been positively icy, which Alexa had initially put down to preoccupation with the forthcoming wedding of Lady Beatrice.

But was this really the case? Or did Florrie's mother suspect her? Was this the real reason she had wanted access to the Facebook account? Had her initial friendliness been flattery to deceive?

It took one very ambitious person to know another, and Alexa sensed that Lady Annabel was fiercely aspirational for her children. Ed, after all, might be slow-witted, plump, and with a face only a mother could love, but he was the family standard-bearer and the future of the line. Florrie's roommate, with her unproven origins, was unlikely to be seen as a suitable partner.

And while in a mere matter of weeks Beatrice would be going up a cathedral aisle to marry a marquess, Alexa guessed that Lady Annabel was looking higher for her beautiful youngest child. There had been the recent near miss with royalty; Alexa could only imagine what Lady Annabel had made of that.

But Florrie's mother was not, she guessed, the sort to give

up easily. She was obviously a very determined woman, who had married into a line of determined people for whom morality and principle were secondary considerations at best. The marriage may have faltered, but there was no wavering in Lady Annabel's sense of position, or her pride as mother of the sole son and heir to the family fortune.

The founding father of this family fortune, Sir Willoughby Whyske, had been interred, as befitted his position, in the family mausoleum at Willoughby Hall. On the front of his magnificent white marble tomb was a large carved plaque upon which he was described, somewhat euphemistically, as "owner of many large plantations in the West Indies." Nor had Ebenezer Cleethorpe, who had married a Whyske in the nineteenth century and brought with him a vast industrial fortune, been noted for his humanity. His money had mostly been made before the Factory Act restricted the working hours of small children in his numerous Manchester cotton mills.

Of the founding ancestors, it seemed only Thomas Trevorigus had no blood on his hands. And yet he might have had something even more unpleasant on them. Trevorigus was a Cornish landowner who had in the early seventeenth century appeared at court in order to appeal for the monarch's assistance with a legal difficulty. What the difficulty was, no one ever discovered; Thomas never saw his native county again.

His bluff West Country manner had apparently proved so immediate and lasting a hit with the King that James made him his Groom of the Privy Closet. This prestigious royal appointment involved attending to the monarch's bathroom requirements in every specific. The remainder of Trevorigus's life was thus taken up with matters pertaining to the regal posterior, and so successful did he prove in the execution of his duties that on his deathbed, the monarch conferred the appointment on the Trevorigus family in perpetuity.

Thanks to developments in sanitary engineering, however, the position was no longer the hands-on responsibility it had been in the past and now involved nothing more onerous than the annual duty of supplying the reigning monarch with twelve months' worth of lavatory paper. Florrie had told Alexa how she could remember as a child seeing the liveried driver of the Harrods truck making a detour to drive with slow ceremony past the Trevorigus-Whyske-Cleethorpes' London residence so it could be saluted by the family before proceeding to the Palace. But due to the time-pressed nature of modern monarchy—that, at least, had been the official reason—this annual parade had some time ago been abandoned, and the supply was now ordered on the Internet from Waitrose and delivered by Ocado.

All in all, Alexa had concluded, it was a family history in which social failure was, and never had been, an option. As soon as Lady Annabel found another prince for Florrie, it was a fair bet that she would be up the aisle with him in short order. And there could be little doubt she was looking for a princess for Ed. If Alexa herself was to have a chance, she must move fast and strike hard.

Chapter Eighteen

"Amazing." Polly shook her head, smiling, at the chilled champagne bottle, the polished glasses, the snowy linen napkins, the plates, the prawns and smoked salmon. "I wasn't expecting anything like this. It's like…like something the Duke of Shropshire might take shooting."

She meant it was excessive, Max knew, with a clutch of shame. And she was right. He wished he hadn't been forced to take it; it was a distraction, an over-opulent infringement on what was intended as an evening of simple pleasures. A drive into the countryside. A drink at a remote pub. Fish and chips eaten out of paper in the Land Rover, looking out at the wonderful view.

But Stonker Shropshire, his host, was an unstoppable force, and when, over the silver chafing dishes that morning, he had winkled out Max's evening plans, he had been determined to make a contribution.

"Taking a girl out, eh?" he had boomed. "Better have one of my Hanky-Panky Picnics then, my boy. I'll get Mrs. Bunion to make you one up. Seafood, champagne. Aphrodisiac City, basically. Then you strike as they're flicking through the newspaper diary page. Never fails with me. Thinking of getting them copyrighted and sold in the estate farm shop, as a matter of fact. With free monogrammed condom in every one!"

Max, coughing into his tea cup, was relieved the duchess was not present.

If Max, now uncorking the bottle, looked red and uncomfortable, Polly hardly noticed. She had now discovered the large lobster. "There's even mayonnaise," she crowed, "here in this little white pot! And lemons! And to cap it all, the *Daily Mail*, too!"

As Max looked even more embarrassed, she decided to stop teasing him. The picnic was a wonderful extravagant gesture and, could he have seen it, would certainly have given her father something to think about.

Dad had hardly looked up from his paper as she'd come into the kitchen earlier that evening, her freshly washed hair bouncing on her shoulders, her new high heels clacking on the tiled floor.

Mum had turned around from the stove and swept her over with an indulgent glance. "Going out with Max, are you? He's a lovely boy." Max had charmed her on his last visit by admiring her garden and telling her that his mother had green fingers too.

Dad had looked up from his paper. "Be careful, that's all," he'd warned. "He does seem all right, I'll give you that. But I don't want you ending up hurt again."

Hurt! Polly thought now as, lying on her stomach, sipping the fizzing wine, she leafed through the *Mail*. It was sweet of her father to care so much—she had forgiven his initial reaction by now—but his concerns were groundless. Unlike Jake, Max treated her like a princess.

He was so romantic. He wanted everything to be perfect. He had turned the Land Rover off the road at the best spot of all, parking on the bright turf edge of high, heathery moorland. They had walked through the carpet of frothing purple, heaving the hamper between them, with the prospect of colored hills in the distance stretching to the blue horizon. Now Max was lying on his back on the grass. He had, she saw, a faint smile on his face.

"Just listen to this!" She smoothed out the diary page and began to read out loud.

Is actress-socialite-whatever Champagne D'Vyne planning an acting comeback? Following her turn as sexbomb architect Bouncy Castle in Bond's last screen outing, she was spotted lunching at thesp hangout Luvvies with hot director Caractacus Pond. "He did mention Hamlet, but I've never been keen on eggs."

"Bouncy Castle!" Polly crowed. "Oh, and you won't believe this!"

London's leading champagnista, party girl Lady Florence Trevorigus-Whyske-Cleethorpe is back with oligarch's son Igor Tchaikovsky after a brief relationship with HRH. But will the irrepressible Florrie make the throne yet? After all, her new position, as assistant to Sir Rupert Backhander MP, will give her some valuable insight into the constitution...

"Unbelievable," Polly cackled. "I didn't realize people really live like that."

"Like what?" Max asked sleepily.

"Oh, you know." Polly flipped the pages of the paper. "Women running around trying to marry princes, that sort of thing."

"You don't approve?" A glimmer of a smile was pulling at his mouth. "You wouldn't like a handsome prince yourself?"

"Of course not!" Polly leaned over and poked him. "I want you, obviously. No prince could come close."

They made love then, unhurried and ecstatic, on the extra-padded blanket that was another feature of Stonker's Hanky-Panky Picnic. The exquisite setting only heightened the perfection of it all; there, among the larks and curlews, under an evening sky that was a decadent riot of violets, golds, reds, and blues. Afterward, he lay for a long time just gazing into her eyes while she stroked his hair.

With incredible speed, it seemed to Polly, she had become part of him. And he, in turn, had become half of her. It was beginning to feel as if Max was the only person who really existed, and she herself only lived when she was with him.

Chapter Nineteen

THE PEOPLE AT THE dining table were roaring with such ear-splitting laughter that Alexa was seriously worried about her eardrums. Just as grand people were entitled to more names than everyone else, they appeared to have more lung capacity too. It was, it seemed, just biology.

"Har har *har*!" bellowed Charlie. He was a chinless wonder with huge ears and a face that drink had made progressively purpler all evening. So far as Alexa could make out, he possessed no brains at all. "Ha ha *har*," screamed back Ed Whyske. His eye caught Alexa's. "Who'd you say you were, again?"

Alexa groaned silently. Appropriately enough given his interests, Ed looked like a cod but had the brains of a goldfish. As he could never remember who she was, Alexa had to start from scratch trying to interest him every time she saw him.

"Flo's roommate! Course you are." But Ed's dead-white, pasty forehead now crinkled in perplexity. "Roommate, is it? Silly bugger, me. Why did I think you were her maid?"

Because I dressed up in a short black dress and frilly white apron and sat on your knee yesterday? Alexa wanted to say but didn't. The confusion was understandable in any case; Florrie certainly treated her like a servant. Her presence as a guest, rather than a waitress, at this dinner party had only been secured after the following exchange:

Florrie (putting down the telephone): Omigod, what a total nightmare from hell. Lulu de Borgia's canceled. I'm a girl short for tonight.

Alexa: I could stand in if you like.

Florrie: *You?* But you're serving all the stuff.

Alexa: Yes, but I could be a guest as well. People quite often cook and serve their own dinners and sit at the table with everyone else.

Florrie: Omigod, how *weird*.

The other guests at tonight's supper—or "din-dins" as Florrie always called it—were Charlie's girlfriend Camilla and someone called Barney van Hoosier. Small, compact, and campy, he was in his early twenties and wore matching shoes, three-piece beige linen suit, and watch chain, a pink cravat and matching rose in his buttonhole the exact shade of the pink pate shining through his carefully combed, side-parted dark hair.

Alexa observed van Hoosier narrowly over the cauliflower cheese. She was struck by his line of talk, a torrent of oleaginous charm, wide-ranging cultural knowledge, and amusing, well-informed gossip. It seemed to her that he used conversation to distract, as she did herself. "Omigod, Barney!" Florrie kept shrieking. "That's *hysterical!*"

Over the rice pudding, Alexa's suspicions grew. She wondered what Barney was distracting everyone from. Did he, like her, come from obscure origins? Had he too largely reinvented himself? Was van Hoosier made up? A clever choice if so, a name so outlandish, no one would ever imagine it was not genuine.

He was, apparently, some sort of historian. She listened to him banging on about his specialist subject, the Tudors. "Sex and executions, basically," he drawled, adding that Elizabeth I had her own recipe for anti-farting powder and the plays of Shakespeare included one hundred fifty words for clitoris. As Florrie shrieked and Camilla and Charlie, cheeks bulging with just-swilled claret, thumped the table in appreciation, a great dark fear gripped Alexa. How could she compete?

What was worse, van Hoosier's curious, assessing gaze was frequently on her; it was as if he too had reached certain conclusions. "Tell me, where did you meet your lovely friend?" he asked Florrie as the roars of amusement died down.

"At *work*!" Florrie shrieked, before collapsing into fresh gales of laughter.

"Work!" everyone echoed, roaring and slapping their sides. Admittedly Florrie and employment had not proved a match made in heaven. The *Socialite* job had lasted less than a week. Florrie's penchant for turning up late or not at all, her hopeless vagueness, her lack of concentration, and her complete inability to spell were, apparently, normal enough for aristocratic members of staff, most of whom, however, managed to muster up some sort of deference to the editor. But Florrie, it seemed, never seemed quite to grasp who the editor was and would stare at her blankly, yawning widely. She was now working for an MP friend of her father's. Only time would tell whether democracy would survive the experience.

Alexa's instinct was to keep a distance between herself and the man with the smiling pink face and matching shoes. She resisted his offers to help her carry plates into the kitchen. But then, as he carried them in anyway, she found herself standing dumbstruck as he placed a pile of ancestral Minton down on the butcher's block and said in an amused voice, accompanied by a charming smile, "You're not making much headway here, are you?"

"Headway?" Alexa said stiffly, yanking open the dishwasher.

Outside, as was usual at this stage in din-dins proceedings,

Florrie and Ed had started throwing bread rolls at each other. Florrie screamed as Ed got her smack in the eye.

"With Ed, of course." Barney had come over and was leaning against the front of the fridge. His beam was undimmed. "You're after him, aren't you?"

"Whatever can you mean?" Alexa met his amused glance with a haughty one of her own.

"Oh, come off it, dear," he said genially. "You're a fake."

"Fake? What do you mean?" Alexa's indignation disguised fear. What did Barney know? Rattled by Lady Annabel's eagle eye, she had recently taken down some of the more blatantly improbable Facebook images. But had she been thorough enough? That one of her whirling between two tartaned dukes at the Royal Caledonian Ball, for instance…

"Oh, it's quite all right, I'm one too," Barney said lightly, fiddling with his watch chain as he kept up his unremitting smile. "I know what you're after. And I can help you get him."

There was a deafening clatter of good silverware as Alexa dropped some spoons.

The company in the dining room roared approvingly.

"Let me give you some advice." Barney folded his arms in their buttermilk linen sleeves. "You're going about it all the wrong way. *Much* too obvious."

"Obvious?" Alexa looked indignantly down at herself. She was a vision of discreet taste in the soberest little black dress she could find in Florrie's wardrobe.

"That frock, for instance." Barney looked her up and down. "*So* tasteful. It positively screams that you don't want to put a foot wrong, and people wonder why you don't. Much better to double-bluff in a tarty dress. People don't take you seriously, and then—*whoosh*"—he raised his arm swiftly—"you move in for the kill and get what you want."

Alexa was piling cheese on the board and trying to ignore him. She didn't need his advice. His or anyone else's. Why was he offering it anyway?

A slight sly smile was playing about Barney's lips. "Wondering why I'm offering to help you?"

"Because you want to marry Florrie and you want me to help *you*?" Alexa hazarded. It seemed unlikely, but it was all she could think of.

"Hardly, my dear," he said roguishly. "I'm as gay as New Year's Eve, as I thought you might have gathered. Mink-lined, gilt-edged, copper-bottomed, one hundred percent proof homosexual." He gave her a dazzling smile.

A terrible suspicion now gripped Alexa. He was not just campy but actually gay. Surely…surely…he wasn't after…

"*Ed?*" she gasped.

Barney's eyes bulged slightly. "Hardly, dear. I have got standards, however low. No, what I'm after is a comfortable berth. I help you marry Ed, and I'm your house guest for life in a range of enticing properties."

Alexa said nothing as she arranged the grapes. Barney's candor had temporarily disarmed her. As she struggled to think, the aroma of ripe Brie floated up into her nostrils.

"We can help each other," Barney pressed.

"I don't know what you mean," Alexa muttered pushing past him with the cheese board and out into the dining room, whose carpet was littered with bread rolls.

"God, what a honk!" yelled Florrie as she made room for the cheese between the candlesticks on the table. "Have you dropped a beast, Ed?"

Alexa studiously ignored Barney as she took a knife to the cheese. She did not want his help. She would do what she had to alone.

She remained aware of his amused stare, however, and was

flustered. She could not shake off the uncomfortable and, for her, unprecedented feeling of someone being several stages in front of her.

"Lexie!" shouted Florrie in disgust. "You've cut the nose off the Brie, you bloody oik."

Chapter Twenty

MAX, LYING ON THE rug with Polly amid the bird calls and heather scents, felt he was in heaven. Then, piercing the mellow sounds of the evening came the shrilling of his mobile from the front of the Land Rover.

"Leave it," Polly murmured, almost asleep under the influence of wine and love.

"I'd better get it," Max sighed, rising and loping over to the vehicle. "Might be an animal."

The caller code was not local; it was none of the estate farmers. The number was Sedona. The caller was the King.

"Father?" he said in surprise. King Engelbert *never* called his son on his mobile. He rarely called him on anything.

Engelbert, who had been preparing himself for hours with measured arguments and reasoned remarks, prefaced by a stream of pleasantries and chatter, now found everything he had so carefully rehearsed flying from his mind. He was not used to persuading people; he was used to ordering them about. What was the point in beating about the bush? He had told Astrid as much after she had confessed her miserable failure at telling Max where his duty lay. "OK then, your turn," she had flung at him.

That it was much easier in theory than in practice, the King was now realizing. He had not factored in his enormous fondness—love, even—for his elder son, and the associated difficulty of making someone you love do something they hate. Overcompensating for this weakness, as Engelbert saw it, made his voice gruffer and snappier even than usual.

"You have to get married!" he announced. Max blinked.

His glance flicked to Polly lying on the rug, the sunset burnishing her hair to a blaze of tangled copper. It was quite soon, admittedly; on the other hand, he was fairly certain she was The one. Why not, he thought to himself.

"Fine," he told his father. He smiled; a feeling of elation was growing within him. "Great," he added euphorically. "Fantastic!" he shouted. Polly looked up from the rug and gave him a puzzled smile.

Engelbert, at his end, felt a mixture of surprise and triumph. What had Astrid been complaining about? Convincing Max was ridiculously simple; he had accepted his instructions without question.

"So you'll come home immediately?" the King growled in relief.

"Come home?" Max frowned. "But I could marry Polly here."

"Polly?" snapped his father. "I'm not talking about Polly. That is an unsuitable relationship," he abruptly informed Max. "It has to end."

Max thought he was hearing things. "What?" he stuttered.

The King repeated it. "She is not a suitable wife," he added.

Max shook his head slowly. "I don't understand," he said. "Who am I supposed to marry then?"

"Someone else!" the King thundered, annoyed at his son's slowness to comprehend the obvious. "Someone suitable, that we'll find for you."

"Let me get this straight." Max was frowning, his eyes darting, nervous and unseeing, about the dashboard. "You want me to drop everything here, come home, and…get *married*? To someone I haven't even met?" He almost wanted to laugh, it sounded so incredible.

The King caught the giddiness in his son's tone. He would

not be mocked, not under any circumstances. "You're heir to the throne of the ancient kingdom of Sedona. You have to get married to someone appropriate."

Someone, Max thought, would wake him up in a moment; this would all be a bad dream. Or a joke, or something else with a sane explanation. "Where did this idea come from all of a sudden?"

The King sensed that confessing it came from a public relations consultant would be ill advised. He chose to ignore the question.

"You must come back," he repeated, as if the mere act of saying it again and again would get the desired result. "That girl Polly is *not* suitable."

"But how do you know?" Max asked, still more confused than angry. "You've never even met her."

"I don't need to. She's not appropriate, that much is clear. She's obviously a gold-digger," the King invented wildly. Astrid, listening keenly from the corridor outside his office, shut her eyes hard. Engelbert had handled it badly from the start. But this was disastrous. Of all the stupid things to say…

Now, finally, Max was furious. "There's no way—*no way*," he exploded, "that Polly is a gold-digger. She's the least avaricious or snobbish person I've ever met."

"Only interested in you because you're a prince, a future king," the King continued. "Sees herself on the throne—"

"I haven't even told her I'm a prince," Max cried, trying to smile as Polly, sitting up on one elbow, waved to him from the rug. He raised his hand with two digits sticking up. *Two minutes*, he mouthed.

"Haven't *told* her?" the King gasped. "Why ever not?"

"Because I didn't want her to know. Because, as you so rightly point out, she might see me differently then."

The King had by now recovered both his equilibrium and his seat on his high horse. "Well, it's irrelevant how she sees you, because she's not a princess. Not an aristocrat. Nothing else will do for a prince of the blood."

Max fought the urge to smash his fist into the metal side of his vehicle. "God, it's so...so...*medieval*."

"Medieval's exactly what it is," the King agreed. "We go back to Maxim the Ugly, who—"

"Took over the kingdom in 1459," Max parroted resentfully. "There's been an unbroken line of de Sedonas on the throne ever since then."

"Precisely. And you're not going to be the one to break it."

"But what if I *am*?" Max demanded passionately. "What if I *refuse* to marry this *appropriate* person you're going to find for me? What if I marry who I like? For *love*?"

There was a brief, horrified silence on the other end of the line. "Then you'll have to abdicate. Renounce your right to the throne."

It was music to Max's ears. Such a simple solution. Why had he never thought of it before? "Great, well why don't I? It's the answer to everything. I could do the degree I want to, marry who I want to..."

"If you do," the King broke in hysterically, "you will bring shame on the family. Sedona will be a laughingstock. Could you really be so selfish? Destroy me? Destroy your mother?"

Max stared at the heather stretching away before him. He was stung. This was a low blow if ever there was one. "Mum?" he flared. "I don't believe for a minute she has anything to do with this."

"Well, that's where you're wrong!" Engelbert raged. "Your mother is completely behind me on this."

Behind him, Max thought bitterly. Where Astrid had always been, in other words: a meek step to the rear of her despotic spouse.

"And," the King added, "she will be as devastated as me if you refuse to cooperate."

"Cooperate!" Max began. What was he, a prisoner? Then he

pictured her sweet, mild face swollen with tears, her big blue eyes red-rimmed. He felt guilt and resignation, then bitterness and outrage. How dare his father demand he come back? And for such crazy reasons. Had he gone mad?

But of course he had, Max realized with a rush of relief. That was his parents, ground down by worry and exhaustion. Obsessed as they always had been by royal duty, they could not see the wood for the trees. Shut up in their palace, in their time-warp kingdom, they did not realize that what they were proposing was impossible and unreasonable in the real world.

He took a deep breath of relief. Even so, on the evidence of this exchange, there was no point in trying to persuade them over the telephone.

Max thought hard. If, on the other hand, he returned to Sedona as requested, he could see his parents face to face. He could reason with them and calm them down. His mother and father were fundamentally sensible; they would see his point. It shouldn't take more than a few days. Then, once everything was sorted out and smoothed over, he could come back to Polly.

"OK," he said to his father reluctantly. "I'll come back."

From the rug where she was lying, Polly heard the Land Rover door slam. As Max came toward her, she saw that, for all his efforts to smile, he looked tense.

"What's the matter?" she asked.

"Oh, nothing. Just that I…er…have got to go away for a bit." His voice, she thought, sounded strained, as if he was struggling to keep it light. He was not quite meeting her eyes.

"Go *away*?" A thousand sword blades of terror jabbed Polly. "Go away where?"

"Oh, just home." He looked at her. For a wild moment, he wondered if he could tell her the truth. For a second, the wonderful prospect of unburdening himself hung tantalizingly in the warm, heather-scented air.

But then, slowly, the prospect receded. It was too much of a risk. She might think he was mad, that he was making it all up. And what she had said about princes earlier had not been encouraging either. Would she still be interested in him if she knew?

Max racked his brains. Polly saw him swallow and knit his brow, and felt more worried than ever. Was something terribly wrong?

"Parent trouble," he said eventually, ruefully. "They need me. I have to go and talk to them." Well, it was true, if not the whole truth.

Polly was all concern. "Oh, poor you." She felt, however, secretly relieved. His face had hinted at something much worse than mild disagreement between his mother and father.

He shrugged. "I won't be long. It should be repairable. I'll be back in a week, with any luck."

Chapter Twenty-One

…request the pleasure of your company
at the wedding of their daughter
Lady Beatrice Clementine Annunziata Augusta
Trevorigus-Whyske-Cleethorpe
to the Marquess of Dymchurch
on Saturday 31 July at 11.30
at Westchester Minster
and afterward at Willoughby Hall, Gloucestershire

On Saturday 31 July, Alexa had been awake since dawn. Today was the day! The day when, as one of a clutch of glamorous, privileged, and titled guests, she would finally knock Ed for six with her beauty and vivacity. The day she would force him to demonstrate before a gathering of high society including his mother that she was the girl for him.

Yet in the midst of her feverish plotting, Alexa now picked up a strange sound. A wailing. It sounded as if it were coming from Florrie's room.

She hurried along the passage. Her roommate, out all last night with Igor and his bottomless pockets, lay in bed, red-eyed and wailing.

"I really do need a Nurofen, darling. Go and get them, would you? They're in my bog."

"Your bag?"

"*Bog*. Khazi. Thunderbox. Shitter. Whatever," Florrie shouted. "Just get them, will you?"

Going obediently to the larger of the flat's two vast marble bathrooms, Alexa tried not to panic. What if Florrie was too ill to go? Lady Annabel would never allow Alexa to attend the wedding alone. As it was, she had only been admitted on the grounds that she would serve as Florrie's dresser before the ceremony.

"Come on," she urged Florrie as she returned with the pills. "You must get up. We've got Beattie's wedding to go to."

As Florrie's face clouded, Alexa's heart thumped. Sometimes, and particularly if she was in a bad mood, her roommate resented her use of private family diminutives. She could be mercurial like that; it was a window that could be slammed shut at any moment.

Today, however, it passed without comment. Florrie, it seemed, had other matters on her mind.

"Wedding!" she groaned. "I can't. I'm not going. I'm too ill!"

"But it's your sister's," Alexa gasped. "You're a bridesmaid."

"So what?" Florrie pushed out her enchanting lower lip like the adorable five-year-old she had once been, and still essentially was. But Alexa was finding her anything but cute at the moment. Fury and fear were roaring like a furnace within her. What if Florrie refused to go? She was more than capable of spurning, on a whim, an event on which Alexa was pinning every hope.

"You'll feel better once you're up and about," she soothed.

"No I won't," Florrie declared stubbornly. "I'm not going."

"But who's going to stay here and look after you all day?" Alexa urged sweetly, dandling her roommate's frail hands with every appearance of deep affection.

Florrie propped her long, slim body up on her elbows and stared at Alexa with wide violet-blue eyes in which nothing but an engaging innocence could be seen. "Why, Lexie, darling," she beamed, her smile lighting up her face and showing a row of small, even pearly-white teeth, "you, of course."

❖ ❖ ❖

In the event, Florrie recovered. A sharp call from Lady Annabel helped concentrate what passed for her mind. Her own impressive stamina in drinking matters did the rest. And so, that afternoon, Alexa sat, after all, in the great aisle of Westchester Minster awaiting the entrance of Lady Beatrice Trevorigus-Whyske-Cleethorpe, soon to be Marchioness Dymchurch.

Alexa was struck by the extent to which the scene resembled her favorite dream. The Bach cantata coming from the great organ could barely be heard above the murmur of the crowd. The place was packed. Royalty was present, as well as the Lord High Sheriff and assembled nobles and notables from several counties around.

Alexa had planned her outfit carefully. Her short violet silk dress, fitted at the bodice and slightly bell-shaped in the skirt, was pure Jackie O, with its scoop neck and narrow bow just below the bust. Violet was Florrie's family color; the ancestral flag showed a boar's head against a background of just this shade of purple. It had been intended as a subliminal message to Ed. She had swept her dark hair back into a chignon.

The air above Alexa smelt damp and cool. It was dancing with dust, which occasionally caught the slants of light from the great stained-glass windows. Painted shields and fringed banners dangled in the gloom of the vaulting, and the walls rioted with memorials. Some were pale and neoclassical, all urns and rippling marble drapes held by great carved tassels. Others were dark and Tudor couples in breeches and farthingales facing each other somewhat combatively over small prie-dieus.

At the front of the Minster, near the gold-draped altar groaning under the weight of ceremonial silverware and statement arrangements from a specially imported Knightsbridge florist, was a richly carved medieval tomb. Inside was what was left of the thirteenth-century queen promoted from the position of king's mistress to monarch's wife. They had married in this very cathedral. Had Alexa known the story, she would have been both interested and envious. Dead she might be, but she'd got her man.

As in Alexa's dream, the glamorous young friends of the bride and groom occupied several pews in the middle of the nave. Long-limbed young men with artfully tousled mops, signet rings, and inherited Savile Row morning suits lounged next to the girls. Everyone was yawning ostentatiously and repeatedly, as if the obligation to be up in the late morning to attend a lavish society wedding was as dull a one as could be imagined.

Alexa knew some of them. She had served them at din-dins or sat up all hours in nightclubs with them, admittedly in Florrie's slipstream. But she could not catch a single eye now. A row of county worthies sitting in gold chains and robes along the pew in front separated her from the rest of the crowd. But Alexa had the unpleasant feeling this was not the reason why people did not look around.

Had everyone been warned not to talk to her? Or had there been some awful mistake with the seating?

Just over there was Lady Tara Shropshire, one of Florrie's closest friends and a frequent visitor to the flat. Yet she kept her bony brown back in its flame-red silk strappy dress firmly turned. Alexa, staring at those skinny Cadillac shoulder blades, could hear her inane gabble from here. "Former hedgie...works in funding for Bollywood films...she's got some pet ferrets and she's had this little palace built for them, so sweet...Jenson Button...Boujis... Keith Richards..."

Ed Whyske, meanwhile, was five rows in front of her, his head turning animatedly to the side as he joked with the girl beside him. Lady Camilla Fish, Alexa recognized with a swoop of misery.

Alexa glared at the back of the Fish head, adorned with a simple circlet of daisies that made her own much-sprayed chignon feel suddenly silly and stiff. She glared at the celebrated tattoo of the Fish family crest, which *Vogue* had recently described as "witty," on Camilla's elegant bicep. The other bicep, Alexa had read in a *Tatler* profile, sported a line of Hindu script meaning "All titles, all wealth, they are nothing."

"Nothing!" Alexa thought heatedly. Easy enough to say when, like Camilla, your father owned half of Hampshire! Camilla Fish, who was more than merely grand and rich, but also effortlessly cool. She was one of those willowy, alternative aristocrats, the sort that appeared on the front of the *Daily Telegraph* in Glastonbury week looking mud-spattered but beautiful in tiny shorts and Hunter wellies and hanging on to Kate Moss's arm.

And now she was next to Ed! How, Alexa asked herself in panic, could she compete? On any level? Camilla Fish was long-legged, long-throated, long-haired, and equipped with the longest of aristocratic lineages. Her cheekbones were as high as her social position and she had the type of breasts that supported themselves (the only part of her that did).

Alexa felt as if she would explode with frustration. There was not the slightest doubt in her mind that Ed and Camilla were purposely placed there, right next to each other. Just as she was placed here, next to no one. Well, there was a person there, but she was obviously no one, a fat woman with red cheeks and an unflattering yellow outfit. She looked, Alexa thought, like a pig in a suit.

Yes, there had obviously been some mistake. And that mistake, Alexa guessed bitterly, was to assume that Lady Annabel would place her with the social lions and not the inconsequentials at the back.

Alexa had seen Lady Annabel pass earlier; she hadn't favored her with so much as a glance. Her toned arm had been lightly threaded through that of her estranged husband, with whom hostilities had evidently ceased for the service, in much the same way as the two sides in the First World War had played football on Christmas Day. Alexa had noted the manic pride in Lady Annabel's tanned face as she stalked by in high pink stilettos perfectly matching the rose-colored sleeveless shift dress that ended bang on the knee. The only positive thing to emerge from her humiliation was that Barney van Hoosier did not appear to be present to witness her humiliation.

Now came the rattle of ancestral carriage wheels, the jingle of polished harness, the clip-clop of proud, high-stepping horses.

"I think the bride's here!" Next to her, the fat woman shifted eagerly in her seat and looked excitedly around. Alexa clenched her fingers over the clutch bag that matched her violet dress. The sight of Beatrice coming down the aisle would, she knew, make her want to throw up. She fixed her eyes in despair on the vast cathedral organ with its Victorian-Gothic-patterned pipes, ranged above the carved stone choir screen that was Gothic from the first time around.

She felt the fat woman next door's spare tires ripple with excitement as the future Marchioness passed the end of the pew.

"Oooh, doesn't she look lovely."

"Gorgeous," Alexa snarled, thinking it was amazing what diamonds could do. Beatrice, who was perfectly acceptable-looking anyway, was elevated to goddess level by the wall of solid carbon otherwise known as the Dymchurch tiara, beneath whose blaze her features appeared in a wildly flattering glow.

Alexa raised her chin and squinted toward the distant altar end. She could just about see the Marquess of Dymchurch, the future husband, staring up the aisle, an expression of characteristic blankness on his strangely flat face.

And now here came the bridesmaids: four of them, all daughters of the nobility. Florrie was the tallest and noblest. As she passed the end of the pew, pure perfection in her close-fitting white satin dress, Alexa was unable to believe this was the same girl who had been poleaxed by a hangover only a few short hours before.

As she came down the aisle, Florrie was giggling and waving to acquaintances as if she were in a nightclub rather than the nave of a cathedral. She was pointing at her head, grinning and turning her eyes up, presumably to convey the severity of the hangover. Spotting Alexa, she even made being-sick gestures, but these were swiftly replaced by a look of puzzlement. "What on earth are you doing sitting *there*?" she demanded deafeningly. "You're in the *public* bit with the oiks."

Alexa, recognizing her chance, leaned forward. "Yes. I know. I think there's been a mistake."

Florrie's enormous violet-blue eyes widened. "But Mummy did all the cathedral seating herself," she exclaimed, before adding with a shrug, "oh, well, nevermind. Who cares anyway?"

Chapter Twenty-Two

AFTER THE SERVICE, ALEXA, the pig in the suit, and the others at the rear of the Minster had to wait for those at the front to exit first. Very possibly, she realized, this was another part of Lady Annabel's strategy: allowing all eligible men to be snapped up by other, more socially elevated single women before the likes of Alexa were released from their pens with the rest of the common herd.

When she finally emerged, blinking into the heat and brightness of midday, the cobbled parvis in front of the Minster could barely be seen beneath the mass of moving pastel, nodding fascinators, and tanned flesh, punctuated by flashes of expensive jewelry as the wedding guests exclaimed excitedly at each other and exchanged handshakes and air kisses.

As hanging about on the sidelines was obviously social suicide, Alexa dove into the crowd. She needed to make friends, fast. Apart from anything else, Florrie was elsewhere being a bridesmaid, and it was not at all clear how Alexa would get to the wedding breakfast. It was some distance away, at Willoughby Hall, and no one had offered her a lift so far.

And would it be worth it anyway? If Lady Annabel had seated her at the back of the Minster for the wedding, there were no prizes for guessing where she would be at the wedding breakfast. On table one hundred million, right by the door, with all the bores, misfits, and commoners Florrie's mother had been reluctant to ruin any other tables with.

Alexa tried to pull herself together. There was no point in being negative. She had to look for opportunities. Create some, if necessary.

"Peregrine!" She hailed the first person she recognized: a tall young man in tails who seemed to be having trouble standing on his own feet. The Marquess of Dymchurch's younger brother had been one of the groomsmen, making a hopeless hash of handing out hymn books and service sheets at the cathedral door. His long face was flushed and spotty, he wore very dark round sunglasses—as indeed he had throughout the service—and his hair stood aloft in dryish brown spikes. "Couldn't bag a ride off you up to Willoughby, could I?" Alexa purred with an ingratiating smile.

Peregrine looked startled. He twisted his fat red lips. "Well, thing is, I've sort of got rather a full car. Taking twenty guys already."

"Surely there's room for a little one," Alexa wheedled. Her situation was desperate. If she couldn't get a lift, she would have to catch the bus. Her ever-delicate finances, strained in the extreme now she was full-time life assistant to Florrie, would not even cover the cost of a taxi.

Tension filled the sunny air. Alexa could see the beginnings of a sweat breaking out on Peregrine's bald pink forehead.

She decided to force the issue. She turned a piteous look on him. "I've got *such* a painful ankle. Twisted it on these wretched cobbles!" She shook her head in just enough mock despair to allow a strand or two from her chignon to pull away from its rigidly hairsprayed fellows and fall winsomely over her face. "I'd be *so* grateful if you could fit me in too."

Behind his sunglasses, Peregrine's face was evidently panicked. "Er…" he stuttered.

Alexa was smiling brilliantly. "So kind of you. You can't imagine how sore my ankle is."

Peregrine's expression had something about it of the rabbit

caught in the headlights. He sensed he was in the grip of a higher power but had no idea how to remove himself from its influence.

Alexa now had complete command of the situation. "I simply can't walk another step." She sighed, performing an apparently agonized hop forward. Quick as a flash, she had grabbed his arm and now hung there like a limpet.

As there was obviously no shaking her off, either literally or metaphorically, Peregrine Dymchurch now accepted the inevitable. "You'd better come this way," he grunted, dragging her in the direction of a large sand-colored vintage motorcar with huge headlights, spare wheel on the back, and a folded-down hood. It was parked at the edge of the cobbled area and was already full of lissome girls and young men with cigarettes at the corner of their mouths struggling with champagne corks. *Pop!* went one of the bottles. There was a roar of approval, followed by shrieks as the bottle's contents gushed onto the antique leather seats.

Rising above them all was the familiar honk of Tara Shropshire. "Chased by a rhino...Tallulah...lost five hundred million in the crash...Guy Pelly...her lips are huge...this *amazing* band, they're all etonians...he giggles if you tickle his beard...Sting...poor her, she got bitten by a tramp...Beast of Blenheim...he looks fabulous in eyeliner...Zen weekend in Tuscany...then we all fell off the yacht..."

The yabbering stopped abruptly. The entire car fell silent as Peregrine approached with Alexa. She could sense him mouthing frantically at them. "No room, no more room," they yelled, as if in response.

But Alexa had not got this far to fail in her mission now. "I've got an idea," she piped up sweetly. "I could," she turned and fluttered her eyelashes at Peregrine, "sit on someone's lap!"

The defeated Peregrine could do nothing but bow to the

inevitable. Sulkily, he opened the car's back door. She was in in a purple flash, her injured ankle miraculously healed, squirming onto the first pair of male knees she found. These belonged to a plump, sweaty young earl whose fortune Alexa knew to be in the low to medium bracket, and whose family chateau in Cornwall was partly ruined. Nonetheless, he was a port in a storm.

"This is cozy!" she exclaimed with every appearance of delight, as the other sullen young things shoved up to accommodate her. From across the back seat, Tara Shropshire shot her a look of loathing. Alexa smiled sweetly back.

The vintage limousine, amid a good deal of convivial roaring, singing of the eton Boating Song and brandishing of champagne bottles, wove unsteadily between the hedges of the narrow country lane for many miles. It then swung in suddenly between a pair of large red-brick gates topped with snarling heraldic beasts in cream-colored stone. The curve was so sharp and sudden that a couple of the champagne bottles flew out into the hedges by the gates, accompanied by howls of disappointment.

Alexa, perched on the lap of the sweating earl, was relieved to be on the estate's private road. The driving had been even worse than she had imagined, narrowly missing a bus, several cars, and a line of cyclists; at least here they would not meet anything oncoming.

Throughout, however, she had directed a bright flow of chat at the earl. At first he had not responded at all, then had done so in unfriendly grunts. After she had begun to grind her bottom subtly but effectively into his groin, he had come alive. "I say," he remarked. "You're not nearly as bad as Beatrice's mother told us all you were."

"Thank you, that's adorable of you," returned Alexa sweetly, not betraying by the merest flutter of an eyelid the wave of fury she felt. But she'd get even with Lady Annabel. *And* seduce Viscount

Whyske. In the course of the journey, she had been forming a plan that even his formidable mother would be unable to stop.

The car was climbing further up into the park and passing over the ridge where the great spread of Willoughby Hall was first seen by the visitor. The view was magnificent and meant to be so; from the elevation of the road, everything from the Hall's grand main entrance to the stable block and kitchens could be seen below, like a small, homogenous, and very highly decorated town, its roofline busy with turrets, towers, pinnacles, and flags.

"I always think," drawled one of the girls beside Alexa, a snooty redhead, "that dear old Willers looks like it's been designed by someone who's never studied architecture but thinks it can't be all that hard."

Honks of supercilious laughter greeted this remark. Alexa smiled with the rest, although she did not agree in the least. To her, Willoughby Hall represented paradise, the fulfillment of all her dreams. To be mistress of such a place, she felt, would be El Dorado, Shangri-La, Elysium, and Nirvana all rolled into one.

The car shot down the final descent to the Hall at an alarming rate, accompanied by screams from the back. Apparently unable to stop, it hurtled toward the great building with a momentum that seemed likely to propel it up the great wide flight of shallow front steps and into the building itself.

There was a small, colorful crowd of guests before the mansion. Alexa recognized Lady Annabel's large pink hat. They watched first in interest, then alarm as the car gained upon them, finally scattering like a flock of multicolored pigeons just as the vehicle described a large and unsteady curve in front of the steps and skidded to a halt, spraying a tsunami of gravel that rained painfully on the assembled hats and the handbags lifted to shield faces.

Lady Annabel was the first to recover, detach herself, and march over, her spike heels biting into the gravel. "For goodness' sake, Peregrine!" she snapped at the driver. "Crash that car and you wipe out five ancient lines!"

Her eyes, glittering in the shade of her brim, now turned on Alexa, still seated on the earl's lap and trying subtly to shift herself from the consequences of what she had started. He really seemed very excited indeed, and besides the insistent swelling in his groin, she could feel him panting rapidly behind her. His hot, sweaty hands, clamped around her bottom, were burning wetly through the thin material of her dress.

As an expression of visceral contempt crossed Florrie's mother's features, Alexa smiled politely back, longing to explain to Lady Annabel that the situation wasn't what it seemed, that she had bigger fish to fry. Some of Lady Annabel's own fish, to be precise.

Yet for the successful execution of her plan, she needed to get into the Hall as quickly as possible, before any of the other guests. Only then would she have the advantage she sought.

Sheepishly, the bright young things emerged from the limousine and set about making up lost ground with their elders. Alexa, meanwhile, slipped away. Willoughby's façade had been built to impress and was extensive; it took her a good five minutes before she found some open double doors leading into the conservatory.

She slipped in, grateful for her silver pumps, which made no sound on the marble floor, and sneaked in the direction of where she guessed the main hall to be. Her heart raced as she hurried through a couple of ornate reception rooms, their heavy furniture slumbering beneath mirrors and chandeliers.

As she had anticipated, the wedding lunch was set out in Willoughby's massive entrance hall, a Victorian extravaganza of marble pillars, statues, gilt torchères, chandeliers, molded cornucopia, and ancestral portraits. She hurried across the mosaic marble of the anteroom, mere feet now from the gilded entrance to the hall and its sea of circular tables draped in white linen.

"Can I help you?" A voice shattered the silence. Alexa froze. Damn. *Damn.*

Chapter Twenty-Three

SHE TOOK A DEEP breath and turned with a brilliant smile. "I'm Alexa MacDonald," she gushed at the morning-suited butler. "Lady Florence's roommate."

It was just possible that a look flashed across the retainer's face, as if he had been told something about this person. But within nanoseconds his long basset-hound features had resumed their normal respectful, attentive expression. "Indeed, modom," he intoned, bowing slightly.

"I'm looking for the loos." Alexa staged a rueful laugh.

"You're in quite the wrong part of the house, modom. The lavatories are outside, in the stable yard, next to the plant shop and the café."

Alexa headed off the way she had come. In the second anteroom, she slipped behind a large brocade curtain and waited until she calculated the butler had gone. Slipping out again, she returned to the hall. She was careful to crouch as she moved between the tables, their surfaces a jumble of white-themed flower arrangements, glasses, bottles of water and table numbers on gilt stands.

She looked about frantically. Where was it?

Ah. There. Between the two alabaster pillars that marked the entrance to the hall from the anteroom on the other side. The table plan.

She hurried over to the easel on which the large, hand-calligraphed document, not unlike the Magna Carta, was propped. She frowned at the details of who was sitting where. Here was the bride's table, the top table, with Lady Annabel on it, of course, and the royals either side of her. Next to the Prince of Wales was Florrie, and seated next to her was Lord Sebastian de Loxley, a trainee duke who was presumably the best Lady Annabel could do for her daughter at the moment. And here, opposite, was Ed Whyske, dammit, next to Camilla Fish.

She searched for her own name, her forefinger following the ornately hand-written rows of Lord This and Lady That. Tables 60 to 70, moving further back in the room. Still no Miss Alexa MacDonald. Her insides twisted with fear. Tables 70 to 80. Still nothing. Her heart speeded up. Tables 80 to 90, oh God, still nothing, it couldn't be true. Tables 90 to…and there, finally, she was. Between someone called Brian Spratt and a Mr. Leonard Donkin. On Table 94, at the far back of the hall. It wasn't so much Siberia as the islands north of it. And the sea to the north of those.

Even though she had been expecting it, Alexa felt the humiliation almost physically. But this was no time for anger. She who hesitates is lost, she reminded herself, before moving rapidly into action. Flitting lightly between tables, glancing hurriedly over her shoulder, she switched the place cards. In a matter of moments, Camilla Fish was between Messrs Spratt and Donkin and Alexa herself next to Viscount Whyske.

And now. Dare she? Her fingers seized the card bearing Lady Annabel's name. Within seconds she had moved it from beside the PoW to next to the Lord Lieutenant of the county. Someone called Mrs. Justice Pomfrey, who had been beside the Lord Lieutenant, was now promoted to royalty. There was just time, too, to move Tara Shropshire from beside Prince Harry and stick her next to the Chief Constable.

She rubbed her hands with glee. But not for long. Now she

heard, like a gathering storm, the rumble of approaching voices coming along from the anteroom. Lunch must be about to start. And she was yet to remove the most important item of all.

Stepping smartly to the entrance, she picked up the table plan and its easel—fortunately it was lighter than it looked—and hurried it away to behind the nearest curtain. With that gone, no one would be any the wiser. People could only locate their seats from the cards on the tables.

Except Lady Annabel, of course, but with the evidence removed, she would be hard pressed to make a fuss. And if the Prince of Wales sat down first, with Mrs. Justice Pomfrey beside him, even she could hardly make them get up again.

Satisfied, Alexa sailed out of the main hall and across one of the sitting rooms. In a side passage she found a downstairs cloakroom and locked herself in. If that pompous bloody butler thought she was using the public loos, he had another thing coming.

She revived her hair and makeup as fast as was humanly possible. She noted with delight the new, bold sparkle in her dark eyes and consolidated the effect with some more mascara, then slicked on a new layer of lip gloss. But that was all there was time for.

With one final triumphant glance in the mirror, one hurried smooth of her hair, she hurried back to the main hall, ready to take her seat next to Viscount Whyske and opposite the Prince of Wales.

She approached the bridal table with a casual confidence. The Prince, rather to her regret, was not yet present, but Viscount Whyske was, sitting in his allotted place and looking around with his accustomed blank stare. "Hello, Ed," Alexa beamed, putting her hand in proprietorial fashion on the slender gilt frame of the seat beside him, pulling it out and sitting down.

Florrie, who had plonked herself down opposite and was slathering butter onto a roll, leaned over. "Oh, sitting there, are you, Lexie? Great. Ma told me she shoved you about twenty tables away."

"Did she?" Well, Ma had not succeeded. Alexa could not resist asking, nonetheless, "Why would she do that?"

Florrie rolled her eyes. "Oh, you know what Ma's like. Convinced you're the most awful castle-creeper. She's been banging on at me all morning about it. Wants you out of the flat and everything."

Alexa did not flinch under these powerful blows. Instead, she gave a pretty laugh. "*Dear* Lady Annabel. Such a *wonderful* sense of humor. Because, in fact"—she reached triumphantly over to pluck the place card from among the shining cut-crystal glasses—"she's put me here…"

Her voice died away. Her throat dried in horror. Her hand shook violently.

There was some mistake. It was not possible. The card that she was looking at bore another name, not hers. In the few minutes she had been in the lavatory, someone had swapped it back.

"Er, hi there." The slow, vague voice of Lady Camilla Fish came from behind. "I, you know, think that's my seat, OK? Is that cool with you?"

Confused as she rarely was, Alexa stood up and in her agitation knocked some of the glasses over. The sharp, insistent ring of ancestral crystal under duress brought unwelcome attention her way, among it the mocking eyes of Lady Annabel showing the Prince of Wales to his seat.

Head bowed to disguise the beetroot red of her face, Alexa made her way as best she could to Table 94, in the seas to the north of the islands north of Siberia. The one time she glanced up, she caught the eye of Lady Annabel's butler. His expression, before it reverted to its habitual deferential blank, might have been that of one who, instructed to watch for someone moving place cards about, had successfully thwarted their endeavors.

As she sat down between Brian Spratt and Leonard Donkin,

Willoughby's head gardener and estate manager respectively, Alexa knew she had lost the battle. Spratt's views on the difficulties of growing tree ferns in a northern climate went in one ear and out the other, as did Donkin's patent method of tackling foot rot in sheep. Filling her head like a scream was the knowledge that Lady Annabel had won the day, that Camilla Fish would win Ed, that she herself would be obliged to move out of Florrie's flat in short order, and that her liaison with the Trevorigus-Whyske-Cleethorpes was over. And that Lady Annabel would trumpet to the whole of Facebook her antics at Beatrice's wedding.

She was staring down at her water glass, wondering whether to smash it, slash her wrists, and end it all now, when she felt a hand on her shoulder and a familiar smooth voice in her ear. "She stiffed me too. Table 110, and so far back in the cathedral I was practically in the bloody bus station."

Alexa twisted around. "Barney!" she said in surprise, recognizing him from Florrie's dinner party. Donkin and Spratt had stopped talking, she saw, and were staring open-mouthed at the vision in three-piece violet linen with a large purple orchid in the buttonhole.

"Join the club," she said ruefully.

Barney's mouth was hissing at her ear. "So why don't we get together? Defeat the common enemy? You'll be needing a place to stay, at the very least."

She had no choice, Alexa realized. Otherwise, it was Mum and Dad's. And there was no chance that she was going home again. Unless the home involved had the word "stately" in front of it.

Chapter Twenty-Four

AT OAKESHOTT, THE GRASS waved and shone in the sunshine and the trees glowed with fresh green leaves. Above, the sky was blue; around, the air was warm and sweet with the singing of birds. But Polly was not thinking of the summer.

"Is there a bottom to space?" she heard Kyle asking, from what seemed a great distance away.

Polly blinked and came back down to earth. She and the children had stopped for lunch and were sitting on the grass at the side of the trench. Kyle had left his group of friends and had come over to where Polly was sitting some distance away, hunched over her knees, sandwiches untouched, her water bottle dangling in one hand. "What?" Polly said, vaguely recalling something about bottoms.

Kyle repeated his question.

Polly took a slug of water and pondered. Of late, as he became more interested, Kyle had been firing questions at her like a machine gun, not just about Romans, with which she was fine, but about everything, about which she could be patchy. He was, for all his shaven head and lack of finesse, an extraordinarily bright child. His brain never seemed to stop; something in it was always digging away, like Napoleon the dog.

Long gone were the days when Kyle thought the ancient world was invented by George Lucas. Now, he could recite most of the main dates in Roman history, even manage the odd sentence in

Latin. "Kylus sum," he would say, banging himself across the chest in a clenched-fist salute.

"I'm not sure that there is a bottom to space really," Polly managed eventually. "Space is, well, infinite."

Kyle, however, had moved on. "And what would happen if Jupiter fell on the earth?"

Polly stretched her eyes and tried to remember about gravitational pull. "Well, it wouldn't because…"

Kyle was opening a bag of potato chips as he listened. "Do you believe in God?" he asked next, stuffing handfuls of Quavers in his mouth.

Polly felt tired. It was all rather intense for a Tuesday lunchtime. "Well, he is a historical figure," she conceded vaguely.

"Do you believe in him or don't you?" Kyle was narrowing his eyes at her; his stubbly hair bristled in the sunshine. He was evidently determined to nail the issue.

"Well, I believe in something more powerful than myself," Polly said evasively, taking another sip of water.

"But that's not saying much, is it?" he said dismissively.

Polly had to grin. No, it wasn't saying very much. And, actually, she didn't need Kyle to point out how unimportant she was.

A week, Max had said. But a week had already gone and there was no word from him. She wasn't seriously worried. Just puzzled. He had given her no contact details; she didn't even know where he was. But he had promised to get in contact, and she must have faith that he would.

Fortunately, there was work, although possibly not for much longer. Polly, in the shallow excavation trench, looked down at the brown soil, which had been worked over and sifted through again and again. It was pretty likely that nothing was left. All that could be excavated had been; it had all been duly drawn, plotted, photographed, and recorded. She needed to let the county council, as well as Mrs. Butcher, know that work was coming to an end. The thought of telling Mrs. Butcher, let alone Kyle, was a difficult one.

Perhaps she would put it off another week.

"But if God created the world in six days, what about the Big Bang?"

Kyle was off again. Polly groped for the answer, even though this very morning on the *Today* program they'd had a Christian fundamentalist and a scientist going hammer and tongs on Creationism versus Darwinism. She racked her brains to remember what they had said.

"What does Mrs. Butcher say?" she hazarded eventually.

"She says that God created the Big Bang."

"Ah." Polly smiled. As neat a way of getting around it as any other. She rose to her feet. "Back to work, everyone."

Of course, there was no work left to do now really. She paced slowly over to her own area of the trench, crouched down, and poked the soil. It was a part that had been examined many times before. Yet something—sentimentality?—was urging her to have one last look. She probed away gently with her trowel, following the progress of the tool with her fingers and thinking of Max. The soil gave way easily. Down and down went her questing trowel; deeper it bit, deeper than previously. She knew nothing was down there, but it was soothing somehow, this peaceful, effortless exploration, feeling the sun on her back, aware of the children chattering and bickering in the background.

What was that? Polly was jolted from her reverie. The edge of the trowel had struck something. She felt her fingers make contact with a smooth object. She stopped digging and felt with sure, gentle, but feverish fingers the small expanse of what had been exposed and which now gleamed gray in the sunshine.

Hardly daring to breathe, she picked up her trowel again and began gently to move the earth around it away. One never expected to find them; the last time had been a complete surprise as well...

Polly glanced up at the children, all frowning over graph paper as they plotted their finds. They were occupied, absorbed. She bent her head; her hair flopped into her eyes. She shook it aside and set to work.

A few minutes later, alerted by some instinct, Kyle looked up. He saw Polly's crouching figure and realized she was, even for her, very absorbed.

Kyle narrowed his eyes. Was she gazing into space again? Her attention didn't seem to be on them anymore. He knew there was something wrong; they all did, and Poppy said it was *definitely* because Miss Stevenson was in love with that good-looking man with the dark hair whose dog had dug up the bone that time and who hadn't been back for ages. "Rubbish," Kyle had said robustly, only to have Poppy snap that it was true and that *she* knew about these things and *he* didn't.

Poppy, who knew nothing about the Big Bang or gravitational pull. Let alone about the Pubic Wars; it was Pubic, wasn't it?

Kyle still felt disappointed that the dog's bone hadn't turned out to be a whole skeleton, but even more disappointed in Miss Stevenson. How silly to be in love. He had thought better of her. He himself was never going to be in love, obviously. But if he ever *had* to, it would be with someone like Miss Stevenson, with her soft hair and the gentle eyes that looked at you in such a kind and friendly way. He felt annoyed with the dark-haired man. How dare he upset Miss Stevenson?

Polly was still working at the soil. His quick, perceptive eye noticed that her movements were unusually swift; there was something excited about them. Had she found something?

Kyle's instinct, never long dormant, to bring noise where there was silence, chaos where there was order, excitement where there was calm, was mixed with a genuine curiosity about what was happening and propelled him to her side.

He stared in amazement at the earth in front of her.

"Miss! *Mi-iss*!" The noise exploded in Polly's ear like a trumpet blast. "*Miss!*" Kyle shrieked. "You've dug up a skull!"

Chapter Twenty-Five

THE ROAD BARNEY LIVED on marked the border between an undesirable west London postcode and its more desirable immediate neighbor. The house containing his flat was on the desirable side but did not get the sun in the morning. Or any other time of day, Alexa now knew. It was small, dark, smelly, and faced directly onto a sink estate.

Strictly socially speaking, this did not matter; the W11 postcode for invitation purposes was the crucial factor. Few of Barney's friends—when he had had them—had ever visited in person.

The flat was entered through a battered front door, whose central panel bore several unsteadily mounted bells of different sizes and vintages, pertaining to the apartments above Barney's. In the few short weeks she had lived in close proximity to them, Alexa had had to get used to the reggae DJ who lived on the top floor and the floor-pounding fitness instructor who lived directly above.

The instructor was at it already, Alexa thought, hearing the usual regular thudding of trainered feet on the flimsy ceiling. She lay on her back and watched the swaying lightshade. It was not a question of if, rather of when the floor would give way and the muscle-bound Greek who lived above dropped into her midst accompanied by shattered floorboards and plaster dust.

Alexa's bedroom was the first door in the grubby hallway. Because it had a high ceiling and the floor space was little larger than the mattress serving as a bed, it looked like a shoebox turned on its end. On the wall opposite the door was a tiny blocked-up fireplace, its mantelpiece festooned with dusty Bollinger bottles with grubby candles stuck in the necks. Next to the grimy window was a small wooden wardrobe on whose ill-fitting, permanently open door Barney's black tie outfit hung, swathed in dry-cleaner's plastic and ever ready on a wooden coat-hanger. Ever ready, but these days hardly ever used.

The room had been Barney's, but now he slept on the sitting room sofa. This gave Alexa's room, grim as it was, a context. It was small, noisy, comfortless, and damp, but at least it was private. She should be grateful.

Alexa got up and found her host in the tiny sitting room.

"Good morning!" Barney trilled. "Marvelous day, isn't it?" He was so positive, he made her feel listless by comparison. He was like an engine that was always switched on. His energy seemed to throb through the room.

He was ensconced in one of the few pieces of furniture: a very tatty winged armchair with a standard lamp beside it, its shade skew-whiff. He wore pajamas of shiny pale pink cotton, trimmed with dark blue piping. Over this was a silk paisley dressing gown, and there were burgundy velvet slippers on his plump little feet. Barney always dressed as if he was breakfasting at Brideshead rather than opposite one of the capital's most notorious council estates.

He, too, had apparently only just got up; the habits of a night owl, he claimed, were hard to break. Although the invitations to white-tie balls or to play poker all night in exclusive Mayfair clubs had dried up, Barney kept the same hours.

He now spent them on Facebook, and with enormous benefit to them both; Alexa had found her page exhaustively updated with awe-inspiring views of Scotland and distant glimpses of baronial towers; the on-site claim being that, due to a family emergency, this was where she had been spending the summer.

Barney was not online now, however. He was reading a newspaper, his brow furrowed in apparent deep concentration. Beside him on the floor was an elegant white and gold cup and saucer. None of his china matched; purloined as it was from various stately homes and grand hotels, his plates, cups, dishes, and ashtrays namechecked palaces of gracious living a world away from the battered kitchen cupboards in which they sat. Reaching up to get a cup down, Alexa would feel taunted.

She padded barefoot over the dirty gray carpet to the small square dining table at which no dinner parties were ever held and lifted up the coffee pot. Her eye fell on a white piece of paper unfolded near the pot: Barney's annual membership renewal letter from the London Library.

"It costs a *fortune*!" Alexa picked up the bill in astonishment.

Barney looked up mildly. "But it's very social. You see influential people in the lift all the time."

Alexa remarked that hundreds of pounds a year was a high price to pay for this privilege; indeed, it was possible that the influencer concerned would privately appear in any elevator Barney cared to nominate for less.

"That may well be true," Barney concurred. "But I can't start removing myself from society."

Alexa pulled out a chair from under the small table and cursed as a pile of magazines slipped off the seat and landed on her foot. Barney's flat was not only cramped and dark, it was squalid and full of rubbish. It needed cleaning, although Alexa had no intention of obliging. Nothing would more eloquently advertise the end of her hopes of advancement than getting on her knees on the bathroom floor and scrubbing out the toilet bowl.

A great wave of misery swept over her. "Oh, Barney," she groaned. "What are we going to do? It's social death!"

Barney looked up from his newspaper. His small mouth was turned upward in a beam. "Precisely, my dear Alexa. That's just what it is."

"Social death?" she repeated. Then why did he look so happy about it?

"Yes! I'm taking you to a memorial service!" There was a silence.

"You're taking me to a *memorial* service?" Alexa managed.

"Lord Bedstead's died," Barney announced cheerfully. "It's a great opportunity for you."

"I may be desperate," Alexa muttered, "but necrophilia's not my thing."

She had heard of Lord Bedstead—not his real name, but a reference to his sexual prowess. Which could have had possibilities had the peer in question not been several decades older than her and with a penchant for Brazilian cross-dressers. And dead, into the bargain.

"He died as he'd have wanted to," Barney told her. "Breathed his last in the arms of a seven-foot-tall transsexual with steel teeth."

Alexa rubbed her face. "What's all this got to do with me?"

"Lord Bedstead's memorial service," Barney said slowly, in the emphatic tones of one speaking to an idiot, "is certain to be attended by a great many male aristocrats of similar rank. Not all of them will bring their wives. Not all of them will be married, even."

In the silence after these words, Alexa felt the pistons in her brain break through the rusty coating left by the last few weeks and start to pick up speed. She could see what Barney was getting at. A cathedral full of peers. Some unattached. Sitting ducks. The service would be of a length to allow her to pick her target from the discreet distance of the pews.

It was ingenious.

There was only one problem.

"I never knew Lord Bedstead," she admitted. "Did you?"

"No, actually."

"So how will we get in?" She felt irritated that he had raised her hopes while overlooking this crucial factor.

"Anyone wishing to pay their respects can apply for a ticket," Barney said gleefully. "I'm applying for two."

Alexa's smile broadened into a grin. It was inspired, it really was. You didn't have to be invited into this social inner sanctum. You only had to buy a ticket to be back in the swim.

"Lord Wimble will be there," Barney added.

Alexa nodded. Wimble was the earl she had all but lap-danced on the way to Willoughby Hall. His family fortune was negligible and his generous proportions gave a whole new meaning to "family seat." But he was a start. Once back on the ladder, she could trade him in for two wings, a dome, fishing rights, and a villa in Umbria.

Chapter Twenty-Six

THE WHITE AND GOLD double doors of the Crown Prince's bedroom swung tentatively open. The anxious, smooth, red face of Monsieur Hippolyte, the royal private and press secretary, peered in and looked nervously about for something small, hairy, and ferocious.

Was the blasted dog there? It had a nasty habit of nipping the ankles of anyone who stepped over the threshold.

"Your Royal Highness?" he murmured.

There was no answer. Hippolyte could make out little in the gloom of the Crown Prince's bedroom. At the tall windows, the thick lined curtains were pulled shut, but with apparent crazed haste and with no eye for aesthetics. Not in a manner, Monsieur Hippolyte concluded, that suggested the Prince's valet had done it, but then the Prince had not allowed his valet near since he had come back from England. He had allowed very few people near, in fact. To say that the heir to the throne was unhappy was not dissimilar to saying that the King was ever more short-tempered and the Queen increasingly tense.

Hippolyte cleared his throat. "Sir?"

There was no answer.

The press secretary felt horribly hot. Summer was gathering its full force in Sedona, blasting the mountainous Mediterranean kingdom with scorching rays even at this time of the morning. Hippolyte fished a crumpled white hanky out of his pocket and wiped his sweating brow. Squinting into the darkness, he pressed his fat little hands together and flexed his flabby biceps beneath his crisp white shirtsleeves. Gingerly, he touched his head. The increasing stress seemed to be increasing the size of the bald patch in the center. Certainly, arranging the hanks of determinedly black hair that covered it was getting more complicated.

But nowhere near as complicated as dealing with Prince Maxim. It was all that wretched PR consultant's fault. It was easy for him to demand the Crown Prince come home and get married for the good of the economy, then to flounce off to his next lucrative engagement, leaving others to actually manage the reluctant heir and find him someone to marry.

Others like Hippolyte. Together with Maxim's parents, he had scoured entire forests of royal family trees and thumbed from dawn till dusk through every gazette of lineage and peerage he could lay his hands on. He had pondered lists of quadruple-barreled arch-duchesses until his eyeballs twisted. Life at the Chateau de Sedona recently had been a whirl of entertaining as every eligible daughter in Europe came to stay. But to no avail.

Engelbert, as the entire castle staff knew, was at his wits' end with his son. "He's just not making an effort," the King would rant, pacing up and down the same patch of carpet in his private secretary's office. "There was nothing wrong with that Spanish girl. She did have a strange laugh, but I told Max the trick was not to tell her jokes, that was all."

But the Prince had been unmoved by the Spanish infanta, as well as the Austrian archduchess, the German baroness, the Italian *contessa*, and the female Scottish laird. Likely candidates were running out. But Maxim had to marry someone. The people of Sedona wanted a wedding. The King wanted a wedding. Everyone wanted a wedding, except the person expected to be the groom.

If Maxim didn't get married…

Hippolyte pushed the hideous prospect away. His main

skill—and he was far from alone among palace employees in this respect—had always been ensuring his own survival.

Monsieur Hippolyte had been counting on royal benevolence well into his dotage. He saw himself, like many a cherished retainer before him, putting his feet up in one of the grace-and-favor flats belonging to the Palace and situated in grand apartment blocks all over Sedona. But how cherished a retainer was he at the moment?

The thought of leaving his comfortable—literally palatial—palace life brought a surge of terror to the private secretary's plump white breast. This was followed by one of pure panic. He could no more imagine life outside a royal residence than a snail could imagine life without a shell.

Was it any wonder he had found himself of late treading the path he had sworn he would never tread again, down a certain Sedona back street and up a certain pink-carpeted strip of pavement to the glossy black door of Madame Whiplash? There, anonymous in a black leather mask, he could enter an entirely different world, where partners were plentiful and no one judged anyone. Although the tall, silver-haired figure who had propositioned him the other night had been *very* reminiscent of a certain eminent French justice who had dined at the chateau on more than one occasion…

But who could blame him for being driven to such lengths? Hippolyte demanded angrily of himself. What other relief was there? He felt utterly crushed under the weight of his problems; it wasn't even as if they concerned Prince Maxim alone. Prince Giacomo had returned in the early hours and subsequently spent some considerable time shouting from the palace windows at his departing fellow carousers. They had left eventually, but not without a great deal of horn-blasting which only by a miracle failed to wake his royal parents.

For Hippolyte, the sound had been the now-familiar reveille; he must get up, ring the manager of La Cage Aux Princes, and spend an hour trying to persuade the nightclub owner not to release information to the press about what Giacomo had been doing, who with, and at the cost of how much. Hippolyte cleared his throat. "Sir!" he said again to Prince Max's bedclothes.

All hell now broke loose. Maxim's wretched dog, which had apparently been asleep, woke up and exploded into a frenzy of yapping. Hippolyte leaped back in terror as it danced along the bed barking at him and glaring with its one eye. It was amazing how much malevolence could be packed into a single small orb. Thank God it was too old and lame these days to be able to get off the bed and bite him—but Hippolyte had thanked too soon. Still yapping furiously, the spaniel now slid itself off the end of the bed and lowered itself by hooking its claws into the bedclothes. Once at ground level, it skittered over the Savonnerie and sank its sharp teeth into Hippolyte's plump ankle.

"Ow!" shrieked the panicking private secretary.

"What's going on?" The Prince's dark head appeared from beneath the heap of crumpled sheets. He sat up in his white pajamas with the royal monogram on the breast. His handsome face hardened when he saw his father's factotum. "What do you want, Hippolyte?"

"Your father would like to see you in an hour, your Highness. You are expected in the throne room at ten o'clock."

Having delivered his message, glancing nervously at the dog, Hippolyte retreated. Max fell back on his pillows and sighed.

Beano looked at him sympathetically with his good eye and loyally wagged his tail. Max tickled the red and white curls beneath the animal's chin. Beano apart, he wished with all his heart that he had stayed in England.

On arriving home, Max found he had miscalculated badly. His assumption that his parents were merely suffering from stress could not have been further off the mark. His father had meant every word about forcing him into marriage for the good of Sedona. There was, Engelbert announced, to be no more studying. Sedona expected a wedding, and a wedding there must be.

Even his mother, to whom he had instinctively turned for sympathy, seemed to be keeping her distance and to be resolutely on the side of his father. There seemed no escape, none.

Max thought about the girls who had been paraded before him over the past couple of weeks. It had all been too excruciating for words. They had trotted past him like prize heifers—if only they *had* been heifers. He would have found them infinitely more interesting.

And like a prize bull himself, he would, Max had gathered, be expected to impregnate any bride in short order. Although the medieval ceremony when this process was witnessed by a bevy of bishops had been allowed to lapse—even Engelbert drew the line somewhere—there was still the horrific prospect of becoming a father just as he emerged from childhood himself.

Max sank back into the pillows. Life seemed suddenly a series of prisons. The prison of marriage, the prison of parenthood, and the prison of royal duty. Not for nothing, he thought bitterly, were there three keys on the Sedona royal standard.

Why had he—*he*—been born the heir to a throne? He felt both resentful and guilty. It was a waste for him to have this position when he didn't want it and when Giacomo clearly adored being royal.

Max almost envied his brother his breezy acceptance of a position in life that put him above other people. An egalitarian by inclination, he himself had attempted to avoid the hooray crowd at university, although not with absolute success. There had been a particularly determined social climber who had been hell-bent on an invitation to the chateau. Now what had been his name? Van something. Van Hoofer? Something like that.

"Hey, boy!" Beano now derailed this gloomy train of thought. The dog had, with considerable difficulty, managed to leap back up on the bed and stood with his stiff legs shaking. The Prince stroked him, not without a twist of the heart. He had been amazed to see, on his return, the extent to which, so suddenly, Beano had aged. Gone was the bounding bundle of red and white curls. Beano's legs were stiff and his one eye looked cloudy and sticky with macular degeneration. He was getting old, Max saw, sadly.

The dog licked Max's hand, and the Prince tickled him fiercely in the way Beano had so loved when he was a puppy. He buried his nose in Beano's long ears and felt like howling for the child he had once been, for whom life was just one long sunny day and who could not even imagine the existence of adulthood and its responsibilities.

The Prince swung his long legs out of bed, padded to the window, and poked his head through the curtains. The sky outside was blue and hot as usual, but he could take no pleasure in it. He missed the gray, cloudy skies of England. He missed the great green rolling estate at Oakeshott. But more than this, he missed Polly. He missed her smile. Her shy way of talking, her unexpectedly loud and gleeful laugh. Her passion for her subject, her stories about the children, her amazing body…

He knew she must be wondering what had happened to him, but what could he tell her? He had, anyway, lost his mobile phone, although now, after days of searching, he was beginning to wonder if someone had taken it on his father's orders. Since when was Sedona a police state?

He felt something soft and wet nudging his hand. He picked his dog up and buried his nose in the animal's curly head. "Oh, Beano. What am I going to do?"

Chapter Twenty-Seven

"It's looking good," Barney whispered as Alexa, aloft on swaying black heels, staggered up the stone path into Lord Bedstead's estate church.

"Suppose so." Alexa looked around. It was a beautiful blue day, and the lane was full of flowering bushes, which in turn were full of singing birds. The church was the small, ancient, gray type with arched mullioned windows and a square crenellated tower. But the shoes were killing her and the English countryside wasn't really her thing. Not unless you owned it, that was.

"Not the bloody scenery," Barney hissed. "Over there!" He gestured to where, on the other side of the lichened churchyard wall, a gleaming line of black helicopters were lined up in the grassy meadow.

Alexa's eyes widened. Lord Bedstead's business interests had evidently ranged as far and wide as his libido and his memorial service was attracting huge numbers of what Barney described as the great and the bad. The lane leading to the lychgate had become a positive showroom of Bentleys and Aston Martins.

All of which had made taking the bus humiliating—Alexa could hardly remember the last time she had been on one. But Barney had made a joke of it, saying they must speculate to accumulate. They had speculated on Alexa's clothes, blowing the last of their combined savings on a tight black dress with a plunging cleavage, a vastly broad-brimmed black hat, and the heels. "I look much too tarty," she had objected.

"Nonsense," Barney riposted. "You can't look tarty enough on occasions like these. Death always makes people horny."

And it was true that, on her way up the path, she had attracted more than her share of attention. "Damned fine filly that," a tall, handsome man with an outdoors complexion, thick silver hair, and very naughty blue eyes had commented as she wiggled past.

"Stonker Shropshire," Barney had hissed excitedly.

"The Duke of Shropshire?" Alexa gasped, reeling under a wave of money-and-title lust. The man who owned almost the entire county where her parents lived.

"Yes, but don't get too excited. He's married. That's his wife over there."

Alexa regarded the short, plain woman with jealous eyes. Next to her tall, elegant, and charismatic husband, she looked like a dull hen bird beside a peacock. How did a woman like that snare a duke?

Inside the chilly—amazingly chilly—church, Barney steered a shivering Alexa into a pew otherwise occupied by a boot-faced trout in a black straw boater and a man whose nose was so pointed and eyes so receding he resembled an eagle in a suit. They both looked her disapprovingly up and down.

Alexa ignored them. She knew that she looked beautiful with a rainbow of colored light from the stained-glass window spilling across her breasts. Aware of a number of interested gazes, she stood as straight as her crippling heels permitted.

The pillared nave and the side aisles were rapidly filling up; it was standing room only at the back under the organ pipes. The sidesmen were running out of service sheets, a thick cream card affair printed by Smythson's and bearing a photograph of Lord Bedstead looking like an enormous ancient baby in his floppy Garter bonnet and ribbons.

"The grieving widow," Barney murmured, nudging Alexa in the direction of a woman with an obviously new facelift sporting a fascinator and an air of undisguised triumph.

Barney was making a great show of waving cheerfully at people, who, having stared back blankly for a few seconds, hesitantly waved in reply.

Alexa was by now shaking with the cold. "It's f-freezing," she hissed at Barney, who was mouthing greetings at a heavy-faced woman in a pillbox.

"Who's that?" the woman in the pillbox could be heard loudly demanding of her neighbor, a stooped-looking man in rusty black.

"Here." Barney surreptitiously passed Alexa a small silver flask of brandy. "Keep your spirit levels up."

They rose for the first hymn: "Abide with Me."

"I'm not sure I can." Barney sighed after the obviously nervous organist fluffed the beginning twice and embarked on it a third time.

In the pew in front, various sleek-looking men had their heads bent respectfully. Leaning over slightly, Alexa could see that the entire row was working away on their respective BlackBerries. These, she assumed, were the helicopter owners.

The eulogy had begun.

"The Lord Bedstead was, above all, a much-loved man…"

Alexa wondered if any old flames were actually present. She was particularly keen to see the one with the steel teeth.

"From his very earliest years, it seems, the earl was looked up to by his fellow man. He was known at school for his firm leadership of the younger boys…"

"Beat them senseless whenever he got his hands on them, you mean," grumbled a fruity voice in the pew behind.

"...and his unorthodox views during the war made him the focus of much controversy."

"Why was that?" a young girl to the side whispered loudly. "Was he against the invasion of Iraq or something?"

Her father, next to her, shook his head. "He thought we should appease Hitler."

The vicar was droning dutifully on.

"He later became well-known for the campaigning green management of his estates..."

There was a disturbance two rows in front. Alexa raised her chin to get a better view of a white-haired old lady with a hearing aid. "He was so stingy he made everyone use tea bags twice," she declared loudly. "There were notices in every bathroom telling you to use one square of loo paper only and not have more than three inches of water in your bath."

There were more hymns for the organist to stumble through before a very small boy in a waistcoat led by a superior-looking blond in a racily short purple tweed skirt mounted the lectern and began to lisp "Jabberwocky."

"The grandson," sighed Barney. "How terribly moving."

The child began. "'Twas brillig and the slithy toves..."

Some of the BlackBerrying helicopter owners looked up in astonishment. "What the bloody hell's he talking about?" Alexa heard one rasp to another.

"Probably autistic," was the answer.

An anthem came next, the very small choir taking what seemed to Alexa an unconscionably long time to get through the handful of words on the service sheet. She had never known "Alleluia" to last so long, and by the time it was finished, her bottom was numb with the cold and she had long since lost contact with her feet.

A lumpy, black-clad woman now stepped up to the lectern.

"The daughter," Barney whispered to Alexa.

"*Remember me when I am gone away…*"

"Husband's a gambler," Barney added with relish, "so she really needed the dosh, but he's left everything in trust for the grandchildren. She hasn't got a brass farthing."

"*Better by far you should forget and smile…*" the daughter concluded through obviously gritted teeth.

"*Than that you should remember and be sad.*"

She shut her book with a grimace and stomped down the lectern steps with a face like thunder.

As the service neared its end, Alexa felt nervous. Once outside there would be only the briefest window to make her move and get her man before everyone started climbing back in their Bentleys. If Alexa failed to get inside a Bentley herself, it would be back on the bus.

"Take your marks…" Barney muttered, as the service ended with "In the Mood" by the Glenn Miller orchestra from a CD player at the back of the church operated by one of the sidesmen. In a matter of seconds, Alexa, clinging to her companion, was down the aisle and outside amongst the gravestones.

"Now listen." Barney was casting an expert view over the stream of alpha males issuing from the church porch. "Wharte-Hogge's your man," he whispered, as a Humpty Dumpty-like figure came wobbling out and stood blinking for a moment or two in the sunlight. "Not gorgeous," he hissed, "but he's just come into thirty thousand acres and a Vermeer."

Alexa needed no second urging. Apparently overcome by emotion, she swooped on Lord Wharte-Hogge quicker than a seagull on a child's ice cream. Weeping prettily, she asked to borrow his handkerchief. The rest—the sudden, further attack of grief; his assumption that she was a close member of the deceased's family; her asking him to give her a lift home to London—had all been well rehearsed.

By the time "In the Mood" drew to a close, Alexa was shutting the door of the Wharte-Hogge Bentley and purring away.

Chapter Twenty-Eight

THINGS HAD CHANGED OVERNIGHT on the dig. The discovery of a skeleton had transformed everything. The small, shallow trench on which previously only Polly and the children had worked was suddenly buzzing with new people. A university archaeology department took charge. Funding was found. There was a site director. Experts converged from all directions, as did speculation. Was it a murder? The outer edge of a Roman graveyard? A small, previously unsuspected settlement?

Or just a skeleton somewhat inexplicably located by an ancient lavatory block? Various and disparate though the new individuals on site were, it seemed to Polly that they were united in their determination that whatever it was, it should be more than that.

The Duke of Shropshire was keeping in close touch with developments. His hopes of a world-class site on his land were, Polly gathered, once again rampant, quite compensating for the fact that half his lawn was being dug up.

More people turned up every day. They seemed to Polly to fit more or less every category of archaeologist she had ever known or worked with. Paunchy and bearded (Neil, the site director), red and scrubbed (Rosamund, his deputy), fastidious and bespectacled (Sven from Sweden who spent all his time working), crusty (Marcus and Sam, students with an MP3 player and speakers in a plastic bag). And inevitably, site bunnies (Rose and Amber, who spent most of their time standing on the sidelines shaking their hair at Sam and Marcus and successfully avoiding heavy work).

Polly missed Kyle, Poppy, and their friends. She had pleaded with Neil for them to stay, but the extra personnel on site, as well as new machinery, meant an increased and unacceptable level of potential danger for small people who didn't always stay in the places they'd been told to.

"Sharp tools, heavily laden wheelbarrows, you get the picture. It's fairly risky insurance-wise," Neil said, shaking his head.

Kyle in particular had taken the news badly. "It's not fair. I found the skull in the first place," he protested, stretching the truth unashamedly and making wild claims for himself. He was, Polly could see, going to make an excellent archaeologist one day.

"Better to have them off site really," Neil added, after Mrs. Butcher had taken her charges away for the final time. "Kids get a bit worried about bodies, you know. Think they're scary and all that."

Glancing after Kyle straining at Mrs. Butcher's leash and looking yearningly back at the skeleton—now discreetly shrouded in tarpaulin—Polly felt that Neil was somewhat wide of the mark.

One more person was expected on site: a Roman specialist from France. Polly did not dwell much on the subject. The only subject she dwelt on was Max. Would he ever come back? Would she ever see him again?

Now it had been a month. Effectively, he had disappeared. As the days, then the weeks passed without word, she became prey to horrible suspicions. First that something terrible had happened to him, preventing him getting in touch. Then that the something terrible was another woman, a girlfriend at home.

It was difficult to know which was worse.

Perhaps it was Dad, positively relishing having his worst suspicions confirmed. His belief that his daughter had fallen prey to yet another feckless charmer was something he had no compunction—and less tact—about transmitting. "You don't even have an address for him? Not even a *phone number*?" he growled disbelievingly.

When Polly was forced to admit that she hadn't, Dad merely rolled his eyes. "Oh, George, for goodness' sake," her mother would expostulate. "That's *enough*."

"It's all right, Mum," Polly muttered, escaping to her bedroom to lick her wounds and brood over the inexplicable and infinite void that now stretched between herself and the person to whom until recently she had felt closest in the world.

Poor Mum. She kept trying to feed her up, but, thanks to a stomach permanently abuzz with nerves, the weight was falling off her. Her hair was losing its shine and her eyes, when she glanced furtively at herself in the mirror, looked sunken and heavy. She had, she knew, become jumpy and irritable. She would go to bed exhausted and then be unable to sleep. She would lie awake as animated sequences from her time with Max rolled across the back of her closed eyes. How could he have gone and left nothing behind, as if he had never existed?

At work, Polly did her best to pretend that everything was normal. She confided in nobody; her hope was that they would assume she was naturally subdued and leave her alone. She kept her distance; she was, for instance, the only one apart from Sven who stayed in every evening. The rest went home, changed out of their mud-spattered working clothes, and reconvened in the Shropshire Arms, where the vast amounts of alcohol they drank left impressively few ill effects the next day.

"Come to the pub?" Sam urged now as they packed up the dig for the evening.

Polly looked up from stretching tarpaulin over a newly dug section of trench. She smiled. "No thanks."

"Come on, Poll," Marcus chipped in. "You look like you could do with some fun."

What bloody business was it of his? But Polly suppressed her flash of annoyance. Marcus was only being kind. As well as curious, which he could hardly be blamed for. Her colleagues were bound to be wondering why she was drifting disconsolately around the site like the Lady of Shalott in a hard hat and wellies. Digs were sociable places—hysterically so at times. She was, Polly knew, sticking out like a sore thumb—one of the few protrusions on excavations that archaeologists had no time for.

Rosamund had offered her a chocolate digestive at morning break, saying that she jolly well needed feeding up; the day before, Neil had asked her, point blank, whether anything was wrong. His interest, Polly suspected, was more of a professional one. She was, after all, occupying a place on a dig that someone more committed could fill. He had been tactful, but Polly was left in no doubt that if she didn't buck her ideas up, her place was in jeopardy.

Chapter Twenty-Nine

It was, as always, like being attacked by a walrus. While the English upper classes were not known for their bedroom skills, this was worse even than usual. Alexa timed her moans to coincide with Lord Wharte-Hogge's sporadic jerks and grunts. He had been at it for hours already, but nothing had happened.

Wharte-Hogge was thrusting faster now and squealing. Come on, boy, Alexa thought. Almost there.

"Nanny!" he yelled suddenly, right in her ear. "Nanny!"

She winced, ears ringing, as he rolled off, his sweaty flesh peeling away from her own like a plaster. From the wall some fifteen feet above her head projected a mahogany half-tester to which the Wharte-Hogge coat of arms—three porkers rampant—was somewhat uncertainly fixed. Alexa had been worried about it falling down and decapitating her during some of the more energetic bouncing, but thankfully it had held fast.

A mobile beep, the sharp sound of a message being received, interrupted the drowsy afternoon air. Alexa had switched hers off; Wharte-Hogg rummaged in the suit on the floor for his phone.

Alexa watched him call up the message. It seemed to have an electric effect. His pink face went white and, suddenly in a hurry, he yanked up his Union Jack boxer shorts. He shot her a terrified glance as he wiped his sweating forehead with a handkerchief produced from his pinstriped pocket. The handkerchief was of fine linen and sported a ducal coronet.

Alexa propped herself up on one elbow. "What's the matter?" Perhaps an ex-girlfriend? She would take care of all that, she thought triumphantly. Now she had a foot in the door.

Wharte-Hogge edged backward over the carpet and around the other side of the bed, as if to put its rumpled bulk between himself and her. He caught his foot in her bra, on the floor, and clutched at the half-tester's red brocade curtains for support. Under the onslaught of so much weight, the Wharte-Hogge coat of arms wobbled dangerously.

"You're Heirfix, aren't you?" he said, looking at her wildly.

"Airfix?" Bits of plastic that little boys stuck together? Or was this some reference to cosmetic surgery?

"*Heir*fix. That's what everyone's calling you. Because you find a title and you stick to it like glue. I've been warned," he added, rather hysterically, clutching the curtains as if for protection.

"Warned? Who by?" Alexa demanded.

As if she didn't know.

"Annabel Trevorigus-Whyske-Cleethorpe. We've all been told to steer well clear of you."

"Who's we?" Alexa had started to get dressed; there was obviously nothing to be gained from remaining naked.

"All us unattached titled chaps. She told us that you were operating mainly at weddings, but I've just got a text from her saying that you'd extended your activities to funerals."

He was fumbling at his wrist. With her eagle eyesight, Alexa spotted the Wharte-Hogge family crest on the cufflinks and felt a sickening pang of loss. This, combined with the insult, sent her into a sudden, mighty spasm of rage.

"And you should be bloody grateful," she snarled. "Do you think I screwed you for your good looks and fascinating personality?"

She slammed out of the bedroom. The loud thump and yell

that followed brought her some mild satisfaction as she stamped down the wide eighteenth-century staircase. The coat of arms had evidently finally detached itself and fallen on Lord Wharte-Hogge's head. Alexa hoped it had knocked it off altogether. Heirfix! The bloody cheek. She'd show them. She'd bloody well show them.

Chapter Thirty

"Come on, Poll." Marcus had squatted down beside her and was grinning into her face. The scent of marijuana drifted from his dreadlocks. "What is it? You can tell your Uncle Marcus. You know what they say about a trouble shared being a trouble doubled… Hang on, I've got that wrong, haven't I?"

Polly forced a smile. Sam and Marcus were always trying to flirt with her and did not seem in the least to mind being given the cold shoulder. On the contrary, they appeared to enjoy it.

"Well, it can't be a broken heart," Sam opined as he laid plastic over his hole. "She's too pretty. What guy in his right mind would mess *her* about?" He gave Polly a longing look.

"You know," Marcus said teasingly, "I once dug up an ice maiden. Inuit princess, three thousand years old. Canadian Arctic, that was."

Polly did not dignify this with an answer.

"I'd leave her alone if I were you," Sam counseled his friend as he shook out a noisy length of thick plastic sheeting. "You're dabbling in the stuff of other people's souls."

"Do it all the time, mate." Marcus, standing up, squinted as he lit a roll-up behind a dirty cupped hand. "Check out the guy over there." He waved a tattooed arm at Polly's skeleton. "Not much privacy for him, for all we're preserving the dignity of his remains by not having him on general display."

He shook the match and made as if to throw it on the ground. "Oops," he said, pulling a face and placing it carefully in the pocket of his filthy combat trousers. "Don't want that ending up in the British Museum, do we? Remember that fag packet on Shetland, Samster?"

Sam, laying the plastic sheeting over his most recent area of digging, looked up and grinned. He had splendid straight white teeth. "You should have been there, Poll. Greatest archaeological mystery of modern times."

"What happened?" Polly slipped her lunchbox into her rucksack. It was, as usual, only half empty.

Sam straightened up, unfolding to his full six foot four. "OK, so we were on Shetland, right. And we found a fag packet. So why was it a mystery?"

Sam's eyes were laughing, but Polly knew she was being tested. Were Sam and Marcus, like Neil, beginning to wonder about her credentials?

She folded her arms defiantly. Part of her, the part that had, since Max's departure, almost lost interest in archaeology altogether, didn't care about the cigarette packet at all. But there yet remained a part that did. She forced herself to think. "It must," she said slowly, "be something to do with where you found it."

"You're getting warm," Marcus said.

Polly returned her gaze to Sam. "You...found it in an unexpected place?"

"Warmer," Sam told her.

"Unexpected? Just a bit," Marcus said, puffing on his roll-up. "We found it under an Epipalaeolithic cairn. That's—"

"Eleven to thirteen thousand years old. I know," Polly grinned, feeling as if something within her that had been frozen was starting to move again. Then she frowned. "But...it was *under* the cairn? That's impossible. They didn't have cigarettes thirteen thousand years ago."

"You reckon?" Sam was chuckling. "The site director asked me if they were still smokable. I said, yeah, they're a bit dry, but they sure knew how to make 'em; these are better than mine."

Polly was still thinking. "So how did they get there?"

"That's the big question, sister." Sam and Marcus were watching her with bright eyes.

Polly unfolded her arms and started to pace up and down slowly. "Someone must have dropped them on the site. They must have got in…down some sort of hole?" She looked hopefully at her inquisitors.

"Yeah!" Marcus punched the air with a taut, tattooed bicep. "That was it exactly. You should have been with us, Poll; it took us a day to work it out. A bloody rabbit had dug a burrow under the cairn. At some stage, it collapsed, and the packet got down there when the soil surrounding the burrow slumped in."

For a few seconds they all just looked at each other in delight. "Bloody amazing, isn't it?" Sam said rather gruffly. "This business we're all in."

"So, you coming to the pub, then?" Marcus put in swiftly. "The new bloke from France is meeting up with us there," he added persuasively. "You'll like him. He's *very* good-looking."

Polly gave him a disdainful stare. "What makes you think I'm interested in good-looking men?"

Sam whistled. "Aren't you? Does that mean there's hope for us?"

"No, it means that I've given up on men full stop."

"Aw, come on," Marcus urged. "I'm sure there's something I could do to change your mind."

"You're incorrigible," Polly said, laughing. But it was hard not to be touched by such friendliness, especially if the alternative was a night at home with Mum worrying about her weight and Dad saying "I told you so." "OK then, I'll come for a drink," she said, trying not to sound as reluctant as she felt.

"The ice maiden thaws!" Marcus grinned at Sam.

❖ ❖ ❖

That night, walking to the Shropshire Arms, Polly was nervous. Intense sociability of the sort that lay ahead was exactly the sort she was most out of practice with. She felt awkward and self-conscious. She could see, through the open door as she approached, Rosamund clutching a pint and furiously arguing a point with Neil; Marcus and Sam, meanwhile, were vigorously chatting up Amber and Rose.

She squeezed her way through the crowds. Standing with Marcus, Sam, and the girls, she saw, was a broad-shouldered blond man in a navy hoody and jeans. He had his back turned. Oxford University Archaeological Society declared his back in white letters.

Polly's insides twisted. It couldn't be.

"Polly!" Marcus and Sam had spotted her. "Over here! Come and meet the new recruit. Polly, meet Jake. Jake, this is Polly. She's given up on men for good."

He turned; she felt the full, familiar blaze of his arrogant eyes. Amber and Rose were staring at him, clearly mesmerized.

"Given up on men?" Jake drawled. He tossed back his sun-bleached locks. "And why might that be?" He grinned.

Chapter Thirty-One

"I'VE GOT ANOTHER IDEA," Barney said genially, looking up from his armchair and *Daily Telegraph*.

"Another?" Alexa was suspicious. The last one had hardly been a startling success.

"I'm taking you to an auction." Barney beamed.

"You're going to sell me to the highest bidder? One social astronaut, slightly foxed—"

"Not at all, not at all," Barney interrupted pleasantly. "It's merely a question of a change of focus," he assured her. "I've just been reading"—he rattled the newspaper for effect—"about this perfectly enormous sale that's taking place up north somewhere. The Earl of Highcastle is selling off things from his attics and it's bound to attract people from all over."

"Antique dealers, you mean?" Was he mad? Alexa thought. She might be desperate, but not so desperate as to want to settle down with a sexagenarian with mustard moleskins, polished brown brogues, and an obsession with Georgian barometers.

"Antique dealers, yes, but not just that," Barney said, his good humor not flickering for an instant. "All kinds of what I could describe as the minor gentry will be there too. Lots of lovely boys work for the great auction houses, as you know."

Alexa did know. During one country house weekend in her halcyon days, she had found herself at dinner next to a beady baronet auctioneer. He had been able to tell her, sotto voce, the value of every item in the room in which they were sitting. Including the people.

"And others will be there out of curiosity, or perhaps to pick up a dining table to replace their rotten Chippendale." Barney twirled a monogrammed-slippered foot. "You might not, at this particular point, be looking at marrying one of the country's more senior titles, my dear Alexa. But you can always begin as many others have, with a small country manor, and trade up."

And so here they were, on the Highcastle estate, awaiting Alexa's opportunity to acquire a small country manor. For the time being, however, they were in a tent.

"Camping!" Alexa had squealed when Barney had first suggested it.

He had explained in his mild yet forceful manner that as they were both absolutely poverty-stricken, as neither of their banks would, in the age of new austerity, lend them any more money, and as the train fares would cost more than they had anyway, staying in a hotel or even a pub was out of the question. The Highcastle estate had a campsite, which would obviously be very handy for the auction. And since the rasta upstairs, with whom Barney was on unexpectedly friendly terms, had agreed to lend them his festival tent, the subject, so far as Barney was concerned, was closed.

"They really are marvelous, these modern tents," he remarked cheerfully as he banged in metal pegs and the water ran off the peak of his cap into his eyes. The tent in question was an arc-shaped two-man affair spray-painted all over with outsize cannabis leaves. Its lurid red, yellow, and black stood out startlingly from the site's green surroundings and had drawn censorious glances from the other campers, all of whom had accommodations in subdued forest colors.

Alexa scowled and folded her arms ever tighter over her best tweed jacket. Purchased in a sale that spring, in the expectation of a winter of shooting parties with Florrie that would never now materialize, it was, Barney judged, nonetheless capable of bagging some reasonably sized game at the auction. "Everyone at these things dresses like one of the Mitford girls," he explained. "Men included."

They spent an uncomfortable night, the water seeping into the tent from below. "Richmond never gave me a groundsheet," Barney complained.

Alexa snorted. "Probably gets so stoned at whatever festivals he goes to, he doesn't even notice the weather."

The inside of the tent, certainly, smelt overpoweringly of weed. Alexa hoped it would not cling to her clothes; the tweed jacket and the miniskirt that matched it were hanging from a loop above her head in the faint hope that they would dry in time. But her suede boots, which she had stuffed with Barney's *Daily Telegraph* and placed just inside the zippered door, were ruined and she had serious worries about her hair.

There was a loo block, but Alexa had not even approached it. To do so would have been to bring home all too starkly the depths to which she had sunk. She would remove her makeup with what remained of her Dr. Hauschka from the good old days and pee behind a tree if necessary. One enduring relic of her time in high society was a disciplined bladder—going to the loo all the time being frowned upon in the best circles.

Happily the auction, which was taking place in a huge white marquee, was supplied with the sort of smart Portaloos that had basins. Alexa planned to commandeer one of them first thing in the morning and stay in for as long as it took to attain the period-sitcom look Barney recommended.

As Barney snored away, Alexa lay awake, looking out of the net-covered window aperture at the great spread of Orion wheeling across the sky. Remembering vaguely that he was the Hunter, she hoped he would grant her a happy hunting day tomorrow.

After the torrential rain of the night before, the day of the auction dawned bright and fresh. The route from the campsite passed Highcastle Hall, an enchanting medieval sprawl of golden stone, turrets and towers, and higgledy-piggledy mullioned windows. Alexa sighed. She had known the son and heir, Percy Highcastle, in better days and remembered with a pang how his party piece had been to swallow-dive onto a table of glasses of Krug.

She felt better, however, as Barney pointed out the row of helicopters parked beside the series of larger, white marquees.

"Serious money." He winked at her. "We may be in luck yet." There was a line inside the marquee to register. "We need a paddle before we can bid," Barney explained. "Then we look round at the stuff and come back this afternoon when the auction kicks off."

Behind the registration desk, a row of auction-house girls presided, clear-varnished nails and understated rings poised over their computer keys. Alexa's eye swept over them worriedly; all dewy eyes, aristocratic high color, and racehorse limbs, they represented serious competition. "All thick as two short planks," Barney whispered at her side. "They entirely lack your killer instinct."

But where has my killer instinct got me exactly? Alexa wondered, as the line moved up and the red-faced wreck in the battered tweed suit in front of them planted a pair of huge purple hands on the registration table. "I'm up shit creek anyway," he barked to the astonished assistant. "You may as well give me a paddle." A wave of fellow feeling broke over Alexa.

"Never say die," Barney added, nudging her. "Or should that be dye?" he added as a pair of superannuated coxcombs in tight jeans and tweed jackets stalked by, hair emphatically dark and lustrous, wattled necks safely hidden by cravats stuffed into their checked shirts.

Alexa's heart was sinking. Almost everyone she could see was a brick-faced old soak or a fearsome old trout in a gilet with Chanel sunglasses rammed into her dyed platinum hair.

Where were the minor lords Barney had promised?

In possession of a paddle, a large piece of card bearing a printed number, Barney and Alexa wandered into the viewing room. This was an enormous marquee whose plastic windows looked out over a grassy area providing a display site for various experienced-looking statues and a couple of collapsed vintage cars.

Alexa stopped to admire a dining table huge enough to fill the entire street outside Barney's house. Beside it was a bucket of Victorian truncheons bearing a royal monogram but also some serious woodworm. The asking price was several hundred. Alexa wondered what possible use they could be to anyone not remaking the *Keystone Kops*.

"Let's put in a bid for that," Barney hissed as a beautiful blond young man in a velvet-collared coat paused to examine a battered Georgian hatbox.

"Oh no, the hammer's already come down," he murmured a moment later as a hard-faced brunette in long boots and a short knitted dress planted a proprietorial kiss on the man's cheek.

Barney steered Alexa toward some enormous William and Mary doorframes. "Stay here. Anyone seriously interested in these either has a house that can fit them in or knows someone who does," he told her. "I'm just nipping out for a fag, by the way."

Alexa turned in surprise. "But you don't smoke!"

Barney rolled his protuberant blue eyes in the direction of a tall and chinless youth who had paused by the outside doors and was looking back in their direction. "Why should it just be you who scores?" he admonished Alexa before mincing off with a wave.

Two antiques dealers in brogues and red corduroy trousers

strolled by, flicking through their thick auction catalogue. "Couple of Georgian crappers coming up later," one said to the other.

"I hear the bottom's fallen out of the night commode market, though," answered the other.

Alexa now noticed a handsome man in jeans and tweed jacket with a sensuous face and center-parted dark hair that curled over his collar. He was examining the truncheons and there was something about the way he was caressing the tip of them that excited her interest. She sidled over. "Going to put in a bid?"

He looked her up and down; his eyes—sharp, gray, and with a sprinkling of gold at the center—looked laughingly into hers.

"Might do." He grinned. "How much are you asking?"

Alexa felt a thrill of pleasure. It was a long time since she had been chatted up simply for fun. Social climbing was bloody hard work, and the foothills, where she was currently stuck, were the hardest work of all.

"You couldn't afford me," she said roguishly, turning, wiggling her bottom and sashaying away.

"I always appreciate a good stuffing, don't you?" he muttered, hot on her heels as she passed the taxidermy.

She was thrilled to find herself pursued into the restaurant marquee. "I'm Ralph," he said, plonking himself thrillingly close to her. "Ralph de Vere Coningsby. Care for a glass of champagne?"

Champagne! She hadn't had it for weeks and now positively craved the taste of bubbles popping on her tongue, the thrilling rush as the alcohol hit her empty stomach.

She had never heard of Ralph de Vere Coningsby, but that was no cause for alarm. He was doubtless a member of Barney's minor aristocracy with medium-sized country estate.

And he had other assets. He was lounging in a chair, legs wide apart, in a manner designed to reveal what looked like a very well-stuffed crotch. Alexa swallowed. With his wolfish handsome-ness, broad shoulders, and slim hips, he was one hundred percent testosterone, pure sex. And it had been a long time since she had had anything decent in that department. She ran her tongue around her lips.

Ralph grinned naughtily at her and rose to his feet. "Don't go away now, beautiful," he growled, loping over to the bar.

You bet, Alexa thought. Wild horses wouldn't make her, unless they were on Ralph's estate, of course. Was it in the New Forest? she wondered. She was about to burst with lust and excitement quite without the aid of alcohol.

Ralph came back, shrugging. "No champagne, can you believe it?"

"Oh *no*." On the other hand, Alexa thought, perhaps it was no bad thing.

"But I've got some Bolly in the Defender," Ralph added. "Auction's not going to start for hours. Why not come and have a drink?"

Why not? Alexa thought. Barney, after all, was having his own fun. And her target had been achieved anyway; within a short time of arriving, she had been approached by Ralph de Vere Coningsby, provincial lord of the manor. He might be a small fish in a large pool, but he was big enough where it mattered. She hurried out of the marquee after him and tried to avoid the puddles as they crossed the grass to where the cars were parked.

Ralph's Land Rover was big and green and very dirty inside. "Sorry about the mess," he apologized, spreading an even dirtier piece of oilcloth across the filthy space inside the open back door. "Come in and sit down while I open the booze."

Sitting, legs swinging out of the back of the Land Rover, Alexa imagined herself living the life of a country gentlewoman. Did Ralph hunt? She imagined herself in a tight red jacket, fully made up, hair bound in a net, magically transformed from indifferent to skilled rider, wheeling an elegant stallion on the lawn at the Boxing Day meet.

There was a grunt and the familiar, reassuring pop of a cork from the front. As he sloshed the foam into a plastic cup and handed it to her, Ralph's eyes crinkled with sensual promise.

By the end of the second plastic cupful, his tongue was exploring her mouth and his hand was up her skirt.

He looked at her, his gray eyes gleaming with a blend of wonder and amusement. "Jesus, baby. How long's it been?"

"Oh God! Now!" she panted, feeling her pelvis was about to explode.

His penis, as it sprang from his fly, was more than a rival for the truncheons, and completely free of woodworm.

Sex in the open air had an edge she had never suspected. It felt primeval, urgent, naughty, and the breeze on her most sensitive regions only added to the thrill. Her cries of fulfillment were masked by some timely bellowing from a group of nearby cows—just as well, given that an elderly couple in metal-framed deckchairs were enjoying tea from a flask just a couple of cars away.

That it was over in minutes was the only disappointment.

"Is that it?" she said, as he swung open the back door, which had been closed during their lovemaking. If one could give it such a leisurely name; it had been more like the frenzied coupling of two animals on heat.

Ralph, bundling his manhood back into his jeans, looked at her affrontedly. "You seemed happy enough at the time."

Something now fell out of his pocket and clanked on the vehicle's metal floor. He picked it up hastily, but not before she saw it was a ring. A wedding ring by the look of it.

Alexa stared at him. "You're married!"

"That's right." Ralph buckled his belt casually.

"But…" Alexa was speechless. Her effort has been entirely wasted. She had been deceived.

"And now if you'll excuse me, I've got to get going," Ralph said briskly.

"Get going?" Alexa gasped indignantly. "Get going where?"

"School run." Ralph glanced matter-of-factly at his watch. "It's my turn to pick the kids up today."

Chapter Thirty-Two

MANY TIMES HE HAD been on the verge of writing, but just as often he had put down the pen.

Perhaps, Max was starting to think now, it was better to let Polly assume that he had simply left her. As he had no idea when he could return to her, especially given that his passport, as well as his mobile, had now mysteriously disappeared, the noble thing to do was to let her go. Let her think the worst. The less she thought of him, the easier it would be for her. If she could bring herself to hate him, it would be easiest of all.

The only positive aspect of the situation was that no new prospective bride had yet been produced. Max's hopes were rising that no one suitable existed, but he also knew that, given his father's determination, it was probably only a matter of time.

With thoughts as gloomy as this in his mind, Max had been pleased, on a rare mooch around Sedona, to encounter the small, neat form of Etienne de Crecy, the local vet, with whom he had done work experience before university. He had been quick to offer his services again; a few hours now and again in Etienne's surgery would be a lifeline. The Sedona vet's stock in trade had never been the large farm animals Max especially loved, but the many small, nervous pedigree dogs that comprised most of the animal population of Sedona, and their even more nervous pedigree owners. But that was better than nothing. Max was glad to accompany Etienne to the surgery.

A rude shock awaited him, however. Dog indulgence had gone off the scale in the relatively short period of time he had been away; Etienne had turned it into an industry. Never slow at spotting a potential income stream, he had gone into partnership with a self-styled canine beautician. The result was that a spa for dogs was now part of the surgery. The facilities of "Canine Chic" included a gym where underexercised pooches worked out on a treadmill, guided by a personal trainer. "It's crazy," Max muttered, as his friend showed him around the premises, all sparkling pink and white, festooned with fairy lights.

Etienne, lightly tanned with neat brown hair, flashed Max a glance through his polished hi-tech spectacles. "*Au contraire*, my friend. It's the future. In Sedona, at any rate."

A giant white poodle was having his fur teased in the treatment rooms. Full body grooming, reiki healing, and a thalassotherapy mud bath were also available. "Dogs shouldn't need to come to a spa for a mud bath," Max muttered, thinking of the way Napoleon rolled in dirt at any opportunity, and Beano too, in his younger days.

Etienne showed Max the spa shop, complete with chewy Vuitton handbag-shaped cushions, gold lamé Roberto Cavalli coats, pet-friendly nail varnish, and designer Perspex dog beds.

"And this is beauty therapy," he announced, leading Max on through a corridor where wooden saloon-style doors painted a pastel pink led into small treatment rooms with mirrors on the walls. "We do olive oil baths for tortoises, hydrating strawberry and vanilla facials for hamsters, milk thistle paw soaks for guinea pigs, and one-to-one consultations for kittens."

"Consultations?" exclaimed Max. "*Kittens?*"

Etienne inclined his head. "Some kittens have issues with their owners, my friend."

Max, looking around, felt he had issues with all of it. Where did people with *real* animals go? He thought longingly of the magnificent beasts the British farmers bred, the shorthorns, the Jerseys, the Galloways with their distinctive wide belts, the shaggy, long-horned Highland cattle. "What happens with the farm livestock?"

Etienne shrugged his elegant designer-suited shoulders. "There are other vets. We rarely get called out for those anymore." He pulled a face. "Thank goodness."

Max left before Etienne could explain about the pet patisserie he was thinking of opening next: centerpiece iced pupcakes. He walked back to the chateau with bowed head.

Stalking through the lofty entrance hall with its painted ceiling and ancestral portraits the size of doors, he encountered Giacomo. "News!" exclaimed the younger prince.

"What news?" Max asked resignedly. It was, after all, unlikely to be the news he wanted, that his passport and mobile were being returned to him and he was being sent back to England with his parents' blessing.

"Gorgeous bird, mate." Giacomo loped over the black and white marble floor and give him a high five.

"What bird?" the Crown Prince asked sharply.

"This Swedish countess the parentals have got lined up for you. Great tits," Giacomo said enthusiastically.

Max rubbed his eyes. So they had found someone else after all. He would have to go through the whole ghastly process again.

Max didn't care about the countess's tits, or even how Giacomo knew about them. It was a fact that Giacomo knew about great tits from one end of Europe to the other. "Anything else interesting about her?" he asked ironically.

Giacomo grinned lasciviously. "Buns of steel."

Max put both hands to his forehead and groaned. Did he want great tits and buns of steel?

Chapter Thirty-Three

NOT WANTING TO FACE the dewy-eyed girls on the front desk, Alexa returned to the auction via the back entrance. As she staggered past, obviously rumpled, the boys on Collections, a raffish lot in dark blue polo shirts embroidered with the auction house logo, turned from maneuvering a vast and ugly carved fireplace to give her an appreciative stare.

The enormous main marquee was fuller than before. Rows and rows of bidders and observers were arranged theater-audience style, divided by an aisle in front of the elegant cream-painted rostrum on which stood the auctioneer. Large flat-screen televisions by the rostrum and at the back of the tent illustrated the lot currently up for sale. At the moment it was a piece of furniture, and the auctioneer had just made a crack about Her Grace's drawers.

A small red-faced figure glided up to her.

"Where the hell," Barney hissed, "have you been?"

"Hello, pot, meet kettle," Alexa retaliated, but without conviction. "You were heading straight for the men's loos when I last saw you."

Barney waved a dismissive hand. "False alarm. He wanted to *talk*, would you believe? So I spent most of the time lining up candidates for you."

"One stuffed mongoose," called the auctioneer, a pleasant patrician type with a gray mullet.

"I had Sir Everard Bream good to go," Barney told her crossly. "Chatted him up for ages, not the easiest of things as he has the most God-awful stammer. He's not married, and he's desperate for a little woman to bring his manor up to date and maybe help convert some old stable block into a boutique hotel. He had your name all over him. All over him!"

Barney drove a frustrated red fist into a matching red palm. "But now he's gone home with a collection of slightly chipped Victorian milking pails."

"One hundred and fifty pounds I'm bid for this stuffed mongoose. Thank you, sir, over there. Gentleman on the aisle. One hundred and seventy pounds, the bid's in the room. Oh, an online bid, one hundred and eighty. Any advance on one hundred and eighty for this magnificent stuffed mongoose?"

Alexa hung her head, feeling not unlike a stuffed mongoose herself. She raised miserable eyes to Barney.

"I saw you talking to Ralph de Vere Coningsby," Barney said accusingly. "He's a notorious shagger. Comes to places like this just to pick up women. I hope you…?"

As Alexa's tragic gaze met his in affirmation, Barney slapped his pink forehead so hard his eyes watered. "God, no. Tell me you didn't."

"I didn't realize. I thought he was available."

"Stuffed mongoose going for one hundred and eighty, then. All done at one hundred and eighty." As the mallet clacked down, Alexa felt she was all done too.

"Come on, Barney," she begged. "Can't we find someone else? I'm here now."

"Yes, and look at you," he fulminated, his voice acid with anger and his blue eyes emitting electric sparks of fury. "Covered in mud and your hair all over the place. Where did he shag you, the back of his filthy Land Rover?"

"As a matter of fact, yes."

"I can't believe it. That old trick!"

There was nothing like sustained attack to revive Alexa's fighting spirit. "Well, if he's so notorious, why didn't you warn me? I'd never heard of him."

Barney's lips were drawn back over his teeth. "I didn't warn you," he growled, "because I never in a million years dreamt I would need to. I thought it would be obvious what he was up to. I can't imagine what you were thinking of."

Alexa looked at him guiltily, knowing it would be pointless to say that even the most dedicated gold-digger occasionally had needs that could not be ignored. That woman could not live by social ambition alone. It sounded ridiculous even to her. He was right; what had she been thinking? Well, she had better put it behind her now.

"Oh, lay off, Barney," she tried to josh him. "If I look a bit scuffed, that's all to the good, surely. People are paying a fortune for it all around us."

A stuffed female deer was up under the hammer now. "Great deal of interest in this," the auctioneer reported excitedly. "Two online bidders...ooh, we're seeing some serious mouse-on-mouse violence here."

The audience tittered.

"Surely there's someone else I can go for," Alexa wheedled, as Barney continued to glare at her.

"No, there bloody isn't. Bream was our only chance. I can't believe you took your eye off the ball like that."

Hardly the *mot juste*, Alexa thought, remembering with a mixture of fury, regret, and wonder what had sprung out of Ralph's trousers.

"Come here, where I can keep an eye on you." Barney grasped her arm hard and led her to a seat beneath the rostrum just as the hammer came down on the deer. "Two thousand pounds, all done at two thousand pounds. A lot of doe, that," the auctioneer quipped, to groans from the audience.

At a right angle from the end of the aisle where they sat stretched the platform on which the row of people from the auction house was handling the telephone bids. Alexa's eyes ran avidly over them. Who was on the other end of their phones? Sheikhs? Oligarchs? Old money?

She suppressed the urge to pull a phone from one of their hands and yell "Marry me!" into the receiver.

"All done at two thousand pounds for the stuffed pike," beamed the patrician auctioneer, banging down his mallet to conclude the sale of a large and mournful-looking fish. "The price has gone off the scale!"

Chapter Thirty-Four

She had tried to avoid him, but Jake made it impossible. He had been assigned his own area of the site by Neil but was constantly coming over to hers.

"Go back to your own pit," Polly told him, her teeth gritted.

"But I like yours," Jake replied easily, grinning up at her from where he squatted at the edge of her trench, his eyes narrowed in the sun.

Polly pressed her lips tightly together. She had no intention of getting into conversation. After that first night in the pub, where surprise and manners forced the exchanging of a few words, she had tried not to speak to him at all. The site was big enough for the both of them, so long as Jake kept to his side. Which, so far, he wasn't.

"It wasn't quite working out in France," was Jake's breezy explanation of his sudden appearance in their midst. "Too many cooks and all that. They'd slightly over-ordered on the expertise."

"What about Miranda?" Polly had said coldly.

"Still there, I believe," Jake said airily, poking idly at an uncharted corner of Polly's trench. "Shagging the balls off someone, most probably," he added casually.

Polly did not reply. That Miranda and Jake had split was not necessarily a surprise. What was, was that he seemed to expect them to pick up where they had left off. "Come on, Poll. I made a mistake with Miranda, OK? It was just a fling, a moment of madness," he pleaded.

Polly continued working in her notebook, saying nothing.

"The main reason I left the French dig was because I heard you were on this one," Jake added hopefully.

Bloody liar, Polly thought. She knew this to be the case because Marcus, who along with Sam resented the way Jake had breezed in and grabbed all Rose and Amber's attention, had been making inquiries on the archaeology bush telegraph.

"Well, of course I have," he defended himself to Polly. "I'm an archaeologist. I delve."

Marcus's delvings revealed the real reason for Jake's exodus from France. "Bit of a tomcat, basically," Polly learned. "I mean, obviously fieldwork means bed-hopping," he added, giving Polly a meaningful look. "But Jake was hopping like a frog with a bomb up its arse. Bad for morale, in the end, because some beds are just not hoppable. Like the site director's wife, say."

"No!"

"Yes. And the wife of the director of the local museum."

"He was sleeping with *her*?"

"I'm not sure how much sleeping they were doing." Marcus gave her a cryptic grin. "But the site director didn't dig it anyway. He sacked Jake and so he got posted here. Apparently he's too brilliant to be wasted," Polly's informant added with a derisive toss of his dreadlocks.

Marcus and Ben, Polly could see, particularly resented the withering manner in which Jake treated those he considered less gifted than himself. This category included just about everyone. Polly, used to it, was less affected; besides, as she knew, Jake, academically at least, was every bit as good as he thought he was. His outward carelessness, even dilettantism, was just a show. As Sam had discovered only yesterday.

Sam, who had a poor opinion of Jake's capabilities, had made some derogatory remark. Jake, in reply, had lit a cigarette and let fly a lengthy broadside about the newest wave of post-processual theory and its implications for research. Sam had almost reeled backward and returned to his pit in silence.

While Polly felt that Jake had used a sledgehammer to crack a nut, she also, more worryingly, felt a sneaking admiration. Jake's looks had always attracted her, but in the heat of their affair, it had been his brains that had excited her the most.

Even so, there was *no* possibility that she was getting back together with him. He could come to her pit and gaze up into her eyes all he liked. It would make no difference. Max might yet come back. And even if he didn't, Jake's own past conduct was warning enough. She would remain oblivious to the charms now turned up to full wattage and trained with all their power on her.

"Come out to supper with me, Poll?" Jake wheedled now. He didn't give up easily, she had to give him that. No doubt he just wanted to override her resistance. Women never refused him normally; she was a challenge.

She could see, glancing over, the rest of the dig looking in their direction. Sam and Marcus were making thumbs-down signs.

"No thanks," Polly said to Jake, gathering her tools together. She felt sticky and hot; the thought of a long, cool shower at home was tempting. Afterward she would write up her notes. It would be dull, but safe. Being with her charismatic, treacherous former boyfriend, on the other hand, seemed increasingly dangerous.

She noticed now that, for practically the first time since he had come over to her trench, Jake's attention was on something other than her. He had been working absently on a corner as he spoke and was prodding excitedly.

"What is it?" Polly crouched down beside him; carefully, they dug the object out. It was both longer and wider than she had antici-pated; a piece of concrete, a fragment of wall?

"Decorated on the underside, with any luck," Jake said. "Then we'd have a palace on our hands."

Such a discovery would, of course, be completely typical of Jake, Polly remembered. As well as being clever, he was lucky. Whatever pit he dug always yielded the best artifacts; he seemed able to charm them to the surface, as he charmed everyone else.

They were both on their knees now, working rapidly. They looked up simultaneously; Polly, staring into handsome eyes full of excitement and suggestion, finally felt her suppressed desire for him break through. Jake saw it and grinned. "Like old times," he murmured, brushing the tip of his nose against hers.

The large piece of concrete was now almost completely out. Would it have a fresco on the hidden side? Heart thundering, Polly helped Jake clear away the last few centimeters of earth. They eased it out, she felt it give, and they lifted it into the air.

Avidly they inspected it, brushing the dust carefully off each side. "No fresco," Polly said, disappointed.

"No, but what's this?" Jake's long fingers were tracing what looked like scratches on the other side.

Polly peered. "Is it writing?"

"Looks like it. Done with a knife. Latin."

They crouched over it, heads together, puzzling it out. "*Marcus hic…*" Jake began.

"Marcus was here," Polly gasped out the translation.

"No I wasn't," came the indignant riposte from a few feet away. "I stick to my own pit, thanks. Unlike *some* people."

"I've got it!" Jake squeezed Polly's hand. "*Marcus cacavit bene.* Marcus had a good shit here."

"I bloody well did not, you bastard."

But Polly was not listening. She was laughing into Jake's excited face. "It's graffiti!" she exclaimed. "Graffiti from the loo!"

Chapter Thirty-Five

MAX TWISTED HIS NECK within his stiff collar and looked down at his white starched shirt front. Across it stretched a pale blue ribbon supporting the elaborate gold and enamel device of the Ancient Order of Swedish Fish Picklers. His father had honored him with it at breakfast; the intention was to flatter the countess from Bergen who was coming this morning.

Pinned just below the top button was the glittering pendant of the Star of Sedona, a courtesy title given to all crown princes on their twentieth birthday. What seemed to Max an entire constellation of other, smaller stars were attached elsewhere across his torso, positioned according to some mental decorations map that the elderly Lord Chamberlain, who had officiated in the robing room, seemed to carry in his head. Elsewhere were rows of gold buttons, pearl shirt studs, and a row of medals almost a foot across. Max felt like a Christmas tree in a tailcoat. He also felt ridiculous—and very bad-tempered.

The valet came running in with a large white portable telephone, the sort, Max always thought, you never saw anywhere apart from sixties films and the chateau of Sedona.

"Max, my friend. Do you have five minutes?" It was Etienne. "I need your help."

"I'm a bit busy," Max said shortly, thinking without affection of Etienne's pink and silver palace of canine pampering. No doubt one of the spa assistants was sick and Etienne needed someone to bath a tortoise or paint a guinea pig's toenails.

"Please, my friend. It is an emergency." Etienne's usually relaxed and assured tones were almost unrecognizably strained.

"What's the matter?" Max asked sardonically. "Run out of pet perfume?"

"Not quite so bad as that, my friend." Etienne, for all his faults, at least had a sense of humor. "No, I have a cow case."

"I thought you didn't do cows anymore."

There was a deep sigh from the other end. "I try not to," Etienne groaned. "But sometimes there is no getting away from them. The usual vet is ill, apparently."

"What's wrong with the cow?" Max asked, as the valet twitched at his white tie. "Milk fever? Mastitis?"

Etienne sighed. "That's just what I don't know, my friend. But I can't go—I've got a poodle with Stockhausen syndrome—although I could drop you off at the farm on my way. And pick you up," he added beseechingly.

"But I'm not qualified," Max pointed out. Inside, however, the excitement was mounting. A cow. A real big farm animal. His favorite sort. "And I've got to meet someone," he added dolefully, thinking of the forthcoming reception in the throne room.

"Max, I *need* you," Etienne pleaded. "A suffering animal needs you!"

"When?" Max heard himself saying.

"Now. I can come and get you? It'll be quick, I promise."

In her golden crown and ermine-trimmed robes of state, Queen Astrid looked utterly serene. She felt, however, the opposite. The chateau throne room, where she sat awaiting the entrance of the

Crown Prince, was, with its thick red carpet, blazing chandeliers, and great plump velvet thrones, the hottest room of the hundred-plus in the building. And especially so today, with the temperature outside in the eighties.

But still it hadn't stopped the band. Nothing ever did. Even though the throne room was at the back and faced over the gardens, she could hear them thumping and blaring away, murdering "The Skye Boat Song" in their usual sensitive fashion. It was incredible that they could function at all, given how the heat must be frying their brains inside their helmets. On the other hand, Sedona's armed forces had never been known for their brains. Nor had anyone else in the Sedona establishment, least of all the royal family. It was Max's misfortune to have been born with at least twice as many brains as usual—brains with a pronounced scientific bent, into the bargain.

Astrid's heavy crown felt heavier even than usual; perhaps the gold had expanded in the heat. The fur trim on her cloak, pressed against her by the weighty gold tassels, made her feel she was either about to melt or else spontaneously combust. Beneath the cloak, her full-length white satin dress was hot and sticky.

She looked despairingly at the four household staff who stood upright against the tapestried walls, staring stiffly into the middle distance. If only they could make themselves useful and wave some fans about. She considered suggesting it but desisted. Waving fans had never traditionally been a duty of the palace household staff, and in the Palace of Sedona, if it wasn't tradition, it didn't happen.

Red-faced and perspiring under his own crown, Engelbert wore the ceremonial uniform of the Royal Sedona Guards, of whom he was commander-in-chief. His sky-blue cutaway coat, fringed epaulettes, and white breeches were set off by a sea-green silk sash and an enameled badge shaped like antlers. This was the ancient order of Norwegian Reindeer Smokers (3rd Class), which had been presented to him many years ago on a state visit to the Scandinavian countries. The ties he had forged then had brought forth today's visitor.

The countess from Bergen sat at right angles to the King and Queen in a smaller gilded throne against the wall. The girl was pretty, Astrid thought, but bored-looking. She had been unimpressed with the chateau. "But where are the gym, the spa, the treatment rooms?" she had exclaimed. "At home we have a heated horizon pool and a Pilates studio."

Astrid shook her head slightly and fingered her own Royal Swedish order of the Golden Cod (2nd Class) anxiously. If this particular fish was to be hooked, she was relying on Max's glamour and reserved charm to do it.

And he would, his mother knew, look particularly glamorous today. Max in ceremonial uniform was a thing of beauty: tall and straight, his wide shoulders narrowing to neat hips and long legs, his dark coloring and sculpted face set off wonderfully by all the white and gold. His obvious loathing of what he wore only enhanced his glamour; his dark blue eyes narrowed resentfully under his brows. There were photographs of Astrid at state occasions with her parents, wearing exactly the same truculent look.

It was, she remembered, this very expression that had caught the attention of the handsome student with whom she had fallen in love all those years ago. He had been fascinated by her unease with her position. The Reluctant Royal, he had called her…How times had changed, mused Astrid, forcing her thoughts back to the here and now. No one watching her this morning in the throne room would suspect she had ever been anything but the most dutiful and content of consorts.

"Where *is* the blasted boy?" grumbled the King. He consulted his fob watch, bringing it right up to his eye to squint at it.

The Queen reached over and patted his hand. "He'll be here any minute," she soothed. There was an itch beneath the tiara that she longed to scratch. She longed even more to be in her garden. But it was her duty to be sweating in the throne room waiting for Max to come and meet his latest possible bride.

Astrid had, countless times over the past few weeks, longed to reach out to Max and tell him she knew how he felt. Tell him the whole story about herself, even. Caution had held her back; the information was sensitive, and Max's mood was wild and volatile. If he broadcast it, it could be disastrous.

And what was the point of telling him anyway? Irrespective of what had happened in the past, Astrid accepted she now owed her loyalty to her husband and position. This being the case, and the King remaining firm about Max's marriage, it must follow that Max must submit, as she herself had done.

It was not easy. Seeing Max's astonishment, then his hurt, and finally his anger had tested her resolve and her legendary self-possession to the limit. More than once she had left the room during a particularly tense lunch or dinner and shut herself away to weep. Or Max would come to see her in her room, where over and over again she forced herself to explain where his royal duty lay. Only for him to look at her sadly and say, "I thought you'd be on my side, Mum."

And I am, Astrid would think. I *am*. But what can I do about it?

Further down the room, Prince Giacomo slumped against the purple velvet back of his throne. He was horribly hung over.

"Sit up, Giacomo," snapped Engelbert from the throne, annoyed by his son's semi-somnolent posture. Giacomo shuffled himself upright slightly, yawned loudly, and stared through the window opposite his chair. It offered a superb view of the mountains and sea beyond. White spots were afloat in the blue, yachts from their luxury Riviera moorings further up the coast.

Giacomo whistled softly. "There's some serious hardware out there today," he remarked admiringly. "Two seventy-two-footers, at least. One with two helicopters."

More minutes dragged by, each apparently lasting an age. Astrid was beginning to despair of ever seeing her elder son when something tall and wild appeared at the door of the throne room. As it strode forward, a strong smell of manure followed.

"Who the…" Engelbert stood up in alarm. He glared at the Lord Chamberlain. "Who *is* this? Who let him in?"

"Nice you could make it, bro," drawled Giacomo, holding apart his golden curtains of hair. He was nearer and had better eyesight than his father.

The Countess, on her seat, gasped with horror.

"Max!" Astrid scrambled up and started hurrying across the carpet.

"I'm sorry, Mummy." The Crown Prince lowered his dirty dark head to hers. "I got delayed. I was helping Etienne with a cow case and—"

"Cow case?" Astrid echoed.

"I couldn't not go." His eyes searched hers, pleading for understanding. "The animal was in pain. It was just mastitis, quite simple really—"

"But your clothes!" Astrid gasped in horror. Filth caked the formerly polished gold buttons, and there were various slimes of unimaginable origin on the epaulettes. Max's shoes, previously gleaming with a mirror-like brilliance, were now covered, along with his trouser bottoms, with something brown, squishy, and evil-smelling. His hands were smeared with mud—or worse—and his fingernails were black.

"The problem is, dairy cows tend to fire from behind without warning…" Max was saying apologetically.

Engelbert was apoplectic. It was an insult to the crown, the throne, the armed services, and everything else he could think of. And most especially to himself. He ground his teeth within his jaw.

But he was the King. He must not reveal his feelings. If he affected not to notice the mess, it followed that no one else could either. He cleared his throat and turned to the guest as if nothing had happened. "Countess, may I have the, ahem, pleasure of presenting my, ahem, son…"

He looked around him. Where was she? The ice blond with the glum expression was nowhere to be seen. Engelbert glared at the Lord Chamberlain. "Well?"

The Lord Chamberlain had been a senior soldier; he did not balk in the face of bad news. "She's gone, your Majesty," he confessed, jerking his head erect and meeting the monarch's eye with his own unflinching orb. "Made rather a hasty exit. Don't think she appreciated the smell."

The King slapped his forehead in exasperation. "Damn it. *Damn* it!" He turned furiously to his son. "Six o'clock," he snapped. "In my office. I think we'd better have another talk."

Back to square one, Hippolyte thought dolefully as he scuttled back to his own office and sought protection behind the bastion of his desk. It was large and ornate, with bulging sides and gold handles, festooned with inlay and topped with gold-tooled green leather to which his fleshy arms tended to stick in hot weather like this.

He had taken his jacket off in concession to the boiling heat and it hung on the back of the antique dining chair before his desk. He stared, unseeing, at the smart Parisian label. What now? the private secretary wondered in terror. What could he do?

The small gold ormolu carriage clock on the mantelpiece had been a gift from the monarch to mark his tenth year at the Palace, and it was at this that Monsieur Hippolyte now glanced. It was only eleven in the morning. A depressingly long way from cocktail time.

On the small bar in the corner, rows of cut-crystal tumblers winked invitingly from behind a small decorative rail. Behind them were stoppered decanters of gin and whiskey. In seven hours' time, a footman bringing a small silver ice bucket would rap at the oak double doors. Then Hippolyte would take the silver tongs and the sliced lemon and pour himself a stiff one. Then another.

But Monsieur Hippolyte could not wait until then. He desperately wanted a drink now. He needed one, and if he didn't have one, he'd be down at Madame Whiplash's later, and he absolutely had to stop *that*. If he didn't, eventually it would reach the ears of the King. Perhaps it would anyway. Perhaps it *had*…

Seized by a sudden hysterical panic, Hippolyte staggered to his feet and lurched toward the bar.

❖ ❖ ❖

"There is another possibility, you know," Astrid said that night as she sat at her dressing table, brushing her pale blond hair over her shoulders.

"There is?" Engelbert groaned from the great four-poster where even two large double brandies had been unable to soothe the agitation of the day. The interview with Max had been inconclusive. Even though he had been the one doing all the talking—or shouting—Engelbert had a feeling he had not won the argument.

Astrid replaced the silver-backed hairbrush on the gilt and walnut dressing table. "I was talking to Stonker Shropshire this afternoon," she remarked neutrally.

Beneath the linen sheets, the King stiffened, as always when Stonker Shropshire was mentioned. That smooth-tongued English bastard. "What did he say?" he growled.

"You know he has a daughter, Tara?"

"Ye-es," Engelbert said carefully. Desperate though he was for his son to marry, he drew the line at any offspring of Stonker Shropshire's. The thought of the urbane British aristocrat swanking around Sedona, dominating events and attracting all available attention, was too hideous to contemplate. The King hoped Astrid was not about to suggest that the two families unite. His fear that they might have already was never far from the surface these days as his wife got ever more testy and withdrawn.

"Tara's engaged to Lord Kensington," the Queen continued, much to her husband's relief.

"Oh. Pity." The King tried to sound sincere.

"But Stonker tells me she has a very pretty friend." Astrid shook her hair and leaned forward to rub in a blob of night cream. "Well connected, single, very beautiful, and apparently perfect for our purposes."

"Titled?" demanded the King.

"Yes."

"Beautiful?"

"Very."

"Rich? She's got to be rich. No point otherwise."

"Very rich."

"Who?" demanded Engelbert excitedly.

Astrid took a deep breath. "She's English. She's young. And yes, before you ask, she's almost certainly capable of childbearing, but of course it's a bit difficult to check that sort of thing these days…"

"Name?" demanded the King, waving all this aside impatiently.

"Her name," the Queen said, "is Lady Florence Trevorigus-Whyske-Cleethorpe."

Chapter Thirty-Six

AFTER THE DISASTER OF the auction, having extracted from Alexa a promise that she would henceforth do exactly as instructed, Barney was soon busily plotting their rise upward again.

They were both in Barney's sitting room, which was shaking under the force of Richmond's bass speaker from above. Alexa was attempting for the umpteenth time to get the Highcastle mud off her suede boots.

Barney was sitting in his Brideshead dressing gown, his Montblanc pen poised over a copy of *Tatler*, which he was cross-referencing with his well-thumbed copy of *Burke's Peerage*. He looked the picture of calm contentment as he perused a piece Alexa had read yesterday, a glowing account of an aristocratic birthday party held on Cap Ferrat. The photographs of the ornate belle epoque villa with its jasmine-scented and palm-shaded gardens and enormous underlit swimming pool, and the elegant guests who had converged on it for the celebrations had sent bitterness convulsing through her.

Ed Whyske was, after all, poised to inherit just such a place; had everything gone according to plan, she herself would have been standing, as the hostess in the pictures was standing, in an expensively simple white column dress at the top of a graceful sweep of stairs.

"You're frowning," Barney chided, looking up suddenly. "Remember that your face is your fortune."

Alexa did her best to smooth out her agitated features with her fingertips. "I'm just a bit worried about what happens next," she grumbled.

Barney put down his magazine, put his fingertips together and smiled. "Obvious, I would have thought," he said.

It wasn't obvious to Alexa.

Barney raised the magazine and waved it at her. "The South of France. The Riviera."

"The *Riviera*?"

"Can't imagine why I didn't think of it before!" Barney rose to his slipper-clad feet. "We might be finished—for the moment— in London—"

"More than London," Alexa put in resentfully. "We're finished all over the bloody country. Not to mention the whole of cyberspace since you-know-who texted the whole of *Burke's Peerage* about us."

Barney smiled serenely. "All the more reason to temporarily remove ourselves. There are no end of avenues to explore in the South." He raised his plump pink fingers and began counting them off. "The yacht crowd in Saint-Tropez and Cap Ferrat, for a start. The Hotel du Cap crowd in Antibes, the Palace crowd in Monaco. So cheer up, my dear!" He caught Alexa by the hands and pulled her up. "We just get ourselves down there, and something's absolutely *bound to* come up."

"But how *do* we get ourselves down there?" Alexa demanded. "We don't have any money. We can't possibly afford to go."

Barney rubbed his chin. "I suppose there is that," he admitted. "But something will turn up."

He was, Alexa thought, like a gold-digging Mr. Micawber.

They slumped into doleful contemplation for some minutes, during which the deep bass boom of Richmond's reggae continued to shake the house. Alexa, staring glumly at her muddy boots, willed herself not to hear it. But it was difficult when your very fillings were rattling.

The letterbox in the hall crashed, heralding the arrival of the post.

Quick as a flash, Barney was on his velvet-slippered feet. It was amazing, Alexa thought as the purple silk blur shot past her, how quickly he could move when he wanted to.

He came back a man transformed. His round pink face was suffused with triumph. He commenced dancing around the room with delight, gamboling over the grubby gray carpet, silk dressing gown billowing out behind him. A terrible fear clutched at Alexa—had he been invited to something she hadn't? An event of resounding brilliance and exclusivity, at which he would be socially rehabilitated, while she remained at home in the dingy flat?

Her mind raced with hideous possibilities. Was it an invitation to dine and sleep at Highgrove? August at Balmoral? She couldn't see any large white envelope in his hand—his haul seemed to be mostly supermarket flyers. But perhaps the precious card was in his pocket.

"Has someone asked you somewhere?" she demanded, eyes blazing.

Barney stopped gamboling like a young gazelle. "Asked me somewhere? Not as such. Actually, that's not quite true." He waved the papers he was clutching. "The Cooperative Society has very generously invited me to come and avail myself of their two-for-one Lambrusco promotion and large discounts on tinned lager and frozen chips."

"So why are you looking so pleased?" Alexa felt her rigid spine relaxing against the hard back of the chair.

He pulled a white envelope from the fistful of flyers. "I've received a check this morning."

"Check!"

"Not a huge one, admittedly, but certainly enough to take us to Cannes and, if we're careful, keep us down there for a couple of months."

"Who was the check from?" Alexa was curious. They had discussed their parlous finances only yesterday; he had not mentioned any imminent payment.

"Oh, a newspaper." Barney gave a dismissive toss of the head. "A little story I was helping them with."

Something flashed in Alexa's brain. There had been, all over the front of one of yesterday's papers, a story about an MP caught in a gay fetish bar. Had Barney, who she knew occasionally went to such places, sold the secret to the highest bidder? That would certainly explain his sudden enthusiasm for getting out of London.

He was looking at her, his small blue eyes gleaming. "Come on!" he urged. "The playground of the rich awaits!"

Chapter Thirty-Seven

On Barney's instructions, Alexa went to Jermyn Street for their travel essentials. Cigars from Davidoff were, he stated, a crucial piece of kit, an air of wealth being naturally associated with the pungent air around a hand-rolled Cuban. Of Alexa's kit he made no mention; paper Davidoff bag in hand, she stood morosely in front of Floris, debating whether or not to splash out on a travel set. Turning away, she almost collided with a beautiful willowy blond in skinny jeans, talking loudly into a mobile.

The voice was unmistakable. As was the long, lustrous hair, lit up like a white flame in the sun streaming down the narrow street. Her face was almost entirely hidden by vast black sunglasses; she was instantly recognizable nonetheless. "Florrie!" gasped Alexa.

More beautiful than ever. And yet, it seemed, still single. According to the diary pages Alexa followed so avidly, Florrie drifted from glamorous party to eligible bachelor apparently insensible to the possibilities. The only comfort the marginalized Alexa could draw from these accounts of hectic popularity and manifold social opportunities was the certainty that Lady Annabel would be as frustrated as she was. Albeit for different reasons.

Florrie, still exclaiming into her mobile, did not appear to see her.

"Florrie!" Alexa repeated, grasping her by the arm.

Florrie looked at her in horror. "Omigod, Camilla, some fucking beggar's bloody trying to assault me…Oh, it's *you*, Lexie."

She shoved the mobile into a large, pink leather bag studded with diamanté hearts. "Hey! Last I heard you were trying your luck with Fatty Wharte-Hogge."

Embarrassment flooded Alexa. "We're just good friends," she muttered.

"That's not what he's saying." Florrie giggled. "According to him, you—"

"How've you been?" Alexa interrupted forcefully. "How's the job with the MP going?"

"Did you know they're calling you Heirfix?" Florrie had pushed up her sunglasses. Her blue-violet eyes were wide and amused.

"You must know all about Westminster now." Alexa stuck doggedly to her subject. "Corridors of power and all that," she added, almost wistfully.

"*So* boring." Florrie pulled a face. "All those dreary constituents ringing up, moaning about their fuel bills. I told one of them that if he was so hard up he should sell some property or shares. He went *ballistic*!" Her eyes were wide with indignation. "Told me that he didn't have property or shares, which is rubbish, obviously. Everyone does."

Alexa felt heartened by the fact that Florrie, even after all that had happened, still seemed relaxed in her company. Might it be possible to claw back some of her old ground?

"Glass of champagne?" she suggested.

"Omigod, yes! I could do with some hair of the dog. There's the Ritz just up there."

Alexa had been thinking more of a small downstairs wine bar. But Florrie, in her silver sequined flip-flops, was already striding ahead along the sunny pavement. She hurried to keep up.

"So no weekends at Chequers with the Prime Minister, then?"

"God, yes. All so dreary," Florrie groaned. "Politics is hopeless socially. You never meet anybody interesting."

They were at the doors of the Ritz now, Florrie striding into the gilded, glittering interior with the familiarity of an owner. Alexa, struggling through the revolving door, saw her pass the gilded cherubs and cream-painted pillars and make straight for the corridor that led to the restaurant. "Don't we want the bar?" she gasped, hurrying after her. She forced herself not to panic; Florrie might only be looking for the loo.

"I'm starving," Florrie declared, not slackening her pace until she reached the restaurant door. "Table for two, please," she barked at the attendant waitress.

Helplessly, Alexa followed Florrie and the uniformed flunky across the thick pink carpet to a central table beneath the richly decorated ceiling. "Boring old place," Florrie hissed in a stage whisper over her shoulder to Alexa. "Daddy brings me here whenever he really wants to tell me off about something. Still, it's close, so it will have to do."

Two waiters simultaneously pulled out the oval-backed chairs; another, meanwhile, shimmered over with two large menus. Who would be paying for this lunch? Alexa wondered worriedly. She tried to push the thought from her mind and use the situation to her advantage. She was with Florrie, after all. And there could be other influential people here.

The room was hushed and, as it was early, largely empty. A pile of old dowagers in one corner, Alexa saw; some businessmen in another, glancing appreciatively at Florrie, who was, as always, oblivious to admiration.

"À la carte for me, I think," Florrie declared happily, closing the menu. Alexa's was still open in her hands. She had taken one frightened look at the prices and was now staring hard at the ceiling, which, ironically given her circumstances, depicted a fantastical sylvan paradise.

She forced herself to look on the bright side; Florrie might be intending to pay. There was, after all, a first time for everything. And there were more important things to think about, such as regaining her old position with Florrie.

Even so, as the wine waiter shimmered up, proffering a vast padded menu, Alexa's insides twisted with terror.

"Oh, we don't need to look at that," Florrie assured him gaily. Alexa's heart soared upward. Was she detoxing? Had her preferences switched to tap water?

"Just bring us a bottle of champagne, there's a darling." Florrie gave the waiter a winning smile.

Alexa swallowed. Another waiter came up. "You are ready to order, mademoiselle?" His attention was all on Florrie.

She flashed him a smile of devastating charm. "I'll start with the foie gras and then perhaps the lobster?"

Alexa was starting to feel sweaty with panic. She had seen the price of the lobster and it had left her shell-shocked. Shellfish-shocked.

"A very good choice, mademoiselle," the waiter assured Florrie smoothly. A pair of warm brown eyes now met Alexa's terrified ones. "And for you, mademoiselle?"

Part of her was surprised he used the term; she had, Alexa imagined, aged several decades in the last few minutes. "Soup, please," she muttered.

"Just the one course, mademoiselle?"

"Yes. Thanks."

The champagne arrived and was opened. Alexa's glass sat full and untouched on the tablecloth while Florrie, sipping away merrily, described her other recent adventures in the world of paid employment. Relentlessly, into her companion's hot and rushing ears, she happily listed squandered opportunities Alexa would have killed for.

The job at the upmarket concierge service, for one. This, Alexa learned between Florrie's mouthfuls of foie gras, bit the dust after Florrie arranged discreet dinners for a wealthy executive and his mistress and the executive's wife and her boy toy in the same sought-after London restaurant on the same night and at adjacent tables. As Florrie began on the lobster, Alexa was apprised of the sojourn in a smart London real estate agent that had ended after Florrie had confused the prices while updating the website. The result had been a mini-meltdown in the international property market.

"I just don't think work's my sort of thing, really." Florrie giggled as she polished off the last of the lobster. Her pretty long fingers, heavy with rings from Tiffany and Chanel, flew to her rosebud mouth. "Omigod, but I haven't told you about my new thing! I've branched out into art!"

"Art?"

"Yes, I'm a leading contemporary artist! I'm painting pictures with my tits!"

The sentence, delivered in an excited shriek, caused mayhem in the restaurant. Forks were dropped, glasses clattered onto plates, people choked and spluttered. All eyes swiveled to Florrie, who as ever couldn't have cared less.

"Met this amazing girl at a party who showed me how. I just did it for fun at first, but now people are actually paying for them! Well, Igor's bought one."

Alexa could only stare, as Florrie wittered on happily about her creative epiphany. "The paint's freezing and there are certain bits where you don't want to get it." She applied it with surgical gloves, she added, and rolled around on a canvas before removing the paint with Fairy Liquid.

"Daddy's not keen on it, though," Florrie added soberly, or as soberly as one who had drained more than half a bottle of champagne could manage.

"What about Mummy?"

Lady Annabel had not been mentioned so far. Perhaps she had spontaneously combusted with her own fury.

Florrie's beautiful face fell further. She tugged moodily on a strand of silver-fair hair. "Actually, she's being a complete 'mare."

"Surely not." Alexa's tone was heavily ironic.

Not that Florrie noticed. Having polished off two glasses of champagne by now, she was nodding at the waiter to fill her up again.

"Lady Annabel's being difficult about the painting?" Alexa prompted.

Florrie crossed her slender arms and looked sulky. "No, about the Prince."

"The *Prince*?" Alexa gasped. "You mean you're back with—"

A whirl of pale gold as Florrie shook her head. "No, no. That's over. He's back with his old girlfriend now. I thought everyone knew that?"

Alexa tried to look as if she were still in receipt of inner-circle gossip.

"So Mummy's simply found another prince to marry me off to. *Such* a bore."

Alexa summoned all her considerable acting powers to look sympathetic. "Poor you."

"Some old git of a duke Mummy knows rang her up and told her about this guy. I was like, 'Thanks a lot, old git.'" Florrie rolled her beautiful eyes.

Alexa grasped her champagne glass and, finally, took a deep slug. "Who is this prince?"

"Someone desperate to marry, apparently." Florrie yawned. "I've got to go and meet his parents next week. The King and Queen?" She pulled a face. "In their chateau?" She mimed being sick. "Wearing the family tiara and *everything*?" She drew a tapered forefinger across her throat. "Can you *imagine*?"

Alexa took another deep and fortifying swig of champagne. "Where is this chateau?" she asked when she had recovered herself.

The beautifully shaped shoulders humped resentfully up and down. "How should I know? Don't even want to think about it. Omigod, got to go," Florrie added suddenly, glancing at her Cartier watch. "Bugworth will be coming in the Bentley. He won't know I'm here; we're meeting outside Paxton and Whitfield."

"Bugworth?" Alexa queried. "I thought your chauffeur was called O'Hagan."

"Whatever," Florrie replied rudely. "Must dash, anyway. You'll get the bill, darling, won't you?"

Chapter Thirty-Eight

AFTER THE DISCOVERY OF the graffiti, because of the bonding experience it had been, but most of all because of the boyish excitement in his eyes, Polly finally gave in. She agreed to have supper with Jake.

Privately, she had also decided to sleep with him. Why resist? That she would do so again had been inevitable from the moment she had seen him in the Shropshire Arms. What did it matter anyway? She had imagined herself in love, but Max had disappeared. He had probably forgotten all about her by now.

Jake might be a bastard, but he was a handsome, brilliant, amusing bastard whose measure, moreover, she had by heart. He was, quite literally, the devil she knew. And what was so wrong with his casual attitude to sex, to taking pleasure as and when he found it? He didn't get hurt, as she had. Or abandoned with no explanation.

So why not allow herself to be seduced; who, otherwise, was she saving herself for?

Jake was evidently of the same view. He had chosen as his theatre of seduction a newly opened pizza restaurant in a nearby town. The building had been an old warehouse and was full of shadowy corners into which tables for two flickering with candle-light had been inserted.

"Like it?" he said, eyes wolfish over the breadsticks.

Polly looked around at the gel-slicked, black-shirted waiters, the bleach-blond waitresses, the light from the pizza oven flickering against the exposed brickwork. "Very sophisticated." She smiled.

They ordered, then he leaned over and took her hand. "I was always thinking of you, Polly, all the time I was on the dig."

She raised a disbelieving eyebrow but smiled. Sitting here, sipping Prosecco, being seduced by a scorchingly gorgeous man, was a pleasant experience. She could see the waitresses looking at her enviously.

"Tell me about the French dig, then," she said. As she had already decided she would sleep with him, there was no need for flirtatious preamble. They could talk about something actually interesting. "Where exactly was it?" she asked; there were, after all, several Roman sites in the South of France.

"Do we have to talk work?" Jake smarmed. "I want to talk about gorgeous *you*."

"Was it near Nice?" Polly pressed. "Somewhere up near the amphitheater?"

He groaned. "Oh, if you must. It was just over the Italian border. Up in the hills."

"But where exactly?" Polly pressed. "La Turbie, that sort of area?"

"Further south," Jake said. "Look," he added, impatiently, "must we talk shop? I want"—he stretched out a hand and touched her face—"to talk about how fantastic you look tonight."

"I like talking shop." Polly broke off a piece of focaccia.

He grinned. "So bloody earnest. By rights you should have thick glasses, a squint, and be pig ugly...Sorry, have I said something wrong?"

"Actually," said Polly coldly, "I did used to have a squint."

"Is that right?" Jake nodded as he tore off a piece of ciabatta. "You never told me that before."

"You never asked," Polly retorted. About that or any other aspect of her life, she now recalled. Whereas Max had been all curiosity.

"You've changed, then," Jake added cheerfully.

You haven't, Polly thought. He still was, always had been, an indifferent bastard. He had no idea—and less interest—in how difficult life could be for people less beautiful and clever than he was. As Max's kind, sensitive face swirled into her memory, she swallowed and felt her eyes prick. Oh Max. *Max.* Where are you?

Aware of making a mistake, Jake was now eager to give her whatever technical information she wanted. "The dig was near a place called Sedona," he told her. "Funny place. Independent monarchy, with its own king and queen. But so tiny it hardly shows on the maps. It's just across the Italian border."

The starters had now arrived and Polly was forking up a mini mozzarella ball. "Like Monaco, you mean?"

"Yeah, sort of. But not so high-profile. It's got a palace, though. A chateau. Fairy-tale sort of place."

"And a prince?" Polly queried, laughing.

"There is a royal family, actually." Jake was shoveling in bresaola. He ate as he did everything—voraciously. "And, yes, a prince. But from what I heard, his life's anything but a fairy tale."

"Really?" Polly said, idly reaching for the olive oil.

"Yeah. He's got some weird despot of a father who's demanding he gets married. Someone who works at the castle told me about it."

Polly looked at him cryptically. "A *female* someone who works at the castle?"

Jake rolled his eyes. "Oh God, Polly, lay off. Yes, as you're asking. Anyway," he went on rapidly, "this prince doesn't want to get married at all; he got uprooted from whatever university he was at, somewhere over here, apparently, and dragged home. The poor bastard's spent the whole summer having to look over a succession of hideous euro princesses and find one to marry."

"How medieval," Polly exclaimed, shaking her head as she forked in another ball.

"Apparently all he wants is to be a vet," Jake chuckled, "but he's under house arrest, or castle arrest, and they're not letting him see anyone…"

Polly's incredulous grin snapped away. She laid down her fork and took a deep, steadying breath.

Her heart began to speed up.

"What's he called, this prince?" she croaked, her throat suddenly dry.

"Maxim. Come to think of it, I've even got a postcard of the poor sod." Jake rose in his seat as he rummaged in his back pocket. "Been using it for notes." He passed over the crumpled piece of card. Polly stared at the back, on which various coordinates pinpointing artifacts had been scribbled, along with mobile numbers with women's names beside them. Slowly she turned it over.

Max's handsome, resigned features stared up at her.

Amazement and relief exploded within Polly, followed by exultation. She had known, just *known*, whatever Dad might think, that there was an explanation for Max's absence. Whether Dad would believe this one was another matter. She could hardly believe it herself. Yet, oddly, it fit; he had said his father ran the family firm, that they lived abroad. She recalled their first meeting in the Lakeshott grounds. Is that where he had been staying? Was Napoleon the Duke's dog? But why had Max been so secretive about it all? Anyone else would have trumpeted it from the rooftops.

She leaped to her feet. "Sedona, you say?"

Jake was startled by her intense stare. "That's right. Hey, what's the—"

"How do you get there?"

"You fly to Nice. Then…I'm not sure. I was in a car. Why do you want to know? Do you *know* him?"

"I've got to go," Polly gasped over her shoulder as she headed across the tiled floor. "Tell Neil I might not be back for a while. Sorry, but it's unavoidable."

Chapter Thirty-Nine

"BARNEY! IT'S FANTASTIC!" ALEXA danced joyfully through the sitting room of the Monte Carlo apartment.

The outside was modern, *very* modern, possibly with something of the termites' nest about its color and design. But the interior was, as Barney said, the last word in tax exile luxury.

The rooms were spacious and furnished in good-weather-rich-casual style: white sofas with aqua-blue cushions, huge glass coffee tables, big lamps, and indecipherable contemporary pictures with suggestions of breasts and bottoms.

The kitchen had a juicer, an ice dispenser, and a cappuccino machine. The fact that there were two bathrooms, as there had been in Florrie's Kensington apartment, was another source of satisfaction.

There were long white muslin curtains and mirrors everywhere, particularly in the master bedroom with the huge black-sheeted bed.

"How did you get it so cheap?" Alexa gasped.

"My secret!" Barney merely beamed.

Alexa swiftly dumped her bags and rushed through the sitting room's floor-to-ceiling sliding doors. The large balcony outside had smart wooden sun loungers, a table shaded with a big white parasol, and wonderful views of the sparkling sea. The good life starts here, Alexa thought exultantly, just as…

Judderjudderjudderwhinescreamscreamscreamdronejudderjudder whinescreamscreamscreamdrone…

The savage beating of the air was terrifying, as of ghastly wings: the Angel of Death, the Horsemen of the Apocalypse. And it was rising, getting closer and louder.

"Barney!" screamed Alexa, half expecting some hideous beast to appear, swoop on her, and take her away at any moment.

Judderjudderjudderwhinescreamscreamscreamdronejudderjudder whinescreamscreamscreamdrone...

"What's up?" Barney asked, appearing through the sliding doors.

Judderjudderjudderwhinescreamscreamscreamdronejudderjudder whinescreamscreamscreamdrone...

"What's that noise?"

Barney cocked his head on one side. "It's the..." he began, at the exact moment Alexa saw the blades of a helicopter rise above the next building. It was unbelievably close. She could not only see the people in it, she could almost see the fillings in their teeth.

"...heliport," Barney finished, as the great black beast rocked itself unsteadily up into the blue sky and veered away. "We're next to the heliport."

As another juddering, screaming noise now started up, Alexa glared at her companion. "It's like living under the Heathrow flight path, only ten million times worse."

"Well, you asked about the price," Barney remarked resignedly, as a second helicopter lifted into the air.

Alexa could not reply. So deafening was the helicopter noise that it was impossible to decide whether you wanted tea or coffee. Let alone plan a trap for a billionaire.

As soon as possible, they went out. As Barney said, there was no time to lose, only opportunities. And, Alexa thought grimly, if they stayed at home, her hearing as well.

Outside the apartment block, the air was dry and gritty and it was blisteringly hot. As her shoulders broiled in her flimsy dress and the sun blazed off the narrow pavements into her face, Alexa gazed longingly at the limousines sliding down the winding streets of the tax haven. The sooner she got on the inside of one of those, the better.

Her head was pounding with the shattering noise of road drills, which seemed to be a feature of every corner. They had to walk in single file over upturned rubble and potholes, a challenge for Alexa's teetering heels. Above his black Ray-Bans, Barney's face was a hot pink and his hair was thin with sweat.

"The aesthetics are hardly the point," he reminded her above the drill noise. He was examining a display of glass pistols in a shop window. "It's an OK place to be rich in," he added, "just not a very good one to be poor in."

They were negotiating the steep pavement up the side of the Casino now; finally, some of the white stucco *fin de siècle* wedding-cake architecture the principality was famous for was revealing itself. If she looked behind her now she would see a harbor so crammed with yachts that you could probably walk over the whole lot from one end of the port to the other and never see a chink of water between.

"I must say," Barney remarked out of the blue, "it would be jolly useful if the papers still published a list of the important people in town as they did in the old days. You knew who you were aiming for then. Gold-digging was a hell of a lot easier."

They stumbled along in silence for a few minutes, Alexa stopping occasionally to gaze at the lurid jewelry in the various windows. Most of it was vile, but there wasn't a single piece she would say no to.

"Here we are," Barney said, as they emerged into a large square that blazed with sunlight. "Our center of operations. Here's where we sit and wait for a fly to enter our web."

"What, here?" Alexa looked doubtfully around. There were cars everywhere and crowds barging in various directions through the middle of pavement cafés.

"Of course not!" Barney pointed over to a palatial cream building festooned with escutcheons, trumpets, and cherubs. "At the Casino."

Alexa stared. "You're going to gamble, you mean? What's that going to do for us apart from lose us money?"

Barney looked affronted. "Well, admittedly, it's been a while since I took up the cards in anger, but I daresay the old magic's still there."

"We can't afford to gamble!" Alexa snarled.

Barney sighed. "On the contrary, my dear Alexa, we can't afford not to. But it's merely a front, I assure you. I look as if I am playing cards but I'm actually sizing up the joint. Spotting who is around, getting a feel for the possibilities. You're doing the same across there." He pointed to a grand white building hung with international flags that filled the entire opposite side of the square.

"Anyone who's anyone visiting Monaco goes to the Hotel des Bains at some point or other, just as they do the Casino," Barney explained. "Pick a seat in the bar with a good view, and when you see someone promising, move in."

Chapter Forty

IT WAS A HOT day at PapPixRiviera, but only in the temperature sense. Otherwise it was as dead as the flies in the bottom of the picture agency's grimy metal-framed windows.

Sweating gently in the soupy air, which the fan seemed only to stir, not cool, Jason Snort, chief of the bureau, sat with his meaty brown legs up on his desk. His baggy shorts, combat vest and big boots reflected his view of his work as a type of warfare. With one hand he fiddled idly with the shark tooth strung around his neck. It had been a gift from an admiring tabloid newspaper editor. "From one shark to another," the accompanying note had read. Jason tugged at it wistfully. Those had been the days.

Would they ever come back? The Cannes film festival was long over, the summer silly season yet to begin. But would it begin? It had been widely reported that, thanks to the credit crunch, many of the celebrities whose yachts, thongs, snogging, and general hijinks made for big paparazzi business during the summer would not be coming this year. The hairdressers of Saint-Tropez were worried. Very worried. The pool boys of Villefranche were in despair. The yacht-polishers of Antibes were being laid off left, right, and center, which made a big change from being laid left, right, and center, Jason mused sardonically. While the tennis coaches of Mougins were at their wits' end—not that that was far.

The slump had even touched the previously untouchably glamorous Hotel du Point on the Cap. Jason had heard they were so desperate you could pay for your drinks with book tokens.

He passed a hand through his trademark zinging auburn quiff. Beneath his tanned and frowning brow, his eyes roamed over his desk. Pinned up behind his computer were printouts of his finest hours, of which there had been many. There he was, grinning between Brad and Angelina. Sharing a beer with Piers Morgan. Mugging with Sharon Osbourne, with Paris Hilton, with Katie Price, with Hugh Grant. Were those days really over? His eye caught his collection of long lenses, lined up on the shelf above his computer ready for him to grab and run at the first hint of a story. But would he ever use any of them in anger again?

Meditatively, Jason swigged a warmish bottle of 33 lager and looked out of the window into the broiling Nice street. Nothing much going on out there. Nothing much going on anywhere. His sidekick, Des, his partner in the bureau, was even out taking pictures at a meeting of the Ventimiglia Narrow-Gauge Railway enthusiasts' Society. Could business get much worse?

Things weren't what they had been. It had been years, for instance, since any of the Monaco royals had put a foot wrong, and back in the day, they'd been an industry in themselves.

The Sedona royals should, strictly speaking, be filling the gap, giving him something to snap; wasn't that what royal families were for? But they kept their noses disgustingly clean; Queen Astrid and King Engelbert were as square as Rubik's Cubes. Prince Giacomo had had potential—there had been the odd good story—but he was obviously practically kettled these days.

And no new crown princess in sight. The royal press secretary Hippolyte had dragged him in endlessly recently to record various horse-faced no-hopers traipsing in and out of the chateau. Only the Babe from Bergen had been more or less as advertised, except that she'd run away from a Prince Maxim covered from head to toe in cow shit. Now that *would* have been a picture. But since then, nothing and no one. When were those bloody royals going to come clean and admit that Maxim was gay?

The large black phone on his desk shrilled. Languidly, Jason picked it up. Probably the Ladies' Circle of Menton calling to ask whether he might be interested in covering their annual general meeting. The awful thing was, given the state of the business, he probably was.

"Yeah?" Jason snarled, as if he had mere seconds to spare before rushing off, lens in hand, to snap some megastar.

"It's Hippolyte."

"Yeah?"

"I've got a tip-off for you."

"Yeah?" This, disbelievingly.

"Yeah…I mean yes," Hippolyte corrected himself.

"Hope it's better than the last one," Jason grumped. "The Babe from Bergen?"

"Much better," Hippolyte promised fervently. "Between you and me, Jason, hopes are high that this might be the next Queen of Sedona."

"Yeah?" Jason snapped disbelievingly on his gum. "Bloke, is he?"

"No," Hippolyte said nervously. What was that supposed to mean? Did Jason know something about him? he wondered. He had long suspected that Madame Whiplash tipped the press off about some of her clients. "Transvestite, then?" the photographer mocked.

Hippolyte felt nauseous. Transsexuals made up a good proportion of the Madame Whiplash crowd. He strove to keep his head.

"A girl," gasped the private secretary. "A lady, in fact. Lady Florence Trevorigus-Whyske-Cleethorpe."

Chapter Forty-One

QUEUING AT THE BAGGAGE carousel at Nice airport, Polly's glance fell on two women. A languid, blond, and very beautiful girl, whose eyes did not lift from her iPhone, was being dragged across the marble concourse by a determined-looking woman. Her mother, Polly guessed. A porter dragging an enormous quantity of Vuitton luggage hurried after them. The mother was glamorous, Polly thought, but in a tough sort of way; there was an aggressive chop to her shining auburn hair and a forbiddingly straight line to her magenta-lipsticked mouth. She wore new jeans, zebra-print ballerina flats, and a white shirt turned up at the collar.

Polly found herself in the line behind them at passport control. The man in the booth held the mother's passport up to his eyes. "Lady Annabel…Tre…Tre…"

"Trevorigus-Whyske-Cleethorpe!" snapped the woman, as if it were as straightforward as Smith.

Polly stiffened at the name. Where had she heard it before? She racked her brain, digging and delving, and eventually, triumphantly, emerged with the information. The girl in the newspaper story she had read that last evening with Max! She had been Lady someone of that name; was this her? Who had almost married the heir to the throne or something? She observed the shuffling blond with interest as, in her skin-tight jeans and sequined flip-flops, she followed Lady Annabel in her high clacking heels through Nothing to Declare. Polly, grasping her battered holdall, followed behind the Vuitton mountain.

In the arrivals hall she watched Lady Annabel head for a driver with a cap sporting the legendary Hotel des Bains. Outside, as Polly waited for the bus in the intense, bright heat, a gleaming black limousine glided by. Lady Annabel was in the back, bolt upright and apparently barking instructions to the driver; Lady Florence, meanwhile, was still slumped over her gadget, texting away. She didn't seem to have raised her eyes once since her arrival. Did she even know where she was? Polly wondered.

Her own hotel, the Splendido, failed to live up to the pictures on its website. Much less the description. "This roomy, light hotel full of old-fashioned charm, offers a traditional Nice welcome in an atmospheric street…" Polly recalled as she stood before the scruffy, peeling building with the broken sign.

There was certainly an atmosphere, if not a particularly encouraging one. The Splendido was in the darkest and most piratical of the many dark and piratical back streets in which Nice Old Town seemed to specialize. As for old-fashioned charm, it had it in spades, if you liked shabby, old-fashioned foyers that smelled mustily of food. The traditional Nice welcome, meanwhile, seemed to involve an elderly hotel keeper who had a grudge against the entire world; Polly lugged her bag herself up a seemingly endless series of cracked and winding wooden stairs to the tiny, smelly top-floor room.

Here there was a narrow, lumpy bed; the view, when one leaned out of the high window with the perilously wobbly sill that threatened to detach itself at any moment, was of loaded washing lines protruding from the windows of the building opposite.

And yet Polly couldn't have minded less about any of it. What did it matter, when tomorrow she would get to Sedona and see Max? She felt almost ridiculously happy. She unpacked her few things and skipped out of the hotel to explore the city, the concierge staring after her in glum amazement.

At the end of the gloomy alleyway containing the Splendido, Polly turned left, under a large archway, and found herself at the edge of a bustling market. Long lines of stalls were heaped with exotica: olives, honey, marzipan fruits, heaps of spices on earthenware, unfamiliar fish, and cheese of all sizes, endless variations on species of vegetables: big potatoes, small potatoes, great flapping red peppers. The salad heaped on the wooden stalls still looked to have the dew on it.

Polly sat down at a bar opposite the flower market and ordered a Kir. Sipping it, she gazed happily at the masses of roses, bucket upon bucket of blooms in shades from cream through orange and yellow to a deep, passionate, velvety red.

Afterward, she continued her exploration. The area around the port, an eighteenth-century rectangle of crumbling arcades, shuttered windows, and peeling burgundy walls, seemed to her wildly romantic. There was about it a salty whiff of older, more adventurous and colorful times.

She liked, too, the tin chairs painted an azure blue that stood about the promenade. A group arranged loosely in a four, with one of them pushed untidily back, suggested some earnest discussion, heads close together, laughter, and then disagreement blazing like a sudden flame, one of the group stamping off, offended.

There were other stories too: the two chairs whose seats faced each other, as if some carefree soul had sat in one with legs stretched out on the other, strumming a guitar. The two chairs close together, tilted toward each other, as if lovers had watched the sunset over the water. Polly sighed and was gripped by longing. Tomorrow, though. She only had to wait until tomorrow.

She sat down in one of the chairs. The sea before her swelled thickly, a great spread cape of glittering blue. Seagulls wheeled and called above in the bright air; the sunshine beat down between the palm trees.

Her gaze followed the points of land stretching out into the sea, one after the other. One of those must be below Sedona. No, it wasn't long now.

Chapter Forty-Two

AT EITHER SIDE OF the throne room entrance stood a herald in red tights, a red feathered bonnet, and a short, stiff tabard embroidered with the Sedona royal coat of arms. Their backs were rigid, their eyes were rigid, the long silver instruments from which the royal standard descended were rigid, ready to play the welcoming fanfare as the new princess-to-be arrived.

In her ermine-trimmed robes of state, Queen Astrid eyed a large fly that was buzzing irritatingly about her crown. It was hot, even hotter than the day the Babe from Bergen had visited. Hopefully Lady Florence was not the fainting sort. Stonker had assured her she was as tough as old boots. Or had that been the mother?

Stonker, who always spoke in terms of horse flesh, had proclaimed Lady Florence to be a deuced fine filly. And as Max obviously preferred animals to women, a filly would probably suit him.

Although of course it wouldn't really. Astrid knotted her fingers and tried to hold back the sickening guilt that every day seemed to press more heavily upon her. The situation was becoming unbearable. At least the confrontations at lunch and dinner were over. These days Max rarely came down for meals. He shut himself in his room and ate from trays. Nor did he seek her out in private any longer. He had, she suspected, completely given up on her.

Engelbert sat beside her, positively radiating heat. As a nod to their English guest, the green satin sash of the Ancient order of

Lancashire Clogmakers was strapped over his generous stomach. Astrid herself sported the blue and white striped riband of the Fellowship of Cheese Rollers. She had no idea what cheese rolling actually was. Perhaps Lady Florence, when she arrived, which should be any moment now, might explain.

Engelbert was shifting and squinting at his watch. "I thought English people were punctual," he grumbled.

He stared, irritated, at his sons. Giacomo was practically supine in his chair, fiddling with a lock of unsuitably long blond hair. At least Max, whom Engelbert had practically frogmarched to the throne room, was here this time. He slumped against his gilt-framed damask seat, the image of misery. Engelbert, who hated his sons to look sulky, leaned over.

"Cheer up, Max," he ordered.

As her elder son raised his head and swept both her and her husband with a single resentful glance, misery almost overwhelmed Astrid.

Hippolyte, proud and upright beside the throne room entrance, was savoring a feeling of blissful relief. Rich, pretty, titled; Lady Florence ticked every box. At last he would be able to relax. And in a manner that did not involve large middle-aged men dressed in tight leather.

All she had to do was arrive. Hippolyte breathed out carefully in his restricting morning suit and ran a finger around the sweaty inside of his collar. How much longer would she be? He had warned her somewhat forceful mother Lady Annabel that being fashionably late was frowned on in Sedona, where the convention was to be royally early. It seemed unlikely they had been held up anywhere; Hippolyte himself had organized the limousine. Lady Annabel had wanted to come by helicopter and had been nonplussed to be told that there was nowhere in Sedona to land one.

❖❖❖

There was a flurry at the throne room's gilded entrance and everyone sat up. The footmen strained even straighter to attention.

One of the household servants was whispering in Monsieur Hippolyte's ear. Max watched the private secretary's red face pale, and Hippolyte reel across the doorway to where the Lord Chamberlain stood sentinel on the other side. As he received the tidings, the old man started, then went gray in the face. A yellowed hand shot up to his throat, as if freeing constricted breathing passages.

"What's the matter?" snapped Engelbert, watching this dumb show with annoyance.

Hippolyte was sweating even more profusely than usual. His face, as he walked toward the thrones, wringing his fat hands, was almost purple.

"Your Majesties, your Royal Highnesses…" He was practically in tears, the Queen saw.

"What?" snapped the King.

"I'm afraid…I'm very much afraid…"

Actually, he was terrified.

"Out with it, Hippolyte."

"It appears there's been a slight confusion about dates and times," the trembling private secretary stammered.

"Confusion about times?" The King looked outraged. There was never confusion about time in Sedona. Unpunctuality was against the law—well, it would have been had he been able to get it onto the statute books. "What on earth do you mean, man?"

"Lady Florence will unfortunately be unable to join us this morning."

"Unable?" repeated the King, surprise temporarily suspending his anger. Then his anger kicked in. "*Unable?*" He glared at the private secretary. No one had ever before been unable to "join," as that fool Hippolyte put it, the royal family at a state levee. To be invited as Lady Florence had been was a royal command.

Hippolyte's expression was a mixture of sickly ingratiation mixed with mortal fear. On top of the already outraged Lady Annabel, he was now about to experience the full ire of the enraged King, following which he would face the fury of a Jason Snort denied his special-access pictures.

"It seems," Hippolyte stuttered, wondering if his heart was about to give way, "that Lady Florence has disappeared."

Chapter Forty-Three

THE DIRECT WAY TO Sedona was by bus, Polly discovered. A bus that, by the time she had acquainted herself with its existence and location, she had almost missed. She clambered on board to discover that, besides her, it contained a great number of middle-aged tourists brandishing guide books with pictures of a fairy-tale castle on the front. She felt a surge of excitement. Max's home!

It was blisteringly hot on the bus—the tourists had immediately bagged the shade and left Polly the frying-pan side. But she was too happy to notice.

As a route to bliss, it was an unlikely one. Having chugged through the city back streets, they crossed a ring road and began climbing a wide motorway leading into the hills. A series of orange-lit concrete tunnels led to more motorway, then suddenly they turned off and the landscape changed beyond all recognition.

It was wild, stony, and sun-blasted territory, a land of dry, rocky, steep-sided mountains. They were, Polly saw, traveling along the sorts of roads that cars veered off in Bond films before exploding into a fireball at the bottom. Bends twisted, steeply and suddenly, above yawning ravines. She had not realized the countryside behind the Cote d'Azur was so wild and elemental.

By the time they had reached the highest point of the road, Polly had counted fifteen hairpin bends offering heart-stopping views of dizzying chasms. From here the road wound gradually down beneath thin ash trees and turkey oaks. The panorama of mountain peaks spread around them like the waves of a choppy sea: gray, green, and, in the near distance, white-tipped—the snow on the Alps.

Far, far below was the bottom of the valley. Trees grew out of the living rock at right angles, stunted and twisted affairs for which life seemed in every sense an upward struggle.

If the bus driver miscalculated a bend, Polly thought, awed, there was a vertical plunge of hundreds of feet into the ravine. Would she reach Max alive? She closed her eyes as another hairpin approached. The driver twisted the wheel and they went into the switchback. At the back of the bend he forced the accelerator down to lift them out of it and the bus roared up onto the straight again. Polly let out a groan of relief. The worst was over and they were still alive.

None of the tourists were taking the slightest notice of the view. The men seemed to be looking at each other's cameras and the women chatting to each other and consulting their guide books: *Le Chateau de Sedona, Der Schloss von Sedona*.

Polly had put her sunglasses on by now, but they made little difference. The light was so white and bright, it was difficult to see anything properly, which was why, at first, she thought the dark shapes standing on an approaching bend were trees. It was only as the bus ground closer and the trees could be seen to be moving, waving, even, that Polly realized that they were in fact people.

It was a young blond couple. They were flagging the bus down frantically, possibly desperately. Had they, Polly wondered, set off for a walk in this hot mountain landscape and suddenly realized what trouble they were in?

Neither of them, she saw as the vehicle slowed, seemed particularly well equipped for walking. The bus driver stopped and opened the doors; without even waiting to be asked, they leaped aboard. The girl had high heels on; her very short dress was flashing and glittering in the brilliant light. Her makeup, Polly saw, was smudged and her very long pale hair tousled. She looked as if she had just stumbled out of an all-night party.

The boy was strikingly good-looking, with large pale eyes and full lips. He had shoulder-length blond hair and wore skinny black leather jeans, pointed black boots, and a silver shirt open almost to the waist. His self-confidence was striking; he grinned as he walked up the bus, pulling himself along by means of the seat tops as the French and German matrons looked on admiringly.

"Good morning, ladies and gentlemen!" he announced cheerfully, flashing a set of beautiful teeth.

The bus driver was craning around in concern. Then the girl, who had remained at the front of the bus, sashayed over, leaned a long, creamy thigh against his ticket dispenser, and smiled at him. The driver stared up at her, dazzled, all thought of intervention gone.

"Going to Sedona, right?" The boy beamed confidently around.

"*Ja, oui, ja,*" came the panting chorus.

"You want a sneak preview of the castle? Well, if you get off the bus just here, you can see down the mountainside right into the back garden. The private back garden," the boy added with another flash of his impossible teeth. "You might see the King in the hot tub if you're lucky; he generally has one at this time of day."

Within seconds, it seemed, the entire coach was empty, the ladies fighting each other to disembark. The bus driver had gone too, in pursuit of the beautiful girl. Polly was left alone.

The young man peered in from the entrance. He called down the bus. "You don't want to see?"

"No thanks. I think the King's entitled to have a bath unobserved."

The handsome youth leaped on board and came up to her with a swinging walk. He bent and looked searchingly into her eyes; his own, Polly saw, were intensely blue. "You might see the young princes too," he murmured. "Very good-looking young men. Charming young men. They often chat to their father while he's in his hot tub. Get through quite a lot of state business that way, or so I'm told."

Polly was up in a second and scrambling out of the bus. "Steady on," said the youth lightly.

Outside, the midday heat hit her like a fist. Wild herbs grew in the scrubland along the route and the perfume pulsed upward in the heat. Her fellow travelers, crowded under the scorched and weather-beaten remains of a pine tree, were peering into the chasm below. They were making puzzled noises.

"You can't see the garden at all," one indignant woman was saying to another.

You couldn't, Polly saw. All that was visible from the cliff top was the shadowy and distant bottom of a ravine. As she stared downward, an engine roared into life behind her. She whirled around, but too late. The bus, with the silver-shirted youth driving it, was pulling away and disappearing around the next bend.

Chapter Forty-Four

IT WAS ELEVEN O'CLOCK, and Alexa was taking her now accustomed place in the corner of the bar of the Hotel des Bains. During the last two days she had surveyed most positions, and this table combined excellent eavesdropping with relative discretion. Also, as it directly faced the entrance, anyone entering from the lobby could be instantly assessed.

The third and final of the table's virtues was its distance from the white-coated waiters behind the long polished bar. They were impeccably polite but persistent, and Alexa had found that there was only so long the cheapest glass of white wine could be made to last. Two hours was her record.

That the staff suspected her morals was obvious; a gray-suited manager came to frown at her every now and then. But she gave them all a sweet smile, rustled her newspaper, and generally faced them down. Alexa was made of stern stuff. And when on the hunt for money, she was made of the sternest stuff of all.

Seated, she fished her copy of the *Financial Times* out of her imitation designer holdall. This choice of reading matter was meant to send subtle signals to any passing captain of global industry that she understood his world; his fortune would be safe with her. So far, though, the signal had been neither seen nor heard.

Perhaps, Alexa thought, it was too subtle. And yet there wasn't much else subtle about her, and in particular about the thigh-skimming leopard skin dress that had once belonged to Florrie and which Alexa had borrowed and conveniently forgotten to give back.

She had settled for careful makeup, a re-Fake Baking of her legs, and brushing her hair until it fell like a sheet of oil over her shoulders. Her new footwear was extreme: high, shiny, open-toed, black, and impossible to walk more than five steps in; the flip-flops in which she had made the actual journey from the flat were stowed in her holdall, along with her makeup, mobile phone, and rapidly lightening purse.

But as yet, there were no takers.

Barney wasn't doing any better. Late last night, over the roar of the helicopters, he had glumly related how the sole occupants of the Casino's main gaming room were a group of tourists from the West Midlands who, on the signal of their tour guide, had departed to rejoin their coach.

Alexa was increasingly, gloomily certain they were in the wrong place at the wrong time. "Everyone must be on their yachts," she grumbled.

"Quite possibly," Barney agreed serenely. "We just have to find a way of getting on them."

Defeatedly, Alexa opened the newspaper. Then, aware of a disturbance, she lowered it. Someone had come in—stormed in was more the phrase—to the empty bar. Horrified, Alexa swiftly raised her *FT* barrier. It may not have attracted a billionaire, but it provided a protective screen from this most dangerous of enemies.

The unmistakable figure at the bar was resplendent in a tight-fitting white silk suit and high silver heels. She wore white gloves, carried a silver clutch, and her wrists, throat, and fingers were positively ablaze with diamonds.

Lady Annabel! Lady Annabel Trevorigus-Whyske-Cleethorpe!

Unable quite to believe this stunningly unfortunate blow, Alexa raised her head and peered in terror over the newspaper's peachy ridge. Lady Annabel would have no difficulty in guessing exactly what Alexa was doing here, and absolutely no qualms about denouncing her as a gold-digger to the bar staff, the lobby, and anyone outside who happened to be passing. In short, if Lady Annabel knew she was in Monte Carlo she would move heaven and earth to run her out of town.

"I'M LOOKING FOR MY DAUGHTER!" Lady Annabel announced in a very loud, very slow voice.

Alexa gasped. *Florrie* was here too?

She risked another peep over the top of her paper. Lady Annabel was peering over the bar as if Florrie might be concealed among the cocktail onions. "SHE'S VERY BLOND!" she was bellowing. Lady Annabel was clearly of the persuasion that if you shouted in English to non-English speakers, they would somehow understand it. "SHE'S VERY BEAUTIFUL. YOU'RE QUITE SURE YOU HAVEN'T SEEN HER?"

"No, madame," the obviously terrified waiters were assuring her.

"HER NAME IS LADY FLORENCE TREVORIGUS-WHYSKE-CLEETHORPE!" Lady Annabel thundered as she rapped the bar. "HAVE YOU GOT THAT? LADY FLORENCE TREVORIGUS-WHYSKE-CLEETHORPE!"

"Yes, madame, *oui*, madame," the waiters gibbered. "Lady Florence…erm…"

"AND IF YOU DO SEE HER YOU MUST LET ME KNOW IMMEDIATELY!" Lady Annabel roared, rapping the bar again. "I AM IN SUITE 404. LADY ANNABEL TREVORIGUS-WHYSKE-CLEETHORPE. *CLEETHORPE*. HAVE YOU GOT THAT?"

Alexa ducked behind her paper again as Lady Annabel turned to face the room and cast a final furious stare around. With a last, audible snort of frustration, she stormed out of the bar.

Alexa waved for a waiter. She looked shakily up at him. "I'd like a gin and tonic please. A double. No, make it a triple."

Chapter Forty-Five

FOR ALL THE BRIGHTNESS of the day outside, the King's study was dimly lit. Its three overlapping layers of chintz curtaining had been all the rage when installed some thirty years ago. Rising in the center like a carved wooden island was a desk piled with books, crystal paperweights, jeweled letter-openers, silver-gilt inkstands, small statues, and red leather boxes containing state papers. Before the fireplace two long, worn damask sofas faced each other. It was on one of these that Max was sitting, leaning forward with his arms crossed as his father angrily held forth from the other. On the worn carpet, his feet beat out an accompaniment to his ire.

Within Max, every fiber, bone, and muscle strained restlessly. Was there to be no light at the end of this long and very ornate tunnel in which he found himself?

"It's high time you took on more royal duties," the King was telling his son. Max's face fell. "You are going to represent me," the monarch continued, "at an important business event tomorrow. Your brother was supposed to be going, but he's grounded."

Sergeant Poivre of the Royal Sedona Police had not spared the details of Giacomo's theft of the bus. The King had been mortified and furious. Thankfully, he had Hippolyte's assurance that the press had not got wind of it

Max did not ask why Giacomo was grounded. He did not care. One puzzle did, however, filter through the outer layers of his preoccupied brain. "But Giacomo never goes to important business events," he pointed out. "He only ever goes to parties on yachts."

"Well, it is on a yacht, as it happens," the King snapped.

"I don't like yachts." Events on yachts, in Max's limited experience, were all about drinking and one-upmanship. He doubted any useful business could be done. "They're full of stupid airhead socialites," he added, to make this point.

The King stared irritatedly at his son. "And what other sort of person do you expect to find a wife among? There's no other type left!"

Max did not reply to this, but his expression was eloquent enough. The King scented rebellion.

"You will go," he said gratingly.

"I'd rather not," Max said quietly.

Fury rose in Engelbert's chest; how dare Max defy him? Even Giacomo, reprobate though he was, never stood up to his father the way Max routinely did. There were times when Max didn't seem like a son of his at all.

"Maxim," he said heavily, as if the sheer weight of his words could crush his son's resistance, "you are heir to the throne of the ancient Kingdom of Sedona. As Crown Prince, it is your royal duty to do as your monarch commands." Engelbert's mustache was bristling defensively, his authoritative bass surprising even himself. "To disobey me is treason!"

Chapter Forty-Six

CROUCHED OVER HIS DESK in his office, Monsieur Hippolyte had one hand placed protectively on his head as he tried to placate Jason Snort. "I'm sorry about Lady Florence," he was pleading desperately. "None of us know what happened to her. But I promise you, as soon as someone else comes along ..."

"But there's no princess, no photos, and so I've got nothing to sell," Snort raged from the other end of the line. "Which leaves me with no alternative but to offer for sale my latest set of pictures of..."

Hippolyte's ears throbbed in panic. His heart soared into his throat. Not Madame Whiplash. Please. *Please...*

"...everybody's favorite playboy prince, Giacomo," Snort finished, as Hippolyte drew a deep, shuddering breath of relief. "Didn't realize he could actually *drive* a coach," the photographer added. "Thought he sat in the back of them and got pulled along by horses."

Hippolyte's relief had been short-lived. Panic was once again thumping in his breast. He knew about the story; Sergeant Poivre had wasted no time in putting the chateau in the picture in the bluntest terms. But he had hoped—prayed, no less—that the incident might have gone unnoticed by the wider world.

"We've got pictures," the paparazzo said gleefully. "My colleague Des passed him on the road. Veering all over the place he was. According to Des, he almost went over the edge."

If only… Monsieur Hippolyte closed his eyes longingly.

"There was a girl on board too," Snort added slyly.

"Who?" gasped Hippolyte in panic. Please God none of the international slappers that Prince Giacomo seemed to find so irresistible.

"I can't say," Snort said cagily, sending the private secretary into a fresh plunge of terror. He did not explain that the reason for this was that Des's pictures were too bad to use. The girl was unrecognizable, as was Giacomo at the wheel. According to Des, before he could get the Prince in focus, the bus had reared at him and he had lost the picture in trying to save his own life. Des's excuses, as well as his pictures, were rapidly getting worse, Snort thought. But the story could still be used as leverage with Hippolyte.

"So we'll run it," he said casually, "if you haven't got any better suggestions."

Hippolyte racked his brains. "Er, there's tomorrow night," he gabbled eventually. "Prince Maxim's going to a party…"

"Prince goes to party! Hold the front page!" sneered Snort.

"…on a yacht. Bigski's yacht."

Bigski. Jason raised an eyebrow. He had heard the tycoon was in town—or in harbor.

"Bigski always has lots of girls at his parties," Hippolyte added, veering off into the realms of the wildest speculation. "It's not impossible that the Crown Prince might meet someone there."

Snort considered this. "OK," he said eventually. "But this is your last chance, Hippo. If I don't get a shot of Max and some totty, you're toast."

Chapter Forty-Seven

ALEXA WAS SUCKING THE last of the gin off the ice cubes in her glass and thinking about leaving. Her equilibrium was quite restored. It now seemed a pleasantly long time since the near miss with Lady Annabel.

She paid the bill, stood up swayingly on her heels, and picked up her bag. Then, suddenly, someone was shooting into the bar and running across the carpet toward her.

"Lexie! Omigod! Lexie!"

Alexa stared at the tangle of blond hair and long limbs.

"Florrie!"

Alexa felt near blinded by the blaze of Florrie's teeth and the dazzle of her eyes. In her simple short white dress with wide, gold-trimmed leather belt, she looked like a goddess; an effect reinforced by silver gladiator sandals. Alexa felt hideously conscious of the leopard skin print dress. Would Florrie recognize it?

Florrie's priorities were elsewhere, however. A long finger flew to the plump, bow-shaped lips. "Sssh!" Her grin was wide and naughty and her violet-blue eyes twinkled with excitement. "I'm in major trouble. Mummy's furious with me."

A burly waiter, bringing up a chair for Florrie, now looked at her closely. Was he remembering Lady Annabel's instructions? Alexa tried to throw him off the scent. "A glass of tap water for my friend, um, *Celia*," she rapped out.

"I'm not called Celia," Florrie began indignantly, before being dug hard in the ribs by Alexa. Only then did the penny seem to drop. "Oh, yah, sorry."

The waiter was still staring at Florrie. "Tap water!" Alexa commanded. There was to be no repeat of the Ritz disaster.

Florrie looked peevish. "I want champagne."

"A glass of champagne, then," said Alexa wearily. Because Florrie just *had* to pay this time. Even by her feckless standards, anything else was unthinkable.

Florrie waved a long, imperious arm. "Actually, we may as well have a bottle. Bring us your best, waiter."

Alexa swallowed. The Hotel des Bains' best champagne would be in the Igor category, pricewise. Florrie *must* be picking up the tab.

Florrie was rummaging in her bag and producing from it an iPhone and a packet of cigarettes.

Tapping at the iPhone and frowning at its screen, she lit up and took a deep drag. The waiters were all staring moonily from across the room and seemed in no hurry to remind her about the smoking ban.

"Omigod, I'm in so much trouble, you wouldn't believe it," Florrie exclaimed to Alexa, glancing up from the gadget.

The burly waiter appeared with a champagne bottle in a chilled bucket, and sashayed toward them, lowering it ceremonially in a fog of cigarette smoke. Florrie, blowing a lungful right into his face, ignored his advent. The waiter stood there as if surrounded by the scents of heaven. "Shall I pour, mademoiselle?"

"Yah, great," Florrie said absently.

"Why are you in trouble?" Alexa asked when the waiter had gone. "What have you done?"

Florrie looked up from laboriously tapping in a message. "It's what I've not done." She grabbed a glass and sprawled back in the chair. "Did I mention that prince guy that Mummy wanted me to meet?"

Alexa confined herself to a short nod.

"Well, the meeting was this morning, in his royal palace or whatever, and I sort of forgot." Florrie exhaled a plume of smoke and jiggled the long legs stretched in front of her.

Alexa remembered the appearance of Lady Annabel in the bar. Her spectacular outfit now made sense, as did her spectacular fury. About to set off to meet the royal family, Lady Annabel was unable to find her daughter. A smile tugged at the edge of Alexa's mouth; she tried hastily to suppress it.

She need not have put herself to the trouble; Florrie was as oblivious as ever to anyone else's reactions. Her attention was once more on her phone; she drained her champagne glass absently. Immediately, three waiters came rushing across simultaneously. "Allow me," said one, grasping the bottle in the ice bucket and refilling the glass. "*Permettez-moi*," said another, straightening Florrie's glass on its white paper coaster printed with the swirly hotel logo. A third proffered a small silver bowl of nuts. Florrie ignored these attentions completely. She was laughing at a message she had received.

Alexa, however, wanted details. "You mean," she said, "that these royals were waiting for you and you didn't turn up?"

"Yah, basically," Florrie said, not looking up. "They were all there waiting in the throne room, apparently. Crowns and robes, the lot. Can you believe it?" She grinned and drew on her cigarette.

"But why didn't you turn up? Where were you?"

Florrie ground her cigarette into the nuts. "Omigod, you sound just like Mummy! I'd had a bit of a hard night, OK? Went to this great club. There was this really cool guy there called Jack." She looked, for a second, smitten. "Omigod, he's *gorgeous*. Here he is." She tapped the screen of her iPhone and held it up.

Alexa stared into a blurred close-up face. She could see up both nostrils.

"It's Jack doing his party piece," Florrie said helpfully.

"Which is?" The picture gave little away.

"He can drink an entire magnum of champagne in under a minute!" Florrie's eyes were sparkling.

"Very impressive," Alexa said hastily. "So, back to these royals. You didn't turn up because…?"

"Jack took me to this, like, really amazing after-party. In this villa up in the hills somewhere. We got a bit stuck."

"How did you get back?"

"Omigod, you won't believe it, but Jack hijacked a bus—actually, that's really funny. Jack…hi*jack*ed." Florrie clutched her arms and doubled up with honking laughter.

"Hijacked…?" Alexa wondered if she was hearing right.

Florrie was still snorting with mirth. "We were," she managed between giggles, "on this kind of really hot mountain road, OK? And he flagged down this bus full of tourists and made them get out while he pretended to show them something. Then, while they were staring at whatever it was, he got in the driver's seat and drove me back to the hotel. Cool or what?"

Alexa was still struggling to believe it. "But…the tourists? What happened to them?"

Florrie shrugged. "God knows. But wasn't Jack cool? Like a sort of highwayman or something."

Alexa decided that the fate of a busload of tourists was none of her concern. She had more important matters afoot. "So what happened at the chateau?"

"What chateau?" Florrie looked puzzled.

"The one you didn't turn up to," Alexa said patiently. "The one with the crowns and the throne room."

"Oh, that one." Florrie rocked restlessly in her seat, evidently bored of the subject. "Um, I'm not sure Mummy actually went. I think she had to call them when she couldn't find me. I think the King was pretty furious, as Prince Whatsisname has to find someone to marry." She gave a disdainful giggle and turned her attention back to her screen.

"Prince Whatsisname?" Alexa felt a crashing sensation behind her forehead, a thousand pennies dropping. Here she was, a desperate gold-digger on the brink of hopeless ruin, while somewhere tantalizingly close was a prince who needed to marry fast. The only link was Florrie. She *had* to remember his name. She leaned forward. "Think, Florrie. What's his name, Prince Whatsisname?" Alexa squirmed in agony.

"No idea, darling." Florrie was absorbed in her texting. "All I know is that he's got to get married. Like, this minute! It sounds as if anyone will do, quite honestly. Apart from me, of course. I've rather fucked it up." She looked up, flicked her hair back, and giggled.

Alexa stared at her with burning eyes. "But what's he called?"

Chapter Forty-Eight

THE ROOM WAS QUIET, full of the padded silence of thick carpets and expensive upholstery. It throbbed in Alexa's straining ears. Every atom of her being, every proton, neutron, and electron, was focused on Florrie. The bar, with its clinks, murmurs, and ogling waiters, receded. Nothing existed apart from the beautiful girl who sat opposite her trying to remember the simplest of facts while her fingers tapped agitatedly on her electronic phone.

"The thing is," Florrie said eventually.

"*Yes?*"

"I just can't remember."

Alexa wanted to scream, but there was no time for that. Florrie was looking restlessly around the room; she might, any moment, decide she was bored and leave.

"Didn't you make any notes about him on that?" Alexa nodded at Florrie's iPhone.

Florrie looked down at the small black rectangle in surprise. "Make notes? On this? I didn't know you could."

"Another glass of champagne?" Alexa offered desperately. She didn't care what it cost anymore. There was a jackpot within grasp, after all.

"May as well, I suppose," Florrie said ungraciously. "Nothing else to do except go up to the room and face Mummy."

Alexa did not allow herself the luxury of being offended. She must focus on the matter in hand. "What's the chateau called?"

"Can't we talk about something else?" Florrie complained.

Alexa wanted to strangle her. The sheer will to survive might release the crucial piece of information. She was determined to keep pushing. She could feel how tantalizingly close the break-through was, that the rusted cogs of Florrie's brain were moving, albeit with agonizing slowness.

She must find the answer. Before Lady Annabel arrived, as surely, soon, she would. Like the princess feeling the pea beneath the layers of mattresses, Florrie's mother would, from the upper floors of the hotel, sense the presence of her daughter in the bar below. Alexa had to get the name before then.

A loud burst of unrecognizable disco was emanating from the iPhone.

"Disconnected, damn it." Florrie shook the instrument. "Probably the reception. I'll go and try it outside. It might be Jack."

She stood up.

"Hang on," cried Alexa.

Florrie couldn't leave now. She just couldn't.

A flame of fury roared up in Alexa. Florrie had not even had the grace to say good-bye, nor had she thanked her for the champagne, which obviously, yet again, Alexa would have to pay for. And now she was walking out, taking all Alexa's hopes with her.

No, Alexa decided, springing to her feet and stumbling after her on her unwieldy heels, she wouldn't let her. Florrie would stay until she told her what she needed to know.

She had reached the door in pursuit when she drew back in terror. Something auburn-haired in white and diamonds, its face contorted with anger, had exploded across the foyer and was hurtling itself at Florrie. There was a shriek. Alexa shot back into the safety of the bar. The waiter put the bill down in front of her. The fact that it was on a silver salver in no way ameliorated the pain of the final figure.

But somewhere nearby there was a prince, heir to a kingdom with a chateau, who needed a wife immediately. He was ready to entertain anyone, and Florrie was out of the running. But who the hell was he—and, just as importantly, *where*?

There was one last hope. Barney. This puzzle was just the type his sly, ingenious brain delighted in. She would text him over at the Casino; her message would be short, dramatic, and intriguing. It would communicate the fact that, after so much disappointment and bad luck, they were finally in sight of what they sought.

Alexa decided on "Fortune Ahoy!"

Another fortune, however, that on the bottom of the bar bill, was still staring accusingly up at her. A glorious idea now struck Alexa; dragging her pen out of her bag, she wrote with a flourish on the bottom "Charge to Suite 404, Lady Annabel T-W-C." Florrie had drunk the lion's share anyway.

"Diamonds Are a Girl's Best Friend" now struck up on her phone. A message. Alexa opened it gingerly; there were, after all, a great many other unpaid bills and general unfinished business left behind in England.

But the message was from Barney. "Fortune Ahoy!" it said.

Chapter Forty-Nine

ALEXA RETURNED TO THE flat to find Barney bursting with self-congratulation. He had got into conversation in the Casino with the Russian billionaire Bigski.

"He's invited us to a party on his yacht tomorrow!" Barney exulted. "Only took a couple of champagne cocktails!" He was rubbing his hands with glee. "Bloody expensive, but probably the best investment I ever made. Once you become Mrs. Bigski and set me up for the rest of my life!"

"But he's already married," Alexa pointed out.

While not resident in Britain, the tycoon was a distant presence on the London rich scene, and Alexa knew all about his twenty houses, fleet of planes, and six ocean-going yachts, each bigger and more expensive than the last. But the wife seemed the most significant factor just now.

"He's not available," Alexa reiterated impatiently.

Barney waved a plump, dismissive hand. "He's been married to Mrs. Bigski since the nineties…" The rest of the sentence was inaudible against the shattering noise of the helicopter now lifting off behind their apartment. "…ready to swap for someone younger and sexier."

Alexa considered this. Ambitious though she was, married foreign billionaire tycoons were slightly out of her comfort zone. "I've got a better idea," she said, and told Barney what she had discovered that afternoon.

Barney was immediately dismissive. "But we don't know who this prince is," he pointed out.

"Well, he lives round here somewhere. According to Florrie, he's got a chateau, the lot," Alexa said stubbornly.

Barney frowned. "Florrie's talking rubbish. You know how thick she is. She'll have got it all wrong. The only prince *I* know round here," he added grandly, "is a fellow I knew at university…"

Alexa was electrified. "Yes? *Yes?*"

"…and he's in England studying to be a vet," Barney finished. "No, my dear." His tone had become authoritative. "There's no point wasting time and energy on some wild prince chase when we've got a Bigski in the hand. You have an affair, he divorces his wife and marries you."

"An affair," Alexa wondered about the practicalities. While she had more or less come to grips with the sexual preferences of the British aristocracy, the international jet set might have entirely different ideas. Would Bigski want her to swing from the chandeliers? Or do something altogether more unexpected with them?

"…need to go shopping," Barney was saying, as the latest helicopter juddered into the distance. "Hit the salons. Big hair, big make-up, big tits."

"I don't have big tits," Alexa objected, looking down at her assets.

"We can fix that," Barney mouthed, before another helicopter drowned the rest of his words. "…getting the right bra," he finished as it faded away again.

Alexa was struck by his air of authority. What did *he* know about women's underwear? Or perhaps she would rather not be told. Once or twice since they had arrived here, Barney had headed off into the night after a fruitless evening in the Casino. She had gathered he was visiting someone called Madame Whiplash.

Chapter Fifty

It was a warm night. A beautiful night. The sea was an opalescent cloak spread at the foot of mountains warmed by the sun's last pink rays. The lights of the Riviera were beginning to glitter, a white diamond necklace lying along the coast. High up in the pearly after-glow of the sunset, a crescent moon as narrow as a fingernail paring hung in the sky. To Alexa, it was an evening of thrilling possibility. They now had a plan, and the means to execute it. Would anything be the same after tonight?

Bigski, unsurprisingly, was berthed in Oligarch's Row, the area of the marina where the biggest and most expensive yachts were parked. Thanks to the harbor lights, it was almost as bright as day. Alexa stared out and up at the blinding white plastic sides of boats as high as apartment blocks, their chrome trimmings blazing.

She felt a wild surge of excitement.

Barney had, during the short journey from the apartment to the marina, been whipping both of them into a state of near-delirium by reading out facts about Bigski's vessel from the latest copy of *Megayachts Monthly*. The fact that its cover feature was on the subject seemed to Alexa more than just coincidence. It seemed like fate.

The Big One, for such was its name, sounded startlingly well appointed. "The master suite spans the full width of the yacht," Barney recited. "The walls are marble, there are mosaic floors in all the bathrooms, and the plumbing is—you won't believe this—platinum. A full tank of fuel costs more than most houses. There's a glass observation floor at the bottom, a cinema, gym, steam room, massage area, missile detection system, four gun emplacements, three helipads, and a mini-sub. Golf range, running track, tennis courts." He grinned at her. "What do you think?"

"I think," Alexa grinned back, "that I'd happily shag the boat, let alone its owner."

Bigski's yacht was not just *The Big One*, they discovered as the taxi drew up. It was the Biggest one, the most brilliantly illuminated of all, lights blazing from every deck. There were shrouded helicopters on the top and serried ranks of jet skis below. Its exterior bristled with tenders, CCTV cameras, and radar equipment.

The taxi driver cranked on the handbrake. As Alexa shuffled across the backseat, Barney placed a hot, restraining hand across her thigh. "Don't let yourself out," he hissed. "You'll look like a nobody. Wait for the driver to do it."

"But what if he doesn't?" Alexa hissed back a few moments later, when the driver had not moved but kept looking at them curiously in the rearview mirror.

"The euro will drop eventually."

It did, but only after yet more minutes of crackling French local radio and the knot of interested onlookers outside on the concrete quay staring at them as they sat there. Then, muttering a curse, the driver flung himself out and lurched around to the back, where, with an expression of the utmost reluctance, he yanked Alexa's door free. He drew the line at helping her out, however, and she emptied herself unsteadily onto the concrete, trying not to fall as she straightened up.

Her glittering silver dress was the tightest and shiniest outfit they had been able to find in Monte Carlo, which probably, Alexa thought, made it the tightest and shiniest outfit in the world. It had also cost a fortune, but Alexa was by now beyond caring what happened to her credit card bill. If all went according to plan, she would never need to worry about money again. If things went wrong…well, she would cross that bridge when she came to it. Possibly jump off it, too. As Barney kept saying, failure was not an option.

In best supporting roles to the dress were blocky Perspex heels in which Alexa was completely unable to walk. "Who's walking?" Barney had asked satirically. "No one wears shoes on deck. And after the party," he added gleefully, "you'll never walk again. Limos, PJs, and yachts from now on, sweetie."

Alexa's hair, spritzed in musky perfume, hung gleaming down her back. Her face was so stiff with makeup she could hardly move it.

They had discussed tactics at great length and had settled eventually on two possibilities. Scenario one was that Alexa faked illness during the party. Taken to one of the bedrooms and her condition promptly worsening, she would assume residence for as long as it took to hunt down Bigski within his own compound. Scenario two was seducing the great man during the two hours of the gathering.

They were being watched, Alexa realized now. Within seconds of their appearance, a pin-neat crew member in white shirt, navy trousers, and gold-braided cap shimmered down the gleaming gangway and unfastened the silver clasp holding the white rope at the bottom of it.

He led them to the first deck. Alexa looked around, gathering a hasty impression of cognac marble and smoked-glass mirrored ceilings. Walls were dotted with heavily gilt-framed oils of garish flowers. Erotic marble sculptures stood about.

"Please to remove your shoes." The gangway man had melted away and a pretty brunette in navy blue shorts and matching polo shirt had appeared with a large basket lined with white linen.

Alexa tugged off her heels with relief. There were others already in the basket. Recognizing Manolos, Choos, and Louboutins, Alexa felt a rush of adrenaline. Competition. She stared at her toes; Barney had been right to insist on a top-grade pedicure.

They followed the brunette up various gleaming mahogany corridors and arrived in a glittering salon the size of a football field. Alexa's feet sank into pale carpet so deep her toes were invisible. It was like walking on sponges.

There were people everywhere; the heavily perfumed air was filled with the tinkle of champagne glasses, exclamatory conversation, and the occasional overloud, overconfident male laugh. In one corner, a man in white tie tinkled a shiny white grand piano.

Everyone in the room had turned to look at them both, and particularly at her. Alexa met the women's gazes boldly but didn't bother looking at the men. There was only one man here of interest to her, and she would find him sooner or later.

"My dear Mrs. Bigski!"

Barney was grasping the tiny, birdlike hand of a tiny, birdlike blond. Alexa swept the world's richest wife with an appraising glance from between her stiff eyelashes.

It was encouraging. Mrs. Bigski was a certain age. Stick thin, with a skull face and sunken eyes. She looked confusedly at Barney. "Do I know you?" she asked bluntly, in a heavy Russian accent.

"Know me?" Barney exclaimed. "My dear Svetlana—I can call you Svetlana, can't I?—your husband and I are old friends! We spent a very interesting evening together in the Casino just the other night."

Mrs. Bigski looked more doubtful than ever. "My husband, he meet a lot of people," she muttered, flicking a nervous glance at Alexa, who met it with a triumphant stare.

She guessed that Mrs. Bigski's life of apparent luxury was actually life on a tightrope. Life in tight everything, frankly; the white trousers she wore tonight with her magenta strappy top were so close-fitting that an eel would have to lie on its back to get into them. Of course, Alexa knew, rich wives dressed like this because they were terrified of losing their husbands to newer, shinier models. Models like herself.

Ironic, she thought. Here they were, on this hi-tech machine, with its guards, its CCTV, its state-of-the-art surveillance systems, its missile detection early-warning whatever. But the most dangerous predators of all, so far as Mrs. Bigski was concerned—women like Alexa, who might steal her husband—could slip through all checks without challenge.

"And this is Alexa!" Barney was saying now.

Alexa smiled the smile on the face of the tiger. Her eyes still on Mrs. Bigski's rubies, she felt a sharp jab in her ribs. Barney's elbow. She looked quickly around.

"Ah, Benny, my friend," the newcomer was saying, clapping Barney heavily on the back.

"Barney, Mr. Bigski." Barney was laughing, as if it was a joke, which Alexa was not sure it was. "And may I introduce my very special friend, Alexa MacDonald? Alexa, Sergey Bigski. I can call you Sergey, can't I?" He trained a sycophantic beam on the tycoon.

Had permission been granted? Alexa was not sure. Bigski had a still, secretive face with pale eyes and paler lashes fringing them. The heavy lids were almost closed, giving him a sleepy look, although Alexa guessed this was deceptive, designed to lull others into a false sense of security. Bigski looked to her like one of those people who saw everywhere at once and could simultaneously listen into several different conversations. He looked like a man accustomed to having whatever and whoever he wanted whenever he wanted it. No wonder Mrs. Bigski, who was now a few feet away talking to a woman in a tiara, was scared.

Bigski spoke. "Alexa! Welcome. Any friend of Billy's is a friend of mine."

Chapter Fifty-One

NOW THAT SHE STOOD in his presence, Alexa saw that Bigski was, in fact, small.

Very small. Even without her shoes, she towered above him. His eyes were on the exact level of the tiny, teasing flash of nipple that her dress's low-cut cleavage revealed.

But the size of his wallet, Alexa thought, was obvious enough. The silk T-shirt smoothly ironed by one of a fleet of servants. Perfectly cut jacket with the Royal Yacht Squadron badge and sleeve landing at just the right spot on the wrist to reveal the topmost model in the Rolex range.

"MacDonald! So you are Scottish!" Lightly he took the end of her extended fingers. "I am very fond of Scotland," Bigski added in a Central Casting rolling accent. "I have several estates there. You are a MacDonald of MacDonald, I take it?"

Alexa smiled. She had long ago learned not to answer this question directly. "But if you want to see what's under my kilt, we'll have to go somewhere else."

She heard Barney's sharp intake of breath. Possibly her rejoinder was a little pushy, and might have been a risk. But she saw the heavy eyelids flicker and knew the suggestion had made its impact. Bigski bowed. "Are you interested in art, Miss—or it is Lady—MacDonald?"

Alexa did not state a preference. He could call her Lady if he wanted. "I adore it," she said.

"Good. I've got some very interesting primeval sculptures I'd like to show you." Bigski's curious light eyes were still on hers. "Later, perhaps," he added meaningfully. He bowed and moved away.

Barney, beside her, was jiggling up and down like a small boy who hasn't been to the loo recently. "You've done it."

"Not yet," Alexa said. But that she would do it, she now felt supremely confident. There was a warm, melting feeling building below her navel, which she recognized as desire.

"Excitement always makes me hungry," Barney remarked. "I could murder some of the things on that buffet." He gestured to where, along one side of the room, lobster and oysters were arranged in row upon shining, seaweed-decorated row. Abutting them was a white-draped table where open bottles of champagne shone through shining ranks of flutes.

Alexa, too excited to eat or drink anything anyway, withdrew to a seat by the wall and eavesdropped on a nearby conversation. One woman was describing to the other three the low-environmental-impact new house she and her husband had recently bought.

"*So* green. We insisted on that. The pool is cleaned with marine salts, never chlorine. The garden is certified pesticide free with organic plants. Watered with Evian..."

Alexa listened with exhilaration. These were wives of the super-rich, women who could tell at a glance the thread count of a Frette sheet, who knew all about advance-FedExing your Hermès luggage. Was she about to join their ranks?

As a new debate began about whether dogs preferred Mozart or Elvis piped into their kennels, Alexa rose to her feet. She had noticed that Bigski was no longer in the room. Was this her opportunity? Was he expecting her to find him?

Her exit was aided by the fact that a huge ice sculpture of *The Big One*, filled with caviar, was making its ceremonial way into the room on a white-draped trolley, to cheers and applause from the guests.

Alexa allowed instinct to guide her and headed for what she imagined was the back of the boat.

She proceeded through a series of passages and lobbies filled with statement blooms, eventually emerging onto a large deck filled with yellow and white striped furniture arranged around a small plunge pool.

Alexa settled herself in the nearest chair, amazed at how confident she felt, how assured in her actions. She would sit and wait to be found. Liaisons like this had no real element of surprise anyway; both parties knew what they wanted. It was just a question of allowing the inevitable to happen.

As she flicked, unseeing, through a glossy magazine on the table beside her, Alexa reflected that she should have tried for a foreign billionaire years ago. The rich deep seas of the international high life seemed both easier and more comfortable than navigating the shallow muddy puddles of the British aristocracy.

Suddenly she looked up from the magazine and stared out across the gentle blue swell of the ocean to the mainland. She had the feeling she was not alone. The hairs rose on the back of her neck as she turned and met, over the striped back of the chair, the pale, intense gaze of Bigski. He was standing quietly in the shadows of the entrance to the deck.

A thin smile twitched the lower section of his long, yellowish face. In return, Alexa favored him with a mysterious smolder. There was no need to say anything.

He padded toward her on bare feet.

Her heart was beating faster. It was a great moment. Never in the entire course of her career had she been in the presence of quite so much money.

"You like it here?" Bigski's smile increased slightly. He looked as if he knew all her thoughts.

"Yes, very much." *Very much.*

"I am glad to have the opportunity to be alone with you." Bigski leaned closer toward her. "You are a very admirable woman, and I would like to admire you more."

As his chill yellow hand placed itself on her fake-tanned knee, Alexa allowed her eyelids to droop slightly and her mouth to drop open, as if this act alone sent ecstasy shuddering through her.

His lizard eyes glowed. He smiled; his teeth glittered in the moonlight. Keeping his gaze intently on hers, he pulled her to her feet. Mindful of his height, she was careful not to straighten all the way up.

As his mouth touched hers, Alexa tried to ignore the faint scent of garlic. Instead, she flicked her tongue lightly between his teeth and was gratified to hear a soft growl. The hands that held her tightened like a vice, and Alexa found herself forcing away images of what they might possibly have done in their pursuit of great fortune.

The hands were pulling her swiftly across the polished deck. Half running to keep up, Alexa followed Bigski through a pair of open doors.

She gasped. She cried out with delight. But Bigski was not even touching her. Rather, he was around the other side of a huge circular bed on which were scattered, as rose petals might be in other circumstances, masses of pieces of paper, which Alexa instantly recognized as money.

Bigski was grinning. "You ever made love on a million dollars before? All new notes. We are first to use."

He looked at her expectantly; she kept her eyes trained on him as, slowly, she unfastened the back of her dress. Shaking it to the floor, she pulled some of her hair forward, not so much to conceal her modesty as to accentuate her nakedness.

"No underwear, huh? Nice surprise." The teeth glistened again.

Alexa arranged herself on the bed. The notes were crackly and rather sharp beneath her; still, if she *had* to have paper cuts, wild sex with a billionaire was not a bad way to get them. Her eyes flicked questioningly toward the open doors of the salon. While fairly confident about what lay ahead, she was not particularly seeking an audience.

"Don't worry," Bigski growled, his eyes gleaming as he lowered himself beside her. "No one will disturb us. They would not dare," he added in a voice that made her think of the strangling hands, now moving to the zip of his trousers. He chuckled. "You're about to see that I'm not called Bigski for nothing."

Chapter Fifty-Two

GIACOMO HAD BEEN WILDLY envious.

"Don't know what you've got to look so fed up about," he had grumbled as he mooched about Max's dressing room, cracking gum in his teeth. "You'll have a great time. Bigski's yacht is one of the most expensive in the world."

Max did not answer.

"You never know," Giacomo added provocatively. "You might even meet a nice girl." As his royal brother shot him a furious look, he said: "Honestly, I don't know what it is about you and girls. You should try them. You might even like them."

Max did not dignify this with an answer.

Now here he was at the marina. A small knot of people had gathered along the quayside and were watching him climbing onto the boat in his black tie and shining shoes. Some of them were wondering aloud if he was the Prince of Spain, others Prince Charles, which seemed especially ridiculous, as the heir to the British throne was nearly half a century his senior and had famously large ears.

Max entered the main reception room of the yacht. As every eye turned to him, the urge to flee the heavily scented room with its braying men and women wearing more jewelry than clothes was almost overwhelming.

Navy-blue-shorted crew members in white shirts brandishing champagne hovered around, and a blond with coat-rack collarbones, who Max assumed was his hostess, hurried toward him, rattling with diamonds. He plastered on a smile; actually, as the woman looked very apprehensive, even terrified, this was easier than he'd expected.

"Mrs. Bigski? I'm Maxim de Sedona."

She extended a hand as small and light as a child's; he followed, through the crowd, a back so skinny that the shoulder blades protruded like Cadillac fins.

"My husband is here somewhere," Mrs. Bigski was saying, in a tone that sounded rather despairing. Her thin head on her skinny neck was turning constantly about. "He was, a few minutes ago."

Suddenly Maxim found his way blocked. A small, grinning, pink-faced man with thin dark hair plastered over to one side was standing right in front of him.

"My dear Maxim! So good to see you again!" A short arm extended and clasped him determinedly at the elbow. He was stuck fast, Max realized.

Mrs. Bigski had stopped too and was hovering, her large, worried eyes darting doubtfully from Maxim to the newcomer. But the newcomer was in supreme command of the situation. "My dear Svetlana—or can I call you Sveti?" he boomed, beaming at his hostess. "This is such a wonderful surprise, I can't tell you. Dear old Max and I go back years! We were at university together…"

"What a very happy coincidence, Mr. von Hoosier," Mrs. Bigski remarked, taking a few paces backward and starting to look about her again, presumably for her missing husband.

"Van Hoosier," Barney corrected with aplomb. It might be a made-up name, but that didn't mean it shouldn't be got right.

Maxim, who felt sorry for Mrs. Bigski, realized that any attempt on his part to get away from the person now grasping him would only present her with another problem. He resigned himself to his fate. "Hello, van Hoosier," he said without enthusiasm.

Just when it had seemed his evening could not get any worse, it had. Barney van Hoosier. At university he had, Max remembered, crossed streets to avoid that oleaginous smile, but that option was not open to him now. Actual streets were one of the few attributes Bigski's yacht lacked; presumably his next model would have them.

Max wished he had brought Beano with him. His devoted spaniel had a sixth sense for people his master disliked; he would have sunk his teeth into the van Hoosier calf with alacrity. But Beano had been sick in the night; Max suspected he had overdone it in the palace kitchens. None of the staff were able to resist slipping him tasty morsels, and the royal supper had been tournedos Rossini last night. Maxim himself had found it impossible to digest it; that a small and elderly spaniel couldn't was no surprise.

Barney, meanwhile, was beaming from ear to ear. He could hardly believe his luck. There had been an awkward moment—well, an awkward half-hour, if he were honest—after Alexa had disappeared, when he had found himself without a single person to talk to. He had sought to address his predicament with the well-worn trick of weaving, smiling, through the crowd with two glasses of champagne, as if heading toward an acquaintance in the corner. This pretense, however, could be kept up only for two or three circuits.

So when he saw, being ushered into the room, an old university acquaintance—a university acquaintance, in addition, festooned with royal orders and bearing himself every inch like the prince he was—Barney lost no time. He literally threw himself on Prince Maxim de Sedona.

"My dear Maxim," he cried, steering the reluctant Prince to the side of the room.

"Such a treat to see you here," he said fawningly. "The dear King and Queen are well, I take it?" His jocosity concealed steely determination. Maxim de Sedona could be as distant and unfriendly as he liked, but Barney was a man on a mission. He had no intention of leaving the exchange without an invitation to the royal chateau, at least.

Max resented the assumed familiarity with his parents and Barney's all too obvious intentions. He looked around for an escape. His hostess might have helped, but he could see her at the back of the room, talking to some of the serving staff, still looking constantly about her. The missing billionaire, bazillionaire, whatever he was, had evidently still not been found.

As, beside him, Barney continued in the same unctuous tone and with the same oily, avaricious little smile, Maxim's dislike of him increased. Barney had just asked, with nauseous elaborateness, whether he was having an enjoyable holiday.

Enjoyable! Max suddenly saw red. "Fantastically enjoyable," he drawled sarcastically. "First I was dragged back from England by my parents who've been trying to marry me off to a succession of women in whom I've no interest. And who have even less interest in me—the latest one, some girl from England, in fact, didn't even bother to turn up. So one way or another, it's rather spoiled my summer."

With that, Max turned on his polished heel and ploughed through the crowds. Barney stared after him, ablaze with excitement. How could he not have realized? Once you put two and two together, it was obvious.

Alexa, and by extension Florrie, had not been talking rubbish after all. Maxim was the prince being prevailed upon to marry. Here was a golden opportunity; Alexa, of course, was currently exploring another. But wasn't that golden opportunities all over? You waited ages for one, then two came along at once.

Barney decided Alexa had to jump horses midrace. However successful she was being—presumably at this moment—with Bigski, her installation as wife apparent would not be immediate. A period of consolidation would be necessary, and it would be complicated.

Snaring Max would be so much simpler. There would be no wife to get rid of—if indeed Mrs. Bigski *could* be got rid of; what was more, there would be a chateau, a title, a crown. So much more glamorous than some shady Russian fortune, and of course infinitely more prestigious. Barney could see himself, morning-suited in the front row of the royal wedding, waiting for the bride—his closest friend—to roll up in her carriage.

He had to find Alexa with all speed. She might be in bed with Bigski somewhere, but there was a much greater and easier chance out here, and she was missing it!

Barney felt sweaty with panic. Of course they could always call on Maxim in Sedona. But appearing at the chateau gate like any old tourist was an infinitely more demeaning way to meet him than at a party on equal ground. Max might refuse to see them anyway; Barney, who for all his ambition was realistic, was under no illusions as to the lack of esteem in which he was held by his royal acquaintance.

Maxim's dark head, a good foot above the rest of the crowd, was at the other side of the room now, almost at the double doors of the exit. Barney made a half-hearted dash after him, although what he planned to say or do, he had for once no clear idea.

Indeed, for someone so customarily cool-headed, he was all panic and indecision, as he saw the greatest chance of his conniving life slipping through his fingers. He pressed on, forging his path through the crowd with sharp little jabs of the elbow, straining to keep track of the dark head of the Prince. He had little interest in who he shoved aside, which was why, when he came up against a particularly difficult-to-dislodge figure, he did not immediately recognize who it was.

"Bloody hell, Barney," snapped Alexa crossly. "Just watch who you're pushing out of the way, will you?"

Chapter Fifty-Three

THE FEW MINUTES THAT had just elapsed had not been the best of Alexa's life. One minute she had been prostrate beneath the powerful thrusts of a panting billionaire. The next all hell had broken loose as Mrs. Bigski burst into the room, eyes straining from their skull sockets, and pointed a pearl-handled gun at her husband. It was at that moment that Alexa realized she had underestimated her rival.

She remembered with terror what Barney had said about her never walking again after this party. Kneecapping would be the least of it; shooting her dead would be the work of a second, and another few minutes would see her stowed below, ready to be consigned to the deep the next time *The Big One* sailed out for the day.

Those who go down to the sea in ships… The words slipped into her head from nowhere. Weren't they—or something similar—used at sailors' funerals?

As Bigski, suddenly not very big in any sense, leaped off her, shot over to the far wall, and huddled, whimpering, with his face buried in the curtains, Alexa realized that the business of being an oligarch's mistress, let alone his wife, was a more complicated matter than it had first appeared.

She was lying on a million dollars in the master bedroom of a luxury yacht while a crazed-looking woman dripping in diamonds trained a lethal weapon right between her eyes. Situations didn't come much more complicated than that.

As neither Mr. nor Mrs. Bigski had moved—the latter, in particular, seemed undecided what to do next—Alexa seized the initiative. She raised herself, heart hammering, onto her knees, before the gunwoman. "Please don't kill me," she begged histrionically.

"Kill *you*!" Mrs. Bigski spat, waving her pistol. "You're not worth it!"

Alexa did not need telling twice. She grabbed her dress and shot out of the room without a backward glance.

"You scum! You trash!" Mrs. Bigski shrieked after her, although she might have been addressing her husband, who, when Alexa left, was still on his knees at the bedside, sobbing.

Alexa shot down the corridor to find a loo to change in. She repaired herself as hurriedly as possible, then went to find Barney.

"Bad news, I'm afraid," she told him. But why was he staring at her as if she were the winning ticket for the National Lottery multimillion-pound rollover jackpot? She had failed in her quest, after all.

Barney sprang into action. "Bad news! On the contrary! It's the very best!" He was almost shoving her through the crowds. Alexa was amazed; it was very unlike Barney to leave the scene of so much free champagne.

But here he was, physically pushing her down the corridor. "Why have you got money stuck to your back?" he asked.

They had reached the shoe basket and she had to concentrate to get hers back on. The girl in charge seemed familiar with that particular model, however, and inserted her deftly.

"You've seen these before?" Alexa asked in surprise.

"All Mr. Bigski's ladies wear them," came the expressionless answer. "That dress, too."

Beside her, Barney was dancing about impatiently in his slip-on loafers. "Come on! Quick! He's about to get into his car!"

"Who is?" Alexa was staggering to her feet.

"Prince Maxim of Sedona!" Barney yelped. "Your future husband!"

"My…?"

"Heir to the Sedona throne, a chateau, a country, you name it." Barney's face was close to hers; his eyes were gleaming diabolically. "Congratulate me," he murmured. "I've managed to find him. The very same spare crown prince that dear old Florrie stood up."

Alexa's eyes were riveted to his. Her heart was thundering, the heat rushing around her veins.

"Where is he? *Where?*" Her growl was animal. Visceral. There was no question of her missing this chance.

Down on the quay, Jason Snort drummed his feet in their rubber Crocs. He was bored, as well as uncomfortably hot.

It was all very well for some, he thought, casting a bitter glance at the royal driver asleep in the air-conditioned comfort of the shining black limousine with the Sedona flag on the hood.

Jason had initially tried to chat with him, get some inside info. But as always with Sedona chateau staff, he had got nowhere. The driver knew nothing about a possible new candidate for crown princess. Perhaps those rumors about Maxim's sexuality were true, Jason thought, before remembering that he had started the rumors himself.

Alexa was stumbling after Barney. Sheer determination, a stronger force than mere gravity, alone kept her upright. She could see her quarry now. He was stepping onto the quayside: tall, dark, and handsome in black tie.

Barney was ahead of her, racing down the gangway at a speed she had no idea he was capable of. "Maxim!" he was shouting. "*Maxim!*"

❖❖❖

From his position on the quayside, large hands planted on huge knees, Jason Snort looked up. High up the dazzling, almost blinding walls of the boat, someone was shouting. Snort squinted. A small bloke. Sounded English. A nobody; at least, nobody Snort recognized. The person he seemed to be shouting at was all too familiar, however. Prince Maxim.

❖❖❖

Alexa felt the breath knocked suddenly out of her. Unaccountably, and just before she could reach her longed-for goal, Barney had come to a dead halt. Unable to stop in her shoes, Alexa cannoned into the linen jacket; rebounding violently backward, she grabbed the rails on either side. They felt flimsy and as if they might give way any moment. Below her, the silver water, pooled with swirls of oil, gleamed greasily.

"Let me past!" She hammered desperately on Barney's back. "Get the fuck out of the way!"

"There's a paparazzo down there," Barney hissed. He half turned, his eyes still trained manically on the quayside. "Here's your chance. Milk the publicity! Snog him!"

He stood aside and let Alexa hurtle past like a greyhound out of a trap, albeit a greyhound waving its arms, tossing its hair and shouting, "Maxim! Darling! Wait for me, you naughty, naughty boy!"

❖❖❖

Snort whistled under his breath as the woman hurried, yelling, down the gangway. Legs, check. Long hair, check. Tiniest dress he had ever seen, check; matched with the biggest heels, check. And, the biggest check of all, she was with Prince Maxim.

"Naughty Maxim! Wait for Alexa!"

Jason could hardly believe his ears. *Naughty!* Sedona's dull-as-ditchwater Crown Prince? The paparazzo's blood was not so much up as crashing through him in a wave. In one well-practiced movement, he was on his big red feet, fingers covering the well-worn button on top of his camera.

"Maxim!" screamed Alexa. "Maxi, darling. Not so fast! Wait for me!"

The chauffeur was asleep, Max saw as he descended the gangway. For the first time he regretted the fact that Sedona royalty routinely went everywhere without bodyguards. There had never been thought to be a need.

Then something grabbed him. Something was suddenly strangling him. Something was on his back.

"Hey! Get off!"

What was happening? Arms were being wound tightly around his neck. Some woman's face was being pushed into his.

"What are you doing?" Max was almost too amazed to be frightened. Was this an assassination? She didn't look like a hit man; looming at him was long dark hair, thickly plastered lipstick, and so much mascara it looked like a row of bees' legs. He tried to pull away as the lips now firmly stuck themselves to his.

Alongside the sound of his own struggles, Max could hear the whirring and clicking of a camera.

"Let me go!" he gasped, as his attacker ground her breasts against him. Then he felt her take one of his hands and place it on her bottom.

Jason pumped his button, his heart dancing. This was better than anything he had ever dreamt of.

Chapter Fifty-Four

As the bus had roared off into the distance, Polly's first instinct had been to run after it, screaming in fury. They had been tricked. Their bus had been hijacked. How was she to reach Max now? Her traveling companions, on the other hand, were having difficulty understanding what had happened. The women with their tour guides and the men with their fanny packs and elasticated leisure trousers seemed to think the bus had rolled away somehow. What they were far more distressed about was that the King of Sedona in his outdoor hot tub was not, after all, visible from the roadside.

Polly could only fume and resent the hours being wasted. She could have been in Sedona now, could have gone to the palace and found Max. By now they could have been doing anything…well, one thing in particular. She closed her eyes longingly.

Things had improved once the rescue coach summoned by the bus driver swung into view around the corner; this, however, turned out not only to be more badly ventilated than the first, but to be taking them all back to Nice. Nice! Despite all her protests, she got nowhere; Sedona, it seemed, would have to wait for another day. Slumped angrily in the backseat, Polly had chewed her nails and burnt with the heat, as well as the frustration of being so near to Max. And yet so far away.

She had taken the first available bus the next morning, and was now, finally, incontrovertibly, unhijackably, here.

Arriving in Sedona Old Town, she found, wasn't so much like stepping back in time as striding backward over millennia. There were no outskirts; everything was within the thick encircling city wall of pale stone and reached via the ancient shadowy archway that pierced it. It had a fairy-tale quality, a whisper of beauties in gowns and wimples, a suggestion of handsome knights in armor.

She walked on, enchanted, through ice-cream-colored streets, past window ledges brimming with bright splashes of geranium, by fountained courtyards where water splashed in the light.

Searching for the Palace, she came to what seemed to be the edge of the town. There was a park here, long and narrow, where smooth walks led past flower beds thick with pink roses, heads heavy with marbled petals, each a scoop of raspberry ripple particularly generous on the sauce. Did the park lead to the castle? It seemed likely. The flower beds alternated with bronzes of mustachioed men in uniform; all called Maxim or Engelbert, Polly saw, pausing. Relatives, no doubt, although she could see little family resemblance in their short, thickset frames.

It would not be long now. She walked on, picturing herself in the chateau, waiting by the fireplace in an echoing vaulted hall; Max running toward her down a sweeping flight of stairs.

She pressed on through the park. The neat red trunks of pines thrust upward either side of her, their green umbrella tops providing an unbroken sequence of shade. Between them stretched an expanse of sea, ruched, glittering, and a heavenly deep blue—a mermaid's party cloak. The sighing of the breeze in the pine canopy was sensuous and soothing; there was a faint scent, a sharp, salty whiff of herbs and sea.

What a wonderful place Max lived in. She had never expected anything like this. And yet despair and impatience were starting to twist within her. Where was the chateau?

Le chateau royal. A small black and gold sign pointed back into the town. Polly followed it along a passage of tempting, glossy shops: bags, shoes, a toy emporium selling child-sized pink tin racing cars of vintage design, an art gallery with what seemed real grass as carpet. She allowed herself one stop only, at a souvenir shop with postcards of the royal family outside. Just to check, after all, that she had not been dreaming.

No, here was Max all right, slightly resentful in his official uniform, a hint of exasperation in his dark eyes. Polly looked with interest at the rest of the family. The Queen, sitting with her ankles crossed in a gold-framed armchair, sweet-faced and Grace Kelly glamorous in a pale blue dress and pearls. The King, she thought, looked squat and pompous. Polly had no doubt which one of them was forcing Max to marry.

And this, presumably, was Max's brother. Polly stared into the laughing face of the blond young Prince Giacomo. Her first impression was how entirely unlike Max he looked. Her second was how closely he resembled the boy who had hijacked the bus. But that, of course, was impossible.

A noise—a blare and a thump. Hurrying along the passage into the full blaze of a cobbled sunlit square, Polly found the castle and the source of the sound simultaneously. The band marched up and down, all gleaming breastplates, whirling pompoms and parping brass. Behind it stood Max's home.

It was bigger than she had imagined—a huge fortress of the same pale stone as the rest of Sedona, and just as fairy-tale, with pointed towers like stone pencils, flags, turrets, carved escutcheons, and heraldic beasts. A setting for a magical story. Would it be her story?

She glanced up at the windows glinting in the sunlight. Was Max behind one of them?

She drew a deep, excited breath and strode confidently up to the first of the two white sentry boxes positioned either side of the great gates. "I've come to see Prince Maxim," she explained to the soldier within, a vision in pale blue, gold buttons, and tight white trousers.

She was delighted as the soldier raised his chin and saluted. Saluting seemed an excellent start.

"Name?" barked the soldier.

"Polly Stevenson."

The soldier consulted a list. "You're not expected."

"I know I'm not expected." Polly smiled. "I'm a…friend. I just happened to be passing."

The soldier looked at her doubtfully. "Members of the royal family are unavailable to casual callers."

Polly felt suddenly desperate. That admittance to the chateau might be difficult had never occurred to her.

"Please," she said, pleadingly.

"You must have authorization," the soldier said sternly.

"So how do I get that?"

"The normal procedure for an audience with His Royal Highness, or any other member of the royal family, is to put any such request in handwriting in triplicate."

"In *triplicate*?"

The soldier bowed his plumed helmet in affirmation. "In triplicate, yes. Twelve months in advance of the desired date."

Polly felt her grip on her temper loosening. "And I suppose it then gets put on a silver salver and handed to the first footman, who puts it on another salver and hands it to the second footman, who hands it to the third, who hands it to His Majesty?"

"Exactly that, yes," the soldier said mildly. "After which, you may, following the appropriate pause, take up the inquiry with His Majesty's private secretary."

"Thank you," Polly said tightly, before turning and walking disconsolately away. There was obviously no point arguing.

The heat beat down. The band thumped on. Polly's head was starting to ache, and hope was draining from her. Max might be within the chateau, but she remained very much outside. And going by official channels, she would be unable to see him for twelve months.

The main square was marked at the four corners by four large cannon mounted on wheels. Polly leaned against the nearest one in despair.

After a number of deep, fortifying breaths, she forced herself to think carefully through the options. Were there any? How was she to get in? Fairy-tale though it looked, the chateau was nonetheless a castle. Strong, ancient, and thick-walled, it had been built to protect the inmates and repel invaders.

She passed the chateau gates again and stood for some minutes looking up at the façade, willing Max to come to a window.

The soldier from the other sentry box stepped forward. "Move along, mademoiselle."

A blaze of fury possessed Polly. All right, then. If they persisted in treating her like a criminal, she'd behave like one. Think like one. Were there, she wondered, any breaches in the fortifications? It seemed unlikely. A high, thick wall began where the gates stopped.

Polly followed the wall until it turned to form the side of a narrow, shady alley. She followed it down; the alley turned again and led through a wide archway into a large, sunny cobbled court-yard. The back of the building, the service quarters, Polly realized, just as a large bright blue van roared into the yard and drew to a screeching halt.

Doors banged; two men in blue overalls sprang out. "We've brought the laundry," one of them called to Polly. "Here, come and help us get it out."

I don't work here, Polly was about to say before experiencing a flash of revelation and hurrying over. Minutes later, her arms piled so high with snowy cotton that her face could not be seen, she was following the two men in blue overalls into the chateau.

She kept her head down and her eyes on the blue trouser bottoms of the van men. The first room they came into sounded big and bustling; Polly's empty stomach surged at the smell of coffee and bacon and eggs. It was evidently breakfast time in the castle.

There were people about; hellos were exchanged, but no one asked the men, presumably a regular sight, their business. They passed on, with Polly following, into another room with a tiled floor. It was shady and very warm and there was a clean smell of soap powder. Drying racks hung from the roof; the walls were lined with slatted wooden shelves. This, evidently, was the castle laundry.

The men, muttering to each other, loaded their piles of sheets onto the shelves. Then, nodding to Polly, they left.

She remained in the laundry, smoothing the top of the sheet pile over and over again, as she reflected on her enormous luck. She was in! She had penetrated the mighty defenses of the chateau. Now, to find Maxim.

Chapter Fifty-Five

THE PALACE BREAKFAST ROOM looked much as usual when Max, Beano limping gamely at his heels, entered it. The big French windows, as was normal at this time of year, were open to the breathtaking panorama of mountains sweeping down to a distant sea. Brightness and air poured into the pretty white and gold chamber.

The King and Queen, sitting at the oval table by the window, looked up in surprise. Max shrugged; admittedly, he had not breakfasted with the family for some time. He had started to wonder, however, whether cooperation with the authorities, at meal times at least, might achieve a better result than continuing resistance. He planned also to capitalize on the fact that he had, as requested, spent the previous evening at Bigski's party. Would he mention the mad woman at the end? Max was not sure. It might worry his mother, and no harm had been done. The girl was obviously insane. She had vanished into the darkness as suddenly as she had appeared. Homeward bound in the cozy darkness of the purring royal car, Max had gradually downgraded his levels of alarm. By the time he reached the chateau, he thought of his assailant more in sorrow than in anger. She clearly needed professional help.

The King and Queen were dressed for the official duties that would make up their day; the King in a suit, the Queen with her usual smooth chignon and in a mint-green sleeveless dress. She was smiling at Max, but her smile looked a little uncertain. "You look exhausted," she said.

The King made a noise that sounded oddly snigger-like. Max ignored it, however; he was thinking and acting positively.

"I'm fine," he said brightly, although exhausted was exactly what he was. After the drama of the party, Beano had not been well again and Max had spent much of the night soothing him.

He was more tired than he thought, Max realized. So tired he was starting to see things. For example, the newspapers his parents were looking at, the front pages of which were turned toward him, seemed to be dominated by a large photograph of someone who looked amazingly like himself. Kissing a dark-haired girl.

It was with a plunge of pure horror that the Crown Prince realized it was no trick of the imagination.

He leaped forward and grabbed the newspaper with shaking hands. The photograph really was of him with the madwoman who had assaulted him on the yacht.

He stared, transfixed, at the headline. *Our Future Queen?* demanded *The Sedonan.* Hot and cold waves of horror coursed through his body. He remembered, as he'd writhed to get free of her grasp, the flashing and whirring of a camera, but had not connected the two events.

That kiss! He looked as if he were devouring the woman. But it had been the other way around; she had hurled herself at him, wrapping every limb about his body, wrenching his head down so his lips met hers.

Max fought the overwhelming urge to run screaming from the room. "It's not how it looks," he gasped. "She was a mad person."

"Mad person? That's not very chivalrous," the King remarked placidly.

His father actually looked pleased, Max noticed. But how could he be?

"You don't understand." Max stared desperately at his parents. "I don't know who took that picture. Or why. I don't know who that woman is either. She just appeared when I was getting off Bigski's boat. Sort of launched herself at me."

His father was still smiling, however. "You hadn't drunk too much?" he suggested skittishly.

"Of course not," Max snapped. "That's Giacomo's territory."

Astrid did not defend her second son. Instead she said, "This girl in the pictures. She's apparently very respectable."

"She wasn't acting very respectably," Max growled.

"She's Lady Alexa MacDonald. Of that Ilk," the Queen added.

"Hippolyte knows all about her," the King chimed in blithely. "According to him, the phones have been ringing off the hook in the press office. It's a news sensation, exactly the sort of thing Sedona needs. Everybody wants to know about you and her."

"There's nothing *to* know!" Max cried. Beano, at his feet, gave a warning growl.

The breakfast room door now opened and Giacomo wandered in, his handsome, sleepy face showing all the signs of an exceedingly late night. His expression altered abruptly when he spotted the newspapers. "Hey, bro," he exclaimed, snatching up one and scanning the front cover. "Good going."

"It wasn't how it looks," Max shouted.

"They all say that," Giacomo drawled, flipping back a shining blond lock of hair. "I'm always saying it myself." He read the report out loud. "After an assignation on a luxury yacht, the besotted Prince sealed his love with a passionate kiss…"

"But I wasn't! I didn't!" Max yelled.

Beano started to bark.

"Shut up!" snapped Engelbert.

Beano looked up at his master with an indignant expression. But

Max, usually lightning-quick to defend his pet, was too preoccupied to notice.

"Hey, what's the problem?" Giacomo grinned. "She looks hot. Well," he allowed, "not bad, anyway."

"A charming girl." The King sniffed, twitching his mustache from side to side. "Hippolyte says she is very well connected at the English court. An aristocrat, no less," he added, his voice lingering over the magic word.

Unseen, the Queen made a slight moue at this. Privately she wondered if well-brought-up girls got themselves photographed kissing passionately on the front pages of newspapers. But perhaps she was being old-fashioned. Engelbert had been delighted that a pretty and, apparently, well-connected girl, to whom Max was clearly attracted, had appeared on the scene.

And yet Max's reaction seemed one of genuine horror. That he would deny all knowledge of it, she had been warned to expect. Yet there was defensive and *defensive*, Astrid thought, and Max's reaction was beyond anything she had anticipated.

Engelbert had sidled up to his son. "Nothing to be ashamed of," he said with a smirk, elbowing Max in the side in jocular fashion. "We all have to sow our wild oats."

Pretending she had not heard, Astrid fiddled with her linen napkin.

Max rounded on his father, eyes sparking with anger and frustration. "Wild oats have nothing to do with it," he cried.

There was a knock; Monsieur Hippolyte entered. His hair was carefully arranged in its usual determinedly black bouffant and his brown face—curiously smooth for his age—was wreathed in smiles. "Very positive press coverage, your Royal Highness," he remarked, bowing in Maxim's direction. "May I offer my congratulations?"

"There's nothing to congratulate me about," the Crown Prince snapped.

Monsieur Hippolyte's round eyes met the King's and they exchanged an understanding smile. "Of course. It's early days," the private secretary said. "There are, to put it mildly, quite a number of newspapers interested in this story, but I'll tell them all no comment, shall I?"

As Hippolyte bowed and withdrew, Maxim turned in despair to his mother. "It's not early days, Mum. It's not 'no comment.' It's not anything."

Astrid looked back at him helplessly, wondering what to think. Suddenly it did not seem at all clear.

Chapter Fifty-Six

IT WAS MORE THAN clear to the King, however.

"Be sensible," he urged his son. His voice was reasonable and friendly. "She looks like good breeding stock, this girl."

To Max it seemed as if everything stood absolutely still. He felt suddenly very cold, despite the summer morning. "You're not..." His teeth were chattering in his skull. "You're not suggesting...I should *marry* this woman?"

"Why not?" The King threw open his arms expansively. "You obviously like her."

"As I've already said, I've never met her before," Max growled beneath knitted brows. "I don't know her."

"Oh well, if you say so," the King said disbelievingly. "But, look, why *don't* you marry her? You have to marry someone, it's your duty, and this woman will do as well as anyone. Bird in the hand, and quite a bird too, eh?" He chuckled at his son and nudged him. "Eh?"

Astrid, who had been listening with growing concern, now interrupted. "But, my dear. Surely it's rather early to be talking in terms of marriage? We really don't know a great deal about her."

"Of course we do!" Engelbert riposted. "We've seen that website, haven't we? The family home is a wonderful chateau in Scotland, and there are photographs of her with practically every crowned head in Europe."

Max said nothing. A feeling of unreality was stealing over him.

He had not imagined that his situation could get worse or more complicated, but it seemed he had imagined wrong.

"You don't have to love or even like her," Engelbert was continuing blithely. "A royal marriage, it's just an accommodation. A piece of business, essentially," he went on happily, oblivious to the steam emerging from the Queen's ears. Then, responding to the urgent face-pulling of his younger son, he seemed suddenly to remember himself. "Except in our case, of course, my dear," he added hurriedly, reaching for his wife's hand.

The Queen snatched her fingers away and stood up. "Excuse me," she said in strangled tones, flinging her napkin on the table.

Max met his father's gaze steadfastly. "Even if I did agree with you, which I don't, it's not a piece of business I can do. When I marry, I marry for love."

His saw his mother, heading for the door, pause at his words. Then she turned, her eyes for the first time fixed on his, full of an expression he could not read.

The King, meanwhile, was bristling with outrage. "Lady Alexa MacDonald of that ilk is a suitable person for you to marry," he rapped out suddenly.

"Don't be ridiculous," Max said quietly.

"She is very presentable and very well connected."

"She's also insane," Max retaliated.

"De Sedonas have married plenty of mad people in the past," the King pointed out. "There's rather a history of it, in fact."

"I won't marry her." Maxim raised his eyes to his father's. Again he had the sensation of the world holding its breath. There was a loud thudding noise, which he realized was his heart.

A heavy silence followed, which was interrupted by Giacomo.

"Will I have to wear a top hat at this wedding?" he asked suspiciously as the dread possibility occurred to him.

"At the very least," said the King drily.

"What's the date?" Giacomo demanded. Ages off, hopefully. Time enough for him to be somewhere else altogether when Maxim went up the aisle. Just not another branch of the bloody military, though. Was space an option? The first royal in space—now that would be cool.

Chapter Fifty-Seven

MAX RAN DOWN THE passageway from the breakfast room as if wild beasts were pursuing him. Which in a sense they were; snarling heraldic creatures leaped on flags and devices the full length of the corridor. The only actual creature on his trail, however, was a Beano ripped untimely from some bacon Giacomo had slipped him and limping determinedly to keep up.

Max was clutching his head with one hand; in the other he grasped the fateful newspaper. Playing and replaying in his mind was the very end to the morning's scene. "What if there's someone else?" he had demanded of his father out of desperation.

"Who else?" his mother had asked sharply from where she stood by the door.

"No one in particular," he had muttered, depressingly aware that it was all too true. Polly would have given up on him ages ago.

"Someone else? Not a problem," the King had responded cheerfully.

"Not a problem?" For a moment Max's heart had lifted. Birds sang, sweet melodies swirled in the scented air. He felt unsteady with relief.

"Not at all," boomed the King delightedly. "Once you've married this Alexa woman, any other totty can be your mistress."

Max had snatched up the nearest newspaper and slammed out of the room. He would go back to his rooms and hide under his duvet, in darkness as black as his future.

Polly, meanwhile, was finding her way around the chateau corridors. From the stone-flagged lower passages she had proceeded upward and was now negotiating long, creaking corridors. They smelt of polish and were lined with red carpet and had vaulted ceilings. The walls were covered with white panelling, interspersed with wide white doors with golden handles. Was one of them Max's?

At first she had tensed in fear whenever she passed another person, but she had gradually learned to relax. With the pile of linen in her arms, no one stopped her; no one asked her anything. Should she, Polly wondered, push her luck and ask for directions to Prince Maxim's room? But places like this were full of protocol; something about the manner in which she asked it, or that she asked it at all, might betray her.

Growing within was the depressing realization that she could wander around here forever. Having got to Sedona despite the hijacking, having gained the castle despite the guards, was she now to fail because of interior geography?

A large staircase loomed at the end of the passage. Polly paused when she reached it. Up or down? Her whole future could depend on it.

Max had almost reached his room now. He felt twisted with anger and, now, guilt. Poor Beano, he realized, had had a devil of a time keeping up. As he approached the double doors of his suite, he stooped and picked up his pet. "Nearly there now, boy."

Polly, coming up the stairs, heard his voice. She scrambled to the top and dashed around the bend, only to tangle her foot in a ruched piece of carpet and come crashing down at his feet.

Max, his dog in his arms, turned at the commotion. Some poor laundry maid had fallen over with the sheets. He shoved the newspaper under his arm, put Beano down and sprang toward her. "Here, let me help you up."

She rolled over, turned her face upward—and burst out laughing. "Surprise!"

"Polly?"

He really had gone mad, Max thought. Lost it completely now. Against the red carpet she appeared as a vision. He had forgotten how beautiful she was. How adorable her freckles were and the tilt of her nose, how full and pink her lips, how thick the fringes of her eyelashes. Only her hair was exactly as he recalled it, the soft brown of bracken on an English moorland, or of autumn fields after ploughing.

She scrambled to her knees and was looking in delight at his dog. "This must be Beano! He's adorable!"

The spaniel ambled over slowly and started to lick her hand. "He likes me!"

"That makes two of us," Max said shakily, pulling her up to standing, still not entirely certain that it wasn't all a dream.

Her eyes searched his. "Are you all right? I've been so worried about you."

He hung his head. "I'm sorry."

"So you should be," Polly said sternly. "It was awful, you running away like that. I was worried that something really terrible had happened. But then I found out." She stopped; he was pulling her into his arms and kissing her.

"We'll talk about all that later," he muttered, holding her to him with one hand, opening his room door behind him with the other.

The ceiling above Polly was a whirl of gold and white. He was carrying her across the room. The ceiling became the pleated canopy of a four-poster bed. Gently he laid her among its unmade and rumpled sheets.

"Oh, Polly." He clung to her as if she were a rock in a rushing river and he were a drowning man. "I've missed you so much." He kissed her eyes, mouth, and neck. There was, for the moment at least, nothing more to say.

❖ ❖ ❖

"Why didn't you tell me?" she asked afterward. "Your Royal Highness," she added, snorting.

"I just wanted you to think I was normal."

"Normal!" Polly smiled. "Most people want to be extraordinary. Rich, famous, whatever."

"Not me." Max shook his head slowly. "Normal's great. Normal will do."

His brain was churning, making plans. She was here, she still loved him; he must act. He had now both the reason and the courage to defy his parents. He rose on his elbows, resolved. There was no better time than now. They might still be in the breakfast room…

Polly stretched luxuriously and turned on her side. Lying on the carpet beside the bed was a crumpled newspaper. Her gaze glided idly over it, taking nothing in, but then something yanked her attention back. A pair of eyes in a photograph. A pair of eyes she knew.

It was in her hands in a second. She gazed, frozen.

Our Future Queen? screamed the headline. *Crown Prince Maxim de Sedona passionately embraces his mystery love.*

A woman who, in the cruelest, most appalling, and unlikely twist of fate, looked exactly, horribly, absolutely like…Allison Donald.

All the delight within her curdled to acid. Max. With an Allison Donald-alike. It couldn't be possible.

"Polly?" Max had heard her gasp. "Polly? What is it?"

There was a thick silence around her ears through which only the doomy thudding of her heart penetrated. She had come all this way. Left her job. Oh God, how stupid. How utterly gullible and stupid.

"Polly! What's wrong?" She had leaped up from the bed and was running across the room.

A puzzled Beano had started to bark. What had made the friendly lady so cross?

Max had seen the paper now. He leaped after her. "Please," he howled. "Come back. It's not what it seems."

How many more times would he say that this morning?

Polly, now at the door, turned. "Makes two of you, then," she wrenched out bitterly.

As she blundered, stunned and tearful, along the corridors, Polly walked directly into someone.

"Hey, gorgeous," the someone said in a tone of ardent appreciation. "What's upset a beautiful girl like you? Why don't you stop and tell your Uncle Jack all about it?"

She found herself staring into the amused face of Prince Giacomo. She recognized him immediately from the postcard, but more than that—there was no doubt about it now—from the hijack too. In the flesh it was more obvious; his good looks, yes, but beyond that, the ineffable self-satisfaction she remembered, the obvious belief that the whole world admired and adored him.

Prince Giacomo clearly felt he could treat people however he liked and get away with it.

It was a trait he shared with his brother.

"I'm sure I could think of something to make you feel better," he added suggestively.

Polly had not imagined she could feel any angrier, but a further surge of fury now swamped her. She raised her hand and slapped the startled Prince hard across the cheek. "That's for the bus passengers," she snapped before stalking off down the corridor.

Chapter Fifty-Eight

"TRAP SPRUNG. CONGRATULATIONS TO US," Barney had said that morning on the balcony of the Monaco flat. He had said more, but a helicopter taking off immediately behind had drowned out his words. Even that, though, could not drown the words printed on the front pages of the newspapers all around their feet.

"...now we can move from this bloody place," Barney had added as the noise died down.

And so, that afternoon, ensconced in the best available suite at the Hotel des Bains, Alexa sipped a glass of chilled champagne and soaked in a vast scented bath. Afterward she climbed into the high, soft white bed, sipped yet more champagne, and inhaled the delicious scent of the many perfumed candles scattered about. She glanced constantly at the newspaper pictures, spread on the bed's snowy surface, of herself apparently being kissed passionately by a prince, and tried to feel as exultant as she knew she ought.

After all the effort and excitement, she was exhausted. But it was more than that. She was also worried. Unlike the bumptious Barney, she felt far from certain about what happened next. She was on the front pages, but what now?

Her suite door opened and Barney appeared, wrapped in a dazzling white bathrobe. He looked, Alexa thought, like a little pink pig, slightly sweaty and steaming. Welded to his hand was his own glass of champagne; like her, he had been drinking it nonstop since the newspapers had come out.

He looked at her triumphantly and raised the glass. "Here's to us!"

"What's next, Barney?"

"Next?" Barney repeated with amused incredulity. "*Next?* Obvious, I would have thought."

"Not to me."

He raised an eyebrow. "Not losing our nerve, I hope?"

"Course not," Alexa snapped. "Just wondered what the plan was, that's all."

Barney took another swig from his glass. "The plan is that we go to the chateau, stake our claim. Consolidate our position, press home our advantage," he added, like a thesaurus.

"Might be tricky," Alexa pointed out gloomily. "What if Maxim's there and says he's never seen me before in his life?"

"He won't," Barney said assuredly.

"What makes you so confident?" Although Barney, of course, was always confident.

Reaching into a minibar that was anything but mini, Barney extracted another bottle of champagne and popped it open.

"Because," he said, flashing her a delighted grin, "we have a friend in high places."

"Do we?"

Barney sat on the edge of the bed. "Yes. Chap I met down at Madame Whiplash the other night." His expression struck her as a peculiar mixture of triumph and shiftiness.

"What?" Alexa exclaimed in disgust. "Some old leather queen who likes a good spanking...oh, sorry, Barney. No offense."

"None taken," Barney said slightly huffily. "But since you put it like that," he added, raising his head, "then yes, an old leather queen who likes a good spanking and who has"—he paused for effect—"*royal connections* is in a prime position to help us get what we want."

Alexa's hands were pressed against the mattress, forcing herself up in excitement. "Not...the King!"

Barney chuckled. "No, although it wouldn't be unknown. Some kings have *very* kinky tastes. But no. This old leather queen isn't the actual monarch."

"So who?" Alexa had sunk back against the pillows.

"All in good time, my dear." Barney was examining his polished fingernails complacently. "So I met him at Madame Whiplash. Very meaty boy. Nervous, but warmed up in the end. Said he was called Henri, but it turns out he's actually Jacques Hippolyte. Private secretary to the King of Sedona, no less."

"Really?" Alexa had shot upright again. She was starting to feel dizzy, especially given all the champagne.

"That's right." Barney grinned. "There was a tiny picture of him in the paper, behind the royal family. He looked different without his leather executioner's mask, admittedly. But I lost no time in calling him."

"What did he say?"

Barney took another long draw on his glass. "He thought the pictures were absolutely kosher and that you'd really met the Prince at the party. I had to explain that there'd been a little artifice and that there might be a spot of resistance. He then got worried about what to do when the Prince said you'd attacked him and he'd never seen you before in his life."

"And?" Alexa demanded from the bed.

"Simple!" Barney was gamboling about the carpet. "I told him to tell the King and Queen that you two had been having an affair for some time. But that the obsessively secretive Prince's first line of defense would be to deny it."

Alexa rolled her eyes. "But no one's going to believe that," she wailed.

There was an expression of self-satisfaction in Barney's blue eyes. "Aha, but they will. My friend Jacques reckons the King's so desperate he'll believe anything. And if he does, the Queen will too."

"But—" Alexa tried to interrupt. Barney held up his plump little palm.

"No buts," he said lightly. "Jacques has a big incentive to make the story work. Otherwise, his august employer gets to know all about his naughty tastes."

"Blackmail!" She felt a kind of thrill. Barney's utter ruthlessness was compelling.

"Quite so!" Barney was as relaxed and carefree as if he was planning a picnic. He was clearly enjoying himself immensely, and Alexa could not help but admire his nerve.

"And I've worked out another little plan with him," he now announced. "You're going to make a visit to the chateau!"

"The chateau?"

"Yes. Meet the folks."

"The King and Queen, you mean?"

"Well, who else?" Barney drawled. "You have to meet them. They'll be your parents-in-law."

Alexa closed her eyes. Images of crowns and thrones reeled through her mind. Could Barney really make it happen? She looked at him in awe. From Florrie's kitchen—to this. They had come a long way.

"Henri—I mean Hippolyte—will get the paps there," Barney was continuing. "They'll take pictures of you, and the story will keep going."

Javelins of triumph shot through Alexa. "I could be a princess!" She imagined Lady Annabel's furious face.

"Could?" Barney looked stern. "*Will.*"

Chapter Fifty-Nine

THE QUEEN'S SITTING ROOM commanded the best view of the gardens of any room in the chateau. A pair of fine white gauze inner curtains fluttered gently about Astrid as she sat on her little balcony gazing down at her rose garden.

Astrid was pleased with her roses. It was an exceptionally good year for blooms. The new assistant royal undergardener had been right in his view that the older bushes should be uprooted and new ones put in their place. "Keeps the stock vigorous," he claimed.

But Astrid's thoughts soon wandered to another, less happy subject. One with just as many thorns, but no blooms whatsoever.

She was now convinced that the proposed marriage to Lady Alexa was a terrible mistake. Everything about it felt wrong. Engelbert's unseemly rush for one thing, and Max's denial that he knew Alexa at all. And then the convoluted reasons Hippolyte claimed were behind this. Had Max really been seeing the woman for months? It seemed increasingly unlikely to the Queen.

But what could she do? Especially as, for his part, the King wanted the whole business concluded as soon as possible. A date had even been fixed for Lady Alexa to visit them at the chateau.

But who was Lady Alexa, anyway? Astrid felt increasingly suspicious about that too. Yet she could hardly launch her own investigation; it would take time, for one thing. And who would help her? Max was speaking to no one. Engelbert, for his part, hardly cared who she was anymore. He was happy with all the publicity and desperate for the economic boost a royal marriage would bring to Sedona. He also wanted to settle the succession. But did this justify forcing his son to do something he was obviously opposed to?

Something she had been forced to do herself long ago.

She pressed both hands to her eyes as the memory flooded back.

The recollections that, over the intervening years, she had almost buried seemed now more alive than they had ever been. The genie had escaped from the bottle—the only thing that had escaped, she reflected bitterly. That last night together, that most secret of meetings. In the morning she was to leave her parents' palace for Sedona and her marriage to Engelbert. He had climbed up the drainpipe and swung over the balcony into her room, like Romeo after Juliet. She had let him make love to her, knowing they would never see each other again.

Astrid pressed one long white hand against her forehead, as if to push away the pictures crowding in. That last evening when they had clung to each other, knowing that it would be the final one.

They could not know how final. Shortly afterward, he was dead, killed in a road accident in America. Astrid, the new Crown Princess of Sedona by then, had had to hide her grief in the alcoves and corners of the chateau. Allowing anyone to see how hysterically distraught she was would have provoked suspicion, as well as possibly endanger the baby, the new Crown Prince, that she was by then carrying.

If Astrid shut her eyes, she could see her student lover: tall, dark, handsome, and with those broad shoulders and deep-set eyes. That smile. But increasingly, she no longer needed to shut her eyes. Her lover was not dead. He lived again, through his son. She had given up the struggle to persuade herself that Max's lofty dark looks were a reference to an earlier, taller generation of de Sedonas. The point at which she had admitted defeat was when the determination to be a vet had surfaced. Her lover had been a medical student...

She made a final effort at devil's advocacy. Was the resemblance just a coincidence? And even if it wasn't, how could she prove it?

The evening sun spread golden over the white walls of her room and burnished the gilt to a rich blaze. Still she sat there, thinking. Eventually it sank behind the mountains, and as the yellow-coral sky deepened to lavender, the slender moon appeared.

Should she rock the royal boat? If he married Alexa, Maxim would become accustomed to his fate in time, just as she had to hers. He would adapt. He would have to make do, as she had. Perfect happiness was not a condition members of royal families should aspire to.

On the other hand, Alexa was not like Engelbert. Not in any way. He had become a good husband. Would Alexa become a good wife? Astrid felt she knew the answer to that.

Chapter Sixty

THE HOTEL'S RESTAURANT WAS magnificent, almost oppressively so, its painted ceiling busy with flowers and cupids and the business of supporting an enormous, glittering crystal chandelier. The cavorting deities on the mosaic floor were obscured at regular intervals by evenly spaced white-draped tables filled with silver, crystal, and fashionable diners. The walls were ablaze with gilt-framed mirrors intended to allow customers not only to check their appearance but also to spy on other diners unobserved.

As Alexa appeared at the door, there was a pause in the conversation. The faces behind the table candles swiveled in her direction. Well, let them look, she thought proudly. Let them remember the first time they ever saw the future Crown Princess of Sedona. The plan Barney had described to her this afternoon was audacious and even shocking. But precisely because of that, it had the promise of real success.

Alexa stood proudly, knowing she looked breathtaking in her perfect evening gown. It was new; she had treated herself as they moved from the apartment to the hotel. What did her credit card bills matter now?

The dress was absolutely black, long, and plain, perfectly cut to fit flatteringly closely and made of a rich, thick material somewhere between silk and satin. It was elegant, the furthest remove imaginable from her revealing outfit at Bigski's party. It was a dress fit for a princess.

Her shoes were—apart from the stunning six-inch platinum heel—as sober as the dress and even more expensive. With her hair high in an up-do fixed with a glittering pin Alexa felt every inch the royal. Probably more inches than Barney would have preferred. Beside her, he looked short but proud in his new black tie. The light of satisfied self-congratulation shone in his small blue eyes.

As she followed the fawning maître d' to a table, Alexa was suddenly stopped. A hand at the end of a gold silk arm had shot out and blocked her path.

"Alexa, isn't it?" The voice was unmistakable. No one else had quite the same supercilious iciness to their tone.

Alexa looked down at the set mahogany features; the lips clamped together and trembling with emotion. "Lady Annabel!" she exclaimed in a high voice unlike her own. "What a pleasant surprise!" She glanced at Florrie, who was sitting opposite yawning extravagantly. Then amazement shot into her violet-blue eyes.

"Omigod, it's you, Heirfix. Didn't recognize you in that get-up."

Alexa's every nerve was so singing with tension she could almost hear it. What would her hated enemy do? Stand on the chair and denounce her to the whole restaurant?

Her Ladyship's well-shaped lip curled. "I saw the newspapers," she spat. "Don't you think you're setting your scheming sights a *little* too high this time? Stealing the man intended for my daughter!"

She had, Alexa realized, mere seconds to save her entire future. Her devious brain whirred and clicked, searching desperately for a solution.

Florrie looked up from the iPad parked by her bread roll. "Omigod, calm down, Ma," she said vaguely. "I didn't want to marry him anyway. Heirfix"—she waved breezily at Alexa—"is welcome to him."

Lady Annabel ignored this. Her nostrils flared and she was almost visibly snorting. It seemed to Alexa she might any moment leap from her chair, dragging tablecloth, china, and crystal in her wake, and charge her like an enraged bull. "I will," she snarled, "be calling Their Majesties tomorrow morning to explain exactly who you are—or aren't."

Her mouth opening and shutting with terror, Alexa still sought the words to extricate herself from the greatest crisis of her career. Then something small, pink-skinned, and blue-eyed shimmered to her side.

"My dear Lady Annabel!" murmured Barney, kissing the redoubtable matron's hand, which, as it was not offered, he had had to bodily lift from the table and press to his lips.

Lady Annabel snatched it back and glared at him.

"You know Alexa's wonderful news, of course," Barney beamed. "She is to be married to Prince Maxim de Sedona!"

Lady Annabel's diamond-studded fist slammed hard on the snowy-white linen of the table. She glared up at them both. "*Marriage!* I didn't realize things had got that far!"

"Oh, yes," Barney twinkled merrily. "Alexa is meeting Their Majesties at the chateau the day after tomorrow."

"Never!" Her Ladyship's voice was so low and acid, Alexa felt it was burning her ears. "Not if *I've* got anything to do with it." Her brittle, tanned chest heaved violently up and down. "If you think I'm going to watch an imposter"—her eyes, brilliant with hate, turned on Alexa—"cheat my daughter out of a throne, you're very much mistaken."

Alexa felt her nerves about to snap. It took all her self-control to suppress the urge to scream hysterically. Barney, meanwhile, placed a reassuring—or was it controlling?—hand on his adversary's thin and somewhat crêpey brown arm. She shook his hand off as if it were a toad.

"Cheat, Lady Annabel?" Barney sounded both hurt and astonished. "Far from it. You see, Alexa was very much hoping that if—*when*," he corrected himself hurriedly, "the wedding comes to pass, your beautiful daughter Lady Florence"—given his short stature, the deep and chivalrous bow Barney now made in Florrie's direction caused him to disappear entirely from view for several seconds—"might do her the great honor of agreeing to be her bridesmaid."

Alexa's fingers crept to her ears to protect her from the explosion she felt certain would come. What was Barney thinking? He was risking everything.

She cast a frantic glance around the restaurant; amazingly, the other diners seemed unaware of the near-nuclear drama. Candles were burning steadily. Waiters in buttermilk jackets glided about bearing silver domes and trays.

Lady Annabel was ashen with anger beneath her tan. "*Bridesmaid?*" she repeated, in much the same manner as Lady Bracknell mentioned handbags. "Never!"

She stood up and towered over Barney in her bronze heels. "Lady Florence," she snarled, placing her face close to his, "is the daughter of an earl, descendant of a long and noble line. There is absolutely no possibility that she would ever—"

"Such a shame," Barney cut in smoothly. "Because of course Prince Maxim has a younger brother, Prince Giacomo, who at the moment remains unmarried and extremely eligible." He paused briefly. "And I'm sure Their Majesties would be only too delighted if someone as beautiful and socially elevated as Lady Florence were in the picture…" He let the rest of the sentence drift elegantly.

Lady Annabel coughed. She reached for her napkin.

Florrie, glancing up from her iPad, now piped up. "Jack, you mean?" she exclaimed, leaning over the table so excitedly that she knocked over a crystal water glass. "Omigod, Ma, he's gorgeous! Totally hot."

Lady Annabel's head was a blur as it twisted confusedly between Barney and her daughter. "You've *met* him?" she stuttered to Florrie.

"Yah, he's a fun guy. We hijacked a bus together."

"You...*what*?"

"Nevermind," Florrie said brightly. Then she added imploringly, "oh, Mumsie, *do* let me be a bridesmaid."

Barney laid his paw on Lady Annabel again, and this time it was not shaken off. "I think," he purred, "that you'll find it more than worth your while. Prince Giacomo is a prince, after all, and anyone he marries would bear the title of princess..."

The conflagration raging in Lady Annabel's eyes now finally died down. She turned to Barney and smiled. She turned to Alexa and did the same. And while the smile did not meet her eyes, it was friendlier than any Alexa had seen in living memory.

"I see," Lady Annabel murmured, "that congratulations are due."

Chapter Sixty-One

SHE HAD GONE; MAX had to accept it. He had lost her for the second time. If once was carelessness, twice was almost too much to bear. She had appeared like a miracle and left like a curse. A mere couple of hours and she had vanished as if she were a dream.

There was nothing he could do, no way he could trace her. Where she had been staying, which flight she had been on, how she had got into the castle even, he had no clue. Not that it would help if he did. She had left in the belief that he was in love with someone else, that he was going to marry them too.

And now he might have to. Lady Alexa was to make an official visit to the chateau two days from now. Where, no doubt, she would find Engelbert a pushover. Her scheming, it seemed, had got her everywhere.

And now, another bitter blow.

Max could no longer avoid the realization that his devoted hound was desperately ill. When Beano was sick in the night again, the Prince knew there was no option but to take him to Etienne. The diagnosis he could guess; verification, however, could come only from the vet's equipment.

The streets of Sedona were as clean and bright as usual, and busy as ever with browsing visitors and locals going about their business. As they greeted him, Max did his best to rise above his misery and smile back. It wasn't their fault, after all.

His path along the street had been so far unimpeded, but now someone appeared to block it. "Your Royal Highness!" Fear leaped in Max's chest—another lunatic? In his arms, Beano lifted his sick head and managed a weak growl.

"Your Royal Highness!" repeated the person. An ancient crone, Max saw, looking down about three feet below him. Stooped, dressed in black, with white hair in a bun and a tanned, wizened face. She was beaming at him toothlessly. He responded with a strained smile. He could not rush off. Duty—damn the word—forbade it. One of the unwritten rules of Sedona was that anyone could stop the royal family in the street if they had something particular to say to them. Accessibility was central to Engelbert and Astrid's monarchical style.

"When's it going to happen, then?" the crone cackled.

Beano tried now to yap; Max tried to soothe him. "What?" he asked reluctantly.

"You getting married." The crone's wagging finger reminded Max of a well-cooked sausage. "You got a lovely girl now," the old woman hectored, her cackling voice echoing horribly around the narrow, peaceful street. "Lady Alexa! Very nice. So when you going to name the day, then? Eh?"

It seemed to Max as if the whole of Sedona was listening. He muttered something polite, clutched the still-yapping Beano close, and hurried off as fast as he could.

❖ ❖ ❖

Etienne examined Beano immediately. He came out of the X-ray room, his face drawn with distress.

"Bad news, I'm afraid, my friend. There is a large tumor."

Max bowed his head. He had suspected as much. He met Etienne's sympathetic brown eyes. "There's no chance?"

The vet bit his lip and shook his head.

Irrationally, suddenly, Max remembered his first date with Polly.

It was moving, seeing the demonstration of a relationship like that. The love a person had for their pet, thousands of years ago.

Like you say, people aren't all that different. I'd probably want to be buried with my dog.

But Beano was going before him to the happy hunting ground. *May there be lots of tasty bits from the celestial kitchens*, Max bid his pet silently.

To Etienne he said, in as steady a voice as he could manage: "Well, you'd better do it then."

Almost the worst of it was that Beano loved Etienne. As the vet approached him, he stood up on his shaking legs and licked him, waving the tail that had once been so magnificently plume-like.

Etienne glanced at Max. "You want to stay?" He was filling up his syringe, and his voice was gruff with controlled emotion.

It was not a case of wanting, not exactly, Max thought wearily. "I'll stay," he said.

He saw Beano hold out his paw trustingly to Etienne and then glanced away. Once the syringe was empty, he picked his dog up for the last time. Beano nudged his nose reassuringly with his own and looked into his eyes. *Don't worry, Master, I've had a good life*, the eyes seemed to be saying. Then he slumped in his arms and was gone.

A quick, awkward squeeze of the shoulder from Etienne and Max walked away, his arms empty. His heart, however, was full. How could something so small leave such a huge absence? Nothing would ever be the same again.

Life as he had known it had ended; all the fun and friendship had gone. What happened now—Alexa's visit included—was a matter of supreme indifference to him.

Chapter Sixty-Two

ON THE MORNING OF Lady Alexa's visit, Astrid rose early. She had slept very little the night before. The laboratory had promised that the results would come today; what would they tell her?

Getting mouth swabs was not the easiest of businesses. After much mulling over potential pretexts, none of which seemed remotely convincing, Astrid had concluded that nighttime, while her targets slept, was the only opportunity. As Engelbert, fortunately in this respect if no other, slept with his mouth open, she had been able to insert the cotton bud with minimum fuss. Giacomo and Maxim had been trickier.

Bending over Max, whose mouth was also slightly open, Astrid was struck by the beauty of his face in repose. Lately it had been rare to see him without a scowl or a frown; the smooth, unlined look of his face in the shadows reminded her of the sunny-natured small boy he had once been. How long ago it seemed.

As she hovered over his mouth with the bud, he turned and opened his eyes. Shocked, Astrid stepped back; realizing then that he was still asleep, she came forward again and dived in with the bud. "Polly!" Max said.

Polly? The name was new to Astrid. Who was this Polly?

She had lingered a few minutes, but as Max said no more, she had stolen out of the room.

Poor Max. Alexa was due today. The Queen's fists clenched. She had to help him.

Normal palace procedure was that the royal post, delivered to the back door in gray Royal Sedona Mail sacks, then went straight to the offices of the royal private secretary. Here it was sorted, placed on silver salvers bearing the individual crests of royal family members and taken out by footmen to arrive at the royal breakfast table at a moment precisely timed to be after the eggs and immediately before the final rounds of toast.

But this, the Queen knew, would be a good two hours after the original arrival of the post. She had therefore decided to get up especially early and be at the chateau's main rear door when the gray sacks first arrived. No one was likely to question her right to find her own mail; if, indeed, anyone was there.

Even as the Royal Sedona Mail van roared out of the chateau's cobbled rear courtyard, Astrid, with the help of a rather surprised cleaner, was dragging the two sacks into the service area by the back door. It was a space filled with boxes and cleaning supplies in which the Queen, with her smooth hair and her pearls, presented an incongruous sight. She took little notice of her surroundings, however, occupied as she was with emptying the post bags out onto the black and white linoleum tiles and scrabbling frantically through the contents.

On her knees amid the envelopes and slithery plastic piles of junk mail, Astrid looked up at the sound of a familiar voice. "Yo, Ma. Whassup?"

Giacomo had clearly just arrived back from a night out. His eyes looked as red as his face, his tailcoat was creased and his white tie noticeably grubby.

"What happened to you?" she asked.

Giacomo shifted from foot to foot. "Had to walk. Left the key in my car, and when I came out, the damn thing had gone."

"Your new Maserati?" Astrid gasped.

"Yah. The very same. Bloody silly, isn't it?"

"*Very* silly." But perhaps the silliest aspect of all was the makers presenting it—for reasons best known to themselves—to Giacomo in the first place.

"I mean"—Giacomo hiccupped—"you'd think the person who got in it would have realized they were in the wrong car. Some people, eh?" He walked unsteadily away.

Astrid tried not to be sidetracked. There would be trouble about the car later, but for now she must concentrate on the job in hand. The first gray post bag contained nothing from the laboratory, and neither, to her disappointment, did the second. She helped the cleaner stuff the post back in the bags and went slowly up to her room.

Some hours later, Max stood outside the front of the chateau. Outwardly he was composed; within, numb. The recent awful events had endowed him with a sense of distance, of unreality. He felt uninvolved in what was to occur; he would move, he would open his mouth. But he would not, in any meaningful sense, be there.

But wasn't that the entire trick of being royal? Distance. Detachment? Did that not cover all the skills? He felt an urge to laugh maniacally.

While Alexa's visit was not a state one, there was nonetheless more ceremony than might have been expected. The usual practice was that visitors were received in the privacy of the Great Hall. But today the royal family had been ordered by the King to be out in the front courtyard to meet the limousine bringing Lady Alexa from the Hotel des Bains. It was, Max understood, to be a semi-public occasion.

Accordingly, a number of press had been allowed in through the chateau gates. Crowds of onlookers had gathered on the other side, alerted by both the photographers and the distant view of the ruling family.

Blue sky stretched above the pointed towers of the chateau. A stronghold, Max found himself thinking sardonically, built to protect the royal line. And yet just one girl seemed about to conquer everything without so much as a drawbridge being raised. The royal standard hung limply against the white flagpole. It looked, Max thought, as defeated as he felt himself. He lacked the energy anymore to rail against what everyone said was his destiny. He was broken; he would submit.

"Cheer up," hissed Giacomo beside him. "You look as if you're at a funeral."

Max said nothing. It was nothing like a funeral; not at all like the one he had held in a corner of the castle gardens for Beano. He had been the sole mourner; he had dug the small hole and buried his dog with his favorite collar and ball and a bag of dog treats for the afterlife. Afterward he had climbed up one of the towers and stared hard at the sea.

The crowds at the gate now divided to let through a shining car. The gates themselves swung slowly inward. Giacomo dug Max in the ribs. "Thar she blows!"

Not wanting to watch the limousine as it advanced, juggernaut-like and unstoppable, Max looked about him. He stood at the top of a shallow flight of steps; beside him was his father in a uniform that seemed all buttons and epaulettes, and what wasn't either of those was sash. Giacomo, meanwhile, looked as louche as ever in some naval get-up. Max too had been stuffed into uniform, and that he looked ridiculous, he had no doubt. But who cared? What difference did it make?

Only his mother was not present. His surliness of late had hurt her most, he knew. But what could he have said to her? She, in any case, had sided with his father. With obvious reluctance, admittedly, but it was the siding that counted.

The car glided up to the steps. The photographers, who had been keeping a discreet distance, now rushed over; there was an explosion of zooms and whirrs. Out of the car emerged a pretty dark-haired girl in a simple white dress, ballerina flats, and a single string of pearls.

"Demure," Barney had stressed. "Think Kate Middleton. Think engagement-era Princess Diana."

A wild cheer now arose from the crowd, and the press within the castle compound went completely crazy.

Sun poured in through Astrid's window as she looked down on the small knot of people gathered around the limousine in the front courtyard. The photographers were going wild. She could see Alexa posing for them and waving at the crowd at the gates quite in the manner of the royal she so obviously aspired to be. Had she *any* idea what it involved? Astrid wondered. How could she? Being royal was like childbirth—you could imagine it, but you could never really understand until it had actually happened to you.

She stood before the long oval mirror in the corner of her room and stared at herself. Her reflection, as always, was as calm as it was lovely. Possibly the gray coat she wore over a gray dress was a little severe, but the occasion, so far as the Queen was concerned, was not one for rejoicing.

She stood patiently as her maid looked the outfit over for loose buttons and stray threads. "Perfect," Hortense murmured deferentially, having twitched a sleeve here and pulled a hem there.

"Thank you, Hortense. You can go now."

Astrid dawdled on her way down the great oak main staircase of the castle. At the foot of it she paused, looking up, as if for the first time, at the vast ceiling frescoed with the de Sedona crest. Three big keys—they suddenly looked very jail-like to the Queen.

Was there to be no escape for Max?

❖ ❖ ❖

The pretty dark-haired girl in the white dress turned on her long, slim, sheer-stockinged legs and waved a demure, white-gloved hand at the people who had come to see her. "Scrub up well, you do, for a commoner," Barney had giggled as he looked her over before departure. He was in the crowd now, Alexa knew, and willing her on in her moment of triumph. The triumph he had worked so tirelessly to create. He was her fairy godfather—in more ways than one.

She looked the part, Max found himself thinking as Alexa bestowed dazzling smiles in every direction. She looked, in fact, perfect. Just the right amount of makeup, the right clothes, exactly the right note struck between girlish freshness and womanly sophistication. The crowd were waving and cheering. The press were fascinated, crouching, shooting, exclaiming superlatives. And his family, standing around him at the top of the stairs, were obviously charmed. The Queen had still not arrived, admittedly, but his father was smiling and Giacomo was whistling under his breath.

Max found that he no longer felt angry toward Alexa. He felt weary and depressed. Her motives were so obvious; it was actually rather hard to hate her. He still had no clear idea of how she had got here, but that there had been subterfuge of some sort he had no doubt. And yet, what difference did it make? She was, after all, only doing what socially ambitious women had done for years, and with possibly more ingenuity than most. Why didn't he just go with the flow and marry her? If he didn't, some other ghastly woman would undoubtedly be produced.

The real problem wasn't even her fault. The issue wasn't that he had been manipulated; it was that he had been born royal in the first place. He would never be free to marry who he wanted, to work as he wanted, and it had been madness to imagine otherwise. Never, it seemed to Max, had he felt quite so lonely, quite so alienated, and quite so out on a limb as now.

He saw how utterly at home Alexa looked as she walked gracefully up the stairs toward them. She exuded the kind of happy, relaxed confidence he personally had never come close to. She turned once more and waved at the crowd, her lithe figure twisting, her dark hair swinging out slightly with the movement. He saw the color in her cheeks and the sparkle in her eye; that she was loving every minute was obvious. She bowed and waved to the snapping, exclaiming press corps and to the exultant crowd.

Beside Maxim, Giacomo leaned forward. "Talk about milking it," he muttered. "Jesus, she's going to make a bloody speech."

Straightening up again, Alexa placed one hand to her breast and shook her head, apparently overwhelmed. "Thank you, everyone, so much," she said in a light yet clear voice. "This has been the most wonderful welcome. A dream come true. I feel," she said, in an ardent, breathy voice, "just like a fairy princess."

Even the King started at this. Giacomo gasped. Max, meanwhile, just slowly shook his head. Clever old her, Hippolyte thought. That's tomorrow's headline written.

The crowd remained silent, in case Alexa had anything else to say. Suddenly there came a cry from several rows back.

"It's her! I told you it was, Selwyn. It's our Allison!"

The girl now reaching the top of the chateau steps seemed to have heard. She turned a face gray with horror in the direction of the voice.

A plump hand was waving above the heads of the crowd.

"Allison! Coo-ee! It's Mum! We're just over on a coach tour. You look very smart. What are you doing here, love?"

Chapter Sixty-Three

IT HAD COME. IN the afternoon post. Finally, Astrid had the envelope with the laboratory stamp in her hand.

Her knees were shaking and her breath was shallow and rapid. Eyes still fixed on her own address, she groped backward to a chair and sat down.

Slowly, carefully, she had opened the envelope and drawn out the letter inside. She read it. Her hand moved through the air to her mouth.

She sat back gingerly in the chair. The letter fell from her hand and she sensed the devastating paper float to the carpet as gently as thistledown, rather than drop like the bomb it undoubtedly was.

After the first shock, she felt an odd sense of relief. The result was, she knew, unquestionably right.

Impressions whirled through her head. She caught the ones she could, examined and absorbed them. Gradually, the storm in her mind calmed down and she could think rationally.

She had sent off her own, Engelbert's, Giacomo's, and Max's mouth swabs for DNA analysis. And the conclusion of the laboratory was that while she was most certainly the mother of both boys, Giacomo and Maxim had different fathers.

Only Giacomo was Engelbert's son.

The swabs had been tested three times, with the same result every time.

Astrid clutched the chair arms. It was a dizzying feeling, knowing she held the fate of the family in her hands. She had suspected as much, possibly even hoped as much. But it was still a shock that His Royal Highness Prince Maxim, heir to the throne of Sedona and about to get engaged to be married, was not actually related to the King at all.

She broke it to Engelbert first. His face, as she began to speak, had been white with horror. He had taken the news without comment and remained ominously silent after she had spoken, staring at the fire irons and avoiding her gaze.

They were sitting in his gloomy study, she on a small, hard chair opposite him on the sofa. Nothing moved apart from the pendulum in the grandfather clock, glimpsed through a glass panel in the base. Watching it swing, listening to its deep, slow, unhurried tick, Astrid felt she was on trial—for her past, for her marriage, for her son.

Waiting for the verdict, she twisted her hands in her lap. She had never liked the royal study, but it had been the only place private enough for the purpose. There were no footmen here. The white and gilt walls had ears everywhere else.

As the silence wore on, fear gathered to a hard knot in Astrid's stomach. She had expected him to be jealous and angry; shocked, too, that she had not been pure when he married her. Double standards, of course; he had had many girlfriends himself, by his own not infrequent admission. Presumably he had slept with some of them. But there had been no child—at least, not so far as she knew. And the child was the thing.

Eventually, she put a hand out and took his. "You can divorce me if you like," she said sadly. She felt very sorry for him. Engelbert had been knocked for six already by the other events of the day. That Lady Alexa was a fraud from the English Midlands whose parents were coincidentally visiting Sedona on a bus trip had been shocking too. Even if, in Astrid's private view, it had a certain comic aspect.

And now this, which of course was not funny at all.

The King made no reply to her offer. He looked utterly crest-fallen. Which was of course only to be expected. Would he ever recover? Astrid wondered miserably. Would their marriage?

But perhaps it was better that they should part. Especially if for Engelbert to look at her from now on was to be reminded that she had once loved someone else. Even if the someone had been before her marriage to him; someone, in addition, no longer alive.

Astrid sighed. Only now, it seemed, did she realize what her marriage actually meant to her. What her husband meant to her.

Engelbert might be pig-headed and stubborn, blinkered and impatient, but she had been by his side for twenty-five years. She knew what a good man he was. This afternoon, for example, following the revelations about "Lady" Alexa, he had not raged and stamped, as she might have expected. He had simply gathered the royal family together and taken them all back inside the chateau. Doors had been closed. No comments had been issued. He had been supremely and impressively in charge.

However much she mourned her first love, it was her second love that mattered now, Astrid knew. But was it too late to convince him of that?

After what seemed an eternity, Engelbert looked up. His face, turned to hers, seemed to have aged a decade. To her horror, the Queen saw his tired eyes fill suddenly with tears. His head plunged into his hands. The royal shoulders began to heave. Engelbert was weeping.

Gingerly she put her arms about him, fearful that he would hurl them off in fury. The King wept on.

"What did you say?" she whispered, catching some unintelligible words. It sounded like "leave."

She swallowed. So he did, after all, want her to go. She could not blame him; it was the risk she had run. She must live with the consequences of her actions. She raised her chin and stood up, slowly detaching her hands from him.

The King raised his head. "I'm so relieved," he hiccupped.

"*Relieved?*" Astrid was electrified. Was she hearing correctly?

The royal red eyes fixed on hers. "I thought that when you said Max was another man's child, you were going to tell me his father was Stonker Shropshire. I think I could bear anything but that."

"Oh, Engelbert!" Astrid was back beside him in a second. "Why ever would you think that?"

The King was gazing at the carpet. His plump shoulders in their gray suit heaved in a mighty sigh. "I've never quite felt I was worthy of you."

"Not worthy of me?" the Queen exclaimed. "Oh, my darling!"

As she drew him into her arms again, he clutched her hard and looked up into her anxious face. "I'm sorry about Max's father," he said softly. "That must have been very difficult."

Astrid kissed the top of his well-combed head. She felt she would burst with love and relief. "It's over now, darling. All over."

Chapter Sixty-Four

IT WAS A BEAUTIFUL soft summer evening with pink-orange light stippling the rocky sweep of hills visible from Max's room. The soft glow slanted through the windows and lit the carved and gilded posts of the bed.

There was a knock at the door; Maxim looked up as his mother came in. She had a piece of white paper in her hand.

"I'll come straight to the point," Astrid said.

"Do." Maxim could barely lift his eyes. He could not imagine what fresh hell was next, nor was he interested. The fracas with "Lady" Alexa outside the chateau had been both undignified and ridiculous. But he was some distance beyond caring. No doubt his mother was coming to advise him that yet another potential bride had been dug up somewhere. The whole circus would start all over again.

"You're going to be very shocked," his mother warned.

The Prince shrugged. He didn't think so. Especially after this afternoon. No doubt his mother meant it was unexpected that they had found someone else so soon. But nothing would surprise him anymore.

"Prepare yourself," Astrid said over the thundering of her own heart.

Max looked up impatiently. "I thought you were going to come straight to the point."

"I will. Maxim, I've done a DNA test at the labs." The Queen took a deep breath. "My darling, you're not royal."

Maxim was completely still. He could feel the news exploding slowly within him. Not royal. *Not royal.* He knew at once that it was true.

You're not royal. He could feel his brain actually seizing on the words, examining them and probing their meaning. He realized that, instinctively, he had known all along. It explained so much. The way he had never felt allegiance to crown and ceremony the way the rest of the family did. The fact that he looked so different from Giacomo and his father. The almost psychotic reluctance he had always felt to take up his royal duties.

His mother had laid her hand over his. She was explaining gently something about an old boyfriend of hers. Maxim wanted her to stop. He wanted to know, of course, but not now. There was not time. There was other business, much more pressing business.

Where did he start?

Over a booming heart, he gathered his thoughts. A wedding. The throne. Surely he could avoid them both now. He could not inherit the throne if he wasn't royal, nor did he need to be married…

"Quite a lot to take in, I know," the Queen was saying. She was looking into his face. She looked, he saw, worried.

Maxim smiled at her. Why was she worried? He leaped to his feet and hugged her.

Her face, as he released her, was a mixture of relief and surprise. "So you don't mind?" Astrid asked slowly.

"Mind?" He beamed at her. "Why should I mind? You're still my mother, aren't you?"

"Yes, but your father. He's not…"

"That doesn't matter either. He's still my father. But even better—I don't have to be king!" He hugged his mother again.

"I don't have to marry!" He felt as if something had detached itself from his shoulders and was floating up, up and away. He felt light. Free.

"I can go back to England!" he exclaimed.

There was no time to lose. It was finished with Polly, of course, there was no hope there. But he could return to his studies. That would be something. Not everything, but something. Slowly, he could rebuild his life.

He rushed to a wardrobe, dragged out a bag, and began throwing a motley collection of objects into it. Odd shoes, magazines, a scrunched-up sweater.

"Wait, though," Astrid advised, hurrying forward to take out the odd shoes. "There's no rush."

"But there is a rush. There's a plane at ten o'clock from Nice." He knew when every flight to London left and had never seen the last one of the day lift into the sky from the airport up the coast without wishing he was on it.

"What—you're going *now*? This minute?" That her son's first instinct was to escape was rather hurtful; in vain did Astrid remind herself that everything she had done recently was to make this moment possible.

❖ ❖ ❖

After Max had left for the airport, Engelbert, pleading a headache, had retired to bed. The stress of recent days, and especially this day, had taken its toll.

And not just that, the Queen knew. Engelbert was still worried about Sedona's future. No royal engagement and wedding meant no publicity bonanza and, consequently, no surge in investment and business. After all the drama, he was back to square one.

Astrid, walking slowly back up the castle drive after waving her son off, wished she had the answer. She was grateful to Engelbert, humbled by his generosity, guilty about the many times she had considered him arrogant and pompous. That, after the revelations, his love for Max had not diminished one whit was one of the many reasons she appreciated him more than ever. Engelbert was a prince among men, even if he did happen to be a king.

He had suggested that, in order to protect the Queen's privacy, Max retain the title of Prince but none of the obligations. As far as the outside world was concerned—and most of those in the chateau as well—Max had, with the full blessing of his parents, effectively resigned his claim to the throne in order to pursue his veterinary career. What business was it of anyone else who his father was? the King had demanded. They would get around the issue by simply transferring the title of Crown Prince to Giacomo.

After the tumult of recent days and weeks, the Queen felt calm stealing through her soul as she arrived at the castle door. Drifting around her nostrils came the sharp, warm scent of the lavender borders; the sky above was full of clouds blushing with the final lingering kiss of a sun evidently reluctant to say its farewells.

Of course, the final part of the jigsaw would be for Max to find someone he loved. Then, Astrid thought, she could finally relax. She smiled as she closed the door behind her. Did one ever really relax as a mother? Wasn't that luxury forever surrendered from the moment you first held your child?

Chapter Sixty-Five

KICKING HER HEELS FOR two days in Nice had been the last thing Polly wanted to do. But since the airline had been unable to find her a seat straight away, there had been no alternative. That it was a night flight back seemed particularly depressing—the last of the day. The end of the line, in every sense, she thought glumly as, finally, she pushed through the revolving airport door.

She had spent the last forty-eight hours resolutely not thinking about Max. She had distracted herself with the English newspapers, tried to people-watch, stared at pictures in art galleries, trailed around gloomy palace museums, looked unseeingly at clothes, trained her eyes on the sea; most of all she had walked, walked, and walked, as if the motion and the intensity of it could give her some relief.

Whenever she had felt a thought about him coming, she had headed it off. She had blocked him, dodged him, ignored him, refused him. But still his image bobbed at the edge of her brain, demanding admittance. So far, he had not succeeded.

But now, out of the corner of her eye, as she passed a newsstand, Polly caught sight of a familiar face. He was not, Polly promised herself, striding past the news stand determinedly, going to force his way in now. Whatever the article was about, she did not care. The couture wedding dress, the celebrity chef, the famous guests, she wanted to know nothing about them. Nothing. She could not care less. Really.

On the other hand, what did it matter? She was flying away from him tonight, escaping from the whole sorry mess. She need never hear his name again. She allowed herself one last glance. The headline stopped her dead in her tracks.

PRINCE CANCELS WEDDING

Dropping her bag on the concourse, Polly dashed across to the shop. Within a minute she had the paper in her hands. Words leaped out at her. *Mistake...impostor...Allison Donald...renounced throne... returning to England...*

Allison Donald! Polly shook her head. It was too incredible for words. She sank down on her bag, stunned.

It was at that moment that Max rushed into the airport for the last plane to London and saw her.

Chapter Sixty-Six

"I was promised a royal wedding," stated Lady Annabel, sitting opposite the private secretary's desk and fixing him with a gimlet eye.

A gimlet eye, indeed, was more or less all Hippolyte could see, the rest of Lady Annabel's face, apart from her bright-pink-lipsticked lips, being covered with bandages. With world press attention in mind she had, it seemed, decided on a little last-minute plastic surgery, calculating that it would be healed in time for the moment her daughter went up the aisle behind the new Crown Princess.

Except that that, of course, would not now be happening.

"I was promised a royal wedding," Lady Annabel repeated. "And now, as it appears that promise cannot be honored, I'd like to ask you what you intend to do about it."

"Do about it?" Hippolyte echoed helplessly. What the hell was he supposed to do about it? Was it his fault that the prospective royal bride had turned out to be an impostor?

"Well, someone has to gather up the reins," Lady Annabel informed him sharply. "Astrid and Engelbert are all over the place; they can't seem to make any decisions. It's up to you and me"—and here Lady Annabel fixed him with her glare again—"to sort this mess out."

A mess, the press secretary mused, was certainly one way of putting it. Not only was there no longer a royal bride, there was no royal bridegroom either. Maxim had resigned his claim to the throne and had waltzed off to England to neuter cats, or whatever vets did. No wonder the King and Queen were shut up in their apartment, not speaking to anyone.

As the eerie bandaged face trained its baleful gaze on him, Hippolyte felt he knew exactly what it was like to be hunted. Was it a coincidence that a leopard-skin print wrap dress comprised the rest of her ladyship's attire? Lady Annabel's face in its normal state was frightening enough. But this white mask with glittering eyes was like some nightmare from a Greek tragedy.

"Well, you'd better do something," the mask said briskly. "Otherwise, it's curtains for Sedona. So far as I understand it, they need a wedding to save the monarchy. Just think about what's going to be lost. All those visitors. All that money that would have come into the country…"

He was sweating. Hippolyte knew. Two separate tides of warm darkness were seeping from under his arms across his chest and would soon meet in the middle. Their progress was speeded by the knowledge that Lady Annabel was right. She had identified the main issues with a clarity that would be admirable were it not so horrific and inconvenient.

He tried to arrange his thoughts, but they remained in utter disarray. "It's a disaster," he moaned, his sweating face in his damp hands. "The publicity is ruinous."

Thanks to that bastard Snort. He had clearly made a killing from photographs of the former Lady Alexa boarding a tour bus from Wolverhampton in the company of both her parents. The only positive thing was that Barney van Hoosier seemed to have disappeared without trace.

Emitting a puppy-like whimper, the private secretary stared at Lady Annabel through his plump fingers. "What can we do?" he whispered brokenly. Somehow, the entire future of the monarchy, as well as that of the economy and relations with most of the rest of the world, rested in his hands. It was not what he had signed up for. Back in those wonderful long-ago days when he had joined as a junior private attaché, the delivery of the royal post was about the extent of his duties.

The mask was nonchalantly inspecting its nails. "I have a plan," it said casually, "in case you are interested."

It occurred to Hippolyte now that this was the entire reason she was here. Of course she had a plan. Was Lady Annabel the sort to throw herself pathetically across his desk and beg him to help her? Or was it more likely that, having devised the solution in every detail, she required his assistance in putting it into action? He did not like Lady Annabel, Hippolyte decided, but he admired her.

"What's your plan?" he asked her.

"Everyone loves a royal wedding, Monsieur Hippolyte," Lady Annabel announced. "And it's up to you and me to provide them with one."

"You and me…?" The private secretary fell back in his chair, disappointed. She had said she had a plan, but they were back where they started.

The mask leaned forward. "Monsieur Hippolyte. There *can* still be a wedding. There *can* still be a bride and bridegroom."

"There can?" Hippolyte wasn't following.

The bandages nodded so vigorously it made the private secretary wince. Didn't it hurt? He watched the magenta lips moving.

"Yes. Florrie can marry Giacomo."

Hippolyte's head abruptly emptied of all thought. Into this silence and vacancy, something appeared. It was small at first, and the press secretary struggled to make it out. Then it got larger, and shinier, until it seemed to fill the whole of his mind with its glow. It was the answer. Lady Annabel's suggestion would save everything.

"Giacomo!" gasped Hippolyte. "His Royal Highness Prince Giacomo?"

"Crown Prince Giacomo, as he is now, of course. And why not?" the mask challenged. "He and Florrie get on enormously well. Possibly better than enormously…"

Hippolyte could only stare ecstatically at the bandaged face before him. The Greek allusion had been right. Lady Annabel was an oracle, no less. The fount of all wisdom.

"The wedding's what matters, and the princess," the oracle was explaining. "Sedona's too tinpot for anyone to give two hoots about which prince it is."

Hippolyte bridled at the tinpot but decided to let it drop. There were bigger issues at stake.

"But…but…" His mouth was opening and closing. "What will Their Majesties…the King and Queen say?"

The mask stood up and put both slender brown hands on its leopard-print hips.

"That, my dear Hippolyte," it pronounced, "I leave to you."

Chapter Sixty-Seven

QUEEN ASTRID WAS RESTING in her room when the white-and-gold door opened abruptly and in stalked Lady Annabel. Her features were set with an expression that betrayed, even from fifty feet away, a determination that brooked no opposition.

A few paces behind her came Hippolyte. He looked worried; he had clearly tried, in vain, to stop Florrie's mother's sudden appearance.

"Lady Annabel." The Queen rose calmly from her chair. "To what do I owe this pleasure?"

Lady Annabel, resplendent in a tight-fitting turquoise silk suit which set off her shining chestnut bob, strode forward, her high-heeled sandals stabbing the cream carpet. Her air, as she came right up to Astrid, was excessively businesslike.

The swelling on her face was calming down now, the Queen saw. She observed with interest the fact that Lady Annabel's visage had apparently retained its deep mahogany tan, even under the bandages. Perhaps, after sufficient exposure to sun or sunbed, it just stayed that color.

Her eyes slid over Annabel's bright-blue tailored shoulder to where Hippolyte was cringing in misery. He looked imploringly at her, made some desperate gesture at Lady Annabel, and held his hands up in defeat.

"A very pleasant day, Lady Annabel," the Queen remarked mildly, as an opening shot.

The other woman, however, clearly had no intention of talking about the weather. "I have come about the jewels," she announced.

"Jewels?" The Queen frowned slightly.

"Your jewels," said Lady Annabel crisply.

As Hippolyte groaned, Astrid smoothed over her amazement with a smile. Experience had taught her that if one stood and waited pleasantly, most things explained themselves. And what her particular experience of Lady Annabel had taught her was that she explained things in a direct manner, to the point of rudeness. Astrid did not bear Annabel any ill will for this; on the contrary, the solution to the royal wedding problem had been ingenious and Giacomo, in particular, was delighted about it.

"I imagine," Lady Annabel said smoothly, "that it is tradition in Sedona for the Queen to lend the Crown Princess the pick of her collection to wear on her wedding day?"

The Queen raised a white hand to stifle a surprised cough. Sedona had many traditions, but this was not one of them. Her immediate predecessor had certainly not been given to such gracious gestures. Engelbert's mother would have taken her entire collection to the cathedral and sat on them throughout the service rather than see anyone approach the altar in as much as an earring that had belonged to her. It was amazing that she had not somehow contrived to take them to the grave.

Nonetheless, Astrid smiled graciously. "I would be more than happy to lend Lady Florence whatever she would like to borrow. If she were to come and see me…"

"Actually," Lady Annabel interrupted. Behind her, Hippolyte cringed again. It was the most fundamental breach of royal protocol to interrupt a member of the royal family when talking.

"Lady Florence," Lady Annabel continued, "is occupied with a shoot for *Socialite* magazine at the moment."

Astrid's eyes widened. Yet more publicity!

With Hippolyte as her terrified executive assistant, Lady Annabel had taken absolute charge of the royal wedding. She had sold to the highest bidders not only the rights to produce commemorative plates and tea towels, but newspaper interviews with the engaged couple, glossy magazine photo shoots, and fly-on-the-wall documentaries on every aspect of the preparations. All the palace staff had been encouraged to blog, which in many cases was an entirely new word in their vocabulary.

Annabel's belief that the whole world, especially the celebrity one, loved a royal wedding had been proved spectacularly true. Heston Blumenthal and Gordon Ramsay had been persuaded to do the catering and Damien Hirst to decorate the cake.

It was Astrid's private opinion that, given her talent for PR, Annabel was wasted being a mere aristocrat. Anyone, after all, could have a title, but it took a particular skill to persuade Kelly Hoppen to decorate the rooms, Elton John to sing at the service, and Carlos Acosta to coach Florrie for the first dance. Nothing was being left to chance—the bride least of all. The future Crown Princess was currently receiving training on everything from how to wave at her subjects to the correct way to sit on the beach.

"I am here instead of Lady Florence and it is I who will choose the jewels," Lady Annabel announced.

The Queen counted to ten under her breath. It had proved, over the years, a useful means of hiding shock or surprise. "I see," she remarked neutrally.

"Actually, I'm rather busy myself..." Lady Annabel added. She was shortly to take a conference call with various heads of state, all eager to impress on her the advantages of a royal honeymoon in their territory.

The Queen seized the chance. "I am sure you are, Lady Annabel. Perhaps we can talk about this later."

"I meant," Florrie's mother said, turning hard brown eyes on Astrid, "that we should look at the jewels straight away."

Five minutes later, in the mahogany closet room filled with velvet-lined drawers and glass-topped cases, Lady Annabel had swooped on the Queen's biggest tiara and plonked it on her head. She snatched up a matching necklace of platinum-set pearls and diamonds and then reached for the earrings as well. "Parures in the springtime." Lady Annabel smiled, making the first attempt at a joke Astrid had heard.

"I need to look quite magnificent myself you know." Lady Annabel was staring at herself assessingly. "As the Crown Princess Mother…"

"The…?" It was not a title Astrid was familiar with.

Lady Annabel turned her glittering head to the Queen. "The Crown Princess Mother. It's what you are before you are…" she paused before adding, triumphantly, "The Queen Mother."

Recognizing that she was surplus to requirements, Astrid stepped away from the closet. Hippolyte slipped after her, his face ashen.

"Ma'am, I cannot apologize enough…"

The Queen placed a reassuring hand on his arm. "It doesn't matter, Hippolyte."

"But to come bursting in like that…" The press secretary wrung his hands in anguish.

"Forget it, Hippolyte. It doesn't matter." The Queen was bending down to a small cupboard and drawing out a bottle of champagne and two glasses. She turned round with a smile. "Fancy a flute?"

Chapter Sixty-Eight

"Stand still, that's it..." Florrie felt her eyes jerk from her sockets as the woman kneeling on the floor below her, mouth full of pins, pulled the pale pink silk of the ballgown hard round her waist.

"Does...it...really...have...to...be...this...tight?" It was an effort to force the words out.

The woman looked up. She was small, dressed in black, and with a pointed, rather pinched face. It was, Florrie felt, rather hard to believe that she was the linchpin of one of the most famous couture houses in the world.

"You 'ave to suffer to be elegant, Madame."

Florrie let out a peal of laughter. "Suffer?" What an absolutely extraordinary idea."

She was simply adoring the photo shoot. So much more agreeable to be photographed by *Socialite* for their front cover than it had ever been to work there. To work anywhere, for that matter. And now of course she wouldn't ever have to work again, unless you counted wearing divine—free—couture, eating delicious food and living in a fabulous palace as work. Omigod, being royal was going to be such fun!

They were shooting in the throne room; the photographer, who had such great ideas, was encouraging her to sprawl across the royal seat and stretch her legs up its purple-cushioned back, just pulling up that bit of her skirt...there, that was it, just to expose a bit more thigh. And for the next shot, perhaps on the throne, sitting up, but with her legs slightly apart in those high heels and her skirt pulled up…? That was it. Yes, and if she could bite that piece of hair and sort of smolder…yeah, great. They were going to call the finished article "Is This The World's Sexiest Royal?"

Florrie's laughter rang through the room as she rattled off a succession of anecdotes. "…he giggles if you tickle his beard… Beast of Blenheim…he looks fabulous in eyeliner…Zen weekend in Tuscany…then we all fell off the yacht…"

The *Socialite* people, none of whom she remembered from her own time there, were all such fun. She might even do a column for them; she wouldn't need to actually write it of course, they would do all that for her…

Florrie whirled and twirled in front of the camera, basking in the admiration of the assistants and the fashion director. They kept telling her how famous she was going to be, which sounded like such amazing fun, omigod, just incredible.

The great double doors now creaked open and Giacomo stuck his handsome blond head through. He blinked slightly as he saw Florrie on his mother's throne in a pose Astrid would never have struck in a thousand years. But Florrie looked stunning—young, beautiful, exuberant, and somehow innocent, for all the exposed leg. She was so high-spirited. Last night they had eaten KFC flown in from Monaco and served by footmen off silver plates in the Great Dining Room. Omigod, Florrie had kept giggling. Omigod! This is crazy! This is cool!

Florrie now looked over and saw him; the hair dropped from her mouth; she gasped and bounced on her velvet cushion. "Jack! Omigod, you're so naughty! You're not supposed to be here!" Her eyes were sparkling; her squeal was that of an excited child.

There was a frisson of excitement among the magazine people

as the Crown Prince slipped through the great tall doors, went up to Florrie, and pulled her to him. He was looking quite devastatingly handsome in a white shirt, sharp dark suit, and black loafers without socks. As he kissed his fiancée, long and lingeringly, the girl assistants sighed enviously.

A familiar large, sweating figure now appeared and hurried across the throne room carpet. Giacomo was still busy with Florrie. Her arms were wrapping around his neck, drawing him down into the purple cushions.

"Ahem." The private secretary cleared his throat. Seeing him redden, the assistants giggled.

"If your Highness will permit me." Embarrassment made Hippolyte's tones louder and more pompous than he intended. "May I remind you the Archbishop of Sedona is anxious to speak to you about the service? And His Majesty's tailor is anxious to measure your Highness's inside leg for trousers. And the Colonel of the Royal Sedona Household Regiment wants to measure your Highness's outside leg for a sword…"

Hippolyte was panicking. He had scoured the entire chateau for the Crown Prince; Giacomo was forever slipping out of his reach. So was Florrie; he got the impression that both the Prince and his fiancée thought that hiding from him was funny.

A royal wedding, Hippolyte had imagined, would solve all his problems. He was now discovering that it had only increased them. His phone was ringing off the hook with excited royal correspondents seeking accreditation. Hippolyte had never appreciated, never even begun to imagine, just how many royal correspondents the world contained. Not to mention photographers, documentary crews, and international news teams from Bangkok to Bradford.

"Look, Hippolyte." Giacomo had reluctantly torn his lips from Florrie's and was looking around in irritation. "It's not convenient just now, OK? Apart from anything else"—he looked back at Florrie, who giggled—"I've got a meeting about the stag night."

As Max was going to be worse than useless at organizing anything sufficiently high-octane, Giacomo was taking personal charge of this most crucial aspect of the celebrations. His favorite option so far was a weekend of blindfold driving with a bevy of glamour models. Transport to and from would be provided by the royal plane—dubbed Heir Force One by the irrepressible new Crown Prince.

"Very good, sir." Hippolyte bowed and withdrew.

Giacomo, meanwhile, slid onto the throne beside Florrie: his father's. He swung his legs over one of the ornate arms and grinned engagingly, tipping his head back over the other arm so the gold of his hair touched that of his fiancée's. The delighted cameraman carried on snapping, knowing these pictures would be syndicated around the world.

Yeah, Prince Giacomo de Sedona told himself. Together he and Florrie were going to shake up this monarchy. Really put it on the map. He drew Florrie onto his knee for the next shot and put his fingers in bunny ears behind her unsuspecting head.

Being Crown Prince was cool, basically. He couldn't understand why Max always had such a problem with it.

Chapter Sixty-Nine

THE BLUE SUMMER AIR resounded to the yells, bells, and cheers of the ecstatic multitude. Flashing in the sun's rays were the lenses of the thousands of TV cameras from all over the world that had converged on the royal wedding.

Jason Snort of PapPixRiviera shook his red quiff in the sunshine and adjusted the lens of his camera. He'd never seen Sedona so crowded. People seemed to be squeezed into every nook and cranny—not just excited locals, but people from all over the world. Each balcony and window that had even the suggestion of a view of the proceedings was stiff with gawping observers.

You could say, Jason thought wryly, that there was a fair amount of interest in the wedding of Lady Florence Trevorigus-Whyske-Cleethorpe to His Royal Highness Prince Giacomo de Sedona. Who was now the Crown Prince, his brother Maxim having apparently passed up his right to the throne so he could shove his arm up cows' arses for the rest of his life. Crazy, Jason thought. On the other hand, who cared. He didn't have a view on what these insane royals did. Apart, that was, from the one down his long lens.

The Marchioness of Dymchurch, sister of Lady Florence, sat in the aisle of Sedona Cathedral. Above her, the ancient stone arches met and mingled; beside her, at the end of the pew, stood a herald in red tights, a red feathered bonnet, and a stiff tabard embroidered with the Sedona royal coat of arms. There were twenty of these heralds in all, reminding Beatrice irresistibly of the farcical trial scene from *Alice in Wonderland*. The heralds stood, backs rigid, eyes rigid, their long silver instruments fluttering with the royal standard pressed to their lips, ready to play the welcoming fanfare as the new princess-to-be arrived. It all felt very old, very traditional, and not very Florrie at all.

And yet it *was* Florrie, or would be. She had done it. She really was about to marry into the royal family. Not the original intended royal family, admittedly, but royal nonetheless, and with much better weather.

Beatrice smoothed the apricot silk and tulle of her bouncy little skirt, teamed with a violet jacket and lime-green heels. "Spirit-lifting," her personal shopper at Liberty had described it, and yet Beatrice's spirits remained uncooperatively low. She had, after all, been bested by her sister, despite her own brilliant marriage to a marquess, albeit one unavoidably absent on this occasion due to an as yet unexplained accident involving a fruit bowl and a plastic bag at the home of a nightclub hostess in Mayfair. She would deal with that, Beatrice thought grimly, when she got back to England.

Next to her and behind, the whole Trevorigus-Whyske-Cleethorpe family had turned out for this most auspicious day in their history. Beatrice glanced at Topaz, one of her many half-sisters, and wondered if the best foil for her huge shoulders and beefy back was the clinging eau de Nil bandage dress she had chosen. Within the family, Topaz was famous for having an edgy take on fashion, but in Beatrice's view it was an edge she sometimes fell right off.

Only Lord Whyske was absent; he had, as at Beatrice's own wedding, suspended hostilities with his ex-wife and was currently accompanying Lady Annabel in one of the bridal procession carriages.

An ancient acquaintance of her mother's, Honoria, Duchess of Crewe, sat beside Beatrice. Her three strands of hair had been drawn back, curled around into a pair of fat ash-blond sausages, and squashed beneath a tiara that looked like a positive fence of diamonds. "So wonderful, isn't it?" Honoria breathed noisily.

Beatrice could not see why anyone might imagine that having her feckless, selfish sister as their ruler was a good thing. She had walked up the cathedral steps through a black plastic forest of long lenses, television cameras, and microphones, all jockeying for position. At the bottom, great crowds had been holding up their mobile phones to take pictures, laughing, chatting, some even singing. Many had small Sedona flags in hand; others grasped bunches of flowers, doubtless intended for the royal bride-in-waiting. The very air seemed to crackle with excitement.

"Here they come!" wheezed Honoria excitedly.

There were TV monitors in the cathedral; squinting at the one nearest to her, Beatrice spotted the royal procession. The crowd cheered madly and waved their flags.

Beatrice stared at the screen: the gleaming carriages, the red coats of the straight-backed outriders, and the gold braid of the postilions flashing in the sun. She could not suppress a certain awe. All this—for her sister? She imagined Florrie inside her state coach looking out at the crowds and wondered what she was thinking. Probably nothing, knowing Florrie. Not even now.

There was a hush outside. The crowd, Beatrice could see on the monitor, was standing almost entirely still. The clippety-clop of hooves and the jingle of the harness came into the cathedral from outside; it sounded merry and irreverent.

The first carriage stopped. The po-faced postilions jumped down, surprisingly light on their feet, and swung open the coach doors in unison. Wild cheers greeted the King and Queen of Sedona. The

Queen was serene in silver as pale as her white-blond hair, the King's color heightened from the confined and airless space of the carriage on such a hot day. They were holding hands tightly, Beatrice saw.

Out of the second coach, helped by liveried footmen, descended a beautiful, slender woman in a flowing lace gown with glossy blond hair under an enormous tiara. Another huge cheer rose from the crowd. "The princess-to-be conquers Sedona with her glamour, style, and charm," a woman with an American accent screeched excitedly into a microphone.

Florrie had changed, her sister thought, squinting to see better. Her hair was shorter. And *what* had happened to her face? She looked older, much older, and not all her features seemed to be in the same place. The strain of the occasion—and Florrie never usually felt the strain of anything—had obviously taken its toll; her formerly peachy sister looked as if she hadn't slept for a century.

Chapter Seventy

"*La bella principessa*"…"*la princesse la plus chic du monde…*" came the whispering voices from the monitor. In response to some unseen sign, the heralds raised their trumpets to their lips; there was a gasp and a rustle amongst the pews, and then Monsieur Hippolyte quickly materialized and whispered something to the chief herald. The instruments were lowered again, and the whisper swept through the cathedral. "It's not her; it's her mother."

The pieces to camera were quickly abandoned "What? Her mother?" exclaimed the American as the news reached her. "*La madre*"…"*la mere…*" gasped the others.

Mother? Beatrice had come straight to the cathedral from the airport; that her mother would be interested in seeing her today of all days was out of the question. She gawped in amazement at the figure on the screen. The blandness was new, of course. But there *was* something of Lady Annabel about the face, albeit with a completely different nose and enormous, fish-like lips. This impression was confirmed now that her father heaved out his big morning-suited body and stood clutching his top hat, frowning under his bushy brows at the unaccustomed bright weather. Unlike the Sedona monarchs, Beatrice noted, her parents stood a good six feet apart and did not even glance at each other. She wondered if, throughout the journey, they had exchanged a single word.

"Your mother," hissed Honoria, "saw this as a simply marvelous advertisement opportunity."

"Advertising what?" Beatrice could not tear her eyes from Lady Annabel's almost unrecognizable visage.

"Herself, of course," Honoria answered placidly. "There are millions watching on TV, and of course all the press coverage. There'll never be a better time to bag another husband, although of course it's a shame the surgery's so recent…"

Another coach drew up, the crown on top flashing in the sun. Florrie? Beatrice watched carefully as a pretty brown-haired girl in cream got out and the crowd erupted again, but her excitement switched to curiosity as she recognized Prince Maxim's girlfriend. The crowd kept cheering; the young Englishwoman, widely credited with putting a smile back on the elder prince's face, was clearly very popular.

More huge cheers as Maxim himself, tall in a dark suit and tie, emerged from the carriage and took his girlfriend's hand, his face split in the broadest beam Beatrice had ever seen. She felt a brief, disastrous wave of envy. Oh, to be with someone you actually *loved*…

Finally, Florrie arrived. She looked stunning, Beatrice saw, excited despite herself at the sheer spectacle. Her sister, descending from a fairy-tale carriage in a cloud of white satin and tulle, her tiara flashing in the sun and her smooth pale hair gleaming beneath the veil. As her foot touched the red carpet, the press contingent exploded into action and the crowd into ecstasy.

Perhaps Florrie would make a good princess after all, Beatrice found herself thinking. She certainly looked the part, turning and smiling dazzlingly in every direction. The crowd adored her, waving and calling her name. The press were fascinated, crouching, shooting, exclaiming superlatives. Beatrice could hear, behind her, Topaz excitedly wondering if Florrie's dress was Victoria Beckham.

"You know, caught in at the waist like that, then flowing out full length, fabulously simple."

She would never know, Beatrice suspected, exactly how this unreal—and yet entirely actual—situation had come about. She suspected sleight of hand on the part of her mother. Lady Annabel was, after all, Lady Annabel.

She could hardly believe how utterly at home Florrie looked on the red carpet with the carriage behind her. She stood there in the sunshine, tall, white, and lovely, basking in the adulation. She seemed instinctively to understand that it was show business. And yet there was a dignity about her too, her sister saw. A poise, a seriousness, an almost royal aura. Where the hell had *that* come from?

It was time to go into the cathedral. Florrie bowed and waved one more time to the snapping, exclaiming press corps and to the exultant crowd.

About bloody time, Jason thought, an hour and a half later, as, veil flung back, smiling all over her beautiful face, the new Crown Princess came out of the cathedral to a fanfare of silver trumpets and a tumultuous peal of bells. As her husband Prince Giacomo, Crown Prince of Sedona, now appeared, handsome in his braided cap, sword and medals blazing in the sunshine, another, even greater cheer went up.

Even Jason, hard-bitten man of the press as he was, could not quite hold back a gasp of admiration. The television crews sent by at least twenty different countries now began to shout twenty different pieces to camera, all right in Jason's ear. "Ze new princess conquers Sedona viz her glamour, style, and charm," a woman with a German accent yelled into a microphone.

"This princess-to-be fully deserves all the adjectives that have been piled on her in recent weeks," a British reporter bawled at the same time.

"*La plus belle princesse du monde*," shouted a hysterical Frenchwoman.

After the Royal Sedona Air Force roared overhead and released slipstreams of red, white, and blue, a hand-picked group of twenty schoolchildren threw pink and white petals over the newly-wed royal couple. Florrie, helped by her prince into the Sedona state coach, was conveyed to the reception at the castle.

"Frightfully moving, the service," Honoria quavered.

"Wasn't it?" said Beatrice, and she realized that she actually meant it.

Chapter Seventy-One

THE SUN WAS SETTING over the chateau of Sedona, and it was a command performance. A deep red sea of cloud was edged by brilliant gold, behind which the yellow sky turned to duck-egg blue and then to purple. It resembled an amazing celestial experiment in the laboratory of a flamboyant God. Ranged before it like the foreground of a stage set were the fantastical spires, turrets, and decorative rooflines of the chateau.

As the music tinkled and boomed throughout the castle—the flown-in-from-Ibiza DJ Florrie and Giacomo had wanted clashing with the piano trio Queen Astrid had insisted on—a couple could be seen stealing through the darkening castle gardens.

"Here," whispered Max, pulling Polly onto a small balcony that jutted out over the very edge of the terrace. There was room for just two people.

Polly looked down to the wrinkled gold sea far below. Then she closed her eyes and drew in a deep, happy breath scented by Queen Astrid's roses. It was a moment she had never dared dream of, would never have thought possible even a mere few weeks ago.

"You asleep? Am I boring you?" he was murmuring into her neck.

She opened her eyes; he looked up. His expression was intent, serious.

"Will you marry me?"

❖ ❖ ❖

Thousands of miles away, another young couple were embarking on another great adventure. Seeing on the TV news monitor in the Air China first-class lounge the brilliant spectacle of the Sedona royal wedding, Alexa scowled into her half-full glass of Dom Perignon. "Could have been me," she muttered.

"Until your parents turned up," Barney, beside her, said easily. "But nevermind, darling," he added, as the waitress topped up their complimentary tipple. "We've got our lovely new best friends Mr. Lu and his wife, and they're very kindly flying us out to Beijing to show them how the English upper class lives. With any luck, you'll find yourself a newly minted components billionaire, and I'll hook up with a rich widow with a chain of power stations. Here's to us." He grinned, chinking his glass with Alexa's. "Onward and ever upward."

She knocked it back in one.

About the Author

WENDY HOLDEN WAS A journalist for the *Sunday Times*, *Tatler*, and the *Mail on Sunday* before becoming a full-time author. She has now published nine novels, all top-ten bestsellers in the UK, and she is married with two young children. Her novels include *Beautiful People*, *Farm Fatale*, *Simply Divine*, *Gossip Hound*, *The Wives of Bath*, *The School for Husbands*, *Azur Like It*, and *Filthy Rich*.

Krestine Havemann